THE BEACON
and Other Mystery Stories

THE BEACON

and Other Mystery Stories

Elizabeth Elwood

iUniverse, Inc.

New York   Bloomington

The Beacon and Other Mystery Stories

iUniverse books may be ordered through booksellers or by contacting:

iUniverse
1663 Liberty Drive
Bloomington, IN 47403
www.iuniverse.com
1-800-Authors (1-800-288-4677)

ISBN: 9781440155734 (pbk)
ISBN: 9781440155758 (dj)
ISBN: 9781440155741 (ebk)

Printed in the United States of America

iUniverse rev. date: 8/14/2009

For Isabel

CONTENTS

The Beacon 1

The Mystery of the Boston Teapots. 39

Reflections on an Old Queen 59

How Do You Solve a Problem Like Maria?. 87

Echo of Evil 105

Who Killed Lucia? 149

The Devil May Care 191

Mary Poppins, Where Are You? 219

Christmas Present, Christmas Past 255

THE BEACON

The beacon was mounted atop a large cylindrical can buoy. The light hovered six feet above the waterline, a bright warning to navigators to stay clear of the rocky bluff that separated Belcarra Park from Indian Arm. The buoy was anchored a hundred yards from the point, and at high tide, boats could pass safely on either side, but the sensible seafarer avoided the shore side. The beacon shone day in and day out, beaming steadily amid the twinkling lights of the North Shore for anyone approaching Deep Cove, and standing out in stark, solitary splendour against the dark, forested banks for the navigator who was heading towards Port Moody.

A cluster of waterfront homes with private docks lined the shore on the western side of Deep Cove. At the point where the cove ended and the coastline curved to stretch westward towards the Second Narrows Bridge, an imposing three-storied house, glass-fronted and built in tiers towards the ocean, dominated the promontory. The plate-glass panes of the windows were dark, but the house was inhabited. A woman looked out from the upper floor. From where she stood, the beacon was a dot in the far distance, but the light seemed to pierce into her brain. The line of an aria persistently rang in her head as she looked out into the night. *Stella del marinar! Vergine Santa, tu mi difendi in quest'ora suprema.*

The woman breathed deeply, trying to ease the palpitations in her chest, willing the tune to stop ringing in her ears. It was the wrong aria, she thought angrily. She was not Laura; she was Gioconda. She was the one who loved with the fury of the lion. It was the other woman who would need protection when they came face to face. She stared at the light, but there was no comfort in the glimmering star across the water for it pinpointed the locality where her rival lived. There was no escape from the relentless beam, for wherever she looked from her house, the beacon could be seen, challenging her to act, reminding her that there was a presence across the water that was causing her life to disintegrate—a presence that had to be eradicated before it destroyed her completely.

* * *

Edwina Beary firmly believed in a mother's right to be kept informed about the daily lives of her offspring. She also maintained her prerogative to offer guidance when the members of her family were not charting courses that met with her approval. While she was proud of her son's achievements—Richard was a detective inspector with the RCMP—she was also irritated by his apparent unwillingness to find a suitable mate and settle down. Richard, in her opinion, was far too occupied with his job and much too lackadaisical about his relationships.

The three Beary daughters were more satisfactory. The oldest, Sylvia, had met and surpassed expectations, for not only was she a lawyer with a prestigious firm, but she had also produced three well-behaved grandchildren, and she ran both home and career with an efficiency that rivalled her mother's formidable management skills.

Sylvia's husband, Norton, fell somewhat short of Edwina's rigorous standards since he had a meek and unassuming personality and, unlike his wife who dealt with lucrative corporate cases, he practised criminal law and spent his days defending people who, in his mother-in-law's opinion, were the dregs of society. However, Edwina preferred Norton to Steven Ayers, who was the husband of her second daughter, Juliette. Steven had insisted that his wife give up her profession and stay home to raise a family while he forged ahead with his teaching career and spent the weekends playing guitar with his country and western band. Still, Juliette was beginning to show signs of independence. She had started a small marionette company, and through this endeavour was gathering prestige and a little extra income so, on the whole, Edwina did not feel there was any major cause for concern.

The youngest Beary daughter, who at that very moment sat opposite Edwina in the coffee shop at Barnet Village, had never caused her mother a single sleepless night. Philippa had always been a conscientious student and a well-behaved girl. Although she had insisted on pursuing a somewhat impractical singing career, she had followed her parents' advice, not only completing her university degree, but also supplementing it with a variety of business and computer courses, so she was well qualified and always able to find work between engagements. However, since daughter-number-three was single, twenty-five, and dutiful by nature, Edwina expected to be informed whenever decisions relating to career or love life were pending. Therefore, the news that Philippa had changed singing teachers without consulting her came as a shock.

Edwina felt slighted.

"Are you sure you've made a wise decision?" she demanded. "Sophie Guttenberg may have been spectacular in her heyday but a great performer doesn't necessarily make a good teacher."

Philippa stared reflectively into the froth on her latte and sidestepped the question.

"She was amazing, wasn't she? Such a huge voice in that tiny little frame. Remember the televised performance of *Gioconda* back in the nineties?"

Edwina nodded, but her expression remained severe.

"Yes, of course I do. That was the production that aroused your interest in opera. After you saw it, Guttenberg became a passion for you." Edwina set down her coffee, picked up her panini, and prodded a stray piece of eggplant back into the flatbread. Having rearranged her sandwich, she assumed the steely stare that had never failed to produce results with recalcitrant students during her long career as an educator. She looked her daughter straight in the eye. "Don't you think you might be switching teachers for the wrong reason?" she suggested.

Philippa was used to her mother's tactics. She shook her head vehemently.

"No! I'm not," she insisted. "Sophie is a fabulous vocal coach. If she wasn't first rate, they wouldn't have hired her to run the Opera-in-the-Schools program. She has such an understanding of the soprano voice and she's opened up my top register incredibly. You'll hear the difference when you watch the show tonight."

"But what about her temperament? One hears such odd things about her."

Philippa paused and considered her words carefully. "Yes," she allowed finally, "she's a strange woman. She has an almost hypnotic ability to help singers achieve the focus necessary to place the voice correctly, but within her own calm exterior, I think there's a bubbling cauldron ready to boil over. She doesn't seem happy—but that doesn't stop her from being a great teacher."

Philippa concluded with an air of finality that implied there was nothing more to be said. Recognizing a lost cause when she saw one, Edwina decided a temporary withdrawal was in order.

"Let's hope you're right," she conceded grudgingly. "Guttenberg's intense personality made her an outstanding Gioconda, so I suppose all that fervour could be inspiring. It's too bad," she added, diverging to a less controversial subject, "that Ponchielli only wrote the one opera. It's such a spectacular piece. Why hasn't Vancouver Opera ever mounted it?"

"Budget probably," said Philippa, relieved that the inquisition had ended. "It would be expensive."

Edwina's mouth set into a disapproving moue.

"What's wrong with the opera auxiliary?" she said censoriously. "Don't they fundraise?"

Philippa had a sudden inspiration. If her mother's energies could be diverted elsewhere, she would be less likely to buffet the members of her own family with her gale-force personality.

"You know," she said casually, "ever since Dad retired from teaching, he's kept himself busy with his work on Council. You ought to get involved in a community project too. You have the time now. Why don't you join the opera guild and help raise money? Then you might have some influence."

Edwina looked surprised, and then her expression grew thoughtful.

"That's not a bad idea," she acknowledged.

Philippa egged her mother on.

"Talk to Mae Fenwick," she urged. "She's head of the guild. She'll be at the performance tonight because her daughter, Joan, is in the ensemble. Mae's the one who booked the Village Theatre so we could demonstrate our mini-*Figaro* to the general public." Sensing that her mother was giving the matter serious consideration, Philippa made one final push. "Dad knows Mae," she pointed out. "She's always calling him over some council issue or other. He can introduce you."

Edwina finally took the bait.

"All right," she agreed. "I'll have a chat with her."

"Great! You'll love Mae. She's another powerhouse just like you." Having achieved her objective, Philippa changed the subject. "Where is Dad, by the way? I thought he was coming tonight."

Edwina sniffed disapprovingly.

"He was supposed to join us, but he had to go out to the boat so he said he'd grab something to eat on the way and join us at the show—and translated, that means he wants a burger and fries instead of something healthy. I don't know what I'm going to do with him. His waistline is virtually non-existent and I'm sure his cholesterol must be right off the chart, but of course, I can never get him to go for a check-up."

Philippa nodded. She adored her father, but on matters relating to health, she sided with her mother. Edwina was meticulous about watching her diet, exercising properly and keeping her weight under control, but having a disciplined, smartly turned-out wife had no effect on Bertram Beary whose response to challenges over his antiquated suits or expanding girth was simply to reply that he was built for comfort, not for speed.

"He probably won't be at the boat club long," Edwina continued. "He just wanted to check the engine fluids and make sure the running lights were working."

"What on earth for? You don't go boating in January."

Edwina rolled her eyes.

"Your sister has given us comps for the Deep Cove Players. When your father discovered that the theatre was only two blocks from the docks, he decided we should chug across by boat to see the play."

"It'll be pitch black. Is he crazy?"

"No more than usual. Actually," Edwina conceded, "there are a lot of lights on the shore—your father says the yellow glow from the halogen lamps at Rocky Point will be enough to light our way—so we should be fine. He does have a point. It's such a long drive around the inlet, but it's a short hop by boat."

"Why has Sylvia given you comps for an amateur show in Deep Cove? Come to that, why does she even have comps?"

"Didn't I tell you? Sylvia and Norton joined their local theatre club, and Norton has a part in the next production."

"Norton! You're joking."

"No. He's really going to be on stage. Sylvia hopes a spot of acting will help him improve his performance in the courtroom."

"I know these amateur groups are always short of males, but they must be absolutely desperate to cast Norton."

"Probably," agreed Edwina. "He's got a key role. They're doing *The Reluctant Debutante*."

Philippa dissolved into giggles.

"He must be playing the excruciatingly boring guardsman who wants to marry Jane."

"Yes, I believe so," said Edwina. "In which case, he really won't have to act that much. But anyway, that's why your father is at the boat club tinkering with the *Optimist*."

Philippa looked anxious.

"Does he know the performance starts at seven-thirty? I'd hate him to miss it, and you know what he's like when he's puttering at the docks."

"Not to worry," said Edwina. "I dropped him there, and as soon as we've eaten, I'll drive back and pick him up. We'll be in lots of time."

Philippa took another sip of coffee and reverted back to the subject of her vocal coach.

"You know," she said, "I'd love to see that film of *Gioconda* again. I have to go downtown tomorrow. I'll pop into Virgin Records and see if it's available on DVD."

"It could well be," said Edwina. "As I recall, it was rather a historic production. Wasn't it after *Gioconda* that Guttenberg's career fell apart?"

"Yes," Philippa admitted ruefully. "She had a nervous breakdown."

Edwina frowned.

"I remember reading about it in the papers, but it all seemed very hush-hush. Do the opera insiders know what actually happened?"

"Yes, it's common knowledge. Sophie's husband had been having an affair with the wife of one of his business associates, and as the marriage disintegrated, Sophie disintegrated along with it. The situation came to a head at a party on her father's yacht. She went quite mad, confronted her husband's mistress and actually threatened her with a flare gun."

"Good heavens. I'm surprised she didn't end up in jail."

"Her husband took it away from her before any damage was done. But it's a horrible story. Sophie must have been in utter despair."

Edwina frowned. "For all her talent, she must be very fragile. No man is worth that sort of grief. She should have divorced her husband, counted her blessings and moved on."

"She did move on. Joan Fenwick says Sophie was really happy when she first opened her studio here. She even started singing again. She didn't want to return to the opera stage—she must be pushing fifty by now—but she'd considered doing a concert. But now she seems to have lost her nerve and she's become quiet and broody again. Something is distressing her, and Joan thinks it's her husband."

"So she married again?"

"Yes. That's why she left Germany. She married a Canadian who was working in Hamburg. They returned here the following year and moved to Deep Cove two years after that. He's a real charmer—tanned, good-looking, very much into outdoor recreation. His name is Leonard Trant. I've met him a couple of times, and Sophie obviously adores him, but rumour has it he has a roving eye."

"Well, don't let his roving eye fall on you or she might go after *you* with a flare gun." Edwina gave her daughter a searching look. "On the subject of roaming males," she added, "how is Adam? I gather he's back in Germany for another year."

Philippa gritted her teeth and waited for another barrage of advice.

"Yes," she said, "but he'll be here for a couple of months this summer. Our agents are setting up a B.C. tour for us."

"A tour of what?"

"Festival events . . . that sort of thing. We're doing excerpts from *Rose Marie*. It's a great act. You'll love it."

Edwina's eyes remained stern.

"Who was this Gretchen he was talking about on New Year's Eve?"

"She's another singer in the company. They're working together."

"I've heard that one before," said Edwina. She downed the rest of her latte and started to gather up the plates and mugs.

"Don't anticipate trouble," Philippa said mildly. She kept her tone deliberately calm, although inwardly she shared her mother's reservations.

"My whole career as an administrator depended on anticipating when there might be trouble," Edwina pointed out, "and you certainly managed to find it at the New Year's Eve ball. I doubt if you'll hear from that nice young officer from New York again. He didn't seem too impressed finding you with two other escorts."

"He'll get over it," said Philippa, "and if he doesn't, it indicates a total lack of humour, so I wouldn't be able to get along with him anyway."

Edwina radiated disapproval. "I hope you know what you're doing, both with your career *and* your love life. Don't say I didn't warn you." She stood up, turned to the mirrors that lined the alcoves along the wall, patted her blonde hair into shape, and returned the dishes to the girl at the counter.

Philippa sighed. Then she picked up her makeup case and followed her mother out of the shop. She gasped as she stepped outside, for the afternoon was bitterly cold, but in spite of the frosty air, Barnet Village looked bright and cheerful. The twinkling lights that had decorated the stores for Christmas still hung in place, and the patches of hard snow dotted along the pavement reinforced the sense that the holiday season was not quite over.

"There's still three hours to curtain time," said Philippa, "but I'm going to head over now. I'm researching grant resources for the arts council and I need to stop in the library. Do you want to come, or are you going to pick up Dad right away?"

"I'll go get your father," said Edwina. "Hopefully he won't be so full of junk food that he'll nod off and sleep through the performance. We'll see you after the show."

Edwina gave her daughter a hug, then turned and marched briskly away, the heels of her dress boots echoing noisily on the sidewalk. A moment later, she disappeared through the glass doors of the underground parkade.

Philippa set off in the opposite direction. She walked through the village and crossed the road to the community complex that housed the theatre and the library. The light was already fading, and the trees behind the glass and concrete building were black against the evening sky. In summer, the trail that connected Rocky Point to the oil refinery at the far end of Old Orchard Road provided an exhilarating hike around the shore of the inlet, but now the woods looked ominous and forbidding. Philippa glanced up as she approached the side entrance. The rotunda at the top of the building was only a dark silhouette against a purple sky, and she was glad to get indoors where there was warmth and light. She entered the library and settled herself at a computer terminal.

By six o'clock, her work was completed and she moved across to the theatre. None of the other performers had arrived yet. She entered the dressing room and, taking advantage of the extra space, spread her things along the counter and applied her makeup in leisurely fashion. Once done, she changed into Susanna's gown, pulling the basque jacket tight, while still leaving room to breathe, and arranging the muslin fichu artfully around her shoulders. Then she moved to the full-length mirror and nodded with satisfaction at her reflection. Being short could be a disadvantage on stage, but the snug bodice and ballerina-length skirt were gratifyingly flattering to her petite figure.

As she was sticking a mobcap on her red curls, the door opened and Joan Fenwick entered the room. Joan was one of those rare singers who never displayed anything that could be remotely interpreted as temperament so Philippa was surprised to see a grim expression on the mezzo's face.

"What's up?" Philippa asked.

"It's Sophie." Joan plopped her case on the counter and looked anxiously towards the door. "She's here . . . in body only. There's something the matter with her. I spoke to her, and she walked right by, and then she turned back and started mumbling something about a light. I don't think she even saw me. She looked absolutely demented. My mother has arranged to have two of our major sponsors here tonight, and if Sophie is sitting out front in that condition, you can imagine the impression it'll make. Somehow we have to keep her out of their way."

"That's easy," said Philippa. "My parents are in the house tonight. They'll help. Before you change, run out front and tell the box-office staff to send my dad backstage as soon as he comes to pick up the tickets. I'll ask him to play watchdog."

"What a good idea," said Joan. She beamed, her good humour restored. "I love your dad," she added warmly. "Councillor Beary can handle anything."

Philippa smiled.

"Except my mother," she said wryly.

* * *

Upon his arrival at the theatre, Bertram Beary left his wife to seek out Mae Fenwick and dutifully reported backstage to find out what his daughter wanted. He listened sympathetically as Philippa explained the importance of keeping Sophie Guttenberg away from the gentlemen from the bank. Beary was perfectly willing to carry out his daughter's directive, but when he returned to the front of house, Sophie had disappeared. A search of the hallways and the auditorium proved fruitless, but a query to the girl at the concession stand revealed that the singer had left the building.

Beary hurried outside, wheezing slightly at the effort of increasing his normal leisurely pace, and scanned the faces of the people in the courtyard. Sophie's gleaming Aston Martin was still parked near the main entrance, but the singer was nowhere in sight. Beary walked along the side of the building and peered around the parking lot. The moon had come up, setting a purple glow across the night sky, and the steady beams of the tall streetlamps lit the ground below. He proceeded along the brick path that led to the grassy amphitheatre at the back of the complex, but this area too was deserted.

He was about to return when he saw a flickering light at the far end of the tennis courts. A walker with a flashlight was moving along the edge of the woods and heading towards the inlet trail. Suddenly the shadowy figure paused and turned back, and the light solidified into a pinpointed beam. For a few brief seconds it shone like a beacon marking the entrance to the path, but then the walker turned away. A glowing green circle appeared briefly against the black wall of trees, and then it faded to nothing as the walker entered the trail and was swallowed up by the woods. Beary looked at his watch. It was almost seven-thirty. The performance was about to begin.

The moon disappeared behind a cloud and the grounds darkened until nothing was visible but the pools of light created by the streetlamps and the golden rectangles of the library windows. He gave up and returned to the theatre. He seated himself by the rear doors where he could watch for the singer's return, but half an hour into the show, she had still not appeared, so he gave up his vigil and concentrated on his daughter's charming rendition of Susanna. He very much doubted if Sophie would show up now, but he was extremely curious to know what she was doing that was more important than her star students' showcase performance.

* * *

Sophie stumbled down a set of steps, and the flickering beam from her flashlight illuminated a patch of worn red bricks inlaid into a bend in the path. The pounding in her chest was getting stronger. She could faintly make out a curved boardwalk at the base of the stairs, but the trail was uneven and the glow from her flashlight was fading.

Suddenly, she tripped on a root that was protruding from the path and as she clutched at a branch to save herself from falling, the flashlight flew out of her hands. It landed with a thud somewhere in front of her, and the light went out. The sky overhead glowed faintly where the moon hovered behind the clouds, but where she stood at the base of the evergreens, she was entombed in darkness. The hoot of an owl pierced the silence, making her catch her breath and clutch at her chest. She fell to her knees, gasping as the icy chill of the rough bricks penetrated the thin wool of her skirt. She reached forward and felt around the wooden surface of the boardwalk, trying to find where the flashlight had fallen. Her hand brushed against something solid, which moved and then was gone with nothing more than a faint plop as it descended onto the semi-frozen quagmire below.

The pressure on her temples made her feel as if her head would burst, and in the inky shadows, an image appeared in her brain, dazzling her senses as if it were brilliantly lit with a spotlight. She squeezed her eyes shut, but the picture refused to go away. She could see the bedroom, with its utilitarian Ikea furniture and faded blue linen curtains. There were magazines littered about the floor—titles she had never heard of—trashy things, she thought bleakly, like the creature who lay on the bed. The wedding picture on the bedside table revealed that the woman had been beautiful, with a beauty-contest type of loveliness that had been eradicated by the shocked grimace that was fixed on her face now. In the photograph, the woman was gowned in white—perfectly coiffed and professionally made-up—and the only splash of colour came from the bouquet of roses she held at her waist. The figure on the bed was also dressed in white, although the flowing summer dress was a simple cotton rather than the gleaming satin of the wedding gown, but the red smear on the front was an ugly bloody stain, spreading outwards from the dagger that had ended her life. The woman lay immobile, with no knowledge of the immolation that awaited her.

Sophie shuddered at the memory of the dagger. The music kept pounding in her head, and a phrase kept repeating itself over and over. *Neither God nor sanctuary can help you now.* She saw the bed burst into flames and she felt a scream welling up in her throat. She wanted the pain to stop. It should be over, but it wasn't. As she knelt on the cold, hard ground, she realized that her husband's betrayal and its terrible aftermath would never be obliterated from her consciousness. Her love was dead. All feeling had departed. She should have burned with the other woman, for there would never be any peace for her now, other than the escape of oblivion.

* * *

Sylvia and Norton Barnwell decided to eat out before going to rehearsal since their favourite waterfront bistro was only two blocks from the theatre. They had just finished their main course when the jingle of a cellphone interrupted their perusal of the dessert menu.

"It's mine," said Sylvia, whipping her phone out of her purse.

Norton sipped his coffee and waited patiently while his wife took the call. She appeared to be listening attentively with the professional calm that she reserved for her clients, but when she rang off, she informed Norton that the call had come from Philippa.

"Sounds like my little sister had quite a night," she said.

"What's up? Did *Figaro* not go well?"

"The show was fine. The big drama was offstage. The lady who coaches the singers—who also happens to be Philippa's voice teacher— was in a most peculiar state and took off before the performance started. Then after the show, when Philippa was leaving the theatre, there were sirens and emergency vehicles racing by and the sky was lit up like a blazing sunset. There was a big fire on the Old Orchard Road."

Norton blanched.

"Not the refinery!"

"No. It was a private house. Anyway, the fire isn't the issue; it's the teacher that Philippa is worried about. Sophie Guttenberg lives only a few blocks from us, so Philippa wants us to run by her house and make sure she's all right. Dad was given the job of keeping an eye on the woman last night, but I gather she disappeared fifteen minutes before the show started. She hadn't reappeared by the final curtain, so he went outside to check if her car was still there. As he came out, he saw it pulling onto the road, so goodness knows what she was doing all through the performance. She hasn't answered her phone all day. Philippa is quite concerned."

"Seems to me, Philippa is overreacting. The woman probably developed a headache and went home to rest."

"Philippa isn't overreacting. It sounds as if this voice teacher has been acting very erratically." Sylvia glanced at her watch, decided there was no time for dessert and waved to the waiter to bring the bill. "Anyway," she continued, "I said we'd run out there after rehearsal."

"For heaven's sake," protested Norton. "It'll be after ten o'clock. Leaving aside the fact that I have an appointment at seven o'clock tomorrow morning, it's far too late to go knocking on the door of someone we've never met and inquiring after their health."

"Yes, I know," said Sylvia, "but Philippa is not prone to exaggeration, so I said we would. Now, finish your coffee. You don't want to be late for your rehearsal."

Norton looked glum. He was not looking forward to the evening ahead. "I know you got me into this with the best of intentions," he said plaintively, "but I must say I find acting awfully difficult. It was very sporting of you to sign up to do props and keep me company, but I honestly wish that I was doing your job and you were on stage."

Sylvia filled in the charge slip that the waiter had deposited on the table, put down the pen and stood up.

"The purpose of joining the theatre club was for *you* to develop your speaking skills," she said briskly. "*I* don't need to be on stage and I'm not there to keep you company. I just want to make sure the director gets a decent performance out of you and doesn't pussy-foot around telling you you're doing fine when you're as animated as a drowned poodle. Good heavens," she added, looking out the window and staring towards the docks. "What on earth is going on down there?"

Norton followed her glance. In the yellow pool of light created by a halogen lamp at the end of the dock, a cluster of people had gathered and appeared to be pointing towards the water.

Sylvia and Norton put on their coats and headed for the door. As they stepped out onto the street, the distant wail of a siren cut the night air. The sound became louder, and the volume steadily increased until, in a blaze of headlights, a fire truck came around the corner and headed down towards the wharf. A police car followed close on its tail. Sylvia could hear another siren in the distance. Presumably an ambulance was on the way. A man in an orange floater coat came running to meet the squad car. Even from where they were standing, Sylvia and Norton could hear the agitated greeting he gave the burly constable who got out of the vehicle.

"There's a body at the end of the wharf. We've pulled him out but he's a goner. I don't think the paramedics are going to be able to do anything for him, but you'd better go round and get his wife. It's the house out there on the point."

The police constable looked alert.

"You know who it is?"

"Of course I do. He owned a big Bayliner so he was a regular at the fuel docks. Everyone round here knew him. It's Leonard Trant."

* * *

Upon receiving news of her husband's death, Sophie Guttenberg's behaviour was bizarre. It was the strangest form of grief Constable Jean Howe had ever seen, if grief it was, for the woman seemed to be in a daze even before she was told of the reason for the visit from the police, and once she knew why they were there, she appeared unsurprised and indifferent. She had uttered only two sentences. "It doesn't matter any more. I'm as dead as they are." WPC Howe had mentally noted the plural pronoun, but Sophie had sunk down onto the chesterfield and said nothing more. The young constable went to the kitchen to find the motherly Filipino woman who had answered the door when the police had first arrived. Having requested a cup of tea for the bereaved widow, Jean Howe returned to the living room and surveyed the details of the décor.

The furnishings were expensive. The room was dominated by a concert grand, placed on an angle so that a student standing in the curve of the piano could enjoy a spectacular view across the inlet; yet if turned towards the accompanist, the singer would be staring directly at the dramatic operatic poster that hung on the wall behind the piano bench. Very good psychology, thought Jean—inspiration from both art and nature. Jean had learned a little about the world of music from her boss, who often talked about his opera-singing sister, and if this case proved to be murder, she knew that Richard Beary would probably have access to a great deal of insider information about the strange woman who sat silently at the other end of the room.

The constable continued her circuit, studying the pictures on the walls as she went. They were all theatrical shots, and one in particular caught her eye. It was a colour enlargement of the woman on the couch, though if it had not been for the strong features and the tortured expression, Jean would not have recognized her, for in the photograph,

Sophie was resplendent in a vivid ensemble with striped skirt and heavily beaded bodice, and her hair was twisted into coils and ringlets which were entwined with beads and ribbons to match the ornamentation on the gown. Now, she was dressed in black, and as she huddled on the couch, her body looked tiny, and her unmade-up face appeared shrivelled and frail. Jean looked again at the photograph. The woman in the picture held a dagger, the hilt as ornate and colourful as the bodice of her dress. The dagger looked familiar. Jean glanced back at the framed poster by the grand piano. It was printed in German—except for the Italian title, *La Gioconda*—and an artist's rendering of the jewelled dagger formed the upright of the letter *L*. Jean looked more closely. There was a written inscription in Italian above what appeared to be the soprano's signature. She was so engrossed in studying the poster that she jumped when Sophie spoke.

"Can a single heart endure so many sorrows?"

Jean was startled.

"What? I'm sorry. What did you say?"

Sophie smiled sadly.

"The inscription," she said. "You were reading what's written on the poster. That's what it means."

She turned her head away and stared out through the glass. Her back stiffened, and Jean went to the window to see what had caused the woman's tension. The day had been cloudy and no stars were gleaming in the sky, but one solitary light burned white in the distance. Just a marker on a buoy, Jean decided. She could not understand why it affected the woman so, but the WPC observed that the singer seemed unable to take her eyes off it.

Encouraged by the fact that Sophie had spoken, Jean made another attempt to draw her into conversation.

"Actually," she said, "I was staring at the dagger. It's very ornamental. It must be a stage prop, but it looks real in the photograph."

Sophie's reaction was far more dramatic than Jean had anticipated. The singer swung back, wild-eyed, and rose to her feet. She took two steps towards the constable. Then, without another word, she dropped to the floor in a dead faint.

* * *

Richard Beary set the autopsy report onto the pile of statements on his desk. The Trant case was becoming increasingly perplexing. The cause of death was not drowning, which was why the body had washed ashore within twenty-four hours of going into the water. Trant had received a heavy blow to the front of the head and the skin on his right arm was severely burned, but even that had not killed him. He had died from a heart attack, most likely brought on by the shock of the assault. Death had probably occurred some time during the evening of the *Figaro* performance in Port Moody. The right arm of Trant's jacket was missing and there were traces of phosphorus on the remaining fabric, which suggested that the burning had been caused by a flare gun.

"Our forensic people found similar traces on the inside wall of the boathouse at the end of Trant's private dock," said Richard. "The attack must have taken place there."

"Lucky his boat wasn't set on fire," said Sergeant Bill Martin, who had been handling the investigation of the inferno on Old Orchard Road and, as a result, had arson on his mind. In spite of statements from sanctimonious neighbours who had pointed out that the victim of the Port Moody fire had been an accident waiting to happen because she smoked and drank in bed, Martin was anxious to see the forensic reports on the cause of the woman's death and the expert opinions on what had triggered the fire. Since the victim's estranged husband was the beneficiary of both life and house insurance policies, the sergeant was inclined to be suspicious.

"Trant's boat wasn't in the boathouse," said Richard. "It's in dry dock. We checked on that. He owned a thirty-foot Bayliner, but it's currently having an engine rebuild. It's been out of the water for two months. The empty boathouse was a perfect place to set off the flare. It would have ricocheted off the side and gone straight into the water."

"What was Trant doing on the dock in freezing January weather when his boat was out of commission?" Martin looked puzzled.

"Fixing storm damage," said Richard. "We had some bad winds before Christmas. According to the Guttenberg's housekeeper, Trant had spent a couple of evenings repairing the roof supports, and he'd declared his intention of finishing the job that evening while his wife was at the theatre. There was a tool kit on the dock and a trouble light hanging over one of the beams. The light was unplugged, but the killer probably did that after Trant went into the water."

"Who was the last person to see him alive?"

"Probably his wife, but she isn't talking. She's still under sedation in Lions Gate Hospital. No one can get a word out of her. Most of our information has come from the housekeeper. She saw Trant around five o'clock that day. She served dinner early as Guttenberg had almost an hour's drive to Port Moody and Trant wanted to get on with his repairs. The housekeeper left as soon as she'd cleaned up, which would have been around five-thirty. Guttenberg left for the theatre at six o'clock."

"How do we know if she isn't talking?"

"The neighbour who lives in the house opposite is a writer. His study window overlooks Trant's driveway. He was working all evening and he saw Guttenberg leave—she drives a silver Aston Martin, pretty hard to miss—and he also saw the car return shortly before nine-thirty."

"That's a useful witness. Did anyone else come to the house that evening?"

"Not in a vehicle. Brady—that's the writer—says Trant's SUV was parked in the drive all evening, but he didn't see any other cars. He also insists that no one came on foot. I gather the drive and front porch are well lit, but we should take that with a grain of salt because presumably the man was looking at his computer screen and not spending the whole evening staring out the window."

"You never know," said Martin. "Maybe he was suffering from writer's block. Did the other members of his household see anything?"

"No. He lives alone. His wife walked out on him last year."

"Does he have any idea why someone would want to kill Trant?"

"Not really. It sounds as if they didn't socialize other than to chat in the front garden. Brady says Trant seemed pleasant enough, unlike Sophie Guttenberg who looked like a startled fawn whenever he spoke to her. His assessment of Guttenberg was that she was totally immersed in her music and didn't register anything that didn't relate to her work, but he said it in a nice way. He said he thought of her as vulnerable and intriguing, whereas Trant was more social. He'd do things like water the garden or feed the pets when people were away on holiday."

"What did Trant do for a living?"

"He was an architect . . . a successful one judging by the family assets. Unless, of course, the wife is the one with the money, but singing teachers don't make big dollars and her career tanked years ago, so she hardly had time to build up a fortune. We'll have to check on the source of their income. The housekeeper filled us in on some of the family background, but she didn't know anything about their finances, other than the fact that they were obviously very well off."

"Does anyone other than the wife stand to inherit now that Trant's dead?"

"Possibly. We have yet to turn up a will. Trant has a son from a first marriage. Darren. He's nineteen. He lives with his mother in one of those water-access-only homes up Indian Arm. They were interviewed yesterday. Mum's an accountant, so she carries out her business from home—easy enough in the computer age—and Darren's a student at Cap College."

"That's quite a commute. How does he get there?"

"They have a fourteen-foot Glasply. He moors it at Deep Cove, and then takes the bus to college."

"Easy enough for either of them to get to Trant's boathouse by water."

"True," Richard acknowledged, "but Darren and his mother say they never have any contact with Trant. The divorce was acrimonious, and Darren can't stand his stepmother. His exact words were, 'She's a scheming bitch who put on the poor-pathetic-me act for my father when he was working in Germany and weaselled him away from my mother who was staying in Vancouver so I didn't have to change schools. And now she's murdered him, and it serves him bloody well right. I'm just sorry they don't have hanging any more because that's what the cow deserves.' For a college student, he's rather inconsistent with the metaphors, but there's no ambiguity about his meaning. The mother was not quite so vehement. She says Trant was a womanizer from day one and if she'd had any sense she'd have ditched him much sooner. She seems to think Sophie did her a favour by stealing him away, but she acknowledges that her son was deeply hurt. Her guess is that Trant reverted to type and was cheating again, and Guttenberg killed him in a jealous rage. She's probably right, though my sister will be madder than hell if we arrest her beloved teacher. Still, the facts look pretty incriminating. The housekeeper admitted that she had overheard her employers having violent rows. The singer was crazy with suspicions that her husband was having an affair—and Jean Howe swears that Guttenberg was in shock even before she was told that her husband was dead. Her history is damning too. She attacked someone with a flare gun once before—her first husband's mistress."

"She actually fired a flare gun at another woman?"

"No. It was taken from her before she could use it, but there's no doubt she's a neurotically jealous woman. I'm very worried about what she said to Jean. 'I'm as dead as they are.' That tells me there's another body out there somewhere. It could even be washing ashore as we speak. Just because no one came to the house by car doesn't mean Trant didn't have a visitor. What if the mistress came over by boat? They could have had a tryst while Guttenberg was at the theatre. Guttenberg left the show early. What if she came home as Trant was seeing his girlfriend off from the dock? She could have heard their voices, gone down and caught them in the act."

"But there wasn't a boat."

"No, but she could have cast it adrift."

"Did none of the other neighbours see anything? Can't Trant's boathouse be seen from the other waterfront homes?"

"Only from the house next door, but the couple who live there are in Florida. There's very little to go on so far. We have to find something to give us a lead on who Trant's mistress was."

"Records of phone calls?"

"Trant used his cellphone all the time, and that's probably at the bottom of the inlet. The house phone appears to have been used strictly for the music studio, or for routine things to do with the running of the household. There was a call the day before Trant died, but it was for Guttenberg, not her husband. The housekeeper answered the phone, and she says the caller was a woman."

"Does she know who it was?"

"No, but she says it was some kind of appointment, because she heard Guttenberg say, 'Yes, all right. I'll be there.' And then she hung up. We are checking on it, but chances are it was an unrelated call."

The door flew open and Jean Howe came into the room. Her eyes were bright with excitement. She held a computer printout in one hand and a lab report in the other.

"Sir, we've got her! Trant's mistress. This has to be it."

Jean set the documents on Richard's desk, waved Bill Martin over and stabbed her finger at the paragraph at the bottom of the lab report.

"This just came in for you," she said. "It's the forensic report on the fire in Port Moody. They found traces of phosphorus. They think it was started with a flare gun!"

"Good God!" said Richard.

"There's more," said Jean, handing him the computer printout. "These are the phone records. The call to Sophie Guttenberg the day before her husband's death came from the house that burned down."

"Janis Edwards," said Bill Martin. "The glamour girl who smoked and drank in bed. And look at this," he added, pointing at the lab report. "We're dealing with a homicide. There was a dagger in what remained of her rib cage, and just in case that hadn't done the trick, the bedroom door was closed and someone had taken the trouble to reverse the lock so that she couldn't get out . . . *and* a piece of metal was jammed in the outside of the sliding window so it couldn't open."

"She must have already been dead," said Jean. "Otherwise she'd have broken the window to escape."

Martin shook his head.

"Not possible," he said. "They were made of Lexan. She probably had them installed for security, given that her garden backed onto a trail. Lexan can't be broken, although it does burn, but by the time the fire got to the window, the whole bedroom would have been engulfed. Poor woman. I hope she *was* dead before the flames got to her. The dagger would have been a blessing."

"Well," cried Jean, "the dagger is going to be a blessing for us too, because I know where it came from. I saw a photograph of it at Trant's house. It belongs to Sophie Guttenberg."

"Bingo," said Sergeant Martin.

* * *

"It's a lost cause and a waste of your valuable time," snapped Sylvia. "It'll be a plea of temporary insanity and any beginning law student could deal with it. Philippa has no business pressuring you to take the case."

Norton looked mulish. "Philippa isn't convinced that Sophie Guttenberg is guilty. And I have to say, after talking it over with her, I think she may have a point. You see, however feasible it is that Guttenberg could attack another woman in a jealous rage, it's unlikely that she would kill her husband. Besides, Guttenberg is a tiny little thing and Janis Edwards was stabbed. That requires a lot more force and actual contact with the victim than simply firing a flare gun. And two weapons imply premeditation—a determination to kill that doesn't fit with the woman's character."

"For heaven's sake," protested Sylvia. "The murder weapon *belongs* to Guttenberg—though why she would want to keep such a souvenir is beyond me."

"It's a beautiful example of a Venetian dagger," Norton pointed out. "She used it in *Gioconda*."

"How on earth could something that lethal have been used as a stage prop?"

"It was retractable," said Norton. "Mind you, prop knives are pretty dicey. They can jam, and there have been instances where actors have impaled themselves on blunt shafts and done themselves a serious injury. But in this case, someone had deliberately fixed the dagger so that it didn't retract any more, and the blade had been sharpened, so it was a pretty formidable weapon."

"Have the police any idea when it was tampered with?"

"Within the last two weeks. The housekeeper told the police that the dagger was kept in a glass case in the front hall. There were guests at the house two weeks ago and the dagger was taken out and passed around. At that time, the blade was still rounded." Norton looked smug. "You realize, of course, that this is another point in Sophie's favour."

"Why?"

"She's a brilliant artist, but she's hopeless at mechanical jobs. Philippa thinks someone who knows her history and emotional state has used that knowledge to frame her."

"That's the most outlandish thing I've ever heard," snapped Sylvia. "Philippa can't be serious."

"Well, she is," said Norton. "And now that Sophie has been arrested, I've agreed to defend her."

"And you'll spend hours going over every detail—retracing her steps, analyzing reports, reviewing articles that go back twenty years—just to come to the conclusion that she went over the edge and committed two murders while her mind was unbalanced. Then my sister will be mad at you because you weren't able to save her precious teacher from her own folly. What do you hope to get out of it?"

Norton smiled. He knew his wife well.

"Well, money for one thing. It turns out that the fortune in the family came from Sophie herself. Evidently her father was a German steel baron. Both parents died in a car crash two years ago and Sophie, being an only child, inherited everything. So I will be extremely well paid for those hours of research. Top dollar, Philippa tells me. She's tracked down the family solicitor who happens to be very fond of Sophie, and he is extremely anxious that there is a proper defence. The neighbour who lives opposite is also offering to help, and all Sophie's students are up in arms on her behalf. Mae Fenwick has volunteered her assistance too—you know, the stalwart lady who runs the opera guild. It sounds as if she never liked Leonard Trant. She considered him a fortune hunter who took advantage of Sophie when she was vulnerable because he knew she was the only child of rich parents. Sophie appears to have quite a few champions."

Sylvia looked slightly mollified, but she still fired a parting shot.

"Well," she said, "if you're determined to take the case, go ahead, but I don't know how you're going to prove Philippa's wild theory when you have a client who won't talk. Anyway, you can stay up all night and figure it out. I'm going to bed."

Sylvia left the room. Norton headed for the kitchen and made himself a cup of herbal tea. Then he returned to the living room and took out the DVD that Philippa had lent him. He switched on the TV, inserted the disc, and settled back to watch *La Gioconda*. It was time to get to know his client.

* * *

The following morning, Philippa drove to Barnet Village, bought herself a latte at the gelato shop, and then set off to explore the inlet trail. As she walked, she reflected on the night of the murders. Norton had faxed her copies of the relevant reports so she had a clear idea of the critical times. Sophie had left the theatre at ten past seven and had returned for her car shortly after eight-thirty. A neighbour had reported the fire at Janis Edwards' house just before eight o'clock, but by that time the blaze had a firm hold. The flare that ignited the bedclothes was probably fired around seven-thirty. Philippa wanted to see for herself just how long it would take to walk from the theatre to Janis Edwards' house. She checked her watch as she crossed the theatre parking lot. It was quarter past ten.

She passed the amphitheatre and continued along the edge of the tennis courts. Then she crossed the railroad tracks and entered the trail. There were two paths that branched to the right. One was a paved bicycle path, which ran alongside the railway line, and the other was a dirt trail, closer to the water and far less even since it followed the rises and falls of the rocky shoreline. Philippa took the top path because she was sure that anyone walking at night would take the upper route. The day was cold and clear, and visibility was good since the branches of the alders and cottonwood trees were bare and the winter sunlight shone through. Further in, the path became darker and greener, for cedars and firs began to appear amid the deciduous trees. After five minutes of brisk walking, Philippa saw a house through the trees, but the area between the path and the residence was overgrown with tangled blackberry brambles and ivy-covered stumps so it was hard to imagine that anyone could penetrate the bushes to reach the home. Philippa slowed her pace slightly, realizing that if Sophie had walked the route at night, she would have progressed with less speed, especially as she had been wearing dress shoes with high heels.

A few minutes later, the bushes to the right parted, and a cut in the brambles revealed a gravel path that traversed the railway lines and led to a row of condominiums. Philippa walked across the tracks. When she reached the other side, the skeleton of Janis Edwards' house came into view. It was easily accessible from the path, for there was no garden fence, and only a row of hydrangea bushes separated the trail from the back lawn. Philippa approached the blackened structure and tried to visualize the house as it had been prior to the fire. The remnants of the back deck were still in place, and she could see that stairs had gone from the deck to the lawn. One end of the house was intact. A small, square window stood open, and as she moved further to the right, she could see the remains of bathroom fittings, but the connecting wall beside the bathroom was non-existent and there was a vacuum where the bedroom should have been. The house must have had a good view of the water, at least in winter, for even from where Philippa stood, she could look back and see the ocean through the bare branches of the alder trees. She glanced at her watch. It was not yet ten-thirty. With a sinking feeling, she realized that Sophie could easily have reached the house and returned to the parking lot with a good forty-five minutes to spare. The picture looked bleak. If Sophie didn't talk soon and give her side of the story, it was going to be very difficult to help her.

Philippa sighed and went back across the tracks. The cut in the brambles continued across the bicycle path and led to the lower trail, so she decided to return via the bottom route. She walked down a series of steps and soon reached a small platform where a hide had been built to overlook the mudflats and the nesting waterfowl. The structure must have been there for years because it was covered in ivy. Below the platform, the bank sloped down to a dock. At present, the tide was in and two children in a dinghy were paddling towards the pilings. As Philippa contemplated their progress, the sharp cry of a blue heron broke the silence; then suddenly there was a flapping of wings as the huge bird took off from the shore. It soared across the water and flew towards Pigeon Cove, where it disappeared into the shadow of the distant trees. The outlook should have been exhilarating, but in her present mood, Philippa was impervious to the beauties of nature.

She continued along the trail, which was little more than a series of dirt paths carved out of the bank and linked by an intricate network of boardwalks and steps. She trod carefully, because in many places, the roots of cottonwood trees jutted up through the earth. At one point, where a black swamp interrupted the track, an innovative engineer had utilized a root to frame several bricks into a small platform to stabilize the planks that traversed the marsh. Philippa imagined that a sea of skunk cabbage would surround the boardwalk in the summer, but now the earth was bare, except for a patch of ivy that trailed down the bank at the far end of the fen. A flicker of light glinted beneath the ivy. The sunlight filtering though the trees appeared to be hitting something metallic. Philippa knelt down and leaned as far as she could over the edge of the boardwalk. She stretched her hand down into the ivy and felt something hard. She pulled up the object. It was a flashlight. Thoughtfully, she put it into her bag and continued on her way.

As she reached the bridge at the end of the path, her cellphone rang. It was Norton.

"Sophie is ready to talk," he said.

* * *

The cold snap had ended, but with the increase in temperature came the rain. It was a gloomy, overcast day and the damp was bone-chilling, but Norton's smile belied the dismal weather. He had been deeply moved by the film of *La Gioconda*. Although unadventurous by nature, he enjoyed melodrama, as long as it was the kind that could be turned off with a switch. The passion and spectacle of the opera had been tremendously stirring and he was still bubbling with enthusiasm when he met Philippa at the hospital.

"That ballroom scene was incredible! The costumes alone made it worth viewing," he trilled. "I recognized the ballet music immediately but I hadn't a clue that it was from *Gioconda*. I always associated it with that silly sixties song about Camp Grenada. But I soon stopped chortling because the choreography was breathtaking."

Philippa interrupted the flow.

"Yes, I know it's a great production, but what about Sophie? What did you conclude from watching her?"

Norton looked reflective.

"If she's anything like the character she was playing, I don't think she could have done what she's accused of. In spite of all the stuff about 'I love the man you love' and 'for his kisses I will kill you', I sensed a woman eaten up by *passion*, but ultimately governed by *compassion*. She might rage or threaten, but in the final analysis, love and pity would be stronger than hatred. But of course, the question is how good an actress is she? That's what she portrayed in her greatest role, but is she like that in real life?"

"I believe she is," said Philippa.

"You know," said Norton, "it's utterly irrelevant, but the one phrase that keeps haunting me is 'Look to the sea.' I keep hearing that over and over. Strange, isn't it? Anyway, enough about the opera. Let's go up and see Sophie. I thought she might be more receptive with you there, so I'm glad you were free to come along."

"She'll be OK with you," said Philippa. "That's one of the reasons I wanted you to defend her. She won't find you threatening. She needs gentle handling."

"Yes, I know," said Norton affably. "That's me. Totally innocuous. That's why Sylvia's got me into this embarrassing mess with the drama group. She wants me to develop more presence in the courtroom, but of course, it's a hopeless cause. My forte is research, not performance. I do hope you're not going to come to the play. It's going to be disastrous . . . well, my part, anyway."

"Oh?" said Philippa, sensing a challenge. "What's the problem?"

Norton hung his head.

"Everyone keeps telling me different things, and the director uses terms like *countering* and *crossing* and *cheating*, and then she gives me long lectures on motivation and I honestly haven't got a clue what she's talking about. And Sylvia is on at me all the time because she says I can't be heard past the second row. It's an excruciatingly miserable experience for me."

Philippa's eyes twinkled. She stepped back to the other side of the corridor and looked at Norton speculatively.

"I'm the audience," she said. She pointed to the garbage can beside the elevator. "That's your co-star. Say one of your lines."

Norton obliged; then he looked across at Philippa to see the verdict.

"Terrible, right?" he said.

"Not at all . . . just the classic beginner's errors. You're letting your head drop because you're tall. Then you've placed your body towards the audience but turned your head to face the person you're speaking to, so of course you can't be heard because you're sending your voice into the wings. We can fix that in an instant." Philippa kept it simple. "Turn your body towards the other actor," she said. Norton did as he was instructed. "Now turn you head towards me but keep your eyes on the garbage bin. There! That's it. That's what your director means by *cheating.*"

"Oh, I see," said Norton. "No one explained that."

"All you have to do is stand up as straight as you possibly can, speak five times as loud as you think is necessary, articulate so clearly that you feel you're ridiculous, don't drop a single *t* or *d* off the ends of your words, and keep your eyes on the person you're speaking with. Forget everything else you've been told and concentrate on those five things. You'll get through with flying colours."

"But won't I be a bit wooden?"

Philippa was too kind by nature to point out that Norton's normal personality was as charismatic as a two-by-four. Instead, she said, "You're playing a guardsman, and he's supposed to be stiff. It'll be perfect."

The elevator arrived. Still looking a little bemused, Norton followed Philippa inside. When they came out on the third floor, they saw a WPC sitting outside a room halfway down the corridor. Norton approached the constable and introduced Philippa as his assistant. Once through the doorway, Philippa made a face.

"Was that necessary?"

"Probably. Especially if we don't want to annoy your brother."

"Richard wouldn't mind me talking to Sophie. He's a good policeman. He always supports anything that will lead to the truth."

"That may be," said Norton, "but the constable outside doesn't know that and I'm in a hurry to get information from this singing teacher that you're so anxious I defend. Now, come on. Let's hope she's awake."

Sophie was hidden from view by closed curtains, but a nurse emerged from the enclosure and planted herself in their path. Norton diplomatically explained why they were there. Reluctantly, the nurse admitted them.

"You can have ten minutes," she said. "The patient's still in a state of shock. I know she wants to talk, but I don't want her agitated."

"I hope you haven't let her talk to the police," said Norton.

"Of course not." The nurse looked indignant. "She won't be talking to them after you leave, either," she added. "Don't worry. I'll keep an eye on her."

She held the curtains aside and Norton and Philippa slipped through. Philippa was shocked to see how frail her teacher looked. At their first meeting, Philippa had been surprised at how tiny the soprano was, for in the televised opera she had appeared larger than life, but now, even her normally petite frame seemed to have shrivelled to nothing. But her voice, when she spoke, was strong, and the tale she told was as riveting as her performance as the ill-fated street singer.

"I didn't kill them," she began. "I don't understand what's happening, but I didn't do it. You have to believe that."

"We believe you," Philippa said gently. "Tell us exactly what happened."

"I knew what was going on," said Sophie sadly. "I didn't know who Leonard was seeing, but I recognized the signs. I'd been through it before, you see, with my first husband. I was angry and upset, and we fought, but he kept denying that there was anyone else. Then I got the phone call. It was a woman, and she said she wanted to talk to me. I could tell from the way she spoke that she was the one. She lived very close to the Village Theatre, so I agreed to see her the night of the show. But I wasn't going to take things lying down. I was furious, and I was determined to make her leave us alone. I didn't want anyone to see my car there—I didn't want people to know about her association with my husband—so I walked around from the theatre. She told me how to get there, and when I arrived, I saw that the doors on the deck were open. I went into the house, but everything was silent. I called out, but no one replied. Then I saw that there was a light in the next room, so I went through. And she was lying there. I could see she was dead, because the knife . . . *my* knife . . . was sticking up through her ribs and there was blood all over the bed. I moved forward to make sure, and as I stared at her, there was a popping sound, and suddenly the bed simply caught fire. I think I froze, and then I heard a bang, and I looked around. The door was closed. I tried to open it, but I couldn't. The fire on the bed was getting bigger, so I ran to the windows, but I couldn't open them either. I tried to break them, but the glass wouldn't break. I was terrified. I thought I was going to die in there with her—and then I saw the beacon in the distance." Sophie's eyes widened and her expression became remote. "Isn't it strange?" she said. "She could look out on it too. Perhaps we had been staring at it at the same time. No wonder I felt haunted by the light."

Norton looked baffled.

"There's a buoy in the middle of the inlet," Philippa explained. "I've seen it when I've been on the boat with Dad. That'll be the light

Sophie's referring to. You can see it from her house. I remember Joan Fenwick commenting on it. She's working on the mezzo aria from *Gioconda*—"

"Ah," Norton interjected. "'Stella del Marinar'—gorgeous piece that."

"Yes," said Philippa. "'Star of the Mariner' . . . Sophie used to tell Joan to sing towards the beacon."

A trace of a smile crossed Sophie's face.

"The beacon saved me," she said. "Somehow it gave me strength. I looked around and saw the other door. It led to a bathroom, and there was a tiny window. It was so small, but I'm small too, and I managed to wriggle through onto the deck. Then I ran down into the garden and back across the railway tracks. I was going to return the way I came, but I heard voices on the path and I could see a flashlight. It looked like a couple with a dog. I didn't want anyone to see me so I ran down onto the lower trail. It was rough, but I had my flashlight so I could see where I was going. But then I fell and dropped the light. I was dazed. I don't know how I found my way back to my car, or even how I drove home. I don't remember anything, except that I got there. I went in and I stayed inside. I didn't dare go out again. And then they came to tell me that Leonard was dead too."

Sophie stared miserably at Philippa and Norton.

"I know they won't believe me," she said. "But that's what happened. You must make of it what you will. I don't really care what happens to me any more, but I do want to know who killed my husband. All I ask is that you find out for me."

* * *

Philippa never had any compunction about nagging her older brother. Richard often complained to Sergeant Martin that his sister was like a ferret hunting its prey when she had a particular object in mind, but secretly he was proud of her perseverance and he valued her judgement sufficiently not to ignore her when she put forth suggestions about his cases. But as he pointed out to her, the charges against her singing teacher were based on strong evidence and he had not neglected to investigate the other people who might have benefited from the victims' deaths. However much she wished it to be otherwise, the fact remained that none of the other suspects could be linked to both victims. Leonard Trant's ex-wife was out of the picture because she had spent the evening with her neighbour and had not returned home until eleven o'clock. Darren Trant had spent the early part of the evening at the pub in Deep Cove and had not set off for Indian Arm until eight o'clock. Since his mother was out, no one could say what time he returned home, so he would have had ample opportunity to moor at the dock by his father's house, but by that time, Janis Edwards was already dead. Edwards' estranged husband had been scrutinized as well, for he certainly had a motive to kill his wife, but the police drew a blank with him too. He had spent the day skiing on Grouse Mountain, and half-a-dozen people attested to the fact that he had not come down until six-thirty. He had his own car, so there were no witnesses to prove that he had driven directly back to his apartment—and therefore, he could have stopped in Deep Cove, left his car at the end of the block, and walked to Trant's house to commit the first murder. However, there was no way he could have arrived in Port Moody in time to kill his wife. So the concept that Sophie had been framed was theoretically possible, but there was no one person who could have set her up in such a deadly fashion.

But like his sister, Richard was not entirely satisfied. Whenever he reached a dead end, he would fall back on a simple tactic. Forgetting about opportunity or physical evidence, he would concentrate on the personality of the victim. He picked up his pen and started to jot down the names of all the people whose lives were impacted by Janis Edwards. When he finished, he stared at the first name. On the basis of the evidence, it didn't seem possible, but every instinct told him that he had the solution. Some vital piece of information had to be missing. He pulled the pile of statements towards him and began to read them all over again.

* * *

The following evening was the opening performance of the Deep Cove Player's production of *The Reluctant Debutante*.

"Should be *The Reluctant Dilettante*," grumbled Beary as he started up the engine on the *Optimist*. "Sylvia had no business forcing Norton on stage, not to mention insisting that we go and witness the fiasco."

31

"Just as long as this crossing isn't a fiasco," snapped Edwina. "I hope you know what you're doing, taking us over at night."

"A breeze," Beary assured her. "I know this area like the palm of my hand."

"I fail to see how," said Edwina. "As I recall, you brought the boat down from the coast so you could go crab fishing through the winter, and it seems to me you haven't gone out once. It's very cramped in here," she added, looking around the tiny cabin that was only just big enough to squeeze in the two lawn chairs that Beary had set up for them to sit on.

"You're welcome to go outside," said Beary, "if you want to sit through Norton's performance in soaking wet clothes."

"Don't be ridiculous," said Edwina. She peered through the rain-swept glass and frowned.

"Are you sure you can see? The visibility in here is terrible."

"Stop fussing," grunted Beary. "Everything's fine."

Edwina pulled her coat tightly around her and stared out the side window. The yellow halogen lights of Rocky Point emanated a comforting glow from the shore, but as the *Optimist* progressed further into the inlet, the light seemed a false security, for when she drew her eyes back to the boat's gunwale, she realized there was only darkness surrounding their small craft. The *Optimist* was nestled low in the water, and the steady bow wave that showed faintly in the port light looked ominous. Edwina was regretting her acquiescence, especially when she remembered that they would have to return the same way. To take her mind off her anxiety, she started to talk about the play.

"We'll have to be polite, no matter what the production is like," she said. "Sylvia's intentions are good, after all. Norton is incredibly dull, and if this experience helps him get ahead in his profession, it'll be worthwhile."

"Norton doesn't do that badly," Beary argued. "He does quite well by his clients. He does his research and digs up the critical points for the defence; then he numbs the prosecutor's brain with minutiae, bores the judge to tears and everyone finally gives in out of desperation. He's certainly no Rumpole, but his methods usually work."

Beary leaned forward and squinted, trying to see ahead. The lights of Deep Cove were now twinkling on the far shore, but the glare combined with the rain was making it hard to see. Edwina noticed her husband's consternation.

"I'm sure you could see better outside," she urged. "You have raingear, and an umbrella would keep you reasonably dry."

"I can see perfectly well," Beary lied.

"No, you can't. It's black as pitch, and all those lights on shore are blinding. This really was a stupid idea. We ought to have driven—"

Edwina's voice faded into a gasp.

Beary swore and yanked the wheel over to starboard. A huge mass loomed across the bow and inexorably bore down on them. For one brief, terrifying moment, the cabin seemed to light up, and Edwina saw her husband, leaning horizontally, holding the steering wheel hard over.

Then, miraculously, the *Optimist* responded, and the wall of metal quietly slid past on their port side.

"Oh, my God," said Edwina. "What was that?"

"The can buoy," said Beary. "I couldn't see the beacon. It was masked by the lights on shore."

Edwina had leapt to her feet without realizing it, and now she sank back onto her chair. She could feel her heart pounding. For once she had nothing to say, but Beary said it for her.

"Well," he announced with amazement in his voice, "that would have been curtains. From this point on, anything we have is a gift. But for the fact that this old tub can't do more than seven knots, we'd have been at the bottom of the inlet. I must say," he added, reverting to his usual irreverent self, "that I made an interesting discovery from that experience."

At last Edwina found her voice.

"Oh, and what would that be?"

"It's quite true when they say that the most common last word of people who die in accidents is the vernacular for excrement."

"Yes, well fortunately, it wasn't your last word, and let's hope you don't have to repeat it on the way back."

"I won't," said Beary breezily. "On the return trip, it'll be easy to see the light because there's nothing but black hillside behind it. It's only a hazard coming from Port Moody." He stopped speaking suddenly and looked thoughtful.

"What is it?" demanded Edwina. "Don't tell me there's some other problem you haven't anticipated."

Beary shook his head. He slowed the engine and pointed ahead. They were passing by the promontory at the entrance to Deep Cove.

"Look," he said, "that's Philippa's teacher's house. See—the expensive pile, right on the point."

"Bought with Guttenberg's inheritance from her parents," Edwina reminded him. "If anyone was going to be popped off, you'd have thought it would have been her. Usually it's the wealthy wife who gets murdered."

The *Optimist* quietly glided past the point. Beary looked ahead. Deep Cove had materialized into a glowing shoreline where shops and docks were visible and growing larger every minute. As the details on land became clearer to his eyes, the ideas in his mind formulated into one cohesive picture.

"I think you just hit the nail on the head," he said slowly. "The more I think about it, the more the pieces seem to fit. We still have half an hour to show time," he added. "I'm going to give Richard a call."

* * *

When the phone rang in his office, Richard was staring at the paper on his desk. As he answered the call, he thought for one eerie moment that his father was present and reading over his shoulder, for Beary was bellowing the name he had written at the top of the list.

"Trant! It was Leonard Trant. He's your killer. I'm ready to bet that he killed Janis Edwards, and attempted to kill his own wife too."

Richard felt a surge of excitement. "Slow down, Dad. Explain. I need to know how you came up with that idea."

"He had a rich, neurotic wife and a troublesome mistress. The mistress was causing trouble and she set up a meeting with his wife. That gave him a perfect opportunity to get rid of both of them. He knew his wife's history, so he formulated a plan that would make it appear that she had killed Edwards, and then got trapped in the blaze that she had started to cover her crime. I think he went to Edwards' house, stabbed her with his wife's knife, which he'd sharpened and rigged so that it worked as a lethal weapon, and then hid in a back room and waited for his wife to arrive. He reversed the lock on the bedroom door and jammed the windows. He knew they were Lexan and wouldn't break. He didn't even consider the possibility that Sophie would escape through the bathroom window because it was so small, but she is a tiny woman, and when you're desperate enough, it's amazing what you can do."

"Sophie Guttenberg didn't say anything about seeing her husband at the house. Wouldn't she have known if he had been there?"

"Not necessarily. He could have hidden and waited for her to arrive. Then, once she walked into the bedroom, all he had to do was fire the flare through the doorway, slam the door shut, and leave, knowing that Sophie would be trapped."

"But how did he get there? His car was home all night, and the neighbour opposite insists that no other cars arrived at the house. Besides, Trant is dead. Who are you suggesting killed him?"

"Not a who . . . a what."

"Stop being enigmatic, Dad. I've got a case to close. What killed Trant?"

"The beacon. It just about killed me and your mother too."

Richard's tone changed.

"What on earth happened? Are you OK?"

"Yes, we're fine, but we nearly ended up at the bottom of the inlet." Beary described the incident with the can buoy. He could tell by the silence at the other end that his son was shocked by the tale. "Trant didn't have to take an hour to drive to Edwards' house. He could get there in half an hour by boat. All he had to do was anchor clear of the shallows and row ashore in a dinghy. There's a small dock just below Edwards' property, so it would only be a short walk up the trail. But on the return trip, I think he made the same error we did and failed to see the buoy because he was blinded by the lights in Deep Cove. If he hit that buoy, his head would have cracked against the dash of the boat. That would explain the wound on his forehead. He'd have been dazed and confused. The boat would have been sinking. What would you have done in the circumstances?"

"Tried to get into the dinghy," said Richard.

"Yes, but what if the dinghy was damaged, or he couldn't get it free?"

"I'd have fired a distress signal."

35

"Exactly. We know the killer had a flare gun. It's quite conceivable that a dazed man on a sinking boat might misfire in some way. Perhaps the boat lurched and the flare ricocheted. Who knows? But if he caught fire, he'd have gone in the water to put the fire out, and it's more than likely that the shock of the whole experience would have brought on his heart attack. I know I just about had one when I saw that bloody great buoy looming out of the darkness. Now I know how the captain of the *Titanic* felt."

"It's an incredibly ingenious theory," admitted Richard.

"Face it. It's the only scenario that fits all the evidence. It has to be the solution."

"But there's one basic flaw." Richard frowned thoughtfully. "Trant didn't have a boat. His Bayliner has been in dry dock for two months. I talked with his neighbours and they assured me he didn't have any other kind of vessel. Not even a canoe. We'd have heard about it by now if he'd borrowed a boat. So how do you explain that away?"

"I can't," said Beary. "But I'm sure I'm right. Can't you send down a diver to see if there's a boat lying on the bottom by the can buoy?"

Beary rang off. Richard put down the phone and pondered his father's theory. Of all the people connected with Janis Edwards, Trant had the most to lose. All the pieces fit in terms of time and motive and character. But was it enough? He was going to have to re-read all the reports before deciding what recommendation to make.

By six o'clock his eyes were fuzzy and fatigue was making him sluggish. He packed away the file and got his coat. Enough was enough. He left his office and headed out, but as he passed the front desk, he saw a middle-aged man speaking angrily to the duty sergeant. Richard was about to slip by when the sergeant called him back.

"You might want to hear this, sir," he said. "This man is the next-door neighbour of your murder victim. He's just got back from Florida. Trant was looking after his place while he was away."

"That's right," said the man indignantly, "and what I want to know is, where the hell is my boat?"

* * *

The eighteen-foot Double Eagle was found at the bottom of the inlet. The bow was smashed, and the scorch marks were still evident on the curved edge of the hardtop where the flare had hit and presumably ricocheted back to burn Leonard Trant. Trant's neighbour became far less hostile once he realized that Sophie Guttenberg was prepared to top up his insurance payment so that he would be able to purchase a brand new boat. He also became more forthcoming, and blithely informed the police that he had seen Trant testing the flare gun in the boathouse to see if it actually worked. And so the mystery of Leonard Trant's death and his mistress's murder was solved.

Sophie sold the Deep Cove house and, to Philippa's delight, purchased an exquisite heritage home in New Westminster which was only a ten minute walk from her own condo. Sophie's former neighbour, Brady, helped her move. He was a constant fixture at the new house and, as Edwina sourly commented, was behaving as if he were planning on becoming husband-number-three. Hopefully, she remarked, the reason his wife left him was not rampant infidelity and Sophie was not repeating the same mistake a third time.

Norton, to Sylvia's disappointment, was deprived of a lucrative brief. On the plus side, however, he surprised everyone by having a great success in his stage debut. The critic for the *North Shore News* praised his delightful comic performance and concluded with the comment: "Norton Barnwell portrayed the ramrod-stiff guardsman perfectly, with a booming monotonous delivery that was absolutely hilarious, making him one of the highlights of the production." All in all, thought Philippa, it was a most satisfactory ending to a distressing episode.

And she could not help thinking, given the operatic soul lurking under her practical everyday persona, that the beacon had, after all, been the Star of the Mariner for Sophie Guttenberg. For there was no doubt, to paraphrase the aria, it had protected her in her hour of need.

THE MYSTERY OF
THE BOSTON TEAPOTS

"We're heading for Boston," said Edwina. "I should be able to get a nice cup of tea."

"We're in America," said Beary. "Why not settle for a nice cup of coffee? Besides," he added, "don't you remember your history lessons? All the tea was dumped into the harbour."

He stuck his head back into his guidebook and emulated the other occupants of the commuter train, who, having seen the available scenery so many times that it had become invisible to them, either had their noses in books or newspapers, or were working on their laptops.

The young woman opposite had not once looked up from her Stephen King novel since she had boarded the train three stations back.

Edwina turned to look at the perpetually moving panorama of fields, forests, lakes and picturesque old houses that paraded past the window of the train. Visibility was good from the top level of the two-tier railcar, and as the train passed the stretches of multi-coloured trees, she could see right down to the forest floor. The underbrush was far less dense on the East Coast than it was in the West. Another train rattled by, going in the opposite direction, but the passengers were invisible behind darkened windows. With a start, Edwina realized that the people in the other train could not see her either. The windows were designed to allow one-way viewing. A voice came over the PA system to announce the next station, and a moment later, the train glided to a halt, discharged a handful of individuals and took on another large batch of morning commuters. Then it smoothly continued on its way. The conductor's capped head emerged from the stairwell and he began his progress along the aisle. Edwina nudged Beary in the ribs.

"Tickets, Bertram. The conductor is coming."

Beary kept his nose in his book. He had flipped the pages to the street map of Boston.

"There," he said, without looking up. He pointed to the back of the seat in front of them. "Didn't you notice the commuters sticking their tickets in the slots? You should really be more observant about the habits of the natives. Now," he added, stabbing a finger at the book in his lap, "this is where we should start. The train will come into the South Station, so we'll exit onto Atlantic Avenue. If we turn right, we should be able to find the site of the Boston Tea Party."

"You won't find much to see," said the conductor as he reached for their tickets. "These days, it's just a construction site. The wharf doesn't exist any more."

"What!" exclaimed Beary. "But that's a historic location."

"Not any more. The whole area was filled in with dirt from the surrounding hills. It's long gone." The conductor gave Beary and Edwina a friendly smile. "Out-of-town visitors?" he asked. "Where are you from?"

Beary told him.

"We're in Massachusetts for a convention," Edwina added. "My husband is a city councillor and one of his colleagues has relatives here, so they're very kindly putting us up. We have a couple of free days, and we were told the thing to do in Boston was to walk the Freedom Trail. So we shall spend a lovely day touring your beautiful old buildings and buying Boston Tea Party souvenirs, even if the original site has disappeared."

"Not to worry, ma'am. You'll find lots of history along the way. You've picked a bad day for it, though. It'll be a wet one. There was an Atlantic low-cloud formation this morning. The sea mist is going to end up as rain."

He moved on to the end of the carriage and disappeared down the stairs.

Edwina looked at her husband.

"How much of this tour is outdoors?" she asked him.

"I've no idea," said Beary. "I've been checking out the pubs and the restaurants. I figured the only thing we'd look at was the Boston Tea Party site, but now I'm told it's non-existent."

"You're impossible," snapped his wife. "Boston is the hub of American history. I thought you were reading up on the directions for the Freedom Trail. For heaven's sake, stop looking for food outlets and find out what buildings we should see. Or give me the book and let me do it."

Beary had no desire to have his day mapped out by Edwina, whose stamina for sightseeing would have qualified her for a gold medal had there been an Olympic category for tramping round museums and art galleries, so he obediently flipped back the pages of the guidebook and began to read. Over his bent head, Edwina noticed that the woman across the aisle was staring in their direction. When she saw that Edwina had noticed her, the woman looked away and began reading her book again. Unusual, thought Edwina. Most Americans were extremely friendly, especially once they realized that they were talking with visitors to their country. This woman's reserve was unusual. She was thin, with wiry red hair, and her navy blue raincoat suggested she was bound for work in an office. Edwina glanced up at the overhead luggage rack. There was a briefcase above the woman's seat.

The voice came over the PA system again. Beary slapped the guidebook shut and slipped it into his backpack.

41

"Come on," he barked. "South Station. This is us."

"It's the end of the line, by the looks of it," said Edwina, noting how everyone in the carriage was getting up and gathering belongings. She stood and followed Beary into the queue that was slowly inching towards the end of the aisle. They got halfway down the stairs, but then they had to wait. The compartment below was already filled with people who had come through the connecting doors between the carriages. A few people from the top level had made it to the bottom. Edwina saw the woman in the blue raincoat wedged into the side seat on the lower landing. Then the train slowed and came to a halt, the doors slid open, and the carriage spewed its occupants into a hurrying mass of humanity hastening towards the doors at the end of the platform.

* * *

"Now this is what I call a railway station," said Beary, looking around the cavernous concourse. "Newsstands, coffee shops, a bookshop, a shoeshine stand . . . look, even a chocolate shop."

Edwina's eyes were purposefully sweeping the end wall. "Never mind the chocolates," she said. "You don't need the calories. Where are the washrooms?"

Beary pointed to a sign to the left of the exit doors. Edwina hurried off, and while Beary waited, he watched the crowds milling around the stands and scurrying between the various exits. Seeing a board that listed the train schedules, he mentally noted the trains to Mansfield Station so that he would know where to look when they were ready to return. Six platforms and twelve tracks, he observed. No wonder the station was so busy.

When Edwina returned, she looked mildly put out. Not that this was unusual, Beary thought, but before they set out on their tour, it might be wise to buy the cup of tea that was obviously on her mind. As for himself, he was quite prepared to sit for half an hour before setting off. However, when he indicated the concession stand and made the offer, his wife shook her head.

"No, I don't want concession-stand tea. I'll wait until we find a nice teashop. There must be something quaint and interesting along the way. I assume New England will have something that resembles an Olde English Tea Shoppe. Let's get started."

Beary led the way to the main doors and they walked out onto the street. The old city was not particularly large, so it did not take long for them to reach the Boston Common where the guidebook indicated that the Freedom Trail began.

"Did you notice the woman who was sitting opposite us on the train?" Edwina asked suddenly.

Beary was surprised. The comment seemed to come out of nowhere.

"No. What about her?"

"She was in the washroom at the station. She was so incredibly rude it took my breath away. She was washing her hands and she'd put her briefcase on the counter. I happened to notice that someone had splashed a puddle of water by the sink and it was pooling against the side of her case. I went to move it and showed her the wet patch— and she glared at me, snatched the case, and marched out without a word."

Beary refrained from pointing out that not everyone appreciated his wife's habit of organizing, assisting and correcting the world at large. What Edwina perceived to be helpful was usually interpreted as bossy interference by the recipients of her attentions. Therefore, he grunted sympathetically and changed the subject.

"Look, there it is. That's where we start."

"What are you pointing at?"

"Don't you see the red brick path? That's what we follow. Just like *The Wizard of Oz*, only a different colour."

"Oh, I see," said Edwina. "All right, off we go. Hopefully, the red bricks will pass my teashop along the way."

With Beary using the guidebook and Edwina keeping her eye on the red brick line, they began the tour. They passed the State House and the Park Street Church, and soon found themselves bringing up the rear behind a group of schoolchildren who were accompanied by two harassed-looking teachers. When they reached the Granary Burying Ground, the schoolchildren were turned loose with instructions to locate and take notes on specific city ancients and revolutionaries, and the cemetery was soon abuzz with sufficient noise to wake the permanent residents. After plodding through wet grass and dodging noisy grade-schoolers for half an hour, Beary was feeling as rebellious as some of the grave's inhabitants, for the day was extremely cold and the air was damp. However, Edwina was determined to persevere, so Beary was forced to follow her through the swarms of children as she surveyed headstones, some of which dated back to Shakespeare's time.

"Oh, look," cried Edwina, pausing by a well-worn piece of masonry. "Paul Revere!"

As they stared, awed and fascinated, at the grave of the legendary hero, the skies opened and the cloudburst predicted by their friendly train conductor erupted. The cemetery instantly became a sea of umbrellas—the schoolchildren had come well prepared—and Beary and Edwina abandoned Paul Revere and ran for the exit. In spite of their rain jackets and one shared umbrella, the torrential rain drenched them before they had gone another block.

The quaint teashop had still not materialized, and Edwina's expression was starting to look as cold and forbidding as the day itself. But rescue was approaching in the form of one of the nation's Founding Fathers. In front of a majestic-looking building which turned out to be City Hall, a statue of Benjamin Franklin held pride of place. Beyond his bronzed shoulders could be seen a green Starbucks sign.

Beary looked at his wife and raised his eyebrows. Edwina had raindrops dripping off the end of her nose.

"Coffee will do just fine," she said.

* * *

After warming her hands around a grande latte and savouring it slowly, Edwina was restored to good humour. It was amazing what a cup of coffee could do, thought Beary. His wife had even managed to shrug off the presence of a particularly loud and uncouth panhandler, who, after being ejected from the shop, had ambled around the outside, knocking on the windows.

"Perhaps he's the village idiot," she quipped. "A bit of local colour."

"Speaking of local colour," mused Beary, "I wonder why Benjamin Franklin was placed opposite a statue of a donkey."

"I have no idea," declared Edwina, "but from now on, I shall always associate Franklin with coffee."

She pulled the guidebook from Beary's pack and looked to see what was next on the route. Beary swivelled round in his seat and peered at the grey scene beyond the window. The rain was still pounding down. He quailed. Then he turned back to his wife.

"Would you like another coffee?" he offered hopefully.

"No," said Edwina. "The Old South Meeting House is just round the corner. You don't have to look like that," she added. "One goes inside. It's an indoor tour."

"Perfect," said Beary. "And then we'll go for lunch."

* * *

The field-trip group was still ahead. When the Bearys arrived at the Old South Meeting House, they found it filled with schoolchildren reenacting the debate over the tea tax. Beary and Edwina beamed approval. As former teachers, they liked to see students enthusiastically engaged in educational activities. They watched the debate for a while, and then circled the room, peering into glass display cases, studying the faces of the town elders, and reading the historical anecdotes that lined the circumference of the walls.

"I'm beginning to understand the Salem witch trials a little better," muttered Beary, eye-to-eye with a portrait of a severely gowned and bonneted woman. She had a thin face and dark hair, parted in the centre and tightly drawn back around her head. Her gimlet eye was so daunting, he thought, that it made Edwina's frostiest expression look like a gentle reproach. He moved on, completing the circuit slowly. The longer he took, the warmer he became and the more time there was to allow his damp clothes to dry.

Once he had examined every glass case and read all there was to read, he trailed after Edwina to the lower floor where the washrooms and the gift shop were situated. Edwina entered the shop with alacrity. Beary followed less enthusiastically. In his experience, very few items in gift shops actually came from the city that one was visiting. Whether one bought socks that advertised a visit to Mount Rushmore or lighthouse ornaments from the Great Lakes, inevitably, somewhere on the purchased item were the words, *Made in China*. He imagined

Boston would be no different. Edwina, who was remarkably efficient when it came to reading labels on food items, was surprisingly naïve in this regard and still firmly believed that "A Gift from Boston" was indeed a gift from Boston. However, Beary refrained from enlightening her, since the result would be a lengthy search to find items that were crafted locally, which, once tracked down, would prove to be six times as expensive.

Happy in her blissfully ignorant state, Edwina immediately lighted on the stationary section. Beary sighed. He suspected that his wife had enough gift-shop notepaper to supply the next four generations of Bearys, but he knew that it was pointless to remind her of the fact, so he dutifully admired the selections she picked out.

"Oh, here's something appropriate," Edwina cooed, picking up a box of thank-you notes that were decorated with teapots. She popped the cards back on the shelf. "I'll have a look around and see what else they have, but I'll probably get these."

Resigned to spending the next half hour in the store, Beary found a book on lighthouses and browsed through it while Edwina made her rounds, scrutinizing jigsaws, postcards, tea towels and coasters. The schoolchildren had not appeared and the store was still quiet. Presumably, the teachers had the wisdom to avoid places where purchases could be made. Out of the corner of his eye, Beary noticed movement, and he looked up to see another customer enter the shop. With a start, he recognized her. It was the woman with the briefcase who had so annoyed Edwina at the train station.

Edwina had her back turned and was engrossed in the children's books so she did not notice the newcomer. The red-headed woman went straight to the stationary section and, without preamble, began to pull the teapot thank-you notes off the shelf. Then, armed with a stack of six boxes, she walked over to the cash desk.

As the cashier was ringing the purchases through, Edwina turned back to Beary to show him what she had found.

"Look!" she cried. "I have gifts for all the grandchildren. Aren't these sweet?"

She waved two soft-cover books under his nose and flipped the pages over to show him the contents. Beary obediently viewed the collection of paper dolls in colonial underwear that appeared to possess wardrobe items for every occasion from cutting wood to attending a society ball.

"They'll be perfect for Chelsea," Edwina declared. "Now, these jigsaws are for the boys, and Jennifer and Laura will like—" She stopped speaking as she caught sight of the woman at the cash register. "Good heavens," she muttered. "What is she doing here? She hardly looks like a tourist."

"She's buying your notepaper," said Beary. "Six boxes of it anyway."

Edwina flinched.

"What! I think there were only six." She strode back to the stationary section and peered at the rack. Then she turned back indignantly and glowered at the woman by the cash desk. The cashier had concluded the sale and was handing an Old Meeting House plastic bag across the counter. The redheaded woman tucked the sales slip into the pocket of her raincoat and walked out of the store.

"Bother," said Edwina. "I really liked those."

She took her purchases to the cash desk and set them down.

"Do you have any more of the thank-you notes with the teapots?" she asked the sales clerk.

The salesgirl was apologetic.

"No, I'm sorry. That was my last batch. But we get them in quite often. I'll have some more by next week."

Edwina looked even more put out.

"I won't be here next week. What on earth did that woman need six packages for? There were twelve in each box. Who needs seventy-two thank-you notes?"

"I did wonder about that myself. She said she was throwing a shower for her daughter and the theme of the event is the Boston Tea Party."

"What are they going to do?" Edwina sniffed. "Throw the bride-to-be off the wharf?"

The salesgirl smiled. "You know," she advised, "if you really want a set, you'll find them in several other stores. All the gift shops along the Freedom Trail stock them. You'll be able to pick some up either at the Old State House or at Faneuil Hall."

Edwina took her purchases and, slightly mollified, returned to

Beary who was hovering impatiently by the exit door which led directly onto the street and back to the line of red bricks. Once through the doors, the Bearys saw that the rain was still coming down, so they were relieved to find that the next stop was only a short distance away.

They walked up the street and came to a halt in front of an impressive red brick edifice topped by a tall white steeple. Edwina craned her neck upwards, admiring the lion and unicorn poised on the gables and the small bull's-eye windows that resembled tiny ship's wheels. A clock hung beneath the elaborate cornice molding at the top of the Georgian façade, and the lower edge of the timepiece was framed by a semi-circular garland of laurel leaves.

"The Old State House," declaimed Beary, his nose back in the guidebook. "Now this is really worth a visit. Boston's oldest public building. This is where the Declaration of Independence was read."

Edwina nodded with satisfaction. "Good," she said. "I can get my cards here."

They went through the front door and found themselves in a hall that, in spite of an elegant curved staircase with wooden banisters, was surprisingly tiny. But then, thought Beary, remembering the size of the uniforms he had seen on display, people were much smaller in the eighteenth century. The foyer was extremely crowded, partly because of the fact that the gift shop was located there, and partly because of the narrow halls that restricted the traffic flow. Beary headed for the stairway to escape the crush. Edwina worked her way towards the gift shop and signalled that she would meet him upstairs.

The top floor was mercifully quiet compared to the hubbub below, and the glass display cases were filled with a fascinating collection of bayonets, powder horns, muskets, bullet molds and powder pouches. Beary made the rounds of the antiquated armaments, intrigued by the old technology and fascinated by the way the outmoded weaponry demonstrated similar concepts to those of modern warfare.

Twenty minutes later, Edwina had still not appeared, but remembering the crowd in the gift shop, Beary suspected his wife was still waiting in a lengthy lineup. He continued his tour of the room, but as he paused to study a set of calipers for measuring bullets, the floor started to shake and a loud rumbling came from below. He looked up, startled.

"Not to worry," said the man at the next display case. "The subway runs underneath the building. You can read about it over there." He pointed to a placard at the far side of the room.

"That's a relief," said Beary. "I thought it was my wife creating havoc in the gift shop." He started towards the next case, which held a fearsome array of cannonballs and a drum from Bunker Hill, but a sharp voice stopped him in his tracks.

"I had every reason to create havoc in the gift shop."

Beary turned to see Edwina at the top of the stairs. Her jaw was set in a tight line, but there was also a satisfied glint in her eye. He noticed that she had not acquired any more shopping bags.

"No luck?" he asked.

"No. You won't believe this. They had ten boxes of those cards this morning, and that same woman came in and bought them all."

"Good Lord," said Beary. "That is strange. Are you sure it was the same woman?"

Edwina nodded.

"No doubt of it. The saleswoman described her. And she said the customer told her they were for a wedding shower."

"Some shower. The bride must have an awful lot of friends."

"I think it's distinctly fishy," said Edwina.

"Odd," agreed Beary, "but not necessarily sinister. I remember you once buying out Safeway's entire stock of birthday party invitations because they were on sale and you said with four children to raise, you'd go through them in no time flat."

"That's different," said Edwina. "Anyway, I've made sure that I'll get my cards when we go to Faneuil Hall. I had the saleswoman phone ahead to the gift store. They're setting a box aside for me."

"I doubt if that was necessary," said Beary. "The bride couldn't have that many friends." He did the math rapidly in his head. "She's already up to a hundred and ninety-two."

"I know." Edwina had the grace to look sheepish. "It is a bit silly to be focussing on cards with Boston teapots when we're standing on one of the major sites of the American Revolution, but that woman really got my blood up, so I wanted to be sure."

"It's your personal Bunker Hill," chortled Beary. "The battle of the teapots. Well, now that you've secured your position, come and look over here."

He led Edwina to the doors which opened onto the balcony where the Declaration of Independence had been read. They stood quietly, absorbing the sense of history, and feeling slightly awed by the significance of the spot. They read the placards, and then looked solemnly at the view down State Street where the Boston Massacre had occurred.

Their silent contemplation was disrupted by the chatter of young voices as the first surge of students from the field-trip group fanned out from the staircase and took over the room. Edwina and Beary decided it was time to depart. They moved away from the balcony, stopping only to admire the model of the USS *Constitution* before making their way downstairs. As Beary descended, he looked over the banister rail and noticed an arrow indicating that washrooms were located on the bottom floor. Knowing his wife's penchant for needing the facilities the moment none were available, he pointed out the sign to Edwina. Her expression grew frosty again and she vigorously shook her head.

"I went before I came upstairs," she said. "It was like being on a ride at the funfair. They should have a warning sign about the subway line."

She hitched her bag over her shoulder and marched out the door. Beary, grinning inwardly at the mental picture that had sprung to mind, followed meekly behind. As he stepped onto the pavement, his tummy gave a growl that emulated the rumble from the subway. He looked at his watch.

"Lunch time," he announced. "Come on. Let's go and eat."

"In a minute. I want to go to Faneuil Hall and pick up my cards."

"Did you pre-pay?"

Edwina nodded.

"Then there's no urgency," insisted Beary. "They'll hold them."

"Well, yes, but—"

"No buts, I want food and I need a rest. My feet are sore. And I know just the place. I read about it in the guidebook. It's only a short hop from here and it's in the direction we want to go." Beary took his wife's elbow and steered her firmly down the street until they reached the Union Oyster House. "See," he said. "Here's your 'Olde English' charm. Another hive of revolutionary activity. It was established in 1826 and it's supposed to be the oldest continuously running restaurant in the United States."

He opened the low door and ushered Edwina inside. In spite of the preponderance of dark wood and mullioned windows, the modern world, in the form of a television set over the bar, had invaded the period atmosphere. The restaurant was busy, and the waiter had to seat them at the counter, so Beary found himself watching the Dow continuing its volatile fluctuations while he tucked into a plate of deep-fried oysters. Edwina had taken over the guidebook, and she browsed quietly while she ate her trio of fish cakes. Beary hungrily devoured his lunch. Then he drew his eyes from the television screen and looked speculatively at the roast potatoes on his wife's plate.

"Are you going to eat those?" he asked.

Edwina looked up from her book.

"Probably not," she said, "but you certainly don't need them. You've already had fries and coleslaw. If you don't lose some weight around your middle, you'll die of a heart attack."

"I'll die of a heart attack if you make me walk much further today."

"No, you won't. The exercise is good for you. Oh, all right." Edwina looked exasperated. She separated the potatoes from the red peppers and slid them onto Beary's plate. "But now that you've eaten so much, you're going to have to walk it off. We'll go to Faneuil Hall to pick up my cards, and then I want to see Paul Revere's house."

They finished their meals and paid the bill. When they emerged from the restaurant, the rain had stopped, and although the day was still cold and damp, the walk through the picturesque cobbled streets became more enjoyable. Faneuil Hall was just around the corner. It turned out to be a magnificent period building on the outside and an arcade of shops of every variety inside, with touristy bric-a-brac mingling with the grandeur of Ionic pilasters. Beary was amused by the contrast of old and new. Edwina stopped by the first gift shop, which was to the right of the main doors.

"It's this one," she said.

She beckoned her husband, but Beary did not respond. He was

staring at a point further up the aisle. Impatiently, Edwina tapped him on the shoulder.

"Sorry," said Beary. "I thought I saw your arch-foe by that rack with the T-shirts."

"Who?"

"Your rival for the teapots. The woman in the blue raincoat."

"You've got to be kidding," said Edwina. Her eyes narrowed and she pursed her lips. "They'd better have held my box of cards," she snapped.

She sailed into the shop and went straight to the cash desk. To Beary's relief, for he had no desire to spend the rest of the day with a wife who was out of sorts, the sales clerk smiled and pulled a box from beneath the counter.

"Here you are, ma'am," he said. "It's a good job you prepaid. I had quite a time holding on to these cards."

"Let me guess." Beary sauntered over to join Edwina. "A woman in a blue raincoat wanted to buy all your boxes because she needed them for a shower she was throwing for her daughter."

The attendant looked at him as if he had sprouted horns and was carrying a trident.

"No, I'm not clairvoyant," said Beary. "She's been in all the other gift shops too. How many boxes did she buy this time?"

"I only had eight. They came in this morning. She wanted them all, but of course, I had the one put aside so I was only able to sell her seven."

Beary did some more rapid arithmetic.

"So if she'd got all the ones she wanted, she'd have had twenty-four boxes of those cards, or two hundred and eighty-eight cards in total. Even if you were as rich and prolific as the Kennedy clan, I can't imagine having a shower with that many guests."

"More to the point," said Edwina acerbically, "if you have that kind of money, you'd have specially printed engraved notes of your own. You wouldn't be rounding up cheap cards from the local gift shops."

Beary took the box of cards and turned it over. As he had expected, the printing at the bottom read *Made in China*. There was nothing else unusual about the box, and he could clearly see the cards below the plastic lid. He shook his head.

"Mystifying," he said.

"Maybe it's some kind of scavenger hunt," suggested the sales clerk.

"Do you keep these cards in stock regularly?" asked Beary.

"Yes," said the clerk. "All the gift shops carry them. They're quite popular. Relatively cheap, and tourists always associate teapots with Boston. They come in batches of twenty-four, so our store shares a set with the shops in the Old State House and the Old Meeting House. We order one two-dozen box from the distribution centre and depending on who runs low first, we divide the cards up so we stay about equal. We've done this for years. There's nothing unusual about it."

Edwina thanked the assistant, slipped the cards inside her Old Meeting House bag, which was hooked onto the clip on her shoulder bag. Then she and Beary left Faneuil Hall and set off again to follow the red brick line.

They soon reached Paul Revere's house. It was a tiny, late-seventeenth-century dwelling with wooden siding and diamond-paned windows, and it nestled snugly amid the high walls of the surrounding buildings. To one side was a courtyard where a solitary tree and the vibrant greens of the boxed herb gardens broke the sea of red bricks that enclosed the property. The field trip had arrived before them and the courtyard was overrun with schoolchildren. Seeing the teachers directing their charges to the back of the quadrangle, Beary realized that the tour must start at the rear of the house. He took Edwina's arm and they worked their way through the crowd until they reached the entrance. The door was so low they had to duck when they entered the house.

Once inside, they found themselves in a dark kitchen, and intrigued by the demonstration of three-century-old domestic ingenuity, they paused to admire the baking oven to the left of the main fire. However, when they turned to move on, they quailed to see the crush moving along the hall. There were tour guides available, but the place was so crowded and the guides in such demand that it seemed wiser to battle through unattended. They proceeded through the halls, reading the signs by the displays and peering into the miniscule furnished rooms, which were dimly lit by mullioned windows. Then they climbed the narrow staircase to the upper floor. Here and there, they heard snatches of explanations as the tour guides elaborated on the customs of the Revere family, but soon the jostling of the crowd and the narrow confines of the house became unbearably claustrophobic and Edwina signalled to Beary that she was ready to leave. The exit was a staircase that led directly from the top floor back to the brick courtyard, and it was with relief that they reached the ground and breathed in the fresh air. Edwina readjusted her shoulder bag. Then she looked down and cried out in panic.

"My shopping bag! It's gone."

She whirled back towards the house. Bracing herself to tackle the crowd one more time, she started towards the entrance. As she headed inside to retrieve her bag, Beary glanced towards the road. Suddenly, he caught a glimpse of a navy blue raincoat at the entrance to the courtyard. But before he had time to react, it vanished from sight behind the brick wall.

* * *

Edwina was livid. Once she had searched the house and ascertained that the bag had neither been dropped nor turned in, Beary told her about the glimpse he had caught of the woman leaving the courtyard. Edwina immediately returned to the house for a third visit and described the redheaded woman to each of the tour guides. Two of them professed to have seen such a person going through, and the attendant on the upper floor had indicated that the woman had not been looking at the displays, but had simply been making her way towards the exit.

"I'm going to the police," Edwina proclaimed resolutely.

"To report what?" said Beary. "It's not as if the woman stole your Tiffany necklace. The woman's behaviour is certainly irrational, but the police will laugh you out of the station."

"I don't care," said Edwina. "There's a principle involved."

Beary knew better than to argue. He patiently tagged along while Edwina asked directions to the police station. Then, wisely suppressing his urge to make remarks about tempests in teapots, he meandered after her as she set off to report her loss. As he had predicted, the officer on the front desk, who was initially concerned that visitors to his city had been robbed, changed his attitude considerably when he was told that the pilfered items amounted to a box of cards, two paper-doll books, two jigsaw puzzles, a story book about Pocahontas and a set of tea towels with lighthouses on them. However, seeing Edwina's expression, which was starting to resemble the women in the Old Meeting House portraits, he dutifully noted the items on a report.

Once they were out on the pavement, Edwina continued to fret.

"He didn't take me seriously," she grumbled.

"I told you so," said Beary, "but you've made the report. You never know what will come of it. Now, why don't we quit for the day and find The Bell-in-Hand. It's the oldest bar in America. I read about it on the way down this morning."

Edwina shook her head.

"Not until we're through sightseeing. We'll go there on the way back from Bunker Hill."

"Bunker Hill is on the other side of town. It's across the bridge. I don't want to walk all that way."

"Of course you do," said Edwina emphatically. "Besides, it's near the USS *Constitution*, and you love ships. We can go over the vessel after Bunker Hill, and then we'll come back to your pub. We still have lots of red bricks to follow. The big marketplace is next."

Beary looked mutinous, but he could tell from the set of his wife's jaw that the only way he would get to the pub was by co-operating and completing the tour. Reluctantly, and inwardly reflecting that the Freedom Trail was not very aptly named, he set off after her. He plodded through Quincy Place, his mouth drooling at the display of lobster, oysters, scallops and Boston cream pie that made him contemplate a second lunch. Sternly, Edwina steered him past the delicacies and out the exit, and they continued along the streets of Boston, admiring the unusual narrow brickwork on the tall, thin houses. They strolled through the Italian district and sauntered through the shady square where the statue of Paul Revere was surrounded by walls decorated with plaques that celebrated the contributions of the city's forefathers. Finally, they hiked across town to Bunker Hill. However, this final endeavour proved to be a failure, for when they climbed to the monument, they found that the museum was closed, and when they returned down the winding streets to the waterfront, the long line of people waiting to board the USS *Constitution* was too much even for

55

Edwina. Resigned, she agreed to pack in sightseeing for the day and seek out The Bell-in-Hand.

By the time they walked back across town, they were both tired, and even Edwina was relieved to enter the quaint, triangular-shaped tavern and settle at a corner table. Beary ignored his wife's disapproving eye and augmented his Guinness stout with three-potato fries. However, Edwina gradually mellowed as her own dark ale started to take effect, and she began to pick at Beary's snack.

"The sweet-potato fries aren't bad," she said. "What are the other ones?"

"Yucca and Idaho," said Beary. He too was feeling significantly better and more benevolent now that he was sitting down and replenishing himself with food and drink. "So, would you like to stop at the Old Meeting House again before we head to the station?" he asked. "I doubt if the police will trace your bag, so you might as well buy duplicate gifts for the grandchildren, even if you can't get your cards."

Edwina sighed.

"Yes, I suppose we'd better. I have to take them something from our trip."

"Never mind," Beary consoled her. "You didn't really need those thank-you notes."

"I know. It's just aggravating. And I still think it's mysterious."

"You know," said Beary, his brain starting to work again now that he was no longer numbed by crowds and aching feet, "the police really ought to follow through on this. What did that store clerk say? The three stores regularly share a case of twenty-four boxes? I imagine that case comes in a crate with quite a few other cases of boxed cards. They come in from China, and they'd be sent to a distribution centre, but the cases would be pre-addressed."

"What are you suggesting?" asked Edwina.

"Well, think about it," said Beary. "We've been wandering about Boston all day and reading the history of the area—a history that includes a high incidence of smuggling. Now, these days, rum isn't the issue so much as—"

"Drugs," finished Edwina. "But those boxes were so small. And we could see the cards through the plastic."

"Yes, but cocaine doesn't take up a lot of room. And a layer of that stuff under the cards would be worth a packet. Especially if all twenty-four boxes in a case contained a quantity of the drug. If I wanted to smuggle drugs into the country, what better way than to have one contraband case in a crate of legitimate items that were going to tourist destinations with impeccable credentials."

"I still don't see what you're getting at," said Edwina.

"What if the labels somehow got switched and the contraband case was sent to the wrong outlet from the distribution centre? What would you do if you were operating a drug-smuggling ring and you heard that your precious boxes had gone to stores where the items could be sold to anyone who happened to fancy cards with teapots on them?"

"I'd hustle down right away and buy them back as soon as they hit the shelves," said Edwina. "Good heavens! Do you think that's what she was doing?"

"I don't know," said Beary. "This is pure speculation. Why don't we call Richard? U.S. Customs will be far more interested in listening to a theory if it comes from an inspector with the RCMP."

"What a good idea," said Edwina. "I hope you're right. That woman really got my goat. I'd be delighted to see her get her come-uppance. You know," she added, "you really can be quite clever when you put your mind to it."

"It's the stout," said Beary. "Can I have another one?"

Edwina sighed. Then she gave in.

"Yes, all right. You've earned it. It's been a long day."

* * *

Beary's conjecture proved to be correct, although he and Edwina did not hear the end of the story until three weeks after they had returned to Vancouver. When Richard contacted U.S. Customs, the officials checked the list of addresses where the shipments of cards were directed. Most of the outlets were legitimate, but there was one privately owned antique store up the coast that also stocked souvenirs, and a police raid of the building resulted in the breaking of one of the major drug rings that had been importing cocaine into the United States for some months. To Edwina's annoyance, the woman in the blue raincoat was not apprehended and the stolen bag of souvenirs was never returned.

However, several weeks after Richard had told his parents about the drug bust, a large parcel arrived at the Beary residence.

"What on earth could this be?" said Edwina. "It's addressed to me, but I don't remember ordering anything from the States."

"Well, open it, why don't you?" said Beary. "It's too big for a letter bomb. Here, use these scissors."

Edwina took the scissors and ran the sharp edge along the brown tape that held the top of the box together. Then she pulled up the flaps and peeled away the bubble wrap. When she saw what lay beneath, her eyes bulged with amazement. She pulled out a card that lay on top and looked at the inscription.

"With thanks," she read. "It's from U.S. Customs."

Beary pulled out a box from the top layer in the case.

"Well, I'm damned," he said. "You won't ever have to buy thank-you notes again." He set the box of teapot cards on the kitchen table. "By my calculations, you have a total of two hundred and eighty-eight cards in that case. The only mystery of the Boston teapots now is how in heaven's name are you going to use them up in the course of your lifetime?"

Edwina's expression was a sight to behold. Beary chortled heartily. Then he patted his wife on the shoulder and picked up the kettle.

"Come on, old girl," he said cheerily. "How about that cup of tea?"

REFLECTIONS ON AN OLD QUEEN

The woman was fair, almost ethereal. Her ringless hands appeared translucent in the glimmering light and the sun catching her hair turned her white-gold curls to gossamer. She made Richard think of The Lady of Shallot, for she was beautiful and remote, and somehow detached from her surroundings. She was dressed all in white, her crisp shirt and Capri pants underlining her air of cool reserve. She stood at the rail, camera at the ready, staring out at the smooth ocean as the *Queen of Tofino* made its way towards Saltery Bay, yet she showed none of the animation of the cluster of Japanese tourists who had been laughing and snapping with enthusiastic abandon ever since the ferry had left Earl's Cove. The deck was otherwise deserted. The spring had been one of the coldest on record, and although it was already May, few individuals were motivated to travel. Richard had counted only a dozen cars on the deck below. Now, finally, a hot day had materialized, miraculously and unexpectedly out of the relentless chill that had dominated the year, but only a handful of people were out to enjoy it.

As the boat cleared Nelson Island, the woman looked back to the shore and raised her camera. It was a mechanical gesture, as if she felt obliged to record some detail about the trip, but something must have malfunctioned, for she lowered the camera again and frowned as she examined it. Richard joined her at the rail.

"Mechanical problem?" he asked.

The woman looked up, startled at being addressed by a stranger. However, she responded politely, though her manner was still distant.

"The battery's dead," she said. "I should have checked before I left."

She put the camera back in its case and slung it over her shoulder.

"It doesn't matter," she added. "I have a backup in the car. I don't really need pictures of the crossing anyway." She noticed Richard's quizzical expression, and suddenly her face lit up with a smile. The transformation was astounding. "I'm on a job," she explained. "I work for a tourist magazine and I've been sent to Powell River to do a story on the restoration of the Patricia Theatre."

"Ah," said Richard. "I thought you didn't have the air of a tourist about you."

"No. I wouldn't be here otherwise. I hate ferry travel."

Richard was surprised at the vehemence in her tone. "The waits can be tedious," he acknowledged.

"I don't mind the waits, I just don't like the boats. My grandparents lived in Victoria, so my parents used to take us to Vancouver Island every other weekend when we were young. I got sick of the interminable rides."

"Have you been on this route before?"

"No. Never. Have you?"

Richard shook his head.

"I've only been on the first leg of the trip. I live downtown, but one of my sisters lives on the Sunshine Coast so I often come up to Pender Harbour."

"Why are you travelling further this time?"

"I'm heading for the Island. I'm booked on a fishing charter out of Campbell River. I came this way so I could visit Juliette, but when I go back, I'll take the direct route from Nanaimo. I only have a few days off."

"Off?"

Richard ignored the query and changed the subject. From past experience he knew that there was little social benefit in letting people know he was a policeman.

"Interesting old boat, this," he observed. "A dinosaur from the past. Obviously kept for short runs on back routes. Do you want to go in and see if we can find the coffee shop?"

"Coffee would be nice. Thank you."

"I haven't introduced myself," said Richard. "I'm Richard Beary."

The woman paused; then with another of the smiles that transformed her face, she replied, "My name's Valerie . . . Valerie Grayle."

Richard opened the door that led to the interior of the ship. He held it for Valerie to go through, and then stepped in after her.

"OK. Which way?" he said. "What's your guess?"

"Down here, I think."

Valerie set off towards the stern. Her instinct proved correct. The cafeteria was in the rear lounge. It was a small area, enclosed by low yellow walls topped with smoked Plexiglas. The décor was utilitarian, with tables of arborite and particleboard. The tops had raised edges to keep items from sliding off. The seats were made from blue plastic and were attached to the same metal frames that held the tabletops in place. The units reminded Richard of school desks. Fluorescent lights, a glassed-in fire extinguisher, and a portrait of the Queen heightened the institutional air, though the austerity was mitigated slightly by the green carpet, which was dotted with diamond patterns that resembled clusters of beige snowflakes.

Only a handful of people occupied the area. A couple with a baby sat at a table near the entrance and a burly man in a Castro cap was reading a newspaper on the other side of the room. A longhaired youth and a pale young woman in a drab floral dress hovered near the counter. To Richard, they looked like relics of the flower-power age. He looked closely at the woman. She appeared nervous, but she did not seem to be afraid of her companion, for when he reached out to touch her, she grasped his hand and rested her head on his shoulder.

Valerie paid no attention to the people in the room. She set her purse on a table at the starboard side of the ship and sat down to wait while Richard purchased two coffees. When he came back to join her, her eyes looked faraway again, but she spoke cheerfully enough when he sat down.

"That's the captain's table," she said, nodding towards a wooden table which was surrounded by four mahogany chairs neatly upholstered with a durable pinstriped fabric.

"Reserved for the ship's officers," said Richard. "Very nice."

Valerie sighed.

"I'd hate to have their job," she said. "Back and forth all the time. How can they stand it? This is lovely," she added, warming her hands around her coffee mug. "Thank you so much."

Richard felt a deep curiosity about his new acquaintance. A cup of coffee on the ferry hardly called for overwhelming gratitude, and yet the woman across the table had shed her remote air and suddenly resembled a happy child on a special outing. The contrast was disconcerting. He probed a little further.

"Have you lived in Vancouver all your life?" he asked.

Valerie began to chatter expansively.

"No," she said. "My family moved to Ontario when I was thirteen. I lived there until just recently, but I moved back after my marriage broke up. My parents are dead, but my sister is here, so I wanted to be near her. We've always got along well. She's the one who recommended me for the job with the magazine. We—"

Valerie stopped suddenly and stared over Richard's shoulder. The happy child disappeared and her expression became withdrawn and remote again. Richard turned to see what had caught her attention. A middle-aged couple had entered the cafeteria. From Down Under, he decided, hearing the strong Australian twang of the woman's voice. Both husband and wife were heavily overweight—a modern-day Tweedledum and Tweedledee, with matching navy shorts, striped shirts and cotton sun-hats. The couple bore down on their table, then continued past, stopping when they reached the pile of trays by the counter. Richard glanced back at Valerie and saw that it was not the noisy Australians who had caught her attention, for she was still looking in the other direction. Her eyes were following the flower-power woman who was walking towards the exit. The woman's long, flowing dress appeared grey in the fluorescent lights and the hair that trailed down her back seemed equally colourless and flat, even though it was interspersed with braids and ribbons. Her partner had disappeared.

"Do you know her?" Richard asked.

Valerie furrowed her brow as if she were trying to remember, but then she said, "No. She looks like a throwback to the seventies."

"It's the Coast culture," said Richard. "There's a big arts community here, and there's still the remnants of the hippie era in pockets. You must have seen the beat-up yellow van on the car deck, the one covered with flags and decals spouting every cause under the sun."

Valerie seemed bewildered.

"Yes, I did," she said hesitatingly. "That's probably what she's travelling in."

She finished her coffee and set down the cup. She shook her head when Richard offered her a refill, but compliantly agreed when he suggested they explore the boat.

They got up and headed into the mid-lounge. Here, three blocks of Naugahyde armchairs filled the room. The area was an unorthodox mix of colours, with turquoise upholstery on the centre rows of chairs and burgundy on the outer sections. The carpet was still green, but had lost its snowflake pattern and was punctured with holes so that it appeared to be covered with orange dots. At the far end of the lounge, extreme-racing and kickboxing video-game machines lined the wall.

Richard and Valerie passed the machines and continued along the corridor that led to the bow. There was a narrow aperture in the left wall of the passageway, and Richard could see a companionway ascending, presumably to a staff area on the upper deck. To his surprise, Valerie stepped over the sill and beckoned to him to follow.

"Come through here," she said. "It leads to a sun lounge."

Richard followed her. He found himself in a claustrophobically small space at the foot of a narrow flight of steps. Valerie was already ascending the staircase, so Richard went up behind her. When he emerged at the top, he found himself in a glassed-in lounge that overlooked an open sundeck at the stern of the ship. He joined Valerie at the window and looked down at the long benches on either side of the lifejacket boxes. The Canadian flag was streaming in the breeze from the flagpole at the end of the deck.

"Look at that," said Richard, pointing to the huge lifeboats hanging at the side of the ship. "The new ferries don't have those any more. This vessel is truly an old Queen."

Suddenly, he sensed eyes on him, and when he turned away from the window, he perceived that they were not alone in the sun lounge. Two people stood in the corner. The man was in officer's uniform and the woman wore the regulation navy pants and white shirt that indicated she was a member of the crew. Judging by the papers in their hands, they had been consulting over some notes, but now they were looking across at Valerie and Richard.

"Sorry," said Richard. "Did we disturb your private space?"

"No," said the man. "This is a public area. It's just that hardly anyone knows it's here and people don't usually stray into it, so we tend to use it as a hideaway."

"It's a fascinating ship," said Richard. "How old is it?"

"She was built in 1960," said the man. "*Queen of Tofino* is one of the original B.C. ferries. Three thousand tons, six thousand horsepower, one hundred and two metres, and she holds one hundred and thirty-eight cars, and over eight hundred passengers and crew. She used to be one of the main ships of the ferry fleet, but the old girl's past that now. She's going to be retired this year. Soon after this crossing actually." The crewmember sighed. "Sad, isn't it?"

Richard nodded gravely.

"Yes," he agreed. "She's part of our history."

He turned to Valerie, but she had drifted away and was not paying attention to the conversation. She was watching the Canadian flag flapping hard against the flagpole at the stern, and she seemed lost in thoughts of her own. Back in her tower, decided Richard, but as the thought crossed his mind, she turned, smiled at him and moved towards the stairs. Richard followed her down to the main deck. Valerie stepped out of the companionway, turned left, and led Richard through the maze-like corridor that meandered its way to the front of the ship.

They passed the men's washroom and entered the small concourse where the first-aid station was located. Here, twin flights of steps from port and starboard merged at a landing, from which a further flight disappeared below decks. Opposite the stairwell was the elevator. On the port side of the area, a row of candy machines lined the wall.

Stairs and steps seemed to be a feature of the old ship, for another short flight led to the forward lounge while a second set descended to the door of the outer deck.

Richard and Valerie went up the short set of steps into the lounge. Richard blinked as they walked in for it appeared that the sea, which had previously been as smooth as glass, had suddenly developed a swell. After a moment, he realized that the windows were made from imperfectly flat glass, which allowed clear vision from close up, but at a distance distorted the view so that the sea appeared to be a mass of undulating waves.

As he moved closer to the glass, the tossing and pitching gradually diminished. No longer pre-occupied with the optical illusion created by the windows, he became aware of soft music to his right. He looked across and saw the flower-power girl curled up in an armchair in the front row of seats. She was very pale, but it was hard to make out her expression because her eyes were hidden by small, lightly shaded glasses in wire frames. Her patterned dress looked grubby and faded in the light from the window. Her companion from the cafeteria was nowhere in sight, but three more throwbacks to the hippie age sat on the floor at her feet. A wiry man with shaggy graying hair and a bushy moustache was strumming on a guitar while a girl in a white embroidered blouse provided a flute accompaniment. Another man, whom Richard assessed to be at least forty, lounged beside the musicians, beating out a rhythmic tattoo on a small bongo drum. He wore black and his long hair was drawn back in a ponytail. Something about his body language made Richard recoil. His policeman's eye told him that the woman in the flowered dress was afraid of the drummer, but from experience he knew that his instinct was worthless unless the woman was prepared to ask for assistance.

Richard turned away and looked out onto the deck where the blue and white B.C. Ferries flag rippled gently at the bow. The speakers crackled suddenly and a voice came over the intercom. The journey was drawing to an end. The girl in the flowered dress uncurled herself from her chair, got up, and drifted past them without even seeming to register their presence. Then she disappeared down the short flight of steps into the hallway. Her companions were packing up their gear.

Richard turned to Valerie. To his surprise, her forehead was furrowed and her face looked pinched. She was squinting as if the light from the windows hurt her eyes, and when she noticed Richard staring at her, she blinked.

"I'm sorry. I seem to have developed a bad headache. The washroom is just round the corner. I'm going to slip in there before we go below. Please don't feel you have to wait for me if I'm too long coming back."

Before Richard could protest, she slipped away. Taken aback by her abrupt change of mood, Richard stood rooted to the spot while the other travellers streamed past him. Valerie Grayle had seemed so serene in her isolation when he had first seen her, yet she had exhibited such a strange mix of personalities when she emerged from her shell that he was beginning to feel a deep sense of concern for her. Something was troubling her deeply.

The lounge was emptying fast. The bongo-drum player had already disappeared, and the flautist and the guitarist were packing away their instruments. Richard wandered to the top of the stairs. He could see a sign by the door of the women's washroom, but Valerie was nowhere in sight. He went back to the lounge and resolved to wait until his strange companion reappeared. He leaned against the back wall, watching fascinated as the undulating waves created by the glass turned the calm ocean into a rolling sea. As he waited, the sun went behind a cloud and the sky darkened. Blue became grey, and with the sudden loss of light, the simulated swell and surge of the water became ominous. For a moment, the scene outside the window looked like a storm at sea, but then the sun emerged from the clouds and the threatening seascape subsided into smooth curving rollers under a bright blue sky. He looked at his watch. It seemed as if Valerie was taking a long time. He wondered suddenly if the trip to the washroom had been an excuse to cut their acquaintance short. Perhaps her increasing remoteness had been a signal that she had been trying to avoid promises of future meetings.

Not sure what to do, he hesitated. He could not delay much longer or the ferry would dock.

And then from the corridor came a piercing scream.

He rushed out of the lounge and ran down the steps. Valerie was leaning against the wall. She was sobbing and hysterical. As he reached her, she hurled herself into his arms, but no matter how tightly he held her, her body continued to heave.

A uniformed officer appeared round the corner. With him came a deckhand and another member of the crew. Richard recognized her. It was the woman who had been in the sun lounge on the upper deck.

"What's going on?" snapped the officer.

"I don't know," said Richard. He moved Valerie away from him and looked into her eyes. "Come on, now," he said steadily. "Tell us what happened."

"He killed her," she sobbed. "He hit her. He dragged her to the rail and threw her over the side. He killed her. He killed her."

The officer paled under his tanned leathery skin, but he instantly leapt into action.

"Sound the alarm," he barked to the deckhand. "I'll drop a marker."

He was through the door to the outer deck before the clamour of the alarm burst onto the air.

Valerie broke down again into sobs. Richard made another effort to get through to her.

"Valerie, look at me. You've got to help us. Who was it? Who went over?"

Valerie looked up at him miserably. Her pale face was stained with tears and her mouth was quivering as she tried to get the words out.

"It was her," she said. "The girl in the flowered dress."

* * *

With the exception of Richard and the two carloads of Japanese tourists, none of the *Queen of Tofino*'s passengers were bound for Vancouver Island; and since Richard was cognizant of the need to be flexible when a police investigation was underway, and the Japanese tourists were happy to have been provided with the chance to get exciting footage of rescue operations in B.C. waters, the ferry crew did not have to deal with complaints about missed connections due to the delayed landing and the lengthy wait at Powell River while the RCMP boarded the ship to conduct their investigation.

Detective Constable Small, whose size belied his name, was on the one hand pleased to find he had a detective inspector on board who had been able to take charge until the ferry docked at Saltery Bay; on the other hand, he was not thrilled to have his authority threatened by the presence of a senior officer. However, he took advantage of Richard's usefulness as a witness. Although Small had talked with Richard very soon after boarding the vessel, he called him back again after the interviews with the other passengers had been completed.

"What's your take on this woman?" he asked, when Richard entered the purser's office. Small had commandeered the space for an interview room. "Did she really see something, or is she a complete nutter? The search came up with nothing, and as far as we can ascertain, everyone who came on board is present and accounted for, including the woman that she insists went overboard. If this was a prank, she should be charged with public mischief."

Richard shook his head.

"No. She definitely saw what she described. She wasn't acting. She was distraught. There was a whole vanload of hippies on the ship, so there could have been another woman who looked similar to the one we saw in the cafeteria."

"Yes, that is a possibility. Miss Grayle did waffle a bit. She thought it had been the same woman she saw earlier, but admitted it might not have been. But my other problem is that she couldn't identify the man. We marched her past every single passenger aboard this ship."

"What about the crew?"

"Her description of the man was pretty clear. Blue flowered shirt, long sideburns and a Zapata moustache. I don't think that's likely to be a crewmember. It sounds more like he belonged with the group of hippies that came up from Roberts Creek—except that none of them meet that description."

"The guitarist had a moustache."

"Wrong hair colour. She distinctly said black. And his clothes were wrong too. It's a real quandary. You're absolutely sure that she wasn't making it up?"

"Yes. I'd bet my life on it. And I'm almost sure that she recognized the woman in the flowered dress."

DC Small frowned.

"Now she was a strange one too," he said. "What did you make of her? She was pretty nervous and withdrawn. Very anxious to assure us she was fine."

Richard didn't pull any punches.

"I'd lay bets she's a victim of physical abuse," he said. "All the classic signs are there. My guess is that the thug with the ponytail probably beats her as often as he beats his bongo drums. I'd sure like to know why this woman had such an effect on Valerie."

The burly policeman looked thoughtful but remained silent.

"You know," Richard continued, "when I first saw Valerie, she made me think of The Lady of Shallot. That's a—"

"Character in a Tennyson poem," said DC Small. "Just because we live in Powell River, it doesn't mean we only know about fish and pulp mills."

"Sorry." Richard grinned apologetically. "Anyway, she had a remote look, as if she lived in an ivory tower, somehow detached from the real world. But when we started to talk, she was charming and approachable and I forgot about my initial impression. Then she withdrew again towards the end of the trip, and when I heard her scream and saw her agonized expression, it made me think of the line near the end of the poem—"

"'The curse has come upon me cried the Lady of Shallot.'" Small recited the lines with a ringing baritone and a dramatic flair that made Richard suspect he had missed his vocation by joining the police force. "Well," pronounced Small, cheerfully oblivious to Richard's train of thought, "the only way we'll know for sure is if a body washes ashore in the next few weeks."

"Even the absence of a body doesn't mean she's lying," Richard pointed out. "Floaters sometimes drift out into the ocean, so you don't always find the remains of people who are lost at sea."

"That might happen on the Victoria run," said Small firmly. "It's not likely on this strip of the coast. However, I'll keep that in mind. In the meantime, I'm taking Miss Grayle in for further questioning. I can't charge her with anything because there's no way I can be certain that she made up the incident, but I'm going to get an assessment from a psychiatrist, because I still think there's a good chance that we're dealing with a head case."

"Look," said Richard, "that could be a dangerous assumption if she's telling the truth. I'm very concerned about Valerie Grayle. I offered to stay here and escort her back to town, but she wouldn't hear of it. She insisted that I carry on with my fishing trip. She said she'd contact her sister if she wanted someone with her, but I'm uneasy. I think the police should keep an eye on her? She could be in danger."

"Don't worry," said DC Small. "We'll keep a watch on her here, and I'll notify the police in town when we send her back. In the meantime, I'll do background checks on everyone who was aboard the ship, including you," he added with a smile, which looked friendly, but Richard was aware that the facial expression did not nullify the intent behind the words. "So I'm going to give the order to release the passengers and crew, but I should warn you, you'll be besieged by the media when you get off. The reporters are waiting at the terminal like a pack of bloodhounds. It's the bane of the cellphone age. You can't contain anything because the spectators get on their phones and start yapping about what's going on, and there's always some bright spark who calls the press and tips them off."

"Thanks for the warning." Richard stood up. "One request," he added before he left. "Could you let Valerie Grayle know that I'll get in touch with her as soon as I return from my fishing trip? I'll be back in Vancouver early next week, so I'll pop round and see how she is. I got her address before she went in for questioning."

The detective nodded and Richard left the office. As he made his way down to the car deck, he heard the throbbing vibration of the engine. The order to unload the ferry must have already reached the captain of the vessel. Sure enough, when Richard emerged from the companionway, the passengers were moving towards their vehicles. The Japanese tourists disappeared into three Toyotas that were lined up along the first lane, and the man in the Castro cap was already sitting in the pick-up truck behind them. A huge Newfoundland dog sat beside him in the cab of the truck. The last car in the row was a Volkswagen Beetle. Richard could not see anyone inside, but the light was dim, so at that distance he could not be sure. A motorhome with Wisconsin plates was parked behind Richard's SUV. It was occupied by an elderly couple. He did not remember seeing them on the passenger deck, so he presumed they had remained below throughout the trip. A cylindrical fuel truck and a long flatbed truck loaded with lumber were lined up behind the motorhome. At the front of the third lane was an empty Chevy Lumina with a rental agreement tucked on the dashboard. As Richard wondered who was driving it, the Australian couple cut across the rows of cars and got in. There were only two vehicles behind the rental car. One was a Volvo station wagon, occupied by the family Richard had seen in the cafeteria, and the last was the decal-covered van. The windows were curtained, so it was impossible to see inside, but he knew a van of that size would seat at least six people, if not more.

Richard strolled thoughtfully between the assembled cars. Several of them had the capacity to bring a stowaway on board. Presumably, the police had searched all the vehicles, but there were a lot of places on the car deck where someone could hide. The ferry was much smaller than the newer boats, but because of this, there were more concealed compartments for equipment that could be brought into use when traffic volume demanded. A hydraulically operated ramp hung overhead, supported with yellow and black striped channel beams. It could be lowered and positioned so that drivers could access the middle car deck, but when out of use, it provided a screened alcove for anyone who wanted to stay out of sight.

The huge doors yawned open and the orange-vested deckhands hooked the safety cables to the landing. The green light was flashing and the first mate was on the phone, so Richard hurried back to his car and prepared to unload. There were only two foot-passengers waiting to go ashore. One was a helmeted, spandex-covered cyclist whose machine, Richard thought ruefully, had probably cost as much as a police officer earned in a year. The other was a lady in hiking gear who was accompanied by a Dobermann as lithe and streamlined as its owner. Presumably, she had stayed below too. Dogs were not allowed on the passenger deck.

The ramp came down and the foot-passengers hurried ashore. Then the signal was given for the first line of cars to disembark. Richard felt troubled as he watched the vehicles leave. Any one of them might hold the solution to the mystery. He hoped that Detective Constable Small was a competent policeman because he had a feeling that there was more to this case than met the eye.

The deckhand waved Richard forward and he drove off the ferry. He felt restless and uneasy, but it was not his case, and Valerie had made it abundantly clear that she did not want him to wait. He made a determined effort to suppress his feelings of disquiet and concentrate on the task at hand, which was to find somewhere to stay in Powell River so he could get away early enough to catch the first ferry to Comox.

The rest of his day proved mercifully uneventful. The cold weather worked in his favour, for tourists were thin on the ground and the first bed-and-breakfast hotel he passed not only had a vacancy, but was also situated opposite an Italian restaurant. He booked a room, then walked across the road and ate a satisfying and substantial meal. After dinner, he strolled along the waterfront, admiring the old houses and peering into the windows of the quaint stores, but no matter how hard he tried to focus on his surroundings, he kept thinking about the drama on the ferry.

The next day dawned bright and sunny. The nagging worry in the back of his mind had caused him to sleep fitfully and he was wide-awake by five o'clock, so he had no difficulty making an early start. After a generously ample breakfast provided by the cheerful owner of the lodge, he paid his bill and set off for the ferry terminal. While he waited in the parking lot, he switched on the radio. As he had expected, the crisis from the previous day was on the news. The announcer, thought Richard cynically, was making the most of the episode. "No, it's not *Murder on the Orient Express*; it's murder on the *Queen of Tofino*." The report was ninety-percent hype and ten percent news, all of which Richard already knew. Irritated, he turned off the radio. Almost immediately, his cellphone rang. It was his sister, Philippa.

"What on earth have you been up to?" she began. "Talk about a busman's holiday."

Richard frowned.

"I assume you're talking about the incident on the ferry, but how the hell did you know I was involved?"

"You were on TV. I came home from rehearsal last night and

switched on the late news and there you were with your arms around a very pretty blonde, though it was obvious that neither of you had romance in mind. There were shots of the rescue crew going out to search for the woman who went overboard. All very exciting. Your photograph is on the front page of the paper this morning too, along with a story about how the handsome detective inspector took charge until the local force boarded the ship, etc. etc. etc."

Inwardly, Richard cursed the ubiquitous cellphone.

"One of those bloody passengers must have filmed the whole thing and passed it along to Global. Still, I'd rather they focussed on me than Valerie."

"Oh, they got her too. Her photo is even bigger than yours."

"Damn. Is it just a picture, or do they have her name?"

"Yes, her name is there." Philippa sounded sympathetic. "Not too good for the poor girl, is it? The whole world knows she witnessed a murder. What's she like?"

"Frail, ethereal, very lovely. A real charmer but troubled in some way. She recently went through a divorce, so that could explain her vulnerable air. I liked her."

"Wow! An intriguing beauty with an air of mystery. Sounds perfect for you. Are you going to stick around and look after her while the locals sort out the case?"

"Believe me, I wanted to," said Richard, "but she was adamant that I should carry on with my trip. So was the investigating officer. Basically I've been sent on my way. 'Go fishing,' they said, and that's exactly what I'm doing. I'm waiting to board the ferry for Little River right now."

"Strange that this woman didn't want you to stick around," mused Philippa. "I mean, if she's as fragile and vulnerable as you say, I'd have thought she'd be the clinging-vine type. Do you think she was put off once she realized you were a policeman? What exactly happened? Do you have enough minutes on your phone to fill me in?"

Richard gave Philippa an outline of the previous day's events. She was as perplexed as he was.

"I know you like this woman," she said slowly, "but are you absolutely sure she's on the level? You say she seemed to recognize the woman in the flowery dress. What if there is some connection between them? You know, one woman's scream sounds very much like another. What if it was the other woman who screamed? Your lovely ethereal damsel in distress could be a murderess with sufficient acting ability to cover up what she did by throwing herself into your arms and making up a story about a dark man with a Zapata moustache and sideburns. Mind you," she added, immediately confounding her own argument, "that's a pretty bad choice of description. If you wanted to make up a mysterious killer, you should at least describe someone who could fit the mould of any number of men on the ship."

"Exactly," said Richard. "No, I'm sure she was telling the truth. But she doesn't want my help, and neither does the detective in charge, so I have to try to put the whole thing out of my mind until I return to Vancouver, because once I'm on that fishing boat, I'm right out of touch with the rest of the world."

"Worrying," acknowledged Philippa. "Do you want me to phone you if there are any developments?"

"You won't be able to. I'll be out of cell range."

"Well, in that case," said Philippa sagely, "I'd advise you to forget about everything except your fishing trip and try to enjoy your holiday. One of the first rules for stress management is not to fret about the things you have no control over."

"Very wise for one so young."

"Not really. Dad's been giving me the same lecture. Octavia Bruni just returned from a trip to Germany and took great delight in phoning to tell me that Adam is living with a blonde mezzo from the Hamburg Opera."

"Ah," said Richard. "Sorry. I guess you're pretty upset."

"Yes, but I'll cope." Philippa was not one to emote a great deal except on the stage.

"Does that mean the summer tour is off?"

"No. We have several bookings. I have no intention of losing a gig as well as a boyfriend." Philippa firmly changed the subject. "Now, getting back to your situation, you should turn your phone off as soon as we end this call. Otherwise every other member of the family will be calling you, because right about now, they'll all be reading the paper over their morning coffees."

"Good idea," said Richard. "I'll phone you when I get back. You take care of yourself."

He rang off, knowing better than to lavish his sister with sympathy. Philippa had always been quiet and self-contained, and since the age of four, she had instinctively dealt with hurt by immediately turning to another activity and becoming totally absorbed. People thought that made her cold, but Richard knew her well enough to understand that she did her grieving privately. He was very fond of his youngest sister.

As Philippa had advised, he turned off his phone and, within ten minutes, he was aboard the *Queen of Burnaby* which was to take him to Vancouver Island. The crossing was uneventful, and after docking at Little River, he only had a two-hour drive along the Island Highway. As the prospect of an offshore fishing expedition got closer, his preoccupation with the *Queen of Tofino* mystery gradually diminished.

He arrived in Campbell River with time to spare. The charter was due to leave at two o'clock, so with a few minutes to kill, he turned on the car radio to see if there had been any progress with the investigation. But as he had expected, there was no new information, so he grabbed his gear, locked up his car and set off for the docks. By that night, he was sufficiently exhausted from the effort of bringing in the day's catch that he slept like the proverbial log.

Five days later, when he returned to shore, he started his journey back to Vancouver. The charter had been a success and the cooler in the back of the SUV was loaded with halibut, salmon and cod. Still in a holiday frame of mind, Richard drove down to Nanaimo in silence, but as he pulled into the ferry terminal and saw the lines of cars and the multitudes of people, he began to reconnect with his normal world. Since he had more than an hour to wait, he decided to find a newspaper. The dispensers were by the washrooms, so he grabbed some change and set off across the lot. As he drew close to the newspaper stand, the headline leapt out at him.

"Murder on the *Queen of Tofino!*"

Richard checked the date at the top of the paper. It was that day's edition. He was disconcerted. Five-day-old news should not be making headlines. He inserted a coin and pulled out a copy of the *Vancouver Sun*. Then, as he started to read, he blanched. His years as a policeman had toughened him to shocks, but his stomach lurched as he read the article.

Valerie Grayle had made the return trip from Powell River to Vancouver the previous day. She had embarked on the *Queen of Tofino* at ten-thirty in the morning, but when the ferry docked at Earl's Cove, her car did not move when the deckhand waved her off. Annoyed, because the driver appeared to be asleep, he rapped on the window to get her attention, but she did not respond. He tried to open the door but it was locked, and the crew eventually had to break the window in order to get into the vehicle. When they opened the door, the reason for her lack of co-operation was apparent. The woman in the driver's seat was dead.

* * *

"Poor woman didn't stand a chance," said Detective Sergeant Bill Martin. "Bloody press gave the killer a road map of how to find her. It wasn't just the stuff on the first day. Someone at the bed and breakfast leaked where she was staying and a newshound caught her on camera the following day as she was getting into her car. Even the blessed licence number showed up in the photograph. So the whole world knew her name, where she was staying and what she was driving."

"She should never have been allowed to travel back on her own," snapped Richard. "I told Small that she ought to have someone with her."

"He obviously didn't take her seriously," said Martin. "That was apparent from the newspaper stories. The press had picked up on the fact that the police were sending her to see a psychiatric specialist and possibly even a hypnotist, and to be fair," he added, "her behaviour was pretty irrational. She clammed up after her first outburst, and when pressed, she started to waffle about what she saw. At the time, it would have seemed as if Small's theory was correct, but in hindsight, my guess is that she was frightened."

"Then why didn't she ask her sister to come up to Powell River? Why did she set off on her own?"

"Small says she insisted that she wanted to be on her own. He says she was completely withdrawn. It was as if she was pulled inside a shell and didn't want contact with anyone at all—as if she could shut out the world, and somehow that made her feel safe."

"Back in her tower," said Richard. He ignored Martin's questioning glance and did not bother to explain the analogy. "I should have stayed with her," he said bitterly. "I let her down."

Martin looked grave.

"It isn't easy to help troubled souls. They have a way of working against you."

"Yes," said Richard. "Well, all we can do now is try to catch the bastard. Small has sent copies of the reports, and it's obvious this killer is a pro. Valerie was killed with a karate chop to the neck. That's not your average Joe's modus operandi for dispatching someone he wants to get rid of. He must have killed her as she was returning to her car because she'd been seen coming down the companionway as the ferry was coming in. She was parked behind a logging truck at the back of the lane on the starboard side of the ship. Her car was tucked between the wall and a forty-foot Winnebago, so it was screened from the view of the other passengers and crew. That made it easy for the killer. As Valerie opened her car door, he simply had to walk by, give her the death chop, slide her into the driver's seat, push down the lock and shut the door."

"She was on the early ferry," said Martin. "That one is loaded with commuters as well as holiday trippers, plus it's the one that the bus goes on. Surely someone saw something."

"No. What makes it even tougher is the fact that several lanes were unloaded before the deckhands discovered her. All the foot passengers had disembarked, the bus had left, and more than fifty percent of the vehicles had gone ashore. There's no way of tracing any of those people, beyond an appeal for them to come forward. One deckhand did report seeing a bus passenger come along that side of the ship, but he was middle-aged, clean-shaven, and balding, so he hardly meets the description of the man we're looking for."

Martin looked dour.

"Well, the karate kid won't come forward, so let's hope the passengers will call in and give us some information."

"You know," said Richard, "this murder may have a connection to Valerie's past. I'm sure she recognized the woman in the flowered dress.

What's more, Valerie said she'd never travelled the Sunshine Coast route before, but she knew her way around that boat. I think she'd been on the *Queen of Tofino* before."

"Then you need to find out more about her background."

"I know. I'll call her sister and see if I can go round for a chat. Valerie said they were close, so I suspect the sister will be able to throw some light on the situation. I ought to see her anyway, simply to give her my condolences."

* * *

Valerie Grayle's sister lived in North Vancouver. Her name was Janet Banks and she worked at a chandler's store close to Lonsdale Quay. Richard phoned the number in the file, but he did not manage to reach her until late evening so she invited him to come around the following morning as she did not have to be at the store until noon.

Richard left for the North Shore early the next day. He had no difficulty in finding the old one-storey house on Chancellor Boulevard where Valerie Grayle had lived with her sister.

The door of the house opened before Richard reached the top of the steps. Janet Banks had been watching for him. She ushered him inside and led him into a small, neatly appointed living room, where a glass-topped coffee table was already laid out with two ceramic mugs, a coffee pot, and a plate of brownies and coconut cookies. Richard declined the baking but accepted a mug of coffee. He studied the woman carefully as she poured the drinks. Janet Banks looked much older than her sister. Her wiry, salt-and-pepper hair and weathered face suggested that she must be approaching fifty, and the only resemblance to her sister came in the neat facial features and tiny build. However, whereas Valerie Grayle's petite frame gave the impression of delicacy, her sister's lean body looked strong and resilient. Janet handed Richard his coffee and settled in an armchair with her own mug.

"My little sister," she sighed. "She was such a happy baby. Valerie was eleven years younger than me, so I always felt responsible for her. She tagged after me everywhere."

"She didn't seem a very happy woman," said Richard bluntly. "Charming, certainly, but very self-contained. Was that a result of her divorce?"

Janet looked surprised.

"No, absolutely not. She'd been like that for a long time."

"Really? I thought perhaps she'd had an abusive husband. Her personality was fairly typical of women who are living with a lot of fear."

"Withdrawn and repressed. Yes, that sums Valerie up all right, but her husband wasn't the cause. Alan is an absolute darling. He's gentle and loving. In my opinion, he was everything she needed."

"Then why did they break up?"

"She left. She just upped and walked out on him and refused to go back."

"Did she tell you why?"

"She didn't have to tell me. Alan and I have had long conversations on the subject. He knew Valerie had a lot of unresolved problems and he was trying to convince her to go for psychiatric help. He was doing the right thing, but she simply withdrew from him. She shut him out of her life."

"Because he was trying to help her?"

"Yes. Astounding, isn't it? I tried to discuss her troubles myself after she came back, but she pulled away from me too. So I backed off. The last thing I wanted was for her to leave. At least with her here, I could keep an eye on her. And she wasn't doing too badly. She had the job with the magazine and she liked that. Mind you, she balked at taking the assignment in Powell River. She had an incredible aversion to boats." Janet set down her cup and her mouth twisted sadly. "You know, I pushed her to go. I thought she should try to get over her phobia, and I thought the trip would take her mind off her marriage breakdown. She'd never been on the Sunshine Coast, and it's such beautiful scenery. I thought it would be good for her. What a fool I was. I'll never forgive myself for making her go."

"When did this aversion to boats start?" Richard asked.

Janet looked thoughtful.

"Way back. She was only four years old. Our grandparents lived in Victoria and our parents took us to see them every second weekend. It was after one of those trips that Valerie started protesting that she didn't want to go, and when my parents insisted, she always threw such a tantrum that one of them ended up staying in the car with her during the crossing. It was around that time that her personality started to change. She was still a well-behaved, sweet little girl, but the bubbly quality had gone. And after that, she started having nightmares, but if we tried to get her to talk about them, all she would say was that there had been a bad storm and big waves."

Richard leaned forward.

"Look. Try to think back. Can you remember when this was?"

"Yes, I can, actually, because for once we were coming back late in the evening. It had been my grandmother's sixtieth birthday party. My grandmother's birthday was the third of August, and I was fifteen at the time, so that would put the date back in 1972. How's that for accuracy?"

"Incredible," said Richard appreciatively. "And *was* it a rough crossing?"

"No. Mom and Dad could never understand why Valerie started having dreams about big waves. The ocean was like glass that day."

"Was it just the nightmares that made your parents think something had happened to upset Valerie?"

"Well, yes, that was the first obvious sign, but then we all thought back and realized that there had been indications at the time that something was wrong. We remembered how Valerie had sat white-faced and silent on the drive home from the ferry. We thought she was sick from eating too much birthday cake, because earlier on, she'd been going on about wanting a chocolate bar from the candy machine." Janet frowned as she tried to recall the trip. "I needed to go to the washroom," she said, "and so did my mother, so Mom said she'd get Valerie a chocolate bar after we'd gone. Valerie was hopping about impatiently, and my mother had to be quite firm with her. She told her to stay in the bathroom while we were in the cubicles, and presumably she did as she was told, because when we came out, she was still there. However, she didn't want the chocolate bar any more and she looked pretty pale. We thought she had an upset stomach." Janet shook her head in bewilderment. "We were only gone a few minutes. Surely nothing could have happened in that space of time?"

Janet looked at Richard for reassurance, but he appeared to be in a trance. When he failed to respond, she leaned across and repeated her question. Richard looked at her strangely.

"I think," he said, "that an impatient little girl who wanted a candy bar would probably have been standing in the open doorway while she waited. She could see a lot in a couple of minutes."

"I don't understand."

"Never mind. Just think about the crossing. Who was on the boat with you? Was there anyone else that you knew?"

Janet looked surprised.

"Yes. There was one person, not that we knew her well. The couple who rented the house next door to my grandparents were young hippie types. My grandparents didn't have that much to do with them, but we saw them occasionally. The wife was on the ferry that evening. She was going to Vancouver to visit her parents."

Richard felt a surge of excitement.

"What did she look like?" he asked.

Janet looked reflective for a moment.

"As I recall," she said, "she had long, straight hair, rather mousey in colour, and she wore those granny-glasses that used to be fashionable. Ugly things, I always thought. And she tended to wear long, flowery dresses."

She looked speculatively at Richard.

"Does that help at all?" she asked.

Richard nodded.

"Yes. This woman is the key to the whole affair. Can you remember anything else about her at all?"

Janet bit her lip. "You know, I didn't really like her because she was so quiet that she didn't seem friendly, but looking back, I'd say she was very tense. With hindsight, my guess would be that she was afraid of her husband."

"Why? Had you seen him act violently towards her?"

"No, but he looked pretty menacing. And according to my grandfather—who, by the way, was a military man who had no time for draft dodgers—the neighbour was a deserter from the States."

"He was a Vietnam vet?"

"I think so."

"Look, this is really important. Can you remember what he looked like?"

"Yes. I remember him fairly well because he looked like he'd

81

stepped off the cover of my *Revolver* album. I was a big Beatles and Stones fan back then."

"Give me some specific details," Richard urged her.

"Well, as far as I can recall, he had longish dark hair, with those sideburns that were fashionable back in the seventies. Half the men went around looking like something from the Victorian era, didn't they? And he had a moustache. One of the ones that made him look like a Mexican bandit. Does that help?"

"You've no idea how much," said Richard. "Now I know what she saw and why she was hysterical on that trip to Saltery Bay."

Janet gazed at him anxiously.

"So why did she break down?"

"Because," said Richard, "I'm willing to bet that the trip you just described took place on the *Queen of Tofino*. That vessel has windows in the front lounge that turn the flat ocean into a mass of rolling hills. To a child, especially in the evening light, that would have looked just like a storm at sea. And I believe that the shock of revisiting the ferry, combined with the sight of a woman whose seventies-style hippie outfit made her resemble your grandparents' neighbour, triggered your sister's memory and caused a major childhood trauma to come rushing back."

Richard shook his head sadly.

"She wasn't lying when she said she saw a murder," he explained, "but it didn't happen two weeks ago. It happened thirty-six years ago."

* * *

"Repressed memory syndrome? Are you serious?" said Sergeant Martin.

"It's the only thing that would explain this whole freakish scenario," said Richard. "I've checked the history of the ship. The *Queen of Tofino* was built in 1960, and during the sixties and seventies, she sailed between the Mainland and Victoria. Valerie knew her way around that boat because she had travelled on it as a child. Small says he's checking on the details of the crossing from Swartz Bay on August 3, 1972, and Jean Howe is going through the missing persons from the relevant period. We're also trying to trace the couple that lived next to Janet Bank's grandparents and I've put a call out for the bus passenger who was seen coming from the vicinity of Valerie's car. If my theory is correct, he's the right age for our killer, because today he'd be in his late fifties or early sixties. The bus company wouldn't have a record of his name, but with the description, they should be able to tell us where he got off. He won't have been on that ferry for any other reason than to murder the one person who witnessed a crime he committed all those years ago—someone who had obviously been terrified or traumatized into keeping silent about what she'd seen, but whose memory was obviously coming back. Think how he must have felt when he read that Valerie was going to be sent for psychiatric treatment and hypnosis."

"There are an awful lot of gaps to fill in. Your hunch doesn't have much in the way of fact behind it."

"No, but there are some pretty dramatic coincidences that can't be simply dismissed. When Valerie was four, she was in the women's washroom, waiting while her mother and sister used the facilities. The doors on the washrooms are open on the ferry, so you can bet she was hopping back and forth over the sill and keeping her eye on the candy machine. If a couple had been quarrelling on the deck, she'd have heard the voices. Perhaps she tiptoed across and peeked through the door. Who knows exactly how it happened. All I know is that two weeks ago, she became hysterical in exactly the same spot on that very same ship."

The door of Richard's office flew open and Constable Jean Howe swept into the room. She waved a printout jubilantly and tossed it on Richard's desk.

"Here's what you want," she said. "August 10, 1972. A woman named Jill Robertson was reported missing by her parents. Look at the description . . . long, straight hair, light brown in colour. She wore granny glasses. Usually wore long skirts or flowing dresses. She lived in Victoria, but had called her parents and told them she intended to leave her husband. He was an American who had served in Vietnam, but since he'd returned from overseas, they'd had a lot of problems. The wife was going to come to live with her parents until she got her life straightened out, and they were expecting her a week before they reported her missing. When she didn't appear, they phoned and her husband told them she wasn't well. He told them she'd call when she was feeling better. They didn't trust him, and they believed that he'd intimidated her into staying. It had happened before, but when a week passed and they still hadn't heard from her, they went to the Island to see what was going on. Their daughter was not at the house, and their son-in-law told them that she had left him. They suspected she'd come to harm and they went to the police right away. It sounds as if there was a fairly comprehensive investigation, but the girl was never found."

Richard read the husband's description at the top of the file.

"Stewart Robertson. Tall, dark-haired, with long sideburns and a Viva Zapata moustache."

"That's him," said Jean. "The case is still open."

"Not for long," said Richard grimly.

* * *

Richard's prediction proved true. Stewart Robertson was tracked down two days later. He lived in Nanaimo and had worked in the shipyard there for the past twenty years. He had a common-law wife, a faded, nervous-looking woman named Joanne, who had lived with him for twelve years. After the deckhand identified Robertson as the same man who had been seen near Valerie Grayle's car on the *Queen of Tofino*, Joanne admitted that she had driven him up to Little River so he could take the ferry to Powell River, but at that point, the case broke down. Everything that linked Robertson to the disappearance of his wife or the murder of Valerie Grayle was purely circumstantial. A good lawyer would have had the prosecution's case thrown out of court. There was insufficient evidence to lay a charge that would stick, and all the police could do was watch and wait.

Two months later, their vigil was over. Richard was at home on his day off. He had slept in and was enjoying a leisurely cup of coffee along with the morning paper. He was engrossed in a story about the latest technology in the treatment of cancer when he noticed a small article at the bottom of the page. His eyes widened as he read it. Then he smiled a tight smile of satisfaction. Charges would never have to be laid against Stewart Robertson now for justice had overcome him another way. There had been an accident in the shipyard. Robertson had been struck on the head. Death had been instantaneous and the case was finally closed.

* * *

A week later, Jean Howe ushered a visitor into Richard's office. It was the woman who had lived with Stewart Robertson in Nanaimo. The first thing that Richard noticed as Joanne came in was that she looked somehow more substantial. The nervous air had vanished, and although she was still pale and thin, her demeanour was quietly confident.

"I had to come," she said. "I couldn't say anything before, though I'd have helped if I could. I was terrified of what he'd do."

Richard was stunned by the implication of her words.

"You knew what he intended to do when you drove him to Little River?"

Joanne blanched at his tone.

"No," she insisted. "I had no idea, and I didn't know what he'd done in the past either. I was simply afraid of opposing him in any way. I was afraid of what he'd do to me. You have to understand . . . whenever I didn't do as he said, he became violent. I didn't know until afterwards what had happened to those other poor women, but he boasted about it when he came back. He threatened that the same thing would happen to me if I told anyone. And he said if I tried to leave him, he'd find me and kill me, the same way he'd killed his wife all those years ago."

"So he actually admitted it?"

"Yes."

"Did he tell you how it happened?"

"Yes." Joanne looked sad. "His wife had left him, and he followed her onto the ferry to ask her to come back, but she wouldn't. They quarrelled, but for once she resisted him. They were out on the deck and he lost his temper and hit her. He was trained to kill in Vietnam, so maybe he didn't mean to kill her with that blow, but he did. When he saw she was dead, he dragged her to the rail and dumped her over the side. But when he looked up, there was a little girl peeking through the doorway. He knew her. She was the granddaughter of his next-door neighbour, so he knew she could identify him. Poor little thing.

85

He went over to her and told her that if she ever talked about what she had seen, he would track her down and kill her."

"And he did," said Richard bitterly. "Though the reality is, the trauma of that incident killed her spirit long before he finally finished her off. Instant death was far too good for him."

"I'm sorry," said the woman. "I hope I did the right thing in coming in. I just thought you ought to know."

"Yes, of course," said Richard. "Thank you. I appreciate the fact that you came. And I'm glad you're free of him at last. You could have been next, you know. Whatever fell on him in the shipyard did you a service."

Joanne had stood, prepared to leave, but now she stopped and looked surprised.

"But surely you know what killed him?" she said.

"No. I just read that there was an accident. I didn't get any details."

The hint of an ironic smile touched Joanne's lips and she shook her head wryly.

"They were dismantling the equipment and items of historic value from the old ferry," she said. "Everything of significance was taken off before the boat was sold."

Richard raised his eyebrows.

"So what fell on him?" he asked curiously.

The smile lingered on Joanne's lips.

"It was the ship's bell," she said, "from the *Queen of Tofino*."

Without another word, she slipped out the door.

HOW DO YOU SOLVE
A PROBLEM LIKE MARIA?

Cilla Buckingham considered her spouse a model husband. Randolph Buckingham was twice as old as his wife, and the combined challenges of age and the control of his various consortiums ensured that he did not make many demands on his spouse. He produced fortunes with the same regularity that other men produce a monthly paycheck, but he rarely had time to spend his money, so that responsibility fell back on Cilla. Randolph did write the occasional cheque, but it was always to benefit his wife. A generous donation to the Burnside City Opera had not been quite sufficient to make up for Cilla's lack of talent and procure her the role of Maria in *The Sound of Music*, but she had happily settled for the Baroness since the part allowed her to wear glamorous clothes instead of drab peasant dresses and a ghastly nun's habit. Another cheque had provided a sable coat and a diamond choker to ensure that she looked every inch the part of the wealthy Elsa. Of course, Randolph never got things exactly right. Cilla would have far preferred a diamond bracelet to the Pekinese with the matching diamond collar that came with the other gifts, especially since the dog was not quite the correct colour to co-ordinate with the coat. However, Randolph meant well so, all in all, she was not too displeased. The wretched dog would die at some point, and after a suitable show of tears, the collar would convert very nicely, with enough diamonds left over for matching earrings as well. Yes, thought Cilla, things were going very nicely indeed.

* * *

Philippa stood in the wings and watched her friend Milton playing a scene with Cilla Buckingham. Milton was amazing, she decided. The Baroness was about as animated as the balcony post she was leaning against, but Milton danced around her and sparkled as if he were playing opposite the legendary Gertrude Lawrence.

A tug at her skirt drew Philippa's attention away from the stage. She looked down to see the little girl who was playing Gretl.

"Maria," the child said solemnly, "I have a big p'oblem."

Gretl could never manage her *r*'s when they followed a *p*.

"What, sweetheart?" Philippa knelt down so that she could talk eye to eye with the little girl.

"The Baroness says we can't walk Pinkerton any more."

"Oh, dear, that is too bad," said Philippa. Privately, she considered Pinkerton as obnoxious as his operatic namesake. Normally, she liked dogs, but the Pekinese had nearly taken her hand off the first time she had attempted to pat it, and its squat little face compressed into a scowl every time she came near. It had bitten several members of the company, but young Gretl had somehow magically won its heart.

"Cilla seemed glad to have you look after the dog," said Philippa. "Why has she changed her mind?"

"It was Liesl's fault," said Gretl sadly. "Last time we walked Pinkerton, Liesl took off his collar and put it round her own neck."

"How did she get away with that? I thought Cilla always sent Marta with you." Marta was Cilla's downtrodden and underpaid personal dresser. Cilla's extravagance did not extend to giving her servants a living wage. Marta was also the only person other than Gretl who could go near Pinkerton without fear of losing a limb.

"Marta's supposed to come," said Gretl. "Cilla says it's in case anyone steals Pinkerton, but she doesn't really care about him," she added indignantly. "She only cares about his collar."

"Surely not," said Philippa.

"No, really. She feeds him too much and she *never* walks him. He's getting awfully fat. And she smacks him if he barks. That's why he's cross all the time."

"You could be right," said Philippa. "Anyway, why wasn't Marta with you?"

"Because if Cilla is on stage, Marta never comes. She just lets us take Pinkerton. But Franz saw Liesl with the collar on, and he told on her."

Right in character, thought Philippa. Proper little Nazi. Rudi Stromberg was good in his assigned role, but Philippa found him an unctuous and unappealing youth offstage. She also suspected he was not as virtuous as he pretended to be.

"Franz is mean," added Gretl, pointing at the shiny red Mary Janes on her feet. "He said my new shoes were ugly."

"That's not true," Philippa assured her. "Your shoes are beautiful. Red is a lovely colour."

"I know," said Gretl. "It's my favourite. But Franz is always teasing us. He's horrid. I feel really sorry for Liesl." Gretl pulled a face. "She has to *kiss* him!"

"She'll cope," said Philippa, reflecting that Little Miss Sixteen-Going-On-Seventeen had had a dozen different boyfriends over the course of rehearsals. Liesl's offstage ensembles consisted of black leather miniskirts and skimpy tank tops, and the way she wore them suggested she knew exactly what to do with what lay beneath. Philippa could well believe she had paraded around the grounds wearing the diamond collar.

"Please," said Gretl, "will you talk to Cilla and get her to give us another chance?"

"I'll try," agreed Philippa, "but she may not listen to me."

"Yes, she will," said Gretl. "You're a p'ofessional. She thinks you're important."

"Well, I'll do my best." Philippa noticed a bandage on the little girl's hand. "What happened?" she asked, pointing at the dressing. "I hope Pinkerton didn't bite you."

Gretl looked indignant.

"Of course not," she said. "He never bites me. I cut myself on his collar. It's really sharp."

A voice from the stage manager's corner prevented Philippa from replying. Jamie Brock sounded annoyed.

"Hey, wake up, Maria, you're on!"

"Sowwy!" wailed Gretl. The *r*'s also disappeared in moments of crisis.

Philippa leapt up, sprang into action and loped onto the stage. As she crossed to stage left and turned back to look at Milton, she glanced towards the wing. Surprised, she saw that the little girl was still there. Gretl was staring at her red shoes.

* * *

Later, in the green room, Philippa learned the meaning of Gretl's peculiar stance.

"Poor little tyke was mortified that she made you miss your entrance," said Sister Berta. "You can always tell when she's done something wrong because she hangs her head and stares at her feet. You should have seen her when Cilla laid into them for removing that pedigree fleabag's collar. I thought Gretl's nose would get stuck between her toes. And it wasn't even the kid's fault. It was that little tart that plays Liesl. And," Sister Berta's tone developed an edge, "speaking of Liesl, I have a bit of a problem. You might be able to help."

"What sort of problem?"

"My boyfriend picks me up after the show, and Liesl has got her beady baby-blues beamed on him. She always gets out of costume and makeup faster than I can—you've no idea how long it takes to fix one's hair after it's been stuck under a wimple for three hours—and she's at the stage door, panting all over him, every night."

"I don't know what I can do," said Philippa. "I don't have any control over the girl. She's a pretty independent spirit."

"A delinquent spirit too. Go ask Jamie Brock." Sister Berta arched her eyebrows knowingly. "Sixteen-Going-on-a-Lot-More-than-Seventeen got pulled in for shoplifting two years ago, and it wasn't just a case of a candy bar from the corner store. She walked out of Holt Renfrew with a Gucci handbag."

"Good Lord! What happened?"

"Nothing. Just a tap on the wrist. She was a young offender. But if she's prepared to steal a thousand-dollar handbag, she certainly won't balk at stealing my boyfriend."

"How do you think I can help?"

"She shares your dressing room. Keep her talking. Give her some stage tips. You're a professional, so she'll listen to you. All I need is an extra ten minutes."

Jamie Brock's voice crackled over the intercom.

"Nuns, Maria, on stage, please."

"Oh, sod it," said Sister Berta. "I haven't gone to the loo yet."

She hiked up the folds of her black habit and lumbered off in the direction of the washroom. Philippa finished her coffee and got up. She was about to leave the green room when the door opened and Milton appeared. He staggered into the room and clutched his chest dramatically.

"I won't make it to the end of the run," he declared. "I shall have a heart attack and die in action. Have you any idea what it takes out of me trying to get any kind of reaction out of Cilla? I don't care how much her husband contributed. She can't act, she can't move and she sings like a constipated crow. Playing Max has to be the worst role of my life. I'm either upstaged by children or dead in the water with the bovine baroness. Couldn't you give her a few tips—a bit of coaching on the side? You're Equity. She'll listen to you."

"You're Equity too. Coach her yourself."

"I tried. I talked to her about her posture. It didn't work."

"What did you tell her?"

"I said just because she had twin Matterhorns on her chest didn't mean she had to carry them as if they were gun turrets on the Nazi tanks. She hasn't spoken to me since—except onstage, of course."

"Do you wonder? You know," Philippa added acerbically, "I don't know why everyone has to come to me with their problems. I have quite enough of my own to deal with."

Milton looked sympathetic.

"Yes, I know, dear. Things haven't worked out the way you hoped. But look on the bright side . . . given the present negative state of your love life, you're perfect for the part of a nun."

"Thanks a lot. You're such a comfort."

"I know. I can cheer you up some more," Milton said breezily. "I have a huge repertoire of nun and Nazi jokes."

"I'm sure you do. Why don't you save them for Cilla?"

"Now *you're* being facetious," said Milton.

He darted off onto another topic. "Have you seen my tiepin anywhere? It seems to have vanished. I can't think what's happened to it."

"Don't ask me," said Philippa. "Maybe you lost it on the Matterhorn."

"You know," said Milton, eyeing his friend severely, "you're very crabby and sarcastic these days. You may be managing to be Julie Andrews on stage, but you're certainly not a spoonful of sugar the rest of the time. Just because Adam is proving to be a rat doesn't mean you have to take it out on the rest of us."

"No, of course not. I'm sorry." Philippa was genuinely contrite. She was very fond of Milton. She gave him a big hug and said, "I promise I'll be more cheerful in future."

"That's my girl," said Milton. "You can do it. Just keep thinking Julie Andrews."

A crackle burst from the intercom followed by a bellow from Jamie Brock.

"Maria, on stage!"

Philippa groaned, grabbed her veil, and took off like a thunderbolt.

"There you are," Milton called after her. "I said you could do it. That was just like the start of the movie!"

* * *

Philippa mediated on behalf of Gretl, and the following week, the children were allowed to walk Pinkerton again. However, resolving

Sister Berta's problem had proved a headache, for Liesl now regarded herself as Philippa's best friend and felt free to unload all her personal problems while they prepared for the performance.

"Liesl is the crappiest part I've ever had," she complained, squinting into the mirror as she glued on an eyelash. "Everyone expects me to be a babysitter. The stupid kids have got a chaperone, but all *she* wants to do is knit and read romance novels, so I get stuck with them every minute, on stage and off." She sat back, blinked, and continued her diatribe. "It wouldn't be so bad if I had a decent leading man, but I'm playing opposite a total slime-ball." Liesl leaned forward and lowered her voice. "You know, he's not as perfect as he makes out. That clean-cut image he puts on for the producer is total crap. Of course, *your* leading man isn't an angel either, but at least he doesn't have a runny nose from snorting coke."

Philippa was taken aback. She was not overly surprised at the reference to Franz's drug habit, but she liked Captain Von Trapp. He had an old-world charm that worked well on stage. He knew his lines, and he was a courteous player who handled all their scenes with panache and gallantry.

"What's wrong with my leading man?" she demanded.

"Oh, he's good on stage," Liesl acknowledged, "but he's into Internet gambling big time. He's in debt up to the sprig of edelweiss on his little Tyrolean hat."

"How on earth do you know that?"

"I have connections."

Now, that I can believe, thought Philippa. However, she merely changed the subject and said, "Have you seen my bone-handled hairbrush? I seem to have mislaid it."

"Haven't a clue," said Liesl. "There's a whole bunch of things gone missing on this show. I lost my sunglasses last week. Someone is taking stuff, but it's never anything valuable. I think we've got one of those what-do-you-call-ems in the cast."

"A kleptomaniac?"

"Yeah, that's it. I think we've got one of those. I figure it has to be one of the nuns, because it would be pretty easy to stuff things under those ugly costumes. It's probably one of the older ones too," Liesl

93

theorized, "because that klepto-thingy is more likely to strike middle-aged women who have emotional problems."

"You know about these things, do you?" Philippa arched her eyebrows.

"My counsellor explained it to me. It's not the kind of excuse you can get away with when you're young."

And I bet you tried, thought Philippa uncharitably, temporarily forgetting her resolution to be Julie Andrews.

The door of the dressing room opened and Gretl came in. Her arms were stiffly extended in front of her, and in her hand, she held a red carnation, but her eyes were fixed firmly on her shoes.

"My mom says I have to give this back," she said sorrowfully.

Philippa looked from the single flower to the elaborate florist's arrangement at the corner of the counter. She had not noticed before, but there was definitely a gap where one of the carnations had previously emerged from the leaves.

"Is that from my bouquet?" she asked.

Gretl nodded, but her eyes never rose higher than Philippa's knees.

"Well, you're welcome to it," said Philippa. "You can keep it."

At last the eyes met Philippa's. They were wide as saucers.

"Can I really? I only took it for my mom. It's so p'etty. I *love* red. It's the best colour in the whole world."

Liesl snorted rudely.

"Maybe you can be a fire engine when you grow up," she said snidely.

"Well," said Philippa, glaring at Liesl and pulling another couple of blooms from the arrangement, "why don't you take your mom a little bouquet? Tell her I insisted you were to have it."

"Thank you," said Gretl. Clutching the treasured flowers, she trotted out of the room.

"You shouldn't encourage her," said Liesl sanctimoniously. "She'll grow up thinking it's OK to help herself."

Thus speaks the pot about the kettle, thought Philippa, remembering the tale that Sister Berta had told.

Philippa finished her makeup and took one last look in the mirror. Yes, her red curls were suitably flattened and her lipstick not too bright.

She shut her makeup case and got up, but as she moved her chair back against the counter, the dressing-room door flew open and Cilla stormed into the room. Her face was contorted into a mask of fury. She marched across the room and grabbed Liesl by the arm.

"Where is it?" she demanded.

Liesl's blasé attitude evaporated. She stared wide-eyed at the seething virago.

"Where is what?" she asked.

"Don't pretend you don't know what I'm talking about." Cilla pushed away the young woman's arm and looked angrily around the room.

"Pinkerton's collar!" she snarled. "It's been stolen!"

* * *

Within minutes of Cilla's departure, Jamie Brock appeared in Philippa's dressing room.

"You're used to dealing with problems," he wheedled. "Can't you calm Cilla down and see if we can deal with this without calling the police? For crying out loud, the curtain goes up in half an hour."

"And I'm on first," said Philippa. "This isn't exactly the best way for me to warm up."

"Just tell her you'll call in your brother if the collar isn't returned. At least that way we can get through the show."

Philippa sighed.

"She's probably already called the police," she said.

"No," said Jamie. "She's gone to her dressing room. I said I'd be down shortly."

"Why did she accuse you, Liesl?" Philippa asked. "Was it just because of the earlier incident with the collar?"

Liesl pouted.

"Probably."

"Were you in her dressing room this evening?"

"Yes. We walked her stupid dog for her as soon as we arrived at the theatre."

"Did Marta come with you?"

"Yes, but she went to the costume room after we came back, and

95

the other kids took off, so it was just me and Gretl who took the dumb mutt back to the dressing room."

"How long were you in there?"

Liesl looked shifty-eyed.

"Not long. A couple of minutes."

Philippa knew perfectly well that the girl was hedging. She continued to probe.

"And what did you do while you were there?" she said.

"Just settled the dog in its basket."

"*You* did that?"

"Well, Gretl did."

"And what were you doing? Come on, I can tell you're covering up something."

Liesl shrugged and looked defiant.

"So I tried on her mink coat. So what? It looks a lot better on me than it does on her."

"Did anyone else come in while you were there?"

"No, but we heard someone coming along the hall, so I took the coat off real quick and hung it up, and then we got out of there and went to our own rooms."

"Did you see who was in the hall?"

"Yeah. It was Sister Berta."

"And where did she go?"

"How should I know? We didn't watch her. I just dropped Gretl off at the kids' room and came back here." Liesl glared angrily at Jamie. "I didn't take the dumb collar. OK? And just in case you're having a blonde moment and think the infant took it, I should point out that Gretl was wearing a little pair of shorts and a T-shirt so there's nowhere she could have concealed it without me knowing. Whoever stole that collar was someone who went in there after us."

Philippa bit her lip. She glanced at her watch, and then looked up at Jamie.

"All right, I'll go and speak to Cilla. You may have to hold the curtain though."

She left the dressing room and found Milton and Sister Berta hovering in the corridor outside.

"Let me guess," said Milton. "You've been given another problem to solve."

"Unfortunately, yes."

"That's what you get for having a brother who's a detective," said Sister Berta.

"Do either of you know anything about what happened?" Philippa asked them.

Sister Berta used an extremely un-nun-like expression.

"That bitch tried to accuse me," she added. "Just because I happened to be outside the door when she discovered it was gone."

"Wait a minute," said Philippa. "Liesl said you were in the corridor when she and Gretl came out of the dressing room. Why were you still there after Cilla came back?"

Sister Berta looked indignant.

"Maria's turning into the Gestapo, is she?" she said snippily. "If you must know, I had time to spare so I went down to the stairwell to gossip with Gurdeep."

Gurdeep was the security guard whose booth was by the stage door. His office was on the landing between the stairs to the lower floor where the chorus dressing rooms were situated and the few short steps to the principals' rooms which were at stage level.

"You were standing by Gurdeep's window?" Philippa felt a surge of excitement. "You can see the door of Cilla's room from there, can't you?"

"Yes. Very clearly."

"Did you see anyone while you were there?"

Sister Berta nodded.

"I saw Liesl and Gretl as I was coming down the corridor," she said. Then, when I was talking with Gurdeep, I heard someone moving, and I looked up to see Mother Superior going back the other way."

"Did you see her face?"

"No, but it must have been her, because she and I are the only nuns upstairs. All the rest are billeted on the lower floor."

"Could she have been coming out of Cilla's room?"

"It's possible," said Sister Berta, "but if she was, it would have been a quick trip. I was only talking to Gurdeep for ten minutes."

"Did you see anyone else?"

"Just Marta returning to the dressing room. Cilla came back soon afterwards. She went inside, and at that point, I decided to go for a coffee. As I went up the stairs, the door flew open and Cilla came out and started shrieking at me. I told her exactly where to get off, and then I went to the green room and told the others what was going on."

"Who was there?" said Philippa. "And how did they react?"

"I was there," said Milton. "I was dreadfully shocked—more by your language, dear, than the theft," he added to Sister Berta. "Such profanity from a nun."

Sister Berta ignored Milton and answered Philippa's question.

"Other than Milton, there were only three people there—your leading man, the head nun, and the nasty Nazi. As I recall, Franz made some spiteful remark to the effect that Liesl was really going to be in for it now, Captain Von Trapp commented that it served Cilla right and she had no business bringing anything that valuable to the theatre anyway, and Mother Superior looked suitably horrified and dropped her hairbrush."

Milton looked puzzled. "What do you mean, she dropped her hairbrush? She didn't have a hairbrush. She was just drinking a cup of coffee."

Sister Berta was adamant.

"She did have one. You probably didn't notice. She stooped down, whisked it off the floor and tucked it back in her robe."

"Hmm," said Milton. "I didn't see her bend down, but she did start so violently that she nearly dumped her coffee—so she could have dropped a brush if it was tucked in her robes, but the funny thing is, I hadn't noticed it earlier."

"What did it look like?" asked Philippa.

"It was like yours," said Sister Berta. "A bone-handled one."

Milton's eyebrows popped up over the rims of his glasses. He turned to Philippa.

"Oh, I say. Was it yours? The one that went missing?"

Philippa nodded grimly. She told him about her earlier discussion with Liesl.

"Well, the naughty old lady," said Milton.

"What did she do after she retrieved the brush?" Philippa asked Sister Berta.

"Took her coffee and hared off to her dressing room."

"Probably to lace her drink from the gin bottle she keeps under the counter," added Milton.

Philippa sighed.

"Thanks, you two," she said. "I guess I'd better go and talk with her. For once, it's going to be the novice putting the abbess on the carpet. I wonder what else she has hidden away in her dressing room."

"Probably my tiepin," Milton called after her. "Make sure you get it back."

* * *

"I'm sorry, dear," said Mother Superior. "My counsellor is going to be so disappointed. I really thought I'd kicked the habit."

Philippa inwardly breathed a sigh of relief that Milton was not present. She could imagine the comment he would make over the unintentional pun.

"It was the stress of the show," the nun continued. "It was just too much for me. I relapsed. Everything is here. I'll give it all back and apologize."

"But why are you stressed?" asked Philippa. "You're a lovely Mother Superior. I've never seen anyone better in the part."

"Well, you see, dear, it's because of Rudi. He got the role of Franz because I recommended him to the director. His mother is a very dear friend of mine, and she's had so many problems with him. Outwardly, he seems like the perfect child, but he's a very sneaky sort of boy. Last year she found out he had started using cocaine and was stealing from her to support his habit. I thought if I could get him into the show, it would get him involved with a different crowd. But I've come to the conclusion that he's never going to change. He isn't a very nice boy, you know. My friend is so happy that he's in the show, and she's over the moon because he's stopped taking money from her. How can I tell her that he's been taking it from me instead?"

"I think you'd better be completely honest with her," said Philippa, "just as you have been with me. Rudi will get help a lot faster if he's made to deal with the consequences of his actions."

"I suppose you're right," sighed the abbess. She got up and went to the cupboard at the side of the room. Opening the door, she took out a white plastic bag and handed it to Philippa.

"There you are, dear. Everything I took is in there."

Philippa opened the bag and looked through the contents. She frowned.

"But the dog's collar," she said. "It isn't here."

"Oh no, dear," said Mother Superior. "I didn't take that. I may have passed Cilla's room, but I never went in there. If the collar's been stolen, someone else is responsible."

* * *

Philippa talked with Gurdeep, who verified what Sister Berta had told her. Next she checked with the Von Trapp children, and they confirmed Liesl's story. None of the children other than Liesl and Gretl had gone into Cilla's dressing room. Gretl's face went white when she heard that the collar had been stolen, but she insisted that Liesl was not the culprit. Uneasily, Philippa noticed that the little girl's eyes were riveted on the cherished red shoes. She knelt and gave the child a hug.

"I know you don't want to get Liesl into trouble, darling," she said, "but you must tell me the truth. Did either of you take the collar?"

"No," said Gretl. "We didn't take it. I don't know who did, honest."

Philippa sighed and got up. There was nothing left now but to talk with Cilla. If the children hadn't taken the collar, there seemed to be only one other person who could have been responsible, and Philippa did not look forward to making accusations against the browbeaten dresser who catered to Cilla's every need. She entered the room, but before she could speak, Cilla embarked on another tirade. She was still fixated on Liesl.

"I don't care what that little tramp says, she took that collar." Cilla compressed her lips tightly and rapped her blood-red fingernails against the makeup counter. "It's quite clear from what you've told me that, other than Marta, those children were the only ones in the room. I saw the collar was missing the moment I came in, and Marta has been here with me ever since, so there's no way that she was responsible, even if she is so destitute that she'd probably rob me blind if she could get away with it."

Philippa looked sympathetically at the thin, dark woman who was quietly brushing Cilla's jacket in the corner of the room. Marta's brooding eyes stared steadfastly at the fabric she was cleaning and she remained impassive, as if impervious to her employer's scathing words.

Philippa glanced towards the other corner where Pinkerton lay in his basket. His pug nose was squished into his blanket and he was sleeping peacefully on his amply padded cushion, blissfully indifferent to his mistress's distracted state. He looked very comfortable. Suddenly, a thought occurred to Philippa. She turned to Cilla and asked a question.

"Has anyone actually searched your dressing room since the collar went missing?" she asked.

Cilla looked blank.

"No. If the collar isn't on Pinkerton, why would it be anywhere else in this room?"

Philippa looked back at Marta. The dresser twisted her hands nervously and glanced towards the dog. A shadow of unease crossed the woman's face.

Cilla finally absorbed the implication of Philippa's words.

"What are you suggesting?" she exclaimed. "That the necklace was hidden so it could be taken later?" She whirled on Marta and her face darkened with fury. "Marta! Is this true?"

"No! I not hide anything," the woman cried. "You go ahead. You search the room."

Marta went to the cupboard and threw open the door.

"There. And here is my coat . . . my bag. You look all you like. I not take anything."

Cilla moved towards the woman's purse, but Philippa stopped her.

"No, not there. Where's the one place you wouldn't think to search?"

She marched over to Pinkerton's basket and, holding her breath in case the little beast woke up and sunk his teeth into her, grabbed it by the edge and quickly tipped it sideways. Pinkerton fell into a heap on the floor. He sat up indignantly and shook his head vigorously.

Then he waddled over to Marta, wagged his feathery tail and jumped up to get her attention. Philippa picked up his blanket. There on the floor, beside the padded cushion that lined the basket, lay the diamond collar.

Marta froze. Terrified, she backed away from Cilla and shrank against the wall. Cilla strode across the room, snatched up the collar and waved it threateningly at the petrified woman.

"I'm calling the police," she snapped.

"No!" cried Marta. "It was not me!"

Pinkerton continued to jump at Marta, and as he strained upwards, Philippa noticed a raw patch on the dog's neck where the collar used to be. She stared at the abrasion, and the red mark reminded her of Gretl's red shoes. *Why had the child been staring at her feet again?* Instantly, Philippa felt a surge of remorse for her suspicions of the dresser.

"Wait," she said to Cilla. "Marta might be telling the truth. Marta," she added to the frightened woman, "go down the hall and bring young Gretl here."

Marta set off. Cilla taciturnly examined the collar while she waited for the dresser to return. Pinkerton transferred his attentions to Philippa and whiffled around her ankles, but wisely she did not bend to pat him, since past experience had taught her not to confuse attention with affection from the pug-faced animal. The interlude seemed to stretch interminably, but it was only a couple of minutes before Marta returned. With her was Milton, who was carrying Gretl in his arms. Pinkerton immediately left Philippa and began to jump up at the little girl. Milton plopped Gretl down by the dog, gave her a smile, and then pointed at the collar in Cilla's hands.

"See," he said. "It's there. Everything's all right."

Gretl's face lit up in a smile.

"Oh, thank goodness," she cried. "You got it back. I was really upset when Maria told me it had been stolen."

Philippa smiled.

"I bet you were. Gretl," she added, "did you notice the sore patch on Pinkerton's neck?"

Gretl held up her bandaged finger.

"Yes," she said. "He got an owie from the collar, just like me." She gave Pinkerton a big hug, and the dog licked her face affectionately.

"And it was rubbing on him and making him sore when he was sleeping," Gretl added solemnly.

"And what did you do to make sure that the collar didn't hurt him?"

"I took it off after his walk," said Gretl, "but I didn't steal it. I just tucked it under his cushion."

Philippa stood up and looked at Cilla.

"There, you see. It wasn't stolen at all. I think you owe a few people an apology."

Cilla glowered furiously and sat down on the chair by the counter.

"Why didn't you tell me?" she snapped at Gretl, but the little girl barely noticed for she was cuddling Pinkerton.

Cilla's eyes narrowed and her blood-red fingernails began to rap an ominous tattoo against the countertop, but after a moment, the tapping ceased and her angry expression was replaced by a look of cunning. Speculatively, she eyed the child and the dog. Then she stroked the diamond collar which lay in her lap.

"Oh, for heaven's sake," she said abruptly. "You might as well keep the dog. He obviously can't wear this expensive collar if it's going to chafe him, and he likes you much more than he likes me. Take him. You can have him."

The look of joy that came over Gretl's face was something Philippa would never forget. The child was stunned into silence. She stared at Cilla, still not believing her good fortune, and Cilla had to repeat the offer several times before the little girl was convinced that Pinkerton was to be hers. Eventually, clutching the Pekinese to her chest, Gretl trotted out of the room. Cilla remained seated, still holding the collar. She had a seraphic smile on her face.

"Well," said Milton, as he and Philippa strolled out into the corridor, "Gretl is the happiest girl in the world, the cast and crew are vindicated, I got back my tiepin, you retrieved your hairbrush, and even the Baroness seems pleased with the outcome. What a rapturous success."

"Our head nun sounds cheery too," commented Philippa, as they passed Mother Superior's dressing room and heard her warming up with her opening song.

"Yes," said Milton, "and I know the answer to the question that she's trilling so merrily."

Philippa groaned and braced herself for another of Milton's quips.

"Go ahead," she said. "Tell me. How *do* you solve a problem like Maria?"

"The answer," said Milton airily, "is that you can't."

"Huh?" said Philippa.

"You can't," repeated Milton, "for the simple reason that *no one* can solve a problem like Maria! Maria," he declared smugly, "is the best problem-solver I've ever met."

ECHO OF EVIL

Suzie Simons propelled herself forward with another strong stroke, flipped neatly around, and pushed off against the mock-Grecian tiles that surrounded the rectangular pool in the basement of her apartment building. One more length and she would have completed her daily quota. Singers needed good lungs, and her daily swimming regime was not only keeping her weight down, but also improving her stamina for performing with the band. Normally she swam with her roommate, but Janice had left Merritt yesterday and driven to Vancouver to visit her mother. Today Suzie was the only occupant of the pool, and, had there not been the young blonde in the red bikini lounging in the hot tub at the far end of the cavernous chamber, she would have found the steaming basement pool a little too isolated for comfort. The lighting in the facility was minimal, and the blue tiles that lined the pool reflected up through the water and cast a ghostly haze about the room. The sound created by her own progression down the pool echoed eerily each time her hand sliced into the water and her body surged forward.

She reached the end of the pool and bobbed up over the edge to make sure that the green towel embellished with golden butterflies was still draped across the wall that separated pool from hot tub. Then she slipped down into the water and turned around, resting with her back against the tiles and her elbows on the steps. Although the heating in the pool was adequate, the room itself was cold. Reluctant to get out of the water, she leaned her head back and luxuriated in a few moments of well-deserved relaxation after the exertions of the past half-hour. As she rested, she heard the door to the poolroom swing open and the sound of footsteps moving across the tiled floor. She was about to draw herself up to see who had entered, when she heard the girl in the hot tub call out. Her voice reverberated as if in an echo chamber, and although her words were audible, they sounded muffled and hollow.

"Over here, honey. I'm in the hot tub."

A moment later, the footsteps were transformed into the swish of moving water as the newcomer joined the girl. Then Suzie heard a man's voice utter a couple of brief sentences. His voice resonated as if he were talking into a loudspeaker, but the words were distinct, even though the tone was distorted and sepulchral.

"Hey, glad you could make it. God, is this hot enough for you?"

There was a feminine giggle, and then the man spoke again.

"Here I come . . . I got you!"

The exuberant exclamation rang out loudly and echoed off the cement walls. A noisy series of splashes ensued, and then the room fell silent. Embarrassed, Suzie slunk lower against the steps. She wondered how long she had to wait before emerging from the pool. Several seconds passed, an interminable interlude, but the room was still quiet—too quiet, she thought suddenly. But as the idea flashed across her mind, she heard movement again, the swish of water followed by the sound of footsteps moving across the room. The door creaked open and swung back, creating a dull thud as it closed. Suzie pulled herself upright and climbed out of the pool. As she walked over to the bench and picked up her towel, it occurred to her that something was not quite right. There had been only one set of footsteps leaving the room, yet the area was now as quiet and still as a tomb. She shivered, suddenly feeling an icy chill, colder and sharper than the air in the room, and she looked over towards the hot tub. There was no sign of occupation, but the brightly coloured butterfly towel still hung over the low wall. Uneasily, Suzie moved forward, and then, as she reached the divider, she froze.

The blonde in the red bikini was still in the hot tub. Her hair, fanning out like a golden butterfly, mirrored the images embossed on her towel, but the face that floated just below the surface of the water was as lifeless as the cold Grecian tiles that framed her body.

* * *

Six months after Suzy Simons discovered the body in the poolroom of her apartment building, Edwina Beary's sister was about to celebrate her ruby-wedding anniversary. Olive Barton and her husband, Harvey, had lived their entire married life in the Nicola Valley, and their daughter, Emily, had organized four days of celebrations in conjunction with the Canada Day long weekend. As a result, several members of the Beary family were travelling to Merritt to join in the festivities.

Bertram Beary quite liked his sister-in-law and her husband, and he had great admiration for their son, Bob, who was an industrious young man working for the British Columbia Forest Service, but Emily Barton had inherited an overabundance of her Aunt Edwina's traits and suffered from an extreme case of terminal bossiness. Emily's invitation had made it quite clear that guests were expected to attend every event on her program, which included a dinner on the Saturday evening, a picnic on Sunday, a museum tour on Monday and an open house on Canada Day, after which everyone was required to troop en masse to the festival site to see the fireworks in the evening. Therefore, Beary, who intensely disliked being told what to do, was not looking forward to the family reunion. However, he was enjoying the road trip since it gave him the opportunity to give his motorhome a good run. Once on the final leg of the trip, he inched his foot down a little further. The vehicle responded with a gratifying burst of speed.

"Slow down, for heaven's sake," snapped Edwina. "You're driving the Coquihalla, not the Indy track."

Beary kept his foot on the accelerator and replied, "Arvy needs a stretch on the highway to burn off the engine deposits."

"That may be, but Arvy is a motorhome, not a Maserati. I want to arrive in Merritt in one piece."

Beary gave way and minimally reduced speed. Then he turned up the volume on the CD player in order to drown out further complaints from his wife. Edwina adjusted her own sound level to compensate.

"We've listened to that soundtrack all the way up. Couldn't we have something different?"

"What! You don't want to listen to *Babes in the Wood* with our grandchildren's voices as bugs and caterpillars, and Philippa as Maid Marian?" Beary's voice was heavy with reproof.

"Not for the entire trip," said Edwina. "We're going to hear it *and* see it at the Canada Day Festival so we don't have to drive to it as well."

"Yes, we do. Oh, I like this bit. It's the rat's number." Beary turned the volume up another notch. "I helped write it."

He added his booming base to the voice emanating from the dashboard.

"There's no more vermin at the castle, they've all moved to city hall;
They're inhabiting the chests of drawers that lean against the wall.
They are doing useful jobs now, writing briefs and quoting stats,
Now they are called—the bureau-c-rats!"

Edwina leaned forward and turned off the power, and the zestful beat of the *Babes* finale was replaced by the drone of the engine and the hum of tires against pavement.

"Enough," she said firmly. "I'm going to have peace and quiet for the last leg of the trip. This is going to be a hectic enough weekend as it is."

"You're the one who wanted to come," said Beary.

"I wanted to come to the family reunion. I didn't expect to have to take in the Canada Day Festival as well." Edwina sniffed indignantly.

"I don't know why our children had to combine work with Olive and Harvey's anniversary," she continued crossly. "It's most annoying. The festival will completely detract from the celebrations. Emily is extremely put out."

In Beary's experience, Emily was always put out. He sprang into defence mode.

"They haven't *all* lined up gigs for the festival," he pointed out. "Richard will be with us all weekend."

"He's the only one," grumbled Edwina. "Sylvia isn't even coming."

"Well, she can't come, can she? She and Norton are in San Francisco."

"That's another bone of contention—she booked their flight *after* Emily sent out the invitations. I believe Sylvia arranged the trip deliberately to avoid coming."

"I believe it too," muttered Beary.

Edwina appeared not to have heard Beary's *sotto voce* interjection.

"Emily has gone to so much trouble," she complained. "She's going to be dreadfully offended when most of our family cut out to do their own thing once the dinner is over."

"Only Philippa and Juliette," said Beary. "Emily won't even notice they're missing."

"And Steven—don't forget his band is playing at the festival."

"Well, Emily won't care if Steven isn't there. She doesn't even like him. Anyway, it's not that big a deal. It's only the one day that our lot will be AWOL."

"Two days," Edwina corrected him. "Setting up Monday and performing Tuesday, which means they'll miss the museum tour *and* the open house."

Beary could always tell when his wife was gearing up for a fit of pique. The pitch of her voice escalated in proportion to the degree of umbrage. He calculated that her tone had jumped a full third.

Edwina started in again.

"What's more, instead of attending the open house, all the guests will be running into town to see our brood perform. And it's not even as if Philippa and Juliette already had the Merritt jobs. They lined up the engagements once they knew they'd be here during the festival. Very thoughtless."

"On the contrary, very thought*ful*," contradicted Beary. "They were probably making a conscious effort to avoid an overdose of your niece's hospitality—and you can bet your SAS sandals that the other guests will infinitely prefer puppets, country and western music and the 'Indian Love Call' to Emily's stultifying agenda. Emily's expectation that grown adults will fall into line like the regimented moppets in her kindergarten class is utterly unrealistic. Besides, she's no fun to be around because she's such a know-it-all. The most irritating thing about Emily is that she always thinks she's right."

"She generally is," said Edwina.

"That's irritating too. Anyway, you can't blame Philippa for grabbing an opportunity to make money. She and Adam are taking their *Rose Marie* act all over B.C., so including Merritt makes perfect sense. You should be encouraging such enterprise."

Edwina tut-tutted disapprovingly.

"I would have preferred her to be doing a tour with someone else. Adam is proving to be far too fickle. I don't want to see our daughter hurt."

"Philippa can look after herself," said Beary.

He pulled into the right lane, and still travelling at highway speed, exited the ramp that led to the outskirts of Merritt.

"Nicola Lake ahead," he announced. "Nearly there. You know," he remarked, noting the cluster of men congregating at the side of the road, "I always think it's so nice when the RCMP put on full dress uniform, complete with Mountie hats, for the Canada Day weekend. The red coats are delightfully ceremonial. Friendly one, that," he added. "Look. He's waving to us."

Edwina raised her eyes heavenward.

"He isn't waving to us," she said acerbically. "He's waving you over. I should say you're about to get a ceremonial Canada Day ticket."

"Bugger," said Beary.

"And," his wife continued frostily, "if you want to expedite the process, I suggest you refrain from asking him where his horse is."

* * *

Ten miles up the valley, a battered-looking Ford Econoline van was travelling down Highway 5A. Adam Craig was intently focussed on the road ahead. His companion in the passenger seat was admiring the ever-changing vista of water, hills and sky.

"I'm so glad we managed to line up this Merritt job," she said brightly. "I've always wanted to stay at the Black Bandit Inn."

"Too pricey for me," growled Adam. "I'm heading for the Riverside Motel. That way I'll be making a profit on my out-of-town allowance." He slowed the van to take a hairpin corner. "Why did we have to come this way?" he grumbled. "The highway would have been much faster."

"Not as pretty though," said Philippa. "This side of Nicola Lake is a glorious scenic drive. The entire valley is dotted with lakes. Besides, the road takes us right to the inn, and then you can drop me off and head into town."

"Why this insistence on blowing a big chunk of your profits on a restored and overpriced wild-west hotel?"

"It's a historic site and it's beautifully renovated—very atmospheric. It's supposed to be haunted, you know."

"Presumably by the Black Bandit, whoever he was. What did he rob anyway?"

"Banks. His name was Mick MacDuggan and he was on America's most-wanted list for over ten years before they finally tracked him down."

"Then why is a Canadian hotel named after him?"

"Because this is where he died . . . right here in the Nicola Valley. He came across the border to visit his sweetheart—she was a local rancher's daughter and he hadn't seen her in over a year. She was working in the haberdashery, which was owned by a good-looking smoothie named Hans Meyerhoff. MacDuggan went to the store thinking his girlfriend would be overjoyed to see him, but instead she called him into the back room and told him she was in love with someone else—and what was more, she was pregnant by this man. There was a terrible row. Several people overheard MacDuggan raging at her, and then he stormed out and went to the inn to get blind roaring drunk. Half an hour later, Meyerhoff ran out and told the townsfolk that the girl had been strangled. The men of the town set out to track MacDuggan down and they found him at the inn. There are still bullet holes in the bar where they gunned him down."

"Sounds like he had it coming to him."

"No. That's the awful part of it. He didn't kill the girl. It turned out she'd been having an affair with Meyerhoff, and he was the one who had got her pregnant. He didn't want his wife to find out, so when he overheard the girl rowing with MacDuggan, he saw his opportunity to get rid of her and put the blame on the Black Bandit."

"Slimy so-and-so," said Adam. "How did they catch him out?"

"His wife became suspicious, and when he realized she was on to him, he tried to kill her too."

"What stopped him?"

"The local doctor. He dropped by unexpectedly and caught Meyerhoff in the act. Then the truth came out. Quite the story, isn't it? According to local folklore, every year, on the eve of his death, MacDuggan walks the halls of the inn. And get this," Philippa added dramatically, "the night of my aunt's banquet is the anniversary of the day before he died."

"How come you know so much about local history?"

"Mum and Dad used to send us to Uncle Harvey and Aunt Olive's hobby farm for a couple of weeks every summer—we loved it, other than being bossed around by Emily—so I know all the local legends. Actually, Emily is probably the reason I know the legends. She's into that sort of thing. She does research for the museum, so don't ask her any questions about the history of the area unless you want to be sat in a corner and lectured for the next three hours."

Adam negotiated another curve, and the bank beside the road glided back to reveal a wide band of deep turquoise water set, jewel-like, in golden, sagebrush-covered hills. Philippa's response was rapturous.

"See what I mean," she exclaimed. "Isn't it breathtaking?"

Adam looked unimpressed.

"You know," he remarked, reverting to the topic that had taken precedence during the majority of their drives between the engagements of their summer tour, "it would have been far more economical and a hell of a lot more fun if we'd taken our two travel allowances and simply roomed together. Then we could have afforded a whole slew of kitschy historic hotels and still had something left over."

Philippa pursed her lips.

"What we'd have left over would be acrimony and the end of a perfectly good friendship. You seem to forget you're returning to Germany in September and heading back to the apartment you share with *kleine* Heidi with the blonde pigtails who bought you that revolting Rheinmaiden T-shirt."

"Her name is Gretchen and she doesn't have braids, and what makes you think I'm serious about her anyway?"

"I don't," said Philippa breezily, "but until you can get serious, don't expect me to be a temporary piece of strüdel."

She smiled sweetly and sat back to enjoy the scenery.

* * *

Emily Barton was well aware of the mutinous feelings of her cousins. She found the Beary clan as irritating as they found her, but she knew their presence would make her parents happy, so she was determined to put up with them. However, she was surprised to find that her friend, Ann MacLeod, was also less than enthusiastic about the coming celebrations.

"It's going to be fun," insisted Emily. "What are you worried about?"

Ann furrowed her brow anxiously.

"My parents. They're upset about something."

"What on earth have they got to be upset about?" Emily kept her eyes on the centerpiece she was crafting for the banquet. "You're about to marry a gorgeous hunk who owns the two businesses that your father wants to merge with. Your parents are getting exactly what they want. I just hope you're getting what *you* want."

"Of course I am. Jason is fabulously good-looking and wonderful company. I adore him."

"I still like Neil better, but I suppose it's your choice."

"Of course it's my choice. I know you were disappointed when I broke off with Neil. He's a dear and he treated me well, but honestly, I could never discuss anything with him."

"So he's the strong, silent type, but he's very reliable."

"So is Jason. He wouldn't be where he is today otherwise."

"Family connections help," said Emily dryly. "Jason is as much 'old Nicola' as you are. The Heinemanns owned the very first lumberyard in the Kamloops area. That's probably the reason your parents think the world of him."

"No," insisted Ann. "They really like him. They're happy about the engagement, but they're edgy. There's something eating at them. My poor mother is a mass of nerves."

"Well," said Emily briskly, "the best cure for your mother is to keep her busy. Get her working on the wedding preparations."

Emily twisted a piece of ribbon into a bow and fastened it to the bells at the centre of her creation.

"There," she said complacently. "That should do. I intend tomorrow evening to be perfect."

Ann smiled.

"I'm sure it will be. Anything you organize always goes beautifully."

Emily picked up a package of name cards and peeled off the cellophane.

"Not necessarily," she said. "You don't know my cousins."

"Yes, I do," said Ann. "We used to play together, remember. Richard was a sweetheart. He used to take us on outings."

"Richard is all right," Emily admitted grudgingly, "but you obviously don't remember how irksome the rest of them can be." She took her script pen and began to inscribe the first name card.

"As I recall, they were very nice children," said Ann. "Independent spirits, but lots of fun."

Emily's hazel eyes glinted. "Yes, well, they're still independent spirits," she retorted. She stabbed a dot over an *i*, added a flourish and slid the card aside. "Sylvia very discourteously opted to go to San Francisco instead of attending the family reunion, and when I complained to Uncle Bertram that I'd already paid for her and Norton's dinners, he had the nerve to say it wasn't a problem because he and Richard could easily polish off the extra plates. On top of that, Philippa and Juliette have lined up engagements at the Canada Day Festival, so they'll attend the dinner and the picnic, then duck out on all the other activities. Very inconsiderate."

"But that'll be lovely," said Ann. "It will make the weekend even more fun for the rest of us. Your guests will have a choice of things to do on the holiday Monday."

Emily grunted. She picked up another name card and changed the subject. "I wonder if the usual horde of ghost-watchers will be at the hotel," she said. "It does rather add spice, doesn't it, having my parents' anniversary fall on the eve of the Black Bandit's death?"

"Well, if the place is full of tourists, don't let them know my family connection with the legend," said Ann. "I have no desire to spend the evening retelling the tale for a gaggle of out-of-town visitors who are dripping with curiosity because the Black Bandit's sweetheart was my father's great-aunt."

Emily stretched and ran her fingers through her cropped, platinum blonde hair.

"Verity MacLeod was such a foolish girl," she said. "It's understandable that she fell in love with Mick MacDuggan. He was probably very dashing and she was too young and silly to know better. Her family did the right thing by coming north to get her away from him. But for her to turn around and immediately have a fling with the haberdasher who gave her a job—that shows the girl was a complete idiot."

"Hans Meyerhoff was supposed to be very smooth and incredibly good-looking," said Ann.

"So what? The handsome haberdasher was the sleaziest character in the history of the town."

"Did you know," said Ann, "that my fiancé is descended from the doctor who stopped Meyerhoff from killing his wife? William Carpenter was Jason's great-great-grandfather."

Emily finished the inscription and neatly placed the card on top of the first one.

"Too bad he wasn't around to save your great-aunt," she said tartly, "though if Verity MacLeod had behaved herself, listened to her parents and acted like a properly brought-up young lady, she'd have probably lived to a ripe old age."

Emily picked up another place card and set to work. Ann looked at her friend with a mixture of exasperation and affection. The most irritating quality about Emily was that she always had the last word and whatever she said was generally right.

* * *

Suzie returned the nozzle to the pump and replaced the gas cap on her Toyota. She hurried inside to pay, hoping that Gary Tindall would not be on the cash desk, and at the same time feeling guilty at not wanting to see him. Ever since the death of his daughter, he had looked on Suzie with aversion, as if she had been responsible for Lisa's death, rather than simply being the person who had reported it. *He thinks I should have cried out or done something to stop it*, Suzie thought. *Subconsciously, he blames me.*

To Suzie's relief, her uncle was on duty in the shop. She could see Gary Tindall in the back, working on an old Cadillac, but he was intent on his task and not looking her way. He was a first-class mechanic, which was why her uncle had hired him, but his grief made him an uncomfortable presence, and if it had not been for family loyalty, Suzie would have filled up at any other station in town, although she knew she was being cowardly and selfish to feel that way. She paid her bill and left quickly. It was only a half-hour drive to Monck Park, but she wanted to get there in time to have a consultation with Steven Ayers about the program for Canada Day. She was looking forward to being the guest vocalist with his band, but there were details that had to be discussed.

She swung left at the Monck Park turnoff, then veered to the right and started up the treacherous road that clung to the cliffs high above Nicola Lake. The breathtaking drive always made her feel both exhilarated and apprehensive, a combination of spectacle and danger, as every curve revealed another panoramic sweep of pale blue sky above and glittering water far below.

Ten minutes later, the switchback road straightened out and began the descent to the campground. Suzie stopped at the entrance gate, and then headed round the ring road in search of Site 83 where the attendant had told her she would find the Ayers' tent.

As she progressed through the park, Suzie looked sadly at the brown trees lining the road. The deadly pine beetle had done its work the previous year, burrowing into the mature trees and starting the process of destruction which had not manifested until the spring. Suzie wondered how many of the sparse number of pines that still remained green were harbouring the larvae that would eat the cambium layer and destroy the trees the following year. She suddenly had a mental picture of Gary Tindall working diligently in her uncle's shop. People could look outwardly healthy too, yet be slowly rotting inside until nothing of their humanity was left.

She continued around the ring road, avoiding vehicles, dogs, and children on bikes or roller-blades. The park was a sea of colourful tents, trailers and motorhomes and the air was redolent with the smell of campfires and barbeques. Suzie steered around a Jeep that was towing a speedboat loaded with shrieking teenagers; then she followed the curve to the lower road. Below a line hung with gaudily decorated beach towels was a post bearing the number 83.

When Suzie got out of her car, she saw that the campsite was a hive of activity. A slender brunette wearing black shorts and a red halter-top was serving hotdogs to a pair of noisy, but apparently happy little girls, while an older Tilley-clad blonde supervised the youngsters and ensured that they ate what was served and retained a semblance of good manners. A corpulent middle-aged gentleman, sporting a Croc Dundee hat and a garish blue shirt covered with fishes, was pouring glasses of wine and handing them around to the adults. Two younger men were grilling burgers on the barbeque. They were closely watched by a sturdy white husky that was tethered to the leg of the picnic bench. Suzie particularly liked the look of the fair-haired, hatless chef, who was dressed casually in jeans and T-shirt, but it was the other man who looked up and noticed her. He was a flamboyant figure in swimming trunks, Hawaiian shirt and cowboy hat, and he beckoned her to join them. As Suzie ducked under the towels, he came forward and took her hand.

"Let me guess. You're Suzie!"

Suzie smiled.

"Yes," she said. "Are you Steven Ayers?"

"I am. Welcome. It's great to have you aboard. I've heard fabulous things about you."

"I bet," Beary murmured appreciatively, joining Edwina at the picnic table. "She looks like a young Dolly Parton."

Edwina sniffed.

"Dolly Parton doesn't have pink hair."

"No one notices Dolly Parton's hair," pointed out Beary. "And it isn't pink. It's strawberry blonde. However," he added thoughtfully, "pretty as she is, she is rather wired. Vivacious, but tense."

Steven gestured toward the picnic table.

"Come and join us," he said to Suzie. "Hotdog or hamburger?"

"Thank you. A hamburger would be great. I didn't have time to eat. The shop closes at six and I came straight over."

"Shop?"

"Literature of Merritt. That's where I work between singing engagements. It pays the rent." Suzie smiled at Steven. "I've heard great things about your band," she said. "My uncle heard you at the pub in Garden Bay. He said you were fantastic. Are you getting enough work to go full time?"

"I wish." Steven donned the self-deprecating smile that he adopted when describing his status in the music world. "My full-time job is teaching. I'm the music and drama teacher at our local high school. The band gigs are just on weekends, but I have my own recording studio, and we're working on our second CD—"

"Introduce the girl, why don't you?" cut in Beary, well aware that Steven could go on indefinitely when presented with a new audience who was not familiar with his musical achievements.

"Oh, right," said Steven. "Meet the family. The gentleman who just interrupted us is my father-in-law, Bertram Beary . . .'"

Suzie proffered her hand, but instead of a handshake, Beary gave her a glass overflowing with Shiraz-Merlot.

"And this is my mother-in-law, Edwina," Steven continued, nodding towards the picnic table. "The rug-rats she's attempting to control are Jennifer and Laura. Last, but definitely not least," he added, pointing to the brunette in the halter-top, "is my wife, Juliette. Oh, and the white fur-ball is MacPuff. Don't give way when he stares at you and looks pathetic. He's on a diet."

Juliette cleared a spot at the picnic table. "Sit here," she invited Suzie. "The girls can move down."

Laura and Jennifer wriggled sideways and Suzie slid onto the bench.

"Are you the opera singer?" she asked Juliette.

"No, that's Philippa. I'm doing the puppet show." Juliette set a hamburger in front of Suzie and reached down the table for the ketchup and mustard. "Philippa's singing at the festival too, but she's not camping in the park. Her agent arranged an out-of-town allowance, so she's staying at the Black Bandit Inn on the other side of the lake. She isn't into roughing it like the rest of us. And you must excuse Steven," she added, beckoning to the good-looking man at the barbeque. "He forgot to introduce my brother, Richard."

"Oh, sorry." Steven grinned and looked totally unapologetic as Richard came to shake Suzie's hand. "We subconsciously try to forget him because he's RCMP."

Suzie paled, and the smile that had started to come to her lips faded. Steven noticed her tension.

"Don't worry, he's on holiday. He isn't likely to arrest you."

"Oh, dear, is it that obvious? I didn't mean to react that way. It's just that I had a horrible experience in the spring, and I spent so much time dealing with the police that I flinch every time I hear a siren or see a uniform."

"What happened?" asked Richard curiously.

"I overheard a murder."

"Good God!" exclaimed Beary sympathetically. "You poor thing. Here." He topped up her wine glass. "Can you bear to tell us about it, or is it still too traumatic? Was it someone you knew?"

"I didn't know the victim, even though she lived in my apartment—I only moved here six months ago—but I've found out a lot more about her since she died, not just because of the investigation, but because my uncle recently hired her father to work at his garage."

"It was a woman who was killed?" asked Richard.

"Yes. Her name was Lisa Tindall. She was a billing clerk at the landfill in Cache Creek, but she lived in Merritt and commuted because her boyfriend works here. He's a driver for HC Trucking, which is owned by Jason Heinemann. Jason is the future son-in-law of Garth MacLeod, the local bigwig who owns most of the property around here."

"We've met Garth MacLeod," said Beary. "He knows my in-laws. Harvey and Olive's hobby farm abuts his cattle ranch, so they're neighbours and good friends. MacLeod made his fortune in logging, I believe."

"That's right. He still has the lumber business, but he's involved in property development too. He employs half the town in one capacity or other."

"We'll be seeing Garth MacLeod tomorrow," Edwina interjected. "Emily persuaded him to bring his RV here for the weekend so it could be used as a base for the festivities. Not Canada Day," she explained hastily, seeing Suzie's uncomprehending expression, "Harvey and Olive's ruby anniversary. The entire MacLeod clan will be at the banquet tomorrow—*and* at the picnic on Sunday, complete with their speedboats, so any of the youngsters who want to water-ski will only have to say the word and they'll be taken out on the lake."

She gathered up the children's plates and indicated that they were free to go. The girls hopped off the picnic bench and disappeared into the green tent at the back of the site.

Beary made another circuit with the wine bottle.

"Why don't you join us for the banquet?" he said to Suzie. "My oldest daughter couldn't make it, so you're welcome to come in her place."

"That's very kind, but I wouldn't want to intrude."

"Nonsense," said Beary. "The dinner has been paid for. Mustn't waste good food. Now, tell us more about this strange experience you had. You say you 'overheard' a murder, but you didn't see anything?"

Suzie nodded.

"So what exactly happened?" asked Richard.

Suzie described in detail how her morning swim had turned into a terrifying nightmare.

"The worst part," she concluded soberly, "is that the crime remains unsolved, so somewhere in town, there's a murderer running loose who knows that I heard his voice and could identify it some day. I dream about that voice," she said wearily. "It echoes in my sleep, just as it reverberated in the basement pool. At the time, I didn't sense anything wrong, but now I hear it as an echo of evil. I wake up sweating and rigid. You know, since that day, I have to sleep with the lights on. It's been horrible—though at least now the local cops have accepted the fact that I was only a witness and don't consider me a suspect any more. It's been the worst experience of my life."

"Do the police have any theories about who was responsible?" said Richard.

"Ricky Granger was the prime suspect. He was Lisa's boyfriend. He lived with her at the apartment so he knew the building and was familiar with her routine—but he has an alibi."

"What sort of alibi?" Richard asked curiously.

Suzie elaborated.

"Ricky has had a history of run-ins with the law. He used to work in the local gun shop, but he was fired for stealing from the till. He was out of work for over a year. Eventually, he managed to get a job with HC Trucking and he's managed to stay out of trouble there, but there's been a recent spate of armed robberies throughout the whole Thompson/Okanagan region, and on the day Lisa was murdered, there was a hold-up at a bank in Kamloops—"

"And he was caught in the act?"

"Not exactly. The robbers wore ski masks, but one of the customers happened to be a regular client at the gun shop and he recognized the tattoo on Ricky's arm. So the police were torn. They had him for armed robbery, but they couldn't get him for the murder, even though he was the most logical suspect."

"Why was that? Did he and Lisa have a volatile relationship?"

"Very, but things looked really black for him once the autopsy results came in. You see, it showed that Lisa was three-months pregnant— and the DNA tests proved that her boyfriend couldn't have been the father."

* * *

Ann MacLeod had been right when she told Emily that her parents were preoccupied. Garth MacLeod was deeply troubled, and the news in the paper that morning had shaken him to the core. He felt a deadly chill as he read the article. Arson was always a terrible crime, but this time, the results had been calamitous. He knew the farm in the story. It was further up the valley, but visible from the highway—an old farmhouse, elegantly restored with a brand new sundeck. The arson attack had occurred three days previously when vandals had broken in at night and set fire to the new deck. But now, the family was dealing with much greater adversity for their entire herd of dairy cows was dead. The animals had broken out of their enclosure and eaten the residual ash, and now it was clear what had attracted the herd.

Analysis had shown that the wood used for the construction of the deck had been treated with chromated copper arsenate. CCA-wood ash tastes salty and animals are naturally drawn to it. But the CCA-treated wood used to build the deck should never have been sold for that purpose. An investigation was underway to trace the source of the treated lumber, and further studies were being carried out to assess arsenic levels in groundwater on surrounding properties.

Garth put down the paper and stood up. He would have very little time over the weekend as he was committed to help with his neighbours' anniversary celebrations, but there were some calls that could not be avoided and he would have to stop by the office to pull some files. He grabbed his car keys and went out the front door. The afternoon was gloriously sunny and the view across the valley was magnificent, but he took in none of the spectacle for his thoughts were dark and turned inwards. The EPA classification of CCA as a restricted-use product had come at a bad time for him. His stockpile of CCA-treated lumber in the late seventies had seemed like a good investment, given the boom in the housing market at the time, but it had become the biggest white elephant in the history of his business. Now he was very much afraid that the elephant might turn round and trample him. He had to get a handle on the situation quickly.

* * *

Suzie remained at the campsite longer than she had intended. Conscious that Beary had refilled her wine glass once too often and that she had to face the death-defying curves of the entrance road in the dimming light, she accepted Juliette's offer of coffee and settled in the canvas chair that Richard drew up beside his own.

Richard looked her straight in the eye, with an expression that mixed admiration and concern.

"Will you be all right driving back?"

"I'll be fine. I'm just going to wait for a bit. After I've drunk this coffee, I'll go for a stroll round the ring road. The park is beautiful in the evening."

"Good idea. I'll come with you."

Ten minutes later, Suzie and Richard set off for their walk. Beary offered to accompany them, but Juliette, having noted the way her brother was eyeing their guest, quelled her father with as steely a look as she, being such a gentle soul, could manage, and he dutifully retreated to his deck chair.

At the western end of the lake, the pale green of the sagebrush-topped hills gleamed brilliantly where the sun was beginning its decline, but the forested trails of the park were already bathed in shadows. The park was on a hillside, so the two longer stretches of the ring road were at different levels, and as Suzie and Richard approached the end of the park, the road curved down towards a wide swath of water, golden in the setting sun and framed by black silhouettes of pine and spruce trees.

The glare of headlights at the entrance gates signalled a late arrival at the campsite. The vehicle, which was towing a Jeep Cherokee, slowly pulled by and turned onto the lower road.

"Now that's a rig!" said Richard admiringly. "You've got to have big bucks to own a forty-foot diesel low-boy pusher unit."

"He does have big bucks," said Suzie. "That belongs to Garth MacLeod."

"No wonder Emily wanted it for the picnic. He could serve the entire campsite out of that unit."

"How well does your family know Garth MacLeod?" asked Suzie.

"My aunt and uncle have known him a long time. I remember him from holidays when I was a kid. He was pretty jolly with us. We were invited to go on trail rides at his ranch, and he'd have us back to the house for hot chocolate afterwards. His wife was a bit of a stick though. We always minded our *p*'s and *q*'s around her. I think she only tolerated us because they had a daughter the same age as Emily—a tiny little thing with dark hair. She tagged along with us all summer long. I expect our motley crew of siblings and cousins was irresistible to an only child."

"That would be Ann MacLeod. She's gorgeous now—nice too. She comes into the bookstore now and then. Every guy in town has been after her at one time or another."

"I know," said Richard. "My cousin, Bob, always had a thing for her, but he never got anywhere. She just considers him a good friend. She got engaged to someone else. My father knows the fellow. He met him when he was fishing at Hihihum Lake."

"You're thinking of Neil Spaulding," said Suzie. "He runs Garth MacLeod's lumberyard in town, but he and Ann are not engaged any more. Ann broke it off last year. Now she's going to marry Jason Heinemann."

"The trucking czar?"

"Yes, but he's in the lumber business as well. He owns a lumberyard in Kamloops. It's the perfect merger actually. Garth MacLeod must be over the moon about the marriage because between him and Jason, they'll control every aspect of the industry throughout the entire Okanagan." Suzie's eyes twinkled. "The ladies in town are happy too," she added. "Now that Ann's taken, there's hope for the rest of us."

Richard looked down at his companion and smiled.

"If you're feeling neglected by the male population of Merritt," he said gallantly, "then every guy in town must have defective vision."

They turned onto the beach trail and walked along the edge of the darkening water. The lights of the Black Bandit Inn gleamed brightly against the shadowy hills on the far side of the lake. Suzie noticed that the air was starting to cool, but the obvious admiration from the man at her side more than compensated for the chill breeze that was springing up on the lakeshore. For the first time in many weeks, she found that she was enjoying herself.

* * *

The following evening, Richard drove his parents to the Black Bandit Inn, thus saving them the inconvenience of unhooking the motorhome. They stopped in town to pick up Suzie, and by the time they arrived at the hotel, the parking lot was already filling up. The front steps were overflowing with women in colourful summer ensembles and men in lightweight pants and short-sleeved shirts, and the crowd from the banquet hall had spilled out onto the terrace at the side of the building. Rather than battle their way through the lobby, the Bearys walked around the garden and joined the guests on the patio. Emily was standing near the tennis courts. She was talking with one of the hotel staff and appeared not to notice the arrival of her relatives from town. Beary took advantage of her preoccupation and kept moving.

"What's she done to her hair? Stuck it in a bucket of ash?" he muttered as he steered Edwina towards the terrace. "Didn't she used to be a brunette?"

"You'd better behave yourself this evening," Edwina warned him. "It's bad enough that you came in that ridiculous shirt, but I'm not going to have you blurting out whatever comes to mind and offending my relatives. And for heaven's sake," she added testily, "take off that hat."

"Merritt," said Beary with dignity, "is cowboy country. My Croc Dundee hat fits in very nicely. I can see at least three Stetsons in the immediate vicinity, one of which is approaching right now."

Edwina looked up to see a burly, middle-aged man coming towards them. He had a bushy moustache that bisected his weathered face, and when he reached them, he gave Beary a hearty slap on the back.

"Beary, you old son-of-a-gun! Good to see you. Nice shirt," he added. "I like the fishes."

"Hello, Vernon," said Beary. "This is Vernon Spaulding," he added to Edwina. "He owns the gun shop in town and his son runs the lumberyard. They spend a week at Hihihum Lake every year. We know each other through fishing."

Edwina recognized the name of the locale even though she had never been there. Hihihum Lake had pleasing connotations because it signified ten days peace and quiet at home while her husband disappeared into the wilds of the Cariboo.

"Come inside and I'll get you a drink," said Vernon.

Beary and Edwina followed him into the hotel, but Richard hung back. Emily was still by the tennis courts, though she was now giving instructions to one of the waitresses. Richard took Suzie's elbow and ushered her forward to introduce her to his cousin.

"Dad said you wouldn't mind if I brought Suzie along," he said to Emily. "I gather there are two extra dinners due to the fact that Sylvia and Norton couldn't make it."

Emily's snapdragon mouth compressed into a smile that implied she minded very much indeed. Her eyes swept briefly over Suzie's fuchsia pink tank top. Then she nodded frostily, waved a dismissal and turned back to the waitress.

"Ooh," hissed Suzie as they moved away. "Are you sure I should have come?"

"Of course," said Richard. "Emily is like that with everyone. You just have to grin and bear her."

"She dresses nicely," said Suzie, glancing back and assessing the impeccable yellow linen dress and the bright sunflower earrings that complemented the perfectly coiffed platinum blonde hair.

"I prefer your outfit," said Richard. "Look, there are the MacLeods." He pointed to a giant of a man standing with a stunningly lovely brunette and two well-dressed women of indeterminate age. "You know them, don't you?"

"Just Ann, but I know Garth MacLeod by sight. Everyone does. Which of those ladies is his wife?"

"The dark-haired one in green. I don't know who the skinny blonde is. Come on, let's join them."

Richard led Suzie towards the group. Ann Macleod saw them approach. Her face broke into a smile and she greeted Richard with a hug.

"Here's the boy who taught me to swim," she cried. "He was so patient," she added, turning to Suzie. "Emily and Philippa and I used to tag around after him. We must have driven him crazy—three silly little girls—no wonder he ended up in the RCMP. He spent most of his teenage years making sure we didn't come to any harm. Are you two together?" she continued. "I didn't know you knew each other."

"We just met," said Suzie. "I'm singing at the festival with Juliette's husband."

"Fabulous!" cried Ann. "We'll be there too. Jason is emcee for the talent show. Have you met my fiancé?" She linked arms with a tall, athletic-looking man who had come to stand beside her. He was tanned and muscular, with chiselled hair and rugged features, and he looked as if he had stepped out of a sporting-goods catalogue. Suzie instinctively distrusted any male who was that good-looking, but she had to admit that his smile was warm and friendly, and unlike Emily, who had looked at her as if she had wandered in by mistake from the local bargain basement, he chatted with her quietly and made her feel welcome. Out of the corner of her eye, Suzie observed Garth MacLeod staring at her. His expression discomfited her, but when he saw that she had noticed him, he took his wife's elbow and guided her towards the door of the inn. However, the blonde woman hung back. Up close,

Suzie could see that the woman must be well into her fifties, but the lines in her face were accentuated by her strained expression. With a start, Suzie noticed that the blonde's eye was twitching. Then, to her surprise, the woman stepped forward and spoke to her.

"Aren't you the girl who overheard Lisa being killed?" she said.

Suzie was shaken by the forthrightness of the question, and she froze, unsure how to respond. Jason Heinemann came to her rescue.

"She probably doesn't want to be reminded of the fact," he said. "Ann told us about your dreadful experience," he added to Suzie. "It must have been pretty traumatic."

The blonde woman smiled nervously. "I'm sorry," she said. "I just wondered if you'd remembered anything more. I'm Mary Cummings, and I knew Lisa Tindall. Before Garth offered me a job as receptionist at the mill, I used to work with her at the landfill office. I—"

Suddenly she stopped speaking and stared over Suzie's head. Suzie swung round to see what had distracted her. Garth MacLeod had returned to the terrace and was beckoning impatiently. As abruptly as she had approached, Mary Cummings moved away. She joined her boss, and he took her arm and led her into the banquet room.

As they disappeared inside, a diminutive redhead emerged. Her short, buoyant curls framed an elfin face with sharply distinctive features, which somehow still managed to look softly pretty, and she wore a dramatically elegant white summer dress, gathered Grecian style at the shoulders. Her face lit up as she noticed Richard and she waved to him.

"My baby sister," Richard muttered into Suzie's ear. "That's Philippa."

"My goodness," said Suzie. "Another stunner. Is she like Emily too?"

Richard laughed out loud.

"No! Perish the thought. You will love Philippa. And all you'll have to do is tell her about your murder in the swimming pool and she'll be your rapt companion for the rest of the evening."

Philippa came down the steps and gave her brother a hug. Then she turned to Suzie with a warm smile.

"You're the country and western performer," she said. "Come inside and I'll introduce you to my singing partner. He's propping up the bar and practising his German on one of the local ranchers, but when he sees you, he'll forget about attempting to discuss cattle breeding in a foreign language."

"Did Mum and Dad find you?" asked Richard.

"Yes. They're already at our table. Come on. Let's join them."

Philippa turned and headed back through the French doors. Richard followed, putting his hand in the small of Suzie's back and steering her through the crush in the banquet room. Philippa led them towards the far rear corner. Edwina was seated at a round table with Jennifer and Laura on either side of her. Juliette and Steven sat on the chairs on the other side of their daughters. Beary was nowhere in sight. The room was crowded, but a light breeze from the doors to the garden made the atmosphere bearable, and a large fan whirring noisily at the back of the room emitted refreshingly cool blasts of air.

"Where's Dad?" Richard asked as he sat down.

"Propping up the bar with Adam," snapped Edwina.

"No, here they come," said Philippa. "Just in time. Emily is taking her place at the head table."

Beary and Adam scurried to their seats. Emily picked up a spoon and banged it against her wine glass, and the roar of the crowd dulled to a murmur as everyone waited for the guests of honour to arrive. A few moments later, Olive and Harvey were escorted into the room by their son and greeted with an enthusiastic round of applause.

Predictably, since Emily had organized it, the evening was a great success. The meal was delicious, and the dance that followed was an exuberant and high-spirited affair. By eleven o'clock the party was sufficiently boisterous that if a posse had entered the bar and peppered the Black Bandit with bullets, no one would have heard the gunshots.

Once the medley of country music and hits from the fifties and sixties deteriorated into rap, Beary got a refill from the bar and retreated to the terrace to escape the noise. Adam had beaten him to it. He was enjoying a solitary cigarette on the porch.

"Bad habit for a singer," Beary remonstrated. "Don't let Philippa catch you smoking."

"No chance of that," said Adam. "She's stomping around the floor with some big lug who works for the Ministry of Forests."

"Her cousin, Bob," said Beary. "Very nice young man. We'd actually thought at one time that he'd be the one to marry Ann MacLeod, but she fell for the son of one of my fishing friends. Then, when that didn't work out, Bob got hopeful again, but he was pipped at the post by the Heinemann fellow. Glad I'm past all those problems." Beary acquired a crafty expression and added innocently, "How's the tour going with you and Philippa, by the way?"

"Great." Adam ignored the probe into his personal life and deliberately took the question to refer to his professional relationship with Philippa. "You'll love our act. McDonald and Eddy have nothing on it."

Beary persevered.

"Philippa said you get a generous travel allowance for these gigs. It must be good if it covers staying at places like this."

"Not that good," said Adam gloomily. "I'm booked into the cheapest motel in town."

"Good," said Beary heartily. "Very sensible of you." Having found out what he wanted to know, he changed the subject. "How are you enjoying our family reunion?"

"Challenging," said Adam. "I keep getting hit on by middle-aged women who want to tell me their life stories." He pointed towards the patio where a fleshy woman in a voluminous floral dress had pinned a youthful waiter against the chain-link fence of the tennis court. "I just escaped from that one," he said. "Someone told her that the ghost of Mick MacDuggan is supposed to walk tonight, so I had to endure a half-hour diatribe about the terrifying experience she had at age ten when her long-dead grandmother materialized and spoke to her. Now she's repeating it again for another poor sucker."

Beary watched as the woman took the waiter's wine bottle and poured herself a refill. "Revisiting her childhood trauma must be giving her a thirst," he noted. "She obviously intends to empty that bottle all by herself."

Adam stubbed out his cigarette. He laughed cynically.

"She's staying here so I guess she figures she can drink as much as she likes, though at the rate she's going, she'll be lucky if she can navigate the stairs. She's completely bombed."

"Who's bombed?" asked Philippa, joining them on the terrace.

"Definitely not you," said Adam. "Where's the lumberjack?"

"He's a forester, not a lumberjack," said Philippa sharply, "and he's dancing with Ann MacLeod. They're old friends. Personally, I'm sorry Ann isn't marrying Bob. It would have been nice to have her in the family, but I have to admit her fiancé is pretty spectacular. He's won the triathlon a couple of times. I'm going to have breakfast with them tomorrow before heading over to the picnic. They're both staying here tonight."

Vernon Spalding came through the French doors.

"Your wife is looking for you," he told Beary. "I think she's ready to leave. She's already dragged your son and his friend off the dance floor."

"Not a problem," said Beary. "I was ready to leave two hours ago. MacPuff has been left far too long. He'll be sitting in the motorhome with his back legs crossed. I shall just make a quick nature call, and then I will report to the lobby."

"It won't be a quick nature call," said Vernon. "The line is a mile long."

Philippa got a key out of her purse and gave it to her father.

"Go upstairs, Dad. Use my washroom. I'm on the top floor."

Beary expressed his appreciation and lumbered away, clutching the key in one hand and his glass of Scotch in the other. Philippa looked at her watch. It was close to midnight. The group on the patio was breaking up. The party was beginning to wind down.

Adam gave her a hopeful look.

"I've had an awful lot to drink," he said. "I'm not really in good shape to drive back into town."

Philippa smiled and dove back into her purse. She pulled out a card and handed it to Adam.

"Merritt's taxi service," she said. "See you at the picnic tomorrow."

She patted him on the cheek and disappeared inside. Adam was about to follow when he felt a hand grip his arm. He looked round to see the rotund woman in the floral gown.

"Time to turn in," she said breathily, emitting fumes that made the air smell like a distillery. Adam hoped she was not offering to share *her* room with him. "I did enjoy our talk," she continued. "I'll look forward to seeing you at the picnic tomorrow. I'll let you know if the Black Bandit visited me in the night," she added coyly.

She relinquished Adam's arm and wove her way into the hotel. Adam mentally counted to twenty and then followed. Philippa was still in the lobby with her mother, but the rest of the Beary clan had disappeared, for Juliette and Steven had already taken the girls back to camp, and Richard and Suzie had gone to get the car. Edwina looked at her watch.

"How long is your father going to be?" she said tetchily.

"He just went to the washroom," said Philippa. "He'll be here in a minute."

The crowd in the lobby had diminished to a handful of people, and the band had ceased playing. The only sounds were the low murmur of conversation from the few remaining guests and the distant clatter of dishes from the kitchen where the final cleanup was in process. Now that the lobby was almost empty, the details of the décor were visible. The vestibule had a faintly Victorian air. The walls were papered a rich maroon colour and the wooden moldings and window frames were dark mahogany. A daguerreotype of a wild-eyed gentleman in a black hat held pride of place on the wall opposite the front doors. A small gold plaque beneath the picture confirmed that this was Mick MacDuggan.

The last of the guests went out into the night and only Edwina remained with Philippa and Adam. Richard's SUV had pulled up in front of the entrance, but Beary still had not appeared. Edwina looked impatiently towards the red-carpeted staircase.

"Do you want me to run up and look for him?" Philippa asked finally.

Her mother nodded, but before Philippa could move towards the staircase, a blood-chilling shriek broke the silence. And then everything went quiet.

* * *

Edwina was tight-lipped on the return drive to Monck Park.

"I told you not to wear that hat," she said.

"Sorry," said Beary. The smirk on his face belied his apology.

"Stop snickering. It isn't at all funny. I'm just glad Olive and Harvey had left so they didn't have to be embarrassed by your antics."

"All I did was go to the bathroom. It wasn't my fault that the lights were off in the second-floor hall. How was I to know that the overblown harpy with azaleas all over her bosom would come upstairs just as I was coming down from the top floor? It was only her over-lubricated brain that made her turn my perfectly ordinary silhouette into the Black Bandit."

"I don't know how I'm going to face her at the picnic tomorrow. Poor woman."

"The poor woman will be so hung-over," said Beary, "that she won't remember anything. Why don't you relax and enjoy the scenery?"

"It's pitch black outside," snapped Edwina. "There's nothing to see."

Since this appeared to be his wife's parting shot, Beary leaned back and stared into the night. It was not true that there was nothing to see, he thought. There was a chilling black void beside the road where the cliff dropped away, but further off, streaks of colour stood out against the night as vividly as the details on a black velvet painting. High above, where the silvery moon illuminated the sky, the inky darkness was transformed to a gleaming cerulean. Below, lights twinkled on the far shore of the lake and created a luminous turquoise band at the edge of the water. The reflectors at the side of the highway lit the edge of the escarpment, and a moving panorama of beige and brown rocks marched towards the windshield in the beam of the headlights. At each corner, as the headlamps hit the sagebrush, patches of shimmering green hovered for a brief moment, and then faded away as the road straightened out again.

Suddenly, two more lights appeared in the distance. Another vehicle was coming towards them. The headlights grew larger and more blinding, and then in a flash, they were gone.

"That was a tow truck," said Beary. "Someone at the campsite must have developed car trouble."

"That's service beyond the call of duty," said Richard. "It's past midnight."

As he shifted gears and negotiated the next curve, a thought crossed his mind. This was not a road where you would want something to go wrong with your car.

* * *

The barbeque the following day did not start until noon, but by eight o'clock, Monck Park was bustling with activity. Tantalising breakfast smells wafted from campsites and the air reverberated with the sounds of children playing and speedboats buzzing up and down the lake. Once the Beary clan had been fed, Richard and his father gathered up lawn chairs and set off down the dirt trail at the edge of the lake. The sun was already hot and they were glad of the patches of shade from the poplars and pine trees that were dotted along the path. Clusters of purple daisies and cornflowers popped up sporadically amid the ferns, but most of the terrain was rock or powdery earth.

Soon they reached the picnic area. A long blue awning had been set up at one end of the grassy strip that abutted the beach, and the site was already filling up with people. Some lay on chaise longues, lathering themselves with sunblock, while others unloaded picnic baskets and set out rows of hotdog buns on the table under the canopy. Garth Macleod was already there, firing up a barbeque, and a tanned young man in a Cabelas ball cap was helping him, though the expression on their faces suggested they were discussing something more serious than wieners.

"That's Spaulding's boy," said Beary. "Good fisherman that. Come on, I'll introduce you."

Beary set off across the grass. Richard was about to follow when he heard someone call his name. He looked round to see his sister approaching. She was accompanied by Ann MacLeod and Jason Heinemann, both of whom were laden with chairs, towels and baskets.

"Ann and Jason gave me a ride," said Philippa as she caught up to her brother. "Is Adam here yet?"

"Haven't seen him."

"What about Mum and Juliette's mob?"

"Stephen has taken the girls swimming, and Mum and Juliette are putting together a salad and looking after MacPuff. It's too hot for him down here. There's no shade. We're going to take turns pet-sitting throughout the afternoon. Here, lend a hand putting out these chairs."

Philippa took two of the lawn chairs and moved them to the shade of the awning. As she bent to open the first one, she heard a voice in her ear.

"Let me help you do that."

She straightened up, ready to retort that she was perfectly capable of setting up lawn chairs, but the words died in her throat. The young man who had made the offer was remarkably attractive, and in spite of the ball cap which hardly did him justice, she was charmed by the sparkling blue eyes and boyish smile.

"You're Philippa Beary, aren't you?" he said. "I'm Neil Spaulding. I know your father. We fish the same lake."

"Of course," said Philippa. "Your father is Vernon, the gun-shop owner. I met him at the dinner last night, but I didn't see you there."

Neil's face clouded.

"No. Some last-minute business came up. I couldn't get away in time. Look," he said, the smile coming back again, "I'm camping in the park for the weekend and I've got my speedboat here. Would you like to go for a tour of the lake after the barbecue?"

Philippa felt flattered. The invitation was sudden and unexpected, considering that they had only just met, but the prospect of exploring Nicola Lake was tempting. She looked at the sparkling expanse of turquoise water, noticing how it disappeared around the corner into the sagebrush hills, and she hesitated, torn between curiosity and caution. Then, out of the corner of her eye, she saw Adam coming across the grass. He was wearing his Rheinmaiden T-shirt and was engaged in animated conversation with a bikinied blonde who was the closest thing to Pamela Anderson that Philippa had ever seen. She turned back to Neil and dazzled him with a smile as brilliant as his own.

"I'd love to," she said. "Just say the word when it's time to go."

However, once lunch was over, Philippa realized that the offer was not exclusive. By one o'clock, most of the people at the picnic appeared to be heading for the water. Neil hailed her and waved towards a Campion Bowrider that was pulled up on the sand. Then he ambled over and issued an invitation to Emily, who was perched daintily on a chaise longue. Emily looked up from the battered-looking volume she was reading, then smiled and shook her head. Neil came to join Philippa on the beach.

"Doesn't Emily want to come?" she asked.

Neil shook his head. "No. I couldn't tear her away from her book."

"What's she reading that's so fascinating?"

"I don't know . . . something that was recently donated to the museum."

"That sounds a dull alternative to a boat ride on a day like this."

Neil shrugged.

"Her choice. Emily's all right. Come on, climb in."

As she climbed into the speedboat, Philippa saw that Ann MacLeod and Jason Heinemann were loading passengers into Garth MacLeod's Bayliner. Neil pushed the Campion into the water and climbed aboard. As the boat drifted out from the beach, Philippa noticed that he was looking back at the occupants of the other craft. Curious to know what had caused him and Ann to end their engagement, she attempted an exploratory foray into his personal life.

"I guess you know the MacLeod's well," she said.

"I handle Garth's lumber sales." Neil's tone was non-committal. He started the engine and moved the boat forward slowly. There were swimmers near the shore, and teenagers on seadoos further out.

Philippa's natural inquisitiveness made her persevere.

"I used to play with Ann during summer visits when we were children," she continued. "She's grown up into a real beauty, hasn't she?"

Her companion's expression became coolly impersonal.

"She sure has. Sit back," he added impassively. "Enjoy the ride."

He thrust the throttle forward and the boat leapt ahead. Within seconds, it had reached the centre of the lake. Realizing that conversation was impossible, Philippa relaxed and emptied her mind of everything but the exhilarating sensations of the sunshine on her face and the warm breeze rippling through her hair. She leaned back and looked up at the sweeping pale blue canopy that formed the sky.

Nicola Lake was longer than she had realized, and it was fifteen minutes before they reached the end. The boat banked as Neil steered it round the curve of the shore, and the angle as they turned made it apparent that, in spite of the lake's great length, it was little more than a mile wide. As they started back along the other shore, Philippa sat up and studied the landscape. She could see the highway that she and Adam had driven en route to Merritt. Where it emerged from the pale green hills, another road branched off and ran down to a trailer park at the edge of the water. The highway followed the lakeshore, but in places, wide flats with willow trees jutted into the water. At one point, a river bisected the shore, bursting out from under a road bridge and streaming into the lake. The boat started to bank again, following the curve of the shoreline, and as the sagebrush-covered hills receded, the campsite came into view. Beyond it, the switchback road climbed steeply and disappeared over the top of the rise. Now that they were coming from a different angle, Philippa could see a cove tucked around the corner from the end of the park. Neil reduced speed and veered toward the shore. He pointed at a grandiose beachfront residence with its own dock.

"That's my old man's place," he said.

Philippa was impressed. Guns and lumber must be lucrative trades, she thought, but before she could say anything, Neil thrust the throttle forward again. The cove flashed by and the Campion was round the point and heading towards the campsite. Neil slowed the boat down as they approached the beach. Philippa surveyed the hurly-burly on shore and sighed. It was very peaceful on the lake, far better for her vocal chords than the picnic ground which was teeming with people. She looked back towards the Black Bandit Inn glimmering in the sunlight on the far shore. Then she peered ahead to the high rocks looming above the end of the lake they had not yet explored.

Neil cut the engine and let the boat drift in. Philippa glanced towards the park entrance and noticed Garth MacLeod's Jeep going out through the gate. She wondered idly why he was leaving. Then the boat rocked and a loud voice brought her attention back to the water.

"Hey, how about taking more on board?"

Adam was clutching the side of the boat, and Richard and Suzie were treading water behind him. Adam grabbed Suzie and boosted her up, and Neil pulled her into the boat. Then, in what seemed like one smooth movement, Adam hauled himself aboard and Richard followed suit.

Neil looked at Philippa and flashed his boyish smile.

"Are you game for another ride?" he asked.

"Yes. Why don't we go up the other end?" she suggested.

Without a word, he restarted the engine and the boat glided forward. Adam climbed up and perched on the bow, and Richard and Suzie settled at the stern. Soon the air became alive with chatter over the sound of the engine. Neil quietly concentrated on steering the boat, but since he had said no more than two sentences the entire time they had been on the water, his silence could not be attributed to the presence of the newcomers. Philippa sighed. Good looks could only go so far, she reflected. If Neil's relationship with Ann had withered, it had probably died from lack of conversation.

The sound of the engine acquired an echo, and the discussion on board became augmented with shrieks and whoops from starboard. Philippa turned to see Garth MacLeod's Bayliner overtaking them. Jason Heinemann was at the helm, one hand on the wheel and one hand holding a beer can, which he waved in their direction as he passed. Neil's expression did not alter, but he veered away until there was a fifty-foot distance between the vessels, and the boats continued more slowly on a parallel course as they entered the eastern end of the lake.

The sun disappeared as they moved into the shadow of the cliffs, and Philippa found herself feeling chilled in spite of the heat of the day. This end of the lake felt almost like a fjord. The shore was steep and rocky, and the road that had disappeared over the hill by the campsite, now reappeared as a ribbon snaking around the edge of the high rocky escarpment that framed the end of the lake. From the water, the height to the top of the cliffs was even more daunting than it had seemed on the drive in. There was a sudden flicker of movement on the cliff-top and a car bobbed into sight, winding its way towards the park. It looked impossibly small, resembling a Dinky Toy as it followed the curve of the road. Suddenly another vehicle appeared, going in the other direction. Philippa recognized it. It was Garth MacLeod's red Jeep.

The Bayliner had pulled ahead and Philippa could see Ann standing in the stern. She too had caught sight of the car, for she was pointing and waving. Jason was starting to veer to port because the end of the lake was approaching, and Ann twisted round so that she could follow the progress of the Jeep with her eyes. Neil held his boat steady on its course, and as it crossed the stern of the Bayliner, Ann's smiling face was clearly visible to the passengers on board the Campion. She continued to wave towards the vehicle on the cliff, but all at once, the light in her face died, and her expression froze into an agonized grimace. Then she emitted an ear-piercing scream.

Philippa whipped around to look at the shore.

The Jeep was no longer on the cliff-top. Silently, smoothly, it was sailing down the side of the escarpment. Then it bounced twice and came to rest on a rocky ledge above the waterline. It hung there for a moment, and then, with a percussive whoosh that seemed to rush at them across the water, it burst into flame.

* * *

The death of Mary Cummings cast a pall on the festivities, and the picnic wrapped up quickly once news of the fatality got back to the park. However, shock was mingled with relief, for if Garth MacLeod had not run low on briquettes and sent his new receptionist into town to pick up more supplies, the body consumed in the fiery inferno at the foot of the cliff would have been his own.

There was also alarming evidence to suggest that the crash was a deliberate attempt on MacLeod's life. A tourist en route to the park had witnessed the accident. He had seen the Jeep careening down the hill, and as it shot past, he had seen the look of panic on Mary Cumming's face. There had been no apparent attempt to slow the car's progress before it hurtled over the cliff. Further investigation revealed a pool of brake fluid where the Jeep had been parked. Since the vehicle had been serviced two days previously, and at that time the brake line was intact, the RCMP suspected that it had been deliberately tampered with.

The Jeep had been used to transport the MacLeods to the banquet the previous evening. There had been no problem with the brakes, either travelling from or returning to the park, so the sabotage must have occurred after their return. However, identifying suspects was proving to be a challenge since, by the time the MacLeod's came back to the campsite, most people had turned in and the area was quiet. The only sign of activity had been further up the circle road, where a small cluster of people had gathered round a campfire. The members of this group had seen the Jeep return, but once it was parked, it was screened from view by the motorhome in the next site. The campers insisted that only three vehicles had come through the park after the MacLeods returned. One had been Neil Spaulding's pick-up truck, one was the tow truck from Baker's garage, and one, from their description, was obviously Richard Beary's SUV. The tow truck had been driven by Gary Tindall who was responding to an emergency call about a broken-down Ford, but it transpired that the call had been a prank and he left the park shortly after midnight. Neil Spaulding had arrived soon after Tindall left. Then the Bearys had come through around twelve-fifteen. The park gates were closed at twelve-thirty, so no other vehicles could have entered during the night. However, that did not preclude the possibility of someone driving to the gates and walking in. There were also hundreds of people camped in the park who would have had the opportunity to tamper with the brakes of the vehicle. The outlook was not encouraging. The only certainty was that the damage had been done some time between midnight, when the MacLeods had turned in, and seven o'clock in the morning when they got up.

While the RCMP investigated, life went on. Mary Cummings had been an unmarried woman with no living relatives, and although people were sorry about her demise, they still turned out in droves for the Canada Day festivities. Richard had spent most of Monday ensconced with the local police force, since the officer in charge of the case had welcomed the assistance of a detective inspector who had been present at the scene of the crime. However, on Tuesday morning, he insisted on leaving the police station by noon as he knew Suzie's act started at twelve-thirty.

When he arrived at the festival site, he headed straight for the bandshell. He was just in time, for as he approached, he heard Stephen's group being announced. The bleachers in front of the open-air stage were packed so he worked his way through the milling throng and found standing room at the side.

Stephen's band was in fine form. So was Suzie, who was resplendent in a white cowboy hat and a pantsuit that sparkled with sequins. As Richard watched the performance, he felt an elbow in his ribs. Philippa had wriggled in beside him. She wore a frilly yellow frock and looked as if she were dressed for a barn dance.

"Good, isn't she?" she hissed, nodding towards Suzie, who was belting out "Before He Cheats" at centre stage.

"I'll say. You look cute. Is that what Rose Marie wears?"

"Sort of. There have been so many versions that anything goes. This is pretty close to the original concept, but Adam is outfitted like the Hollywood version. It isn't accurate but it's what people expect."

"Where is Adam?"

Philippa nodded towards the back of the bandshell.

"He can't fit through the crowd. You'll see what I mean once we're on. Never mind the concert. Tell me what the police have found out."

"Not a lot. Garth MacLeod is very worried about something, and it's more than the fact that someone tried to kill him. I think it may be related to his business and an enquiry that's being undertaken by the Ministry of the Environment. Someone has been illegally selling CCA-treated lumber, and there's a possibility it may be traced back to MacLeod's company. He had a large stockpile of the toxic wood and insists that he got rid of it, but he says it's possible some of it may have gone astray. The driver who was to take it to the landfill was Ricky Granger —that's Lisa Kendall's boyfriend—and I can't help wondering if Lisa's murder was related to the theft and resale of the lumber. She worked at the landfill and she might have been killed because she knew too much."

"But Suzie said that the killer talked as if he were Lisa's lover? And she was pregnant by someone other than her boyfriend, so she was obviously having a secret affair."

"Yes, but what if the man had begun the relationship with the intention of using her connection to the landfill to pull off some kind of swindle."

"Did you suggest that possibility to Garth MacLeod?"

"Yes. He pooh-poohed the idea. He said she didn't have control of anything other than the invoices. He doesn't believe her death is related to the attempt on his own life."

Philippa frowned.

"It wouldn't hurt to cross-reference the people who had the

opportunity to commit each crime. You could have a hard look at anyone who makes both lists."

"Half MacLeod's employees and most of his family were at the campsite that night," Richard pointed out, "so it's a pretty long list. The only people we can eliminate are Ann and Jason because they were staying at the hotel, and from what Ann told the police, they spent the night together. I gather they had separate rooms, but Jason only used his for the sake of appearances. One of the maids saw him tip-toeing back around four in the morning."

Philippa looked thoughtful.

"If Ann was asleep, she might not have noticed when he went back to his room," she said. "He could have left her much earlier."

"Perhaps, but according to the maid, he was in bare feet and pajama-bottoms, which is hardly the right attire to hop in his car and drive round to the other side of the lake."

"It's possible though," said Philippa. "He seemed pretty tired the next morning."

"Hung-over, more like. He was packing the booze away at the anniversary party, but I think we have to rule him out. There was a night crew doing bridge repairs from twelve-thirty until five in the morning. No one came across. You can forget about watercraft too. There was a couple night-fishing off the shore of the park and they insisted that there were no other boats in the area."

Suzie swung into a rousing rendition of "Redneck Woman" and Philippa's eyes went back to the stage.

"I've got to go," she said. "This is the last number. We're on next. Look, there's Mum and Dad. They're up in the bleachers with Juliette and the girls. Why don't you join them?"

Philippa disappeared into the crush and Richard wove his way to the stands. He climbed up the steps and wriggled in beside his parents.

"This is quite the event, isn't it?" he said. "Are you having fun?" he added to Laura, ruffling her hair.

"They don't have pony rides," said his niece. She stuffed a large piece of pink candyfloss into her mouth.

"They don't need pony rides," Beary pointed out. "Children up here ride horses."

"Hush," said Edwina. "Philippa is on next."

Stephen Ayers had removed his cowboy hat, set down his guitar, and taken up his position at the synthesizer.

"Multi-talented fellow, our son-in-law," muttered Beary. "Bit of a change—from country and western to operetta. Hope the crowd is appreciative. I'd hate my daughter to bomb."

"Of course she won't bomb," Edwina said indignantly. "*Rose Marie* is a lovely operetta. I get so annoyed when people make fun of it." She had no sooner finished speaking when there was a huge guffaw from the crowd. Edwina whipped round to face the bandshell. Philippa had twirled onto the stage and was posing coyly, one hand to her forehead as if peering towards the horizon, and Adam was slowly emerging from the wings. He wore full Mountie regalia, and around his middle hung a birchbark canoe. He sedately paddled across to Philippa and began his serenade.

* * *

"Quite delightful," said Beary, when the concert had ended.

"For those who like comedy turns," Edwina said huffily.

Philippa gave her mother a hug.

"Come on," she said. "Adam did finally get out of his canoe and we sang the love duet straight at the end."

"Yes, you did," said Edwina, "and I hope you noticed how the crowd settled down and lapped it up when you did it properly."

"Where's Adam?" asked Beary. "Still paddling down river?"

"Navigating the media probably. I have to go back to join him. The organizers want to get some pictures. I'll meet you at the children's tent. Juliette's already headed over. She and the girls are on in half an hour."

Philippa slipped away, and Richard and his parents started to make their way through the cluster of people gathered at the foot of the bleachers. As they reached the edge of the stands, Suzie bobbed into sight at the edge of the bandshell. She beckoned to them, and they worked their way over to her. As they crossed in front of the stage, Richard noticed Jason Heinemann moving into position to introduce the talent show.

"It's easier if you come round the back," said Suzie. "Follow me."

She led them round behind the stage. Here the grounds were less crowded. Two tents had been set up as dressing rooms on the long strip of lawn between the bandshell and the fence of the enclosure, but other than a few performers lolling on the grass or doing warm-up exercises, the area was clear. At the far end, near the gate, Richard could see Philippa and Adam posing for photographs. Adam was still in his canoe.

As Richard started to follow Suzie across the grass, there was a crackle from the loudspeaker. An echoing, amplified voice came over the sound system.

"Hey, there! Glad you could make it. So, is it hot enough for you?"

Suzie froze.

"That's him!" she gasped.

Wild-eyed, she turned to Richard and clutched at his arm. "It's his voice!" she insisted. "That's the voice I heard in the pool."

"But that's Jason Heinemann. You've heard him talk before. You didn't recognize his voice during the banquet."

"I only talked with him briefly, and he spoke very quietly. It was totally different."

"You're quite sure?"

"Yes. It's him. I know it is."

"It's the echo of the mike," said Beary. "That's what she'll have heard in the pool. His voice would have reverberated."

Suzie nodded.

"Yes, that's exactly what it was like. What should I do?"

Richard set his jaw.

"Come with me," he said.

He took Suzie's arm and led her back the way they had come. Beary and Edwina followed. They pushed their way back through the crowd at the side of the stage. Richard positioned Suzie in front of him. Beary and Edwina moved beside her.

"Now, watch him," Richard told Suzie. "Stare at him. Make it obvious that you're paying close attention."

Jason continued with his introduction, but as his eyes swept the crowd, he noticed the cluster of solemn individuals scrutinizing him from the side of the bleachers. One figure seemed to leap out from the rest. Suzie Simons was white. She appeared petrified, rooted to the spot with terror, but the look of recognition on her face was unmistakable.

Richard watched the emcee closely, and he saw the apprehension grow in the other man's eyes. Heinemann's fear was almost palpable. He faltered, then pulled himself together and finished introducing the first performer. As the young dancer came on stage, he put down the microphone and slunk back into the shadows. Then he inched over to the far wing.

"Watch it," hissed Beary. "He's going to bolt."

Richard lunged forward and shoved his way through to the other side of the stage, but by the time he was clear of the crowd, Jason Heinemann was halfway across the green. He was sprinting at top speed and making a beeline for the entrance gates.

Richard accelerated, but he knew there was no way that he could catch up. He cursed inwardly, remembering that the man was a triathlon winner. The photographers were still snapping Adam and Philippa in front of the gate. Behind them, Richard could see a security guard. He stopped running and bellowed to the guard.

"Stop him! Don't let him get out."

The guard looked round and saw Richard waving. At last he registered what Richard was saying, but by the time he sprang into motion, Heinemann was already too far ahead. The photographers heard Richard shout. They lowered their cameras and glanced about, trying to see what had caused the outcry. Adam and Philippa appeared confused. The chase on the green was blocked from their view and they had no idea why their session had been interrupted.

Heinemann elbowed his way past the photographers, viciously slamming the cameramen aside. Then he put his head down and lunged for the gate. Adam swung round to see what was happening and the canoe swung with him.

Heinemann's run at the gate was halted by the crashing impact as the boat made contact with his head. He dropped like a stone, and when Richard reached him, he was still groaning on the ground.

Adam looked bewildered.

"Did I do that?" he said. "This thing's only wood-framed canvas."

"You must have got him with the gunwale," said Richard. He

hauled Jason Heinemann to his feet, read him his rights, and led the abject man away.

Adam had far too much self-assurance to be discomposed for long and he never passed up an opportunity for a potential headline. He turned to the astounded photographers and flashed a dazzling smile.

"Don't look so surprised," he said.

Raising his arm, he pushed his hat forward across his forehead and struck a manly pose.

"Everyone knows," he told them smugly, "that the Mountie always gets his man."

* * *

At ten o'clock that evening, the fireworks began. The Bearys found a spot on the bleachers and watched as the starbursts and rockets lit up the sky. But although their eyes were on the pyrotechnic display, their conversation was dominated by the subject of Jason's arrest.

Richard was able to fill in the gaps.

"Once Ricky Granger was told that Jason Heinemann had murdered Lisa, he sang like a bird," he explained. "Jason hired Granger because of his criminal record. He realized he could use him for under-the-counter deals, and when Garth MacLeod had to get rid of a huge stockpile of CCA-treated lumber, Jason saw an opportunity to make a tidy profit. Lisa had become besotted with him, so it was easy for him to persuade her to make out an invoice billing the trucking company for disposal of the wood. Then he billed MacLeod for the transportation and disposal—and believe me, it would have been a big bill. Getting rid of dangerous goods is expensive. But of course, neither the load nor the portion of the fee for disposal went to the landfill."

"So where did it go?" asked Philippa.

"I'm getting to that. MacLeod had a new stock of lumber treated with Alkaline Copper Quaternary compounds, which is the new process that's classified environmentally acceptable. There was a big shipment due to go to his lumberyard in town, so Granger reversed the orders and delivered the ACQ-treated lumber to Heinemann's yard in Kamloops and took the toxic load to Macleod's lumberyard in Merritt. Heinemann was able to sell the ACQ lumber for a tidy profit since he hadn't paid anything for it in the first place. Also, he knew that any

145

problem with the illegal wood would be traced back to MacLeod and not to him. But then Lisa got pregnant, and she was ready to blow the whistle if he didn't break off with Ann and marry her. So he killed her."

"But what about Garth MacLeod?" chimed in Edwina. "Why would Heinemann want to kill his future father-in-law?"

"MacLeod was getting too close. He was worried sick about the fact that the toxic wood might have come from his yard. He was investigating the trail. Jason had to get rid of him."

"I thought you said it would have been impossible for Jason to get across the lake to the campsite that night," said Philippa. "How did he manage to sabotage the brake line on the Jeep?"

"Granger told us that too. Actually, the solution is pretty obvious when you remember that Heinemann was a triathlon winner."

"Oh," cried Philippa. "I get it. He swam across."

"Exactly. The night-fisherman would have seen a boat, but a swimmer could have easily slipped by."

"Poor Ann," said Juliette sympathetically. "What a nasty character."

"Better that she found out," Edwina stated firmly. "She's had a lucky escape."

"Maybe she'll go back to Spaulding now," said Beary. "Nice young man, and a good fisherman too."

Philippa glanced towards the end of the bleachers where Neil Spaulding was sitting with her cousin, Emily, who was chattering nonstop in his ear while he viewed the fireworks with the same steady gaze that had been fixed on his face throughout the boat ride. They looked very comfortable together.

"You know," she said slowly, "I suspect Neil has moved on."

"Good heavens!" exclaimed Beary, following his daughter's glance. "The Spaulding lad doesn't deserve to be landed with Emily."

"Actually," said Philippa, "it could be the perfect match."

The last starburst raced up into the sky and exploded into a ball of red. Then the night grew hazy with the smoky air and the crowd started to move away. Emily and Neil walked over to the Bearys and stopped to say goodbye.

"Have they got enough proof to convict him?" Emily asked Richard.

"I think so."

"Good. I always thought there was something shady about him. And last week I found something that backed up my instinct that he was a bad lot."

Beary rolled his eyes.

"Here we go again," he muttered.

Emily ignored the interruption.

"The book I was reading at the picnic was the diary of Martha Gray," she said. "Martha was the town midwife during the late 1870s. She knew all sorts of family secrets, and although she kept her knowledge to herself during her lifetime, she wrote everything down in her diary. Jason, as we know, is descended from one of the oldest families in the area, and his great-grandfather was George Carpenter, the only child of William and Ethel Carpenter. Well, it turns out that Ethel Carpenter couldn't have children, but she had a younger, unmarried sister who became pregnant. George Carpenter was really the sister's child, but to cover up the scandal, Ethel and William adopted the baby and registered it as their own. The only person who knew the truth was the midwife, Martha Gray."

"Is there a point to this history lecture?" asked Adam.

Emily gave him a frosty stare.

"Yes, of course there is," she snapped. "The point is that Martha Gray knew who the real father was. He couldn't marry Ethel's sister because he was already married. And guess who he was."

"I know," squealed Philippa. "I bet it was that haberdasher . . . the awful one who got Verity MacLeod pregnant, and then killed her and blamed the Black Bandit."

"Yes," said Emily, looking extremely self-satisfied. "Hans Meyerhoff—and you must see what that means."

"Well, I'm damned," said Beary. "Jason Heinemann is descended from a ruthless murderer."

"Exactly," said Emily smugly. "I told Ann she shouldn't have broken off with Neil and got engaged to Jason."

Smiling sweetly, she tucked her arm under Neil's and led him away.

The others watched speechlessly as the retreating couple disappeared into the smoky night. At last, Beary broke the silence.

"And the most irritating thing about Cousin Emily," he said, "is not that she always thinks she's right . . ."

Philippa, Juliette and Richard finished the sentence for him. In unison, they chorused:

"It's the fact that she always is!"

WHO KILLED LUCIA?

Philippa Beary was feeling sorry for herself. The summer tour had been a success, but it had also made her realize that nothing permanent was ever going to come of her relationship with Adam. To add to her misery, the day after he returned to Hamburg, she came down with a nasty cold.

"It's not fair." Philippa's voice had dropped a full octave. She glowered at her father who had dropped by bearing nose drops, decongestant and goodwill. "I could deal with the bust-up with Adam if I could keep busy, but this virus has gone down into my throat so it'll be a couple of weeks before I can sing again. I can't even sit in on chorus rehearsals because I might give the bug to someone else—and

I was so looking forward to *Lucia*. Robin is coming back from New York to debut the role here."

"Study the score and listen to the recording," suggested Beary. "I know you have the Sutherland version because I gave it to you a couple of birthdays ago. Amazing woman, that," he digressed. "She sang Lucia in Vancouver a few years after she'd wowed the world in the Zeffirelli production at Covent Garden. Your mother dragged me to it on one of our first dates. I can still remember her gluing herself to the backdrop like a frightened moth and chirruping the coloratura like a songbird in May—Sutherland, that is, not your mother. When *she* goes mad, she chatters like a kingfisher and barks like a pit bull."

Philippa sniffed despondently. "It's not the same," she moaned. "Everyone else is starting on the music, and I'm stuck here keeping company with a vaporizer."

"Very sensible," said Beary. "You won't get better if you don't stay home and rest."

"I know, but I can't concentrate on anything. I'm just sitting around spitting nails because I've lost my voice and my boyfriend in one fell swoop."

"Your voice will come back," Beary pointed out, "and as for Adam, you're better off if he doesn't come back. You were always a bit more smitten with him than he was with you. You can do better."

"He said I was boring," said Philippa indignantly. "He said Gretchen was more exciting because she was unpredictable."

She disappeared under a towel and took another deep breath.

"She probably is," said Beary. "That's a reality of life. People who are even-tempered, reliable and dutiful are often considered dull, especially by those who lack the same qualities. And if you're clever as well, you'll be classified as a nerd and a lot of people will resent you unless you make an effort to disguise your brains. Being the good daughter is a thankless task. Look where it got Cordelia. And that," added Beary, continuing to wax philosophical, "is why virtue has to be its own reward, because it's not guaranteed to bring any other benefits with it."

Philippa was barely listening. She re-emerged from the steamer and carried on where she had left off.

"Being a singer is like being an athlete. Nothing interferes with

Adam's exercise regime when he's in training. Why should he expect me to be any different?"

"He probably doesn't," said Beary. "And if you were prepared to wait out assorted flings with unpredictable bimbos, he'd probably be delighted to marry you at some point, but do you want to spend the rest of your life turning a blind eye and being the loyal one he comes back to?"

"No, of course not."

"Well then, stop grumbling." Beary dove into his bag and pulled out a large, utilitarian-looking paperback. "Here, I brought you something to occupy your mind. A work of Sir Walter Scott to put your romantic trials and tribulations into perspective."

Philippa studied the book in her father's hand.

"*The Bride of Lammermoor.* You know, I've always thought it would be interesting to read Scott's original story. Does the opera follow it closely?"

"There are similarities," said her father. "The family feud, and the concealed letters to make the lovers believe that each has forgotten the other—but the villain in the book is the mother, not the brother. Plus there's a ton of other stuff . . . background on Scottish politics and how the feud developed. It's quite fascinating. But what you'll find really intriguing is the fact that Scott based his novel on a true story. The prologue talks about the history of the real Lucia. Her name was Janet Dalrymple. Your operatic heroine really existed."

Philippa's eyes widened.

"And did she really go crazy and attack her husband on their wedding night?"

"Read it for yourself," said Beary. "The most interesting detail is the fact that the husband survived."

"Why is that so interesting?"

"Because Janet didn't. She died two weeks later. Nobody really knows what happened. Scott tries to explain it in his novel, and he may well have reconstructed everything accurately, but the reality is that he was just speculating from stories that had been passed down through the generations by people who were related to the family of the bride. And since he was writing in the early 1800s and Janet Dalrymple died in 1669, there was a lot of time for the stories to become distorted."

"Are there no records? Surely the husband had something to say after he recovered?"

"No," said Beary. "He refused to say anything, and he banned anyone from enquiring how he had received his wounds."

"Really?"

"Really." Beary planted the book in his daughter's lap. "In the final analysis," he concluded, "it's a mystery."

Philippa did not reply. She flipped her towel aside, picked up the book and opened it to the prologue.

Beary smiled to himself. She was already reading intently as he crept out the door.

* * *

Richard Beary stopped at the Cactus Club on his way home from work. His day had been gruelling, and cooking was the last thing he wanted to do, but he was ravenously hungry. He barely noticed the pretty young hostesses who opened the doors to welcome him, neither did he respond to the flirtatious smile of the nubile blonde who took him to a Plexiglas-lined booth and poured him a cup of coffee. He slid onto the padded seat and ordered a large steak. Too tired to think about anything beyond the anticipated meal, he drank his coffee and stared blankly at the thick round lights on the ceiling. Idly, he counted them—nine in total—and mentally noted how their red glow matched the colour of the vertical lights above the dividers between the booths. He was trying to decide whether the pink tinge of the mock-brick wall was a product of the lights, or whether the fake stones were really tinted that colour, when his reverie was interrupted by the ring of his cellphone.

As he answered the call, the waitress appeared bearing his order. She set the steak on the table, produced a black-pepper shaker and left with a smile when Richard waved her away. With eyes and ears divided, Richard stared hungrily at his slab of prime rib and listened to the voice of Sergeant Martin emanating from his phone.

"It's a stabbing." Bill Martin went right to the point. "This one's going to be dicey. It happened after a Sikh wedding."

A surge of adrenalin obliterated Richard's feeling of fatigue, though he knew that his tiredness was only masked and that his body was starting to run on nervous energy.

"A gang killing?"

"No," said Martin. "Nothing that straightforward, and nobody is dead . . . yet. But we're dealing with wealth, influence and race. Gurinder Madahar was present."

"The former Attorney General?"

"Yes, it was his nephew's wedding and he's demanding to speak with someone high up. You'd better get over there right away. The brother's house is in the Deer Lake area." Martin gave Richard the address. "The situation looks ugly," he concluded.

Richard drew in his breath.

"Who's the victim?" he asked.

"Victims," Martin corrected him dourly. "There are two of them. It's the bride and the groom."

* * *

Philippa finished the prologue and set down the book. Thoughtfully, she headed to the kitchen of her small apartment and put on the kettle. Being a singer, she had always tended to let the drama of *Lucia di Lammermoor* take second place to the music, for she had worked on sections of the role and understood the fiendish discipline that was required to handle the part. Now that she had read Scott's account of the sad story of Janet Dalrymple, the frail heroine of the opera took on new life.

Janet Dalrymple had been the daughter of the first Lord Stair and Dame Margaret Ross, a lady of high birth and higher ambition, who helped her husband rise to such eminence that rumours abounded that her success was due to witchcraft. Janet secretly became engaged to Lord Rutherford. She did not dare let her parents know for she knew they would disapprove of her suitor, both because of his political beliefs and also because of his lack of fortune. The lovers broke a gold coin and each kept half as a token of their faith, but soon afterwards, Janet's parents presented her with another suitor, David Dunbar of Baldoon, and urged her to accept his proposal. Janet refused, and eventually admitted to her parents why she did not want to marry Dunbar. They insisted that she accept, and at last she assented. When he heard of the engagement, Lord Rutherford wrote and demanded his rights, arguing that the vow that he and Janet had taken could not be arbitrarily set aside. Lady Stair wrote back, reminding him that Levitical law dictated that a daughter could not be bound by a vow if her father disapproved, whereupon the young man insisted on a meeting with Janet. He was allowed to see her, with her mother present, and he urged Janet to tell her mother her true feelings. However, Janet remained mute, and, at her mother's command, returned the piece of broken gold to Lord Rutherford. He raged at the pale, motionless girl and left in a tremendous temper, and the marriage between Janet and Dunbar went ahead. On the wedding day, Janet was "sad, silent and resigned". Her young brother, who rode with her to church, reported later that her hand was "as cold and damp as marble". The wedding took place, followed by feasting and dancing, but soon after the bride and bridegroom retired, terrible shrieks were heard from the bridal chamber. When the door was opened, Dunbar was found wounded and streaming with blood. At first Janet could not be seen, but then they found her hiding in the corner of the chimney. Her shift was covered in blood. She was quite mad, and two weeks later, she died. Dunbar recovered from his wounds, but he refused to talk about that night. Thirteen years later, he was killed in a riding accident, never having revealed what had happened in the bridal chamber.

Philippa mulled over the bare details of the tale as she added honey to her lemon tea and brought the drink back to the living room. Two phrases from Scott's prologue seemed particularly revealing.

> "It was difficult at that time to become acquainted
> with the history of a Scottish family above the lower
> rank; and strange things sometimes took place there,
> into which even the law did not scrupulously inquire."

The other sentence that Philippa deemed worthy of attention was even more tantalizing, for Scott acknowledged that his friend, Mr. Sharpe, had given another version of the tale. According to Sharpe, the bridegroom had wounded the bride. Torn between embarking on the novel or trying to discover more about the history of the Dalrymples, Philippa paused. She looked at the book, lying open beside the comfortable armchair, and then she glanced at her computer desk. Feeling a sneeze coming on, she set her mug down. By the time three hearty sneezes had erupted, coming from her throat rather than her head, a feeling of debilitation washed back over her and she picked up the mug and sank back into the armchair. Research would have to wait. She took up the novel, swallowed a comforting gulp of tea, and began to read.

* * *

At the turn of the century, Deer Lake had provided a rural summer playground for Vancouver's wealthy citizenry, but over the years, urban sprawl had reached, surrounded, and ultimately overtaken the lake so that the body of water was now a shining, but sadly polluted pond near the geographic centre of the Lower Mainland. The country estates had changed hands many times over the years, and gradually the city had bought up properties until more than half the lakefront was parkland with public access. However, on the south shore, a few privately owned estates still existed, and when Richard turned onto Stag Lane, he perceived that his destination was one of them. He did not have to look for house numbers, for already two police cars and a van were pulled up by the Madahar's property, and a cluster of curious neighbours huddled on the road, watching the proceedings as two uniformed officers secured the area.

The word *home* was inadequate to describe the Madahar residence. The house must have been one of the original Deer Lake mansions, gloriously restored and renovated. Richard estimated that it was set on at least three acres. He was also willing to bet that a hundred yards of that acreage was lake frontage. He knew that the Madahar's main claim to fame was the success of Gurinder Madahar in the world of provincial politics, but he vaguely recalled that there were several brothers and that the family was a big player in the textile industry. He also recollected a couple of incidents with arrogant young men of that name who drove expensive cars and showed a lot of attitude. Clearly, there was money in fabrics. A bright-looking constable stood guard under a basketball hoop, which was incongruously attached to a triple garage that still looked like the turn-of-the-century carriage house it had once been. Richard recognized the officer right away. Constable

155

Shields. One of the new recruits that Bill Martin had predicted would go places.

"Sergeant Martin just called from the hospital," Shields reported briskly. "It sounds as if the girl is not likely to make it, though they think the groom will pull through."

"Has either one of them said anything?" Richard asked.

"No. Neither one is conscious, and the doctor told DS Martin to buzz off and let the hospital staff do their thing because there weren't going to be any questions for some time. The forensic team is already here," the constable added, "and WPC Howe has got the groom's family rounded up in the living room."

Richard was surprised.

"The parents too? Did they not go to the hospital to be with their son?"

"The mother went down with the ambulance, but once she was told her son would pull through, she came back. I suspect it was because she knew the police were here. She must be the one who called their in-house family lawyer."

"Gurinder Madahar?"

"Yes. The ex-A.G. Anyway, she got a ride back from the hospital with him, so if you want to talk with them on the premises, you can. Otherwise, we can bring them down to the station." The constable grinned. "It might be worth it, just to see the expression on the all-high Gurinder's self-righteous mug. The minute he got here, he started ordering us about telling us what we could or couldn't do with his precious family."

"Keep your perspective, constable," said Richard. "We're not here for a political vendetta."

Privately Richard fully intended to get formal statements down at the station, but those were for later. Right now, he wanted to see the initial reactions of the members of the household, and the more informal the better. He knew full well that in a few days, the Madahars would have closed ranks and the stories would become a composite of everyone's ideas and impressions. He turned back to Constable Shields. "Where exactly did the attack happen?" he asked. "Were there any witnesses?"

"No, it happened in the bedroom. The groom was naked. It looked like he'd just got out of the shower. The girl was still fully dressed."

"Were they preparing to go somewhere else?"

"No. The house belongs to Gurinder's brother, Navraj Madahar. The groom—his name's Arjan—is Navraj's youngest son. He has his own suite in the family home, so he and his bride were to live here." The constable rolled his eyes. "Poor girl," he added. "Wait till you see her mother-in-law—talk about Catwoman in a sari. Definitely not the classic image of the subjugated South Asian lady."

"Do we know who the bride is?"

"Yes, her name is Amanpreet Loti and her father owns half the construction companies in the Lower Mainland."

"Presumably an arranged marriage."

"Probably. Mind you, they'd retired to their rooms by seven-thirty, so maybe they were actually keen on each other and raring to go."

"Wasn't there a reception or party? I thought Sikh weddings went on for hours."

"They do, but the wedding was in the morning. There was a lunch at the temple afterwards, but the big banquet was to be tomorrow evening. So after taking photographs in the park, they all went to the bride's house where she said goodbye to her parents and left for her new home with the groom's family."

"You've found out a lot in a short time," commented Richard.

"One of the brothers came out and spent half an hour telling me exactly what had happened and what the police should do about it."

Richard raised his eyebrows.

"He did, did he? I thought you said there were no witnesses."

"Presumably he can see through walls," said the constable cheerfully. "He acted like he was lord of the universe, and since he's the oldest son in the family, he probably is. His name is Joban. You won't be able to miss him. He'll be the one with the scowl on his face. He was very put out when his Uncle Gurinder arrived and told him to go inside and keep his mouth shut."

"And what was Joban's version of events?" asked Richard. "Before his uncle arrived and took over, that is."

"He says Amy—that's what they call Amanpreet—had a friend at university who was keen to marry her. A fortune hunter, he says.

Evidently this boy kicked up a real fuss when Amy's parents told him to get lost and pointed out that she was engaged to Arjan."

"Is this boy also East Indian?"

"No. White. His name's David Darraby. According to Joban, about half an hour after Amy and Arjan went upstairs, there was a series of horrible shrieks and screams from their suite. He and his father and brother went rushing up to see what was going on. The door was locked and they had to break it down, but as they burst into the room, he says he looked out the window and saw a man running across the garden towards the lake. He swears it was Darraby. He also says Darraby was carrying something and he's pretty sure it was a kirpan."

"A kirpan? I thought this fellow was white."

"Joban says Amy had given Darraby a kirpan six months ago."

"Well, the doctor will be able to tell us whether or not the wounds were made with a kirpan," said Richard. "What about the husband's kirpan? Presumably he had one."

"It's in the suite, still in its holster. It doesn't look used. Forensics will check it, but I doubt if they'll find any traces of blood. It would have been impossible to clean in that short a time."

Richard gave the constable a quizzical smile.

"Looking to go into the detective branch, are you, constable?"

The young policeman smiled sheepishly.

"Well, yes. Either that or the dog squad."

Richard blinked.

"Well, that certainly puts my job in perspective," he said finally. "OK, I'm going to tackle the family now. You can come in and take down information for me."

Richard was shown into the house by a white-jacketed servant. He found himself inside a high entrance hall, which so combined late-Victorian architecture with Indian décor that he felt he had walked into a BBC drama about the last days of the Raj. A wide stairway led to an upper floor, and beside it, a long hall extended to the rear of the house. Three doors opened off the hallway. One of these was open, and Richard could see through into what appeared to be a study. The servant who had let him in signalled him to come forward, but before Richard could respond, the door to the right of the hall flew open and a tall man appeared. He abruptly dismissed the servant, then turned to Richard and offered his hand. Richard looked curiously at the newcomer. The smooth politician's manner had not left Gurinder Madahar, even though it was some years since he had been in office. He was an impressive figure, with dark, intelligent eyes framed by a black beard and navy turban, but from the neck down, his powerful body was dressed in a western-style beige tailored suit.

"Inspector Beary," he began, "my brother and his wife are extremely distressed. I understand that you must speak with them, but I shall of course be present as the family's legal representative. As Joban already told your constable, you will find that this terrible crime was committed by one who is an outsider to us, but all the same, discretion is essential. We are relying on you. Come." He gestured for Richard to follow him. "I will take you in to meet the members of my family. My niece is preparing tea. I am sure you would like some refreshment."

Richard held his ground.

"I am fine, thank you," he said politely, "but I'm sure your family will appreciate the tea. You have all had a terrible shock. While you are serving refreshments, I will speak to each member of the household individually—including the servants who were here this evening."

A frown flickered across Gurinder's features.

Richard kept his voice smooth. "Perhaps you can introduce me, and then we can retire to another room," he suggested. "The study would be fine," he added, indicating the open door. "I'm sure that would be preferable to bringing everyone down to the station." He looked the ex-minister directly in the eye. Gurinder returned his stare, and for a moment Richard expected him to argue. But then he conceded and said, "Of course. But not the study—the Guru Granth Sahib is there. That is where we held our morning prayers. We will use the dining room."

Gurinder looked at Richard closely and there was a flicker of amusement in the dark eyes as if he were waiting for a response.

"Your holy book. Yes, of course," said Richard. He mentally said a prayer of thanks to the powers-that-be who had drilled multicultural religious procedures into trainees for the force. He had just stopped himself in time before demanding to speak with the Guru as well as the family.

Gurinder nodded as if Richard had passed a test, and he turned and went through a door to the right of the hallway. Richard followed and stared at the group assembled in the room. Under WPC Howe's watchful eye, everyone sat silently. Richard's eye was immediately drawn to the only other woman present, partly because of her stunning midnight blue sari, which was edged with gold and further ornamented by glittering jewellery, but also because of her commanding presence. He had no difficulty identifying her as Constable Shield's Catwoman. She was an impressive woman, probably in her fifties, but her hair was still jet black and her face relatively unlined. Her features were strong rather than beautiful and her expression implied authority. Any bride who came into this household would have to toe the line, Richard thought, feeling a sudden wave of sympathy for the girl who was at present fighting for her life in the emergency ward of the hospital.

Two young men stood by Mrs. Madahar, presumably her sons. Richard eyed the taller one who was staring at him, or perhaps at Gurinder, with unveiled hostility. This must be Joban, he reflected. An older man sat on the far side of the room. Like Gurinder, he wore a western suit, but the eyes below the turban looked tired and sad, and unlike his brother's, his beard was greying. He sat bowed and defeated, his grief painful to see. Richard decided to see him first, and once Gurinder had introduced him, he stated his intention. Right away, he noticed a flicker of alarm cross Mrs. Madahar's face. Joban opened his mouth to speak, but his mother put a restraining hand on his arm. Looking intently at her husband, who had slowly risen to his feet, she said, "Can you cope, Navraj?"

Without looking at his wife, the man nodded, and still with his head hung low, he turned towards the door. Gurinder gave a reassuring nod to his sister-in-law, and then followed his brother from the room. As Richard went after them, the thought crossed his mind that Mrs. Madahar's question had sounded more like a warning than a statement of concern about her husband's condition.

Constable Shields stood in the hallway, notebook in hand. Richard gestured to him to follow and entered the dining room. Richard sat at the head of the long mahogany table and Constable Shields quietly took his place at the far end. Gurinder led his brother to a chair at the side of the table, then walked round and seated himself directly opposite. Richard waited a moment to let them get settled. He was about to speak when, suddenly, the constable's eyes lit up and his face broke into a wide smile. Richard swung round to see what had elicited this response. A young woman had entered the room. She was carrying a tea tray. The girl was exquisite, thought Richard. She was gowned in a pink choli dress, richly embroidered with silver and pearls, and the fabric floated gracefully as she moved. She looked towards her uncle, but Gurinder shook his head and signalled her away. She bowed her head slightly, and taking the tray, disappeared as quietly as she had come.

Richard turned to Navraj.

"Your daughter?"

The man nodded, but Gurinder replied.

"Yes," he said. "That is Arjan's sister, Jasmeet."

"I will need to talk with her too."

"Is that necessary? She knows nothing more than the rest of the family, and she did not go upstairs when we heard the cries. She remained with the children and her sister-in-law."

"Young people often know things that their parents do not," said Richard. "Her perspective may be useful."

Gurinder frowned, but said nothing. Richard turned to Navraj Madahar and asked him to describe the events of the evening. The man looked blank, and then glanced at his brother. Gurinder nodded encouragement.

"Go on, Navraj," he said. "Tell him what you heard and saw."

Navraj hung his head again and stared at the gleaming surface of the table. After a moment, he began to speak.

"We gathered here at the end of the day. It had been a wonderful wedding. My youngest son—"

"I think just the details of the evening—" Gurinder broke in.

Richard interrupted.

"No, that's fine, Mr. Madahar. Please. Tell us about the day. I'd like to hear."

Navraj Madahar raised his head and his gentle brown eyes seemed to visualize the scene.

"We commenced the day with prayers," he said softly. "Our family assembled here with great joy. My brother presented Arjan with the ceremonial sword—"

Richard cut in. "Was this different from the kirpan?"

Gurinder answered.

"Of course. It is a long sword that is used for special occasions. Arjan's kirpan is only nine inches in length."

"Where is the ceremonial sword now?"

"It was returned to me after we left the gurdwara—our temple. It is back at my own home. It did not enter this house after the wedding."

Richard decided not to debate the point. He asked Navraj to go on.

"We travelled to the temple together," Navraj said slowly. "The Loti family was waiting to greet us. We performed Ardas, and then we exchanged garlands. We had set up a magnificent tent beside the gurdwara and there we had tea before the ceremony."

Richard interrupted again.

"How did the young people behave?" he asked. "Did they seem happy?"

"Arjan was in a most good humour." Mr. Madahar appeared surprised at the question. "It was an excellent match."

"What about the bride? Ama . . ."

"Amanpreet. She is a quiet girl, but always most gracious. She had willingly accepted the marriage."

"So it was an arranged marriage?"

"Of course. But with the willing consent of both partners."

"So you sensed no tension between them. You felt that Amanpreet was as happy as your son?"

"I believe so. She was calm and serene throughout the day."

Gurinder broke in. "Amy is a most dutiful girl, but studious and serious—she was in her third year at UBC—and never a girl to giggle or laugh. Her behaviour was no different from any other time."

"So you do not believe her friend from university had meant anything to her?"

The Madahar brothers were startled by the question. Navraj appeared uncertain and apprehensive. Gurinder looked irritated.

"Your constable has obviously passed on what my nephew told him," he said.

"Yes." Richard turned back to Navraj. "Did you ever meet this young man?"

Navraj shook his head.

"Had you heard about the friendship?"

"A little. My daughter, Jasmeet, had mentioned that Amy had a friend from her classes."

"Did this not concern you?"

Navraj looked surprised.

"No. My wife said that a boy in Amy's class had misinterpreted her friendship. He had caused an embarrassing scene at the Lotis' house, but he had been made to understand that his feelings were not reciprocated. My wife was most insistent that there was nothing between them and no bar to Amanpreet's marriage to Arjan."

"Did your daughter agree with your wife?"

Again Navraj looked surprised.

"Of course."

And, thought Richard, I bet nobody disagrees with Mrs. Madahar. He resolved to find out Jasmeet's opinion of the relationship. He asked Navraj another question.

"Who was at the house this evening when the couple retired for the night?"

"Myself and my wife; our sons, Joban and Ramandeep; our daughter, Jasmeet; and Joban's wife, Nimrit, and their two sons."

"Is Ramandeep married?"

"Yes, but his wife is expecting a child in October and she did not feel like coming back after the festivities, so she went home. Both Joban and Ramandeep have their own houses. Only Arjan was to live here, along with his bride."

"Where is Joban's wife? I didn't see her when I came in."

"Joban sent her home along with the children. He did not want his family exposed to such a sorrowful situation."

Constable Shields coughed.

"That must have happened before we arrived, sir," he said. "We didn't let anyone leave."

Richard nodded and turned back to Navraj.

"Joban's family was here when you heard the screams from the bedroom?"

"Yes."

"Then I will need his address, and we will need to speak with his wife and children as well. Who went upstairs after the screams were heard?"

"I did, also my two sons. The door was locked." Mr. Madahar suddenly looked very old. "Joban had to break it open. When we saw what was inside, I called out to my wife not to let the others come up. Then I went to my son."

"Did he say anything?"

"No. I think he was conscious for a moment. He just looked at me, and then he slipped away. I thought he was dead."

"Then what did you do?"

"I held him. I think my wife had come up by then. She was in the room. I heard her talking to our sons."

"Who called for the ambulance?"

"I don't know. Perhaps my wife . . . or maybe Joban."

"Where was Arjan lying?"

"On the floor. He was leaning against the bed."

"And where was Amy?"

"She too was on the floor, but a little way from him. She was near the wall."

"Did you look out of the window at all?"

"No, I had eyes only for my son."

"So you didn't see the man running across the garden . . . the one that Joban saw?"

"No, I saw nothing."

"Did you not look up when you heard Joban cry out?"

"Cry out? What do you mean? He did not—"

"Navraj is tired and confused," Gurinder cut in. "He was preoccupied with Arjan. He would not have noticed anything else."

"Please don't answer for your brother." Richard was annoyed, but he kept his voice even. He rephrased the question.

"Did you hear Joban say anything when you were in the bedroom?"

"I don't remember. He was talking, I think, to my wife. They were saying something about a cellphone . . . they said the police had to be called. My wife asked me how Arjan was. I think after that, they left the room. Ramandeep came to kneel with me by Arjan. He told me that the ambulance was coming. I do not recall anything else."

"You are aware that Joban said he saw someone running across the garden?"

Navraj paused. "Yes, I believe so," he said finally.

"When did you realize that he had seen an intruder?"

"I . . . I am not sure. I—"

To Richard's annoyance, Gurinder interrupted again.

"Perhaps when they left the room," he suggested. "Did Joban tell you he was going outside to look for the man?"

Navraj looked relieved.

"Yes, I think that was it," he said quickly. "He was going to look for the man. I stayed with my son until the ambulance came." As if seeing the terrible sight again, Navraj stared into space and his eyes went blank. Suddenly a racking sob erupted from his throat. "He was a good boy," he cried. "He did not deserve that."

Richard gave up and ended the interview. He had already discovered what he needed to know.

* * *

Sergeant Martin was having his own difficulties at the hospital. He was finding the mother of the injured girl very hard to take. Sukhmani Loti had sent the rest of her family away, insisting that she alone would keep vigil over Amanpreet and deal with hospital staff and inquisitive policemen. She sat, dragon-like, in the waiting area, her intense glare putting off all but the bravest individuals from speaking with her. Bill Martin disliked her on sight, but he kept his face impassive as he approached her.

"Mrs. Loti, I need to ask you some questions."

He was rewarded with an icy stare.

Martin persisted. "Who notified you that your daughter had been injured?" he said. "Was it the hospital staff, or did the Madahars call you?"

Mrs. Loti glowered at him balefully but she answered the question.

"It was Manreet," she said. "Arjan's mother."

"What did she say to you?"

"She said there had been a terrible accident and that Amy had been hurt."

"An accident?"

"Yes. She told me that Amy was being taken to hospital and that she would join me there."

"Where is she? I haven't seen her."

"She came and went. Arjan is going to be all right. She did not stay."

"Did she speak to you about what happened?"

Sergeant Martin did not think it was possible for the woman's expression to grow any darker, but Mrs. Loti's face suffused with rage as she spat a reply.

"Yes. It was that boy. The one who had been harassing Amy. He broke into the house and attacked them."

"Did Mrs. Madahar tell you any details? How did the boy get in?"

"No. It does not matter how. He did it."

"Who is this young man?"

"His name is Darraby. He was a student in Amanpreet's English class. It was a Shakespeare course. They worked on a project together. He was nothing to her."

"Did you ever meet him?"

Mrs. Loti's eyes narrowed ominously.

"Yes. He came to the house. He asked to court our daughter. We told him she was already engaged to Arjan and he went away."

"Could your daughter not have told him about her engagement?"

"She had told him, but he refused to accept her word."

"But he accepted yours?"

"He was very angry. He threatened us, and he threatened Amanpreet."

"In what way?"

"He said he would make her suffer. Amy cried bitterly. He made things very hard for her."

"Is it possible that your daughter really loved this man in return?"

"Of course not. It is out of the question. She was a dutiful girl. She understood that the marriage we had arranged for her was a good one."

"So it was an *arranged* marriage?" said Sergeant Martin. As an afterthought he added, "And not a *forced* marriage?"

Sukhmani Loti turned on him furiously.

"That is an outrageous suggestion," she snarled. "How dare you suggest anything of the kind?"

I dare, thought Sergeant Martin dourly, because I grew up in Britain, and I've seen more horrible happenings in the name of ethnic traditions than you've seen in a month of Diwalis or Gurpurbs.

He was prevented from further comment by the appearance of a doctor. The man's expression was sombre, and sensing bad news, Martin stepped back and let the surgeon approach Mrs. Loti.

"I'm so sorry," the man began. He got no further. Sukhmani Loti stood up and addressed him calmly.

"Amanpreet is dead?"

"Yes. I'm afraid we could not save her. The wounds were too severe."

Mrs. Loti's face revealed no emotion. It could have been carved out of stone.

"It is better so," she said. Leaving the doctor stunned and silent, she picked up her bag and walked away.

* * *

Richard's instincts told him that the Madahars were concealing information. The story from each person was identical, which meant it was either true, or had been carefully memorized in the period of time between the call to the RCMP and the arrival of the first member of the force. He replaced Jean Howe with another constable and sent her to interview Joban's wife and children. He was curious to see if their stories tallied with those of the people who had remained at the house.

There was no question that Joban, Ramandeep and Mrs. Madahar had the details down pat. The screams had been heard around eight o'clock. Navraj, Joban and Ramandeep had run upstairs. Amy had been lying against the wall, still fully dressed, but bleeding profusely from the stomach and already unconscious. Arjan lay against the bed. He was naked, but a bloody towel lay halfway between the couple, and Ramandeep had used it to try to stop the bleeding from the wounds in his brother's chest and shoulder. Arjan too was unconscious. The French doors that led to a small balcony off the bedroom were open. Joban had gone onto the balcony and had seen someone running across the grass towards the lake. There was enough light spilling from the windows for him to get a good look at the man and he was ready to swear that it was David Darraby. Joban had come back inside and gone to the living room to tell his mother what had happened. Then his mother had gone upstairs while Joban ran outside to look for the intruder. He ran down to the small dock at the lake edge but could see nothing. However, he thought he could hear a splashing sound on the water. By the time he went back upstairs, his mother had called for an ambulance. At that point, he called the police.

By ten-thirty Richard was exhausted and feeling irritable. The manservant had proved useless. His English was poor and Gurinder's translations revealed absolutely nothing. Richard resolved to see the man later once he had acquired a translator through the station. The only person left to see was the daughter of the house. Richard suspected that she would have more insight into the true nature of the love triangle between her brother, his bride and David Darraby, but whether or not she would be forthcoming was another matter.

When Jasmeet entered the room, Richard saw that she had changed out of her outfit for the wedding and now looked like a typical Canadian student, although the jeans and shirt that she wore were of a brand few university students could afford. She was the first family member who appeared unaffected by Gurinder's presence and she settled at the dining table with a friendly smile. To Richard's surprise, she began the conversation.

"I didn't see anything, you know," she said. "I heard the shouting upstairs, but I didn't go up. Someone had to keep an eye on Jasdeep and Manvir. They wanted to go and see what was happening, and Nimrit was hysterical. She'd never have been able to stop them."

Richard put up a hand to stop the flow.

"You say you heard shouting as well as screams. Could you hear anything that was said?"

Jasmeet paused and thought carefully.

"No. I think by the time my attention was caught, they were screaming."

"They? Both of them? You heard a man and a woman?"

"Mostly her, I think. I heard Amy screaming. She was shrieking hysterically. I think I heard her cry out, 'No!' . . . and then I heard Arjan's voice. He sounded as if he was hurt badly. And then everything went quiet." Jasmeet frowned and pursed her pretty mouth. Finally she said, "It sounded like a terrible struggle was going on. That was the impression I had. I can't tell you any more than that."

"Tell me what everyone did after the screams stopped."

"My father and brothers went upstairs. Then a few minutes later, Joban came back and got my mother. He told me and Nimrit to stay in the living room with the boys, and then he went out and shut the door. About ten minutes later, he came back and told Nimrit to take the boys home. Then he told me to watch for the ambulance."

"The living room backs onto the garden, doesn't it?" said Richard. "Did you look out at all?"

Jasmeet shook her head.

"No. The curtains were drawn. I didn't see anyone running across the grass, if that's what you mean."

"And you didn't see your brother go outside to look for an intruder?"

"No. I think he went out while I was waiting with Nimrit and the children. I did hear the back door open soon after he'd asked me to stay with them. About five minutes later, I heard the door again and there were steps in the hall—that's when Joban came back and told Nimrit to take the boys home, so I guess that was him outside."

"When did you first hear about the intruder in the garden?"

"After the ambulance had left. My mother went to the hospital with Arjan, and then Joban came in and asked me to make tea. He said the police would be coming soon and would probably have to talk with us. He told me Arjan and Amy had been attacked by someone who had climbed the ivy and got in through the French doors. He said he'd caught a glimpse of the man running away and he was sure it was David." She turned to Gurinder. "And he said that you'd been called, Uncle," she added, "and that we weren't to answer any questions unless you were with us. So here I am," she concluded, turning back to Richard. "I hope you catch whoever it is. I'm glad Arjan is going to be

OK, but I'm so sorry for Amy." She looked very young, suddenly, and her eyes grew sad. "Is she going to die?"

Richard did not want to give false hope.

"Probably," he said. "It's not likely that she'll pull through."

Jasmeet looked close to tears.

"She was really nice," she said sadly. "It's so unfair."

"Was she your friend as well as your brother's fiancée?"

"We've known each other for a long time, but not really well. Our parents know each other through business, and we'd see each other at the temple, but we became friends through university. We ended up in some of the same classes and worked on a few projects together."

"Is that how you know David Darraby?"

For the first time, Jasmeet looked evasive.

"Yes. He was in a couple of classes with us. There was a whole group of us who became friends. We'd go to the coffee shop together or hang out at the beach, and we'd visit each other's homes."

"Is it true that David Darraby fell in love with Amy?"

Jasmeet sighed.

"Yes. He had it pretty bad."

"What about Amy? How did she feel about him?"

From the corner of his eye, Richard saw Gurinder give his niece a warning glance. Jasmeet paused, and then she looked rebellious.

"She was crazy about him too," she said. "Well, she was," she said defiantly to her uncle. "It didn't mean she did anything about it. She was far too timid to challenge her parents, but she did love him. You see," she continued, turning back to Richard, "Amy was really shy, so she didn't find it easy to make friends. She'd never got involved with boys because she was much too aloof to attract their attention. So when David decided he wanted her, *he* made the advances. No matter how inept she was at responding or flirting, he just kept on chatting to her until he broke down her reserve. And once she let go, she fell head over heels, even though she knew her parents would never approve. It made her very unhappy. Poor Amy. She was torn apart."

"Her parents would not have allowed a mixed-race marriage?"

"The Lotis? No way. They are hard-nosed traditionalists," said Jasmeet. "But to be fair," she added, "David would not have made a good husband and Amy was sensible enough to know that her parents were right."

"What was wrong with Darraby . . . other than the fact that he wasn't a Sikh?"

"He was a professional student—living on grants and taking courses, but no direction in life. He wants to be a writer, but he does very little except talk a lot and write the odd piece for the student newspaper. And he's so hot-tempered. Amy was really romantic, and I think she thought he was a sort of Byronic figure. He was always texting her with lines of poetry, or he'd get in a black mood and send her messages about killing himself if he ever lost her."

"Do you think he meant it?"

"No. He was just being dramatic, though he did have a genuine dark side, rather like Amy herself. He and Amy had both lost people they loved. David's high-school girlfriend died in a car crash the year they graduated, and Amy lost her older sister in a climbing accident. I think that's what brought them together because the subject came up during a seminar on Shelley. After that, they became constant companions on campus. David had Amy in absolute turmoil, and he kept insisting that they had to talk with her parents and convince them to let her marry him. Of course, that terrified Amy because she knew how her parents would react."

"So you believe she was happy about her marriage to your brother?"

Jasmeet paused again.

"You know, I don't think Amy was ever very happy about anything," she said wistfully. "She was so quiet and withdrawn you never knew what she was thinking. The only reason I know how she felt about David was because we went to a series of Shakespeare movies together when we were taking English 365. At the end of the di Caprio *Romeo and Juliet* she was bawling her eyes out, and she broke down and told me how she felt about David. But the next day, when I tried to talk to her, she clammed up again and refused to discuss it."

"She wouldn't talk at all? Not even to unburden herself to someone her own age?"

"No."

"How did her engagement to your brother come about? Did he hang around with your set at university too?"

Jasmeet looked surprised.

"No. Arjan is five years older than us. The marriage was arranged through our parents."

"Amy didn't have any problem with that?"

"Of course not. My parents will probably arrange a marriage for me too. Why should we object?"

"You seem like a thoroughly modern young woman," commented Richard. "Why would you not want to pick your own mate?"

"I will have a choice. My parents would never make me marry someone I didn't want. But what is wrong with them trying to find someone who will be a good husband to me? It's no different from Internet dating. Lots of Western women do that. In fact, we have all sorts of Internet sites available where we can look for potential matches. Besides, if I meet someone suitable myself, my parents would be perfectly happy to accept him. We simply approach the issue of marriage from a practical point of view and use every resource available to find the best options. Then the final choice lies with the woman herself. It is a very sensible system."

"So you will not be forced to marry against your will?"

Jasmeet laughed.

"No. You should see my aunt. She is thirty-five years old. She lives in Toronto and has a successful career as a lawyer. She says she's tried dating men that she meets *and* men that her parents have picked for her, and her final conclusion is that she has done just as well as they have in coming up with total deadbeats so she's going to stay single and enjoy her career. My grandparents aren't particularly happy about it, but they won't pressure her to change. They're very proud of her achievements."

"Your family is obviously sensible and caring," observed Richard. "Would you say that the Lotis are like your own parents?"

Gurinder had remained silent until now. Richard sensed that he was very proud of his bright, articulate niece, but now he interjected.

"The Lotis are a well-established family," he said. "They have been in Canada for twenty years and have been highly successful in the construction industry. They are a good family."

"I'm sure they are," said Richard evenly, "but according to your niece they are 'hard-nosed traditionalists'. How much choice would Amy have had?"

Jasmeet looked contemplative.

"I don't know," she admitted. "Amy's mother is very forceful. I think there would be a pretty big row if anyone went against her. Her father has quite a temper too. But it's not as if they'd picked someone awful for her. It's not like they'd forced her to go back to India to marry some friend they wanted to bring to Canada. Arjan is good-looking and lots of fun. Amy got along fine with him. She may not have been crazy about him, but she didn't dislike him. And let's face it," said Jasmeet, "if my brother is right and David is the one who broke in and attacked them, the Lotis were absolutely right about him." Jasmeet's pretty face assumed a fierce expression. The resemblance to her father faded and suddenly Richard discerned that she was her mother's daughter too. "He's obviously a maniac," she said angrily, "and if we were in India, he'd get what he deserved."

Before Richard could respond, his cellphone rang. He answered the call and listened gravely. Then he turned off the phone and looked solemnly at the pair seated at the table.

"There's no point in keeping this from you," he said. "I just heard from my sergeant at the hospital. I'm afraid it's bad news. Amanpreet Loti died half an hour ago."

Gurinder's face remained inscrutable, but Jasmeet's eyes flew wide and she gasped. She stared at Richard in disbelief, then her face crumpled and she burst into sobs. Her uncle put an arm round her shoulders to comfort her, but she continued to cry as if her heart would break.

* * *

Before Richard left the house, he went upstairs to check on the progress of the forensic team. Arjan Madahar's suite was luxurious, but it smacked more of the long-term male occupant than the newly arrived bride. The bedroom itself was more gender neutral, and would have had the air of a well-kept hotel room, had it not been for the white-clad figures working in the area and the bloodstains at the foot of the bed, against the wall, and on the carpet in between. Richard saw that the French doors were closed. Mary Wai, the petite woman who headed the forensic unit, noticed where he was looking.

"The doors were open," she said. "We've finished out there if you want to take a look."

"Can you tell if anyone came over the balcony?"

"It's possible. There's a patch of ivy to one side that looks as though it's been beaten up pretty well. I don't think the prints will tell us much because anyone who pulled himself over the rail would also have had to slide his whole body across, so the prints would be wiped out. But we'll check. And of course, anyone breaking in with intent to kill would have worn gloves."

"There may not have been intent to kill," said Richard thoughtfully. He was going to be very interested to hear David Darraby's side of the story.

He opened the doors and went out onto the small balcony. The lights from the arts centre on the far side of the water glimmered in the distance, but the inky blackness below the balcony revealed nothing of the garden or the lake beyond. Richard noted that all the downstairs lights at the back of the house were turned off, so he called to Constable Shields, who had followed him upstairs, and told him to run down and switch on the lights. A moment later, a single stripe of shimmering green appeared directly below the balcony. It was probably enough to illuminate a retreating figure, Richard decided, but hardly sufficient to guarantee an identification. He returned to the bedroom. Mary Wai was bagging and labelling a blood-soaked towel.

"There were two of these," she said. "One was a bath towel, and quite wet, and since I gather the groom was naked, my guess is that he'd had a shower and come out of the bathroom wrapped in the towel. The shower had been used. The other towel was smaller and quite dry except for the blood. It was probably used by the father when he tried to stop his son's bleeding."

"Is there blood anywhere else?"

"No. Just spattered in this one area. There was obviously quite a struggle."

"What about the groom's kirpan?"

"We've taken it, but honestly, I don't think it'll show anything. Clean as a whistle. This is interesting though," Mary added. "It's an old newspaper cutting. I found it in the girl's purse." She handed Richard a folded piece of paper. He opened it out and drew in his breath. He remembered the article well. The summer of 2000. The sad case of Jaswinder Kaur Sidhu, commonly known as Jassi. The Indian police were still trying to extradite the members of her family who they believed had ordered the girl killed. Amanpreet Loti had not defied her parents the way Jassi had, and Richard suddenly wondered if her compliance was motivated by fear? Uneasily, he remembered what Jasmeet had told him. *Amy's sister had died in an accident.* He resolved to review the records involving the girl's death.

Mary Wai spoke again and disturbed his reflections.

"There's something else rather interesting about this girl's purse," she said.

"Oh. Let me see the contents," said Richard. Mary was extremely sharp and he always appreciated any details that she brought to his attention.

"It's not what's in the contents," said Mary with an enigmatic smile. "Test your detecting skills," she challenged him. "See if you can figure out what's missing."

* * *

Bill Martin had strong views about the oppression of women in non-Western cultures. Having grown up in Britain and served briefly on the force there, he had dealt with several cases of killings in the name of family honour, and he had become familiarized with the issues of forced marriages, female circumcision, dowry murders, female baby killings, mutilations, and even bride burnings. As a result of his experiences, Martin had come to the firm conclusion that racial equality meant that members of minority cultures had the right to be villains as well as underdogs. He recognized that between the fairytale surrealism of Bollywood fantasies and the horror stories at the other end of the spectrum, there were a mass of nice families going lawfully about their everyday business, but his blood was up whenever he sensed that a young woman was being terrorized or put at risk because of relatives who put adherence to ancient traditions above a daughter's physical and emotional well-being.

"Canada is way behind Britain," he grumbled to Richard. "England has enacted legislation to deal with the issue of forced marriages, but here they're still refusing to send over the family members who ordered the killing of that poor young woman from Maple Ridge. How much is it going to take before we wise up? I really get the pip from these bleeding-heart politicians who say they're both feminists and supporters of multiculturalism. Haven't they figured out that the two don't go together?"

"Since you're so hot on the subject," said Richard, "I'd like you to check the details on the death of another South Asian girl. Amy Loti's sister died in a climbing accident two years ago. See what you can find out?"

Martin flinched. "God, two in one family. Yes, I'll check up on it all right. Incidentally, on the subject of murdered women, the autopsy results are in. Amy's wounds were definitely made with a kirpan—about nine inches, the pathologist reckons. But it wasn't the one belonging to Arjan Madahar, because Mary Wai called to say there were no traces of blood on the kirpan in the bedroom."

"Darraby was supposed to have a kirpan," said Richard. "We'll have to bring it in. He's in the interview room right now. I'm going down to talk with him, but before I do, I wanted to know if Jean Howe has reported back. I'd like to know the results of her interview with Joban Madahar's family."

"She'll be in shortly. She went to the photographers to pick up copies of the wedding photos that were taken after the ceremony, and then she ran by the Shadbolt Arts Centre to see if anyone had seen Darraby last night."

"And had they?"

Sergeant Martin grinned. "No, but she got lucky at the canoe rental. Turns out Darraby worked there all summer, and around seven o'clock yesterday evening, he popped in to pick up his cheque."

"Well, I'll be damned. So he *was* there. Joban's story could have been correct." Richard stood up and headed for the door. "This interview is going to prove very interesting."

When he reached the interview room, David Darraby was seated next to a sandy-haired woman whom Richard recognized as a particularly irritating legal-aid lawyer who tended to automatically equate poverty with innocence and rarely bothered to look at any evidence that contradicted her opinion. Constable Shields sat cheerfully on the other side of the table, his face vaguely reminiscent of a terrier eyeing a pile of dog biscuits. Richard eyed Darraby curiously. He could see why Amy had fallen for him. The man was incredibly good-looking, with black hair and deep blue eyes, and with the gypsy air of a Heathcliff, which would have appealed to a girl who was an ardent lover of romantic literature. Yet something about the man grated on Richard. Style but no substance was the thought that came to mind.

As soon as Richard sat down and declared the interview open, Darraby's lawyer spoke.

"My client is prepared to make a statement," she said. "David spent yesterday evening at the Shadbolt Centre for the Arts. He was attending a play at the James Cowan Theatre. The curtain was at eight o'clock and the show was not over until eleven. There are witnesses who saw him there. Since the attack at the Madahar residence occurred around eight o'clock, he could not possibly have been involved and I am demanding that he be allowed to leave immediately and not be subjected to further questioning."

Richard ignored the lawyer and turned to David Darraby.

"David, if you cared about Amy Madahar, I presume you want her killer caught. Therefore, you will want to assist us in any way you can."

Darraby hesitated, seeing the snare but not knowing how to avoid it. He glanced uneasily towards his lawyer. She tightened her lips, then nodded briefly. Darraby turned back to Richard.

"I don't know what I can tell you. Amy and I loved each other, but her family bullied her into accepting an arranged marriage and she broke up with me."

"Were you angry when she rejected you?"

"Of course I was angry, but there was nothing I could do about it. I just told her what I thought of her and her family and her customs. And that was that."

"When did this break-up happen?"

"In the spring."

"And yet you got a summer job just down the lakeshore from her fiancé's home? Wasn't that rather an odd thing to do?"

Darraby grinned unpleasantly.

"Not really. I was hoping to see her and make her change her mind."

"Didn't it upset you, having failed, to go there on the night that she had married your rival? Why put yourself through the torture of seeing the house across the lake where you knew she was spending the night with her new husband?"

Darraby looked uneasy but he answered the question.

"I was there because I had tickets for the play," he said. "And I was owed money from my summer job so I decided I'd go early and pick up my cheque."

"You say there are witnesses who saw you at the play. Did you sit with these friends?"

"No, but I had coffee with them during the intermission."

"Did they see you before the play started?"

"I doubt it. I went for a walk around the gardens. I didn't go inside until just before the curtain."

"So unless we can find a witness who can vouch for your attendance during the first half of the play, there's nothing to say that you did not arrive until the intermission—in which case you would have had all the time in the world to take a canoe across the lake and go to the Madahar property. You'd better give us your seat number so we can check with the people who were sitting around you."

Darraby shifted uncomfortably.

"It was festival seating," he said, "and there weren't many people there. I sat at the back, but that section of the theatre was empty. I doubt if anyone saw me."

The carrot-topped lawyer cut in firmly.

"I'd like a private word with my client," she said.

Richard nodded. As he got up, he fired off one more question.

"Did you make any attempt to contact Amy on the day of her wedding?" he asked.

The gimlet eye of the lawyer prevented Darraby from answering, but to Richard's intense satisfaction, he flushed dark red and the furious scowl on his face was as clear an affirmative as if he had signed an oath of confirmation. Richard turned back as he reached the door.

"So what did the text message say?" he asked.

"Inspector!" Sandy-hair's eyes bulged over the top of her spectacles.

Richard smiled and left the room. Constable Shields followed him out. He looked annoyed.

"You're not going to let them off that easily, are you, sir?" he protested.

"They can stew for a while," said Richard. "I'm going to have a coffee. That legal-aid harpy may be a pain in the backside, but she won't let her client make a total fool of her. She'll dig the truth out of him, and when I come back, Darraby will either refuse to say anything, in which case we'll know he was up to no good, or he'll spill the beans and in the process, hopefully, point us in the right direction."

"What was that about a text message?" Shields asked. "Don't we have her phone?"

"No," said Richard. "Mary Wai brought my attention to that. Amy's cellphone wasn't anywhere in her purse or in the room. And that tells me there must have been something on it that someone did not want us to see. I think Darraby tried to contact her that day. Remember how Jasmeet Madahar said he was forever texting her. I think he made one last attempt to get Amy to run away with him."

Constable Shields looked excited.

"That would explain why he was at the arts centre. He could have let her know he was waiting, ready to bring a canoe across the lake to get her. It was dark. No one would have seen. All she had to do was slip out to the bottom of the garden."

"So did he actually come across," pondered Richard, "or did someone else see the message that was intended for Amy? That's what we have to find out."

"Jesus," said Constable Shields. "What if the groom had seen that message? You know how proud these East Indians are. Do you think Arjan turned on her? He could have been wounded as she tried to defend herself."

"It's frighteningly possible," said Richard. "But of course there's one fatal glitch."

Constable Shields looked blank.

"What, sir?"

"Come on, Shields, think," snapped Richard. "If you want to become a detective, you'll have to do better than that."

Shields looked taken aback for a moment, and then the light came on.

"Oh," he said. "The knife. There was no weapon in the room."

"Exactly."

Before Shields could reply, Jean Howe came down the corridor. She was carrying a folder, and when she reached Richard, she opened it and revealed the contents.

"It's the wedding photographs, sir," she said. "Just the proofs, but it's what we need. Look at her, poor girl. One of the Madahar grandchildren told me that he held her hand before they went into the temple and he said it felt as cold as ice."

Richard stared at the photograph at the top of the pile. It was a group picture of the bride and groom with their parents. Arjan Madahar looked proud and happy, and his father was beaming with delight. Arjan's mother was also smiling, though her bearing was more dignified and reserved. But the Lotis presented a totally different picture. The parents' smiles looked forced, and more triumphant than joyful, but it was Amy's face that chilled Richard's blood. It was a ghost face, pale and expressionless, as if the person behind the features had already left and was somewhere on a far plain, or even in another world. There was no more life in the figure in the photograph than in the sad remains that lay in the morgue.

Jean Howe interrupted his thoughts. "Sir," she said, "I managed to talk with Nimrit Madahar and both her sons before her husband returned last night. It's significant."

Richard looked up from the wedding picture. "Go on," he said.

"Nimrit Madahar didn't see anything that night, but she did admit to me that Amy Loti was pressured by her parents into accepting the marriage. She doesn't like the senior members of the Loti family at all. Evidently Nimrit was a friend of Simar Loti—Amy's sister—the one who died two years ago. Nimrit says that Simar was being pressured to go back to India to marry a cousin who wanted to immigrate to Canada. The man was a lot older and he'd been married before. Nimrit also seemed to think he'd been abusive to his first wife. Anyway, Simar was taken back to India to meet the man, and after their first meeting, she tried to kill herself by drinking bleach. She recovered and was brought back to Canada, where she continued to defy her parents and hold out, but finally they broke her down and she agreed to the marriage. The next day, she went up onto Burnaby Mountain and threw herself off the cliff at the top. She killed herself rather than go through with the match."

"Good God," said Richard. "Then didn't Nimrit Madahar have reservations about the marriage that had been arranged for Amy Loti and Arjan?"

"Not really. She could tell Amy was being pressured, but she felt it was a different situation because Arjan was young and attractive. She believed Amy would have learned to love him once she got over her passion for the Darraby boy."

"What was her assessment of Arjan? Did he know about Amy's love for Darraby?"

"Good grief, no," said Jean. "I gather that was a well-kept secret among the womenfolk."

"Would Arjan have been jealous or angry if he had found out?"

"I asked her that," said Jean. "She said there might have been a bit of a row, but she said Arjan was a kind young man at heart, and as long as it had been only a friendship and not an affair, he would have been understanding. To be honest," said Jean, "it sounds as if Arjan really was a more decent man than Darraby, but of course, that's irrelevant when dealing with a young girl's emotions—look at all the tales of woe from Victorian novels. Anyway," she continued, "that was about all Nimrit could tell me, but her sons were little mines of information. Their names are Jasdeep and Manvir and they're as cute a little pair of devils as you've ever seen. They're going to create havoc with a few female hearts when they're older. Incidentally, they told me it's quite possible to climb up the ivy to the balcony off Arjan's bedroom because I gather they do it all the time."

"Do they, indeed?" said Richard. "That might explain the bare patch beside the railing. They didn't happen to be up there that night, did they?"

"No. They wouldn't have been that naughty. Actually, they were playing basketball in the front yard. I guess that was more interesting than the boring grown-up talk in the living room. But after the attack, their mother called them inside. She said she was taking them home, but Manvir had to go to the washroom before they left, and he says he saw Joban go by with a bundle. It looked like a towel. And there's something else that's going to knock you sideways," Jean added triumphantly. "I asked them about their uncle's kirpan and they waxed most enthusiastic and gave me a complete description. It was a brass hilt with a steel blade, nine inches long, and it has the sign of the Khalsa on the top."

"Yes, we know that," said Richard. "It was in the room, still in the holster. There's no blood on it. It wasn't the weapon that killed Amy."

Jean looked smug.

"Yes, but as the boys pointed out, kirpans come in a lined box. Did you find a case like that in the room?"

"No, we didn't actually. But that's hardly relevant. It could have been kept anywhere."

"Maybe," said Jean, "but it's my bet that someone moved it."

"Why would they do that?"

"Because," said Jean, "it was a double case for a set of two. Arjan had two identical kirpans. Look on the Internet. You can see the exact same model. It comes as a set."

"What do you know?" Richard shook his head. "Well done, Jean."

"And I'm willing to bet," Jean concluded, "that the second knife was in the towel that Joban was carrying when he went out into the garden. And right now, it's probably buried in the mud at the bottom of Deer Lake."

"Along with Amy's cellphone," said Richard.

"What about Darraby, sir?" asked Constable Shields. "We still haven't finished with him."

"No," said Richard, "we haven't. I'm going back in there to put the heat on him. I want to know exactly what that message said. I have a feeling it's going to prove to be the thing that triggered the final tragedy."

But before Richard could return to the interview room, Bill Martin came into the hall and called him back.

"Darraby can wait," said Martin. "I just received a message from Gurinder Madahar. Arjan is conscious and he wants to talk to us."

* * *

As Richard prepared to tie up the Madahar case, his youngest sister had sunk into a state of utter despondency. Her virus had mutated and turned into strep throat, and she had been ordered by the doctor to rest her voice for three weeks. As a result, she had been forced to withdraw from the opera chorus for the next production. When her father came to visit, even though her voice was on the mend, he found her in a singularly gloomy frame of mind.

"Perk up, old girl," said Beary. "Missing one opera is not the end of the world. And look at it this way, you'll be able to sit out front with the rest of us and see Robin's debut as Lucia from the house."

"But I was so looking forward to being on stage for the mad scene. It's different close up. You get to act out the story. You're a part of it. It's exhilarating."

"Yes, well that may be, but you'll have to exhilarate from the lower orchestra. Now, stop feeling sorry for yourself and tell me what you've gleaned from reading the book I brought you."

Beary's tactic worked, as he knew it would. Philippa was diverted.

"It's a fascinating story," she said. "Scott's tale is like a casebook on brainwashing. It sounds as if the mother simply isolated her daughter and systematically broke her will. It's certainly feasible, especially given the limited rights that daughters had and the power their families exerted over them. So it's definitely possible that the real-life Janet broke under pressure and went berserk on her wedding night. But it bothers me a bit." Philippa frowned. "Everything points to her being such a gentle girl. Would madness change that basic character? It's not quite right."

"So what do you suggest?" asked Beary.

"I'm not sure. I did a bit of research on the Internet—it was fascinating. Did you know that Joan Sutherland went to visit the grave of Janet Dalrymple? There's a photo of her in the churchyard. Anyway, there are all sorts of different versions, and each one shows up if you go to the Baldoon Castle site, so obviously the historians have not accepted any one version as correct. So if you approach the incident from the point of view of a detective story, you have to look at the basic facts."

Beary smiled and nodded. He had always enjoyed encouraging his children to play deductive games. "And what are the basic facts?" he said.

Philippa shrugged. "Janet died. The groom survived."

"Exactly," said Beary. "And where does it go from there?"

"I don't know. I suppose some things are a given. She had a proud family who had pressured her into giving up the man she loved and marrying the man of their choice. Her lover had railed at her and probably hurt her deeply by turning on her when she renounced him. Her younger brother reported that her hand was icy cold on the way to the church, which would suggest that she was suffering from a combination of stress and fear. She was obviously depressed, frightened and deeply troubled. What happened after that is anyone's guess. One story says Janet attacked Dunbar. Another says Dunbar attacked her. And a third story says her lover, Lord Rutherford, broke into the bridal chamber and attacked them both. The most baffling thing of all is the fact that the groom flatly refused to say what had happened and remained silent until the day he died."

"So," said Beary smugly, "what you have to do is think up a scenario that fits all those pieces of evidence. And that," he added firmly, "should keep you from feeling sorry for yourself until it's time for the opera to open. I shall offer you a deal. I will treat the family to top-price tickets for the best seats in the house, and in return, I expect a brilliant theory to be forthcoming in time for opening night."

* * *

When Richard and Sergeant Martin reached the hospital, they found Gurinder Madahar waiting for them by the information desk. He took them up to the private room where Arjan was recovering from his wounds. Arjan was sitting up in bed. His colour was good, and only the bandages around his chest and shoulder indicated why he was hospitalized. His mother sat in the chair by his bed, and his father stood behind her. Joban stood a little apart, staring out the window.

Navraj Madahar greeted the police officers courteously. Then, without waiting for any intervention from his brother, he said quietly,

"My son would like to tell you what happened. Go on, Arjan," he added, looking towards the bed.

Arjan appeared apprehensive, but he took a slow, careful breath and began.

"Amy was very quiet all day," he said. "I put it down to her usual shyness. I knew she had been friendly with a boy at university who had asked her to marry him, but I had no idea how deeply she felt about him. I thought her decision to marry me had been made willingly. But as the day went on, she seemed even more subdued, and when we retired for the night, I could feel her tension, so I tried to give her some space. I told her I was going to have a shower, and I took my time. But when I turned off the water and stepped out of the shower, I felt a cold chill in the air and I could hear crying. I wrapped a towel around myself and went out to see what was wrong. Amy was standing out on the balcony, looking across to the far side of the lake. She was sobbing her heart out. I saw that she had her cellphone open in her hand. I don't think she even noticed when I took it from her. There was a text message. It said, 'I'm standing watching you from the far side of the lake. You can't go through with this, not knowing I'm here. Just give me the signal and I'll come across to get you, and if you don't come, just remember . . . I'm here . . . I'm watching your window. *I'm watching you with him.*'" Arjan's face twisted at the memory. "He was very cruel," he said. "If only he had left her alone, I could have made her happy in time."

"Perhaps," said Richard, "but she wasn't given time. I think she was afraid to disobey her parents, and between their coercion and the pressure from Darraby, she was tormented to distraction. What happened to cause the struggle? Were you angry when you read the message?"

"No," protested Arjan. "Well, yes. I was angry with the man. I wasn't angry with Amy. I was sorry for her. I put down the phone and went to comfort her, but when I put my arm around her, she pulled away and ran back into the bedroom. Her crying turned into the most dreadful sound I've ever heard. She pulled my kirpan out of the holster and held the blade against herself. She kept crying that she couldn't go on . . . for me to stay away from her. I tried to get the kirpan away from her. I grabbed her wrist and pulled it away from her body, but she resisted and flailed with her arm, and the blade sliced into my chest and up through my shoulder. I guess I let go and clutched at myself, and—"

The young man caught his breath and fell silent. His father moved forward and gently put his hand on his son's shoulder.

"Go on, my son," he said.

Arjan composed himself and looked Richard in the eye.

"As I let go, Amy's arm shot back towards her body and the blade went right into her stomach. I saw her eyes roll back in her head. She fell like a rag doll. I think I staggered towards the bed where the phone was. I knew I had to get help. And then I must have passed out. I remember nothing else until I awoke here in hospital." Arjan looked imploringly at Richard. "You must believe me," he said. "That's exactly how it happened. She may not have meant to kill herself . . . but she was pulling so hard, and when I let go . . . it was just a terrible accident."

Richard nodded.

"I believe you," he said, "but that still doesn't answer all my questions." He looked long and hard at Joban, who remained skulking by the window. Richard turned back and stared at Mrs. Madahar. She looked back defiantly and spoke. Her voice was icy.

"It was not Joban's fault," she said. "He did what I told him to do. I told him to take the phone and the kirpan and throw them in the lake."

"And to replace the kirpan with the duplicate and dispose of the box that came with the set?"

"Yes."

Richard looked back coldly.

"You also told him to pin the blame on David Darraby."

"Why not? It was his fault. He caused nothing but trouble. He should have left Amy alone."

Navraj broke in.

"Please, we know it was wrong, but we did not know what had happened. We were ashamed, and we were afraid."

Gurinder had been silent all this time, but finally he spoke.

"My sister-in-law knows that her behaviour was wrong," he said, "but I hope you will show discretion and pity for a mother who was desperate to protect her son. When she read the message on the cellphone, she was afraid that Arjan had turned on Amy in anger. She was beside herself with fear. But as soon as she discovered the truth, she called me and explained that we had to let Arjan talk to the police. I am sure in this unhappy situation, now that your case is concluded, you will not proceed with charges of perverting the course of justice." Gurinder gave Richard a calculating glance. "The RCMP has many more important cases to solve," he said. "And after all, justice has not been perverted, has it?"

Richard's mouth tightened and he was about to answer when Navraj stepped forward and quietly addressed him.

"Inspector Beary, we hope matters will go no further, but we are, of course, prepared to answer for what has been done. You must make your own decisions as to how to proceed. For above all, I wish you to understand that we are a proud family and a good family, and we are able to follow both our faith and the laws of our chosen country without conflict or reservation. I thank you for all your help."

He put out his hand, first to Richard and then to Sergeant Martin.

When they were outside the room, Richard shook his head wearily. Lack of sleep and the tension generated from tiptoeing through the minefield of a culturally diverse investigation had caught up with him. Sergeant Martin was the first to speak.

"The old boy seems a pretty good sort," he said dourly, "and Arjan is probably all right. But that Joban is an arrogant bugger, and so is his uncle. The mother's a pain too. As far as I can see, Gurinder and the Queen Bee are so full of themselves I'm surprised they don't detonate. But the worst villains in this are the Lotis and pretty-boy Darraby. They're the ones that really perverted justice. The official ruling may end up being either suicide or accident, but the reality is, between them, they murdered the poor girl."

He banged the button to summon the elevator and scowled at the doors until they opened.

Richard felt his shoulders sagging as he followed Martin into the elevator.

"Yes," he agreed sadly. "Poor little Amy didn't get any justice at all."

* * *

The Queen Elizabeth Theatre was buzzing with excitement. Robin Tremayne had wowed Vancouver audiences in 2004 when she had stepped in at the last minute to replace Lisa Metz as Turandot. Since then, her career had shot steadily upwards, and her return to her home city to make her debut in *Lucia di Lammermoor* had been eagerly anticipated by local opera buffs.

Philippa made her way through the crowds in the lobby, stopping to chat with acquaintances who were pleased and surprised to see her out front for once. Then she joined her brother and parents in the lower orchestra.

"You took your time," said Beary. "I thought we had a deal."

"We do," said Philippa, "and I'll tell you my theory at intermission. I couldn't help being slow. Everyone I met wanted to know why I wasn't on stage. I'll have another bout of laryngitis just from having to explain why over and over again."

A burst of applause erupted as the conductor entered the pit. Philippa and Beary fell silent and turned their attention to the stage. The audience waited patiently through the narrative of the opening scene, and then the lights dimmed a second time and the glorious sound of the harp interlude rippled through the auditorium.

When the lights came back up, Robin was poised at the edge of the fountain. She looked ethereal, and deceptively frail—for the demands of the role called for an iron constitution—and as she started to sing, her voice seemed to float as eerily as the spectre of the fountain, a fusion of darkness and brightness that hinted at the instability to come. Philippa ceased regretting her temporary exile from the chorus and watched enthralled as her friend negotiated the gloomy foreshadowing of "Regnava il Silenzio" and the brilliant coloratura of "Quando Rapito in Estasi". Suddenly grateful to her father for his gift, she saw depths in Lucia that she had never noticed before.

At intermission, the Bearys trooped out to the lobby. Taking advantage of Edwina's sighting of an old school friend, Beary trundled over to the bar and returned with two large Scotches for himself and Richard, and a bottle of water for Philippa. He handed round the drinks, and then looked expectantly at his daughter.

"Well," he demanded. "Don't you have something to tell us?"

Philippa smiled.

"All right," she said. "Here goes. I started to make progress when you posed the question: 'Is there a scenario that fits all the evidence?' I thought about that for a long time, and ultimately, there was only one solution I could come up with."

"Fill me in," said Richard. "Is there some mystery I haven't heard about?"

"A literary one," said Beary. "Don't worry. The RCMP doesn't have to get involved. Go on," he added, turning back to Philippa.

"Everything I read suggested that Janet Dalrymple was a gentle, passive girl," said Philippa, "which was why she was so easily manipulated and bullied into submission by both her mother and her lover. But because of her benign nature, I honestly couldn't see her attacking someone with a dagger. But there was no doubt that she was in a terrible state by the time she was on her way to church. Remember how her brother said that her hand was cold. That suggests she was frightened and stressed, but she was obviously resigned to her fate. Then I thought about the story that said Lord Rutherford was present that day and had carried out the attacks. Well, that seemed ludicrous too, but if he was still railing against his rejection, he might have been close by, maybe outside the castle, or somewhere en route. What if he had contacted Janet again on her wedding day? That might have been enough to send her over the edge into utter despair. Then there were the stories that her new husband attacked her, but that seemed ridiculous too. Why would he draw a dagger on his new bride, no matter how upset she was? And then a possible answer occurred to me. What if Janet was so distraught that she grabbed her bridegroom's dagger and threatened to kill herself? What if Dunbar tried to stop her? Both could easily have been wounded in the course of a struggle, but of course, Janet's wounds proved ultimately fatal and she died two weeks later. And that," said Philippa triumphantly, "would explain why the groom refused to say what happened and maintained silence for the rest of his life. Suicide was a mortal sin. If he'd indicated that Janet's wounds were self-inflicted, she would not have been buried in consecrated ground. Wouldn't a gentleman have taken that position in order to protect the lady he'd married? If he had an ounce of decency, and the reports one reads suggest he was a nice enough young man, then he would have tried to protect her memory—and if you look at it from that point of view, it explains all the bits and pieces of information that people came out with. Anyway, that's the conclusion I came to. At last I said to myself why couldn't all the stories be true?"

"Well thought out, young lady," said Beary. "A reasonable explanation for the tragic mystery of Janet Dalrymple. Everyone conspired to break her spirit but her husband tried to save her soul. Why shouldn't that be the solution?"

Richard had been standing on the sidelines, but he had been listening fascinated while his sister talked. To his father's surprise, he entered the conversation with three simple words.

"Why not indeed?" he said.

He drained his glass, set it on the ledge by the bar and walked back through the doors to the auditorium.

Philippa and Beary looked at each other, surprised. But before they could comment, the chimes started ringing. The legendary Mad Scene was about to begin.

THE DEVIL MAY CARE

"Very devilish," said the saleswoman in the costume boutique. "In the glamorous sense, of course."

"Perfect," said Philippa. "That's exactly the look I want."

"New boyfriend?" The assistant, whose name was Katya, smiled wisely. "Or getting even with the ex?"

"Possibly both," said Philippa. "I'm going to the opera guild's costume ball at the Pan Pacific and my mother has paid for a table of eight. She gave one of the tickets to a new lawyer at my sister's firm, and according to Sylvia—that's my sister—he's extremely hot."

"So are you in that outfit," said Katya. "Are you with the opera?"

"Yes, I sing in the chorus. I gather you're giving us discounts for the event."

"Yes, that's right. This boutique is simply a retail outlet that's owned by Dresco."

Philippa recognized the name. The company was a major supplier for the theatre and movie industry. She turned back and studied her reflection in the long mirror. The black velvet leotard was cut low and swirls of red sequins curled like flames from the thighs and the shoulders, making her slender figure look even more streamlined than it was. The fishnet tights were flattering to the legs too, Philippa thought, swinging this way and that as she scrutinized her image in the mirror. She raised her eyes and examined her face, which looked rather washed out under the deep bangs of the shoulder-length red wig.

"You don't think the wig is too cheap-looking, do you?" she asked. "I love the devil's horns sticking up from the crown, but the colour is pretty flashy."

"It's Halloween," Katya pointed out. "You want to be flashy. Besides, you aren't wearing any makeup. Once you paint your face to go with the costume, you'll look perfect."

Philippa nodded. She had to concede the point, and she rather relished the prospect of going to the ball as the very antithesis of Cinderella. Adam's defection had put her in a rebellious frame of mind.

"This goes with the costume too." Katya whipped out a glittering black mask. "If you don't want to use a lot of makeup, you can just wear this and you'll only need lipstick. Either way, you're going to look fabulous."

"Do you really think so?"

"No doubt at all. Have you rented from us before?" Katya asked.

"No," said Philippa. "Usually, if I need a costume, I get something from one of the theatre companies. I did that for my brother—I borrowed a policeman's outfit from *Penzance*—but my mother and I decided it would be fun to go all out for this event. She came in last week, but I've been so busy that I haven't had a chance until today."

"What costume did your mother choose?"

Philippa smiled.

"A very appropriate one. She's the most imperious lady I know."

"Ah," said Katya. "Good Queen Bess."

"That's the one."

"She is rather autocratic," said Katya. "She was very annoyed that your father refused to rent a costume."

Philippa laughed.

"Yes. He's going to the ball on sufferance. He said if he had to endure a dinner dance, he'd at least be comfortable, so he's putting together some old sheets and going as Julius Caesar."

Katya clucked her tongue disapprovingly.

"That won't complement your mother at all. She looked quite magnificent."

"I know. But Dad dug in his heels, so my mother will probably stick him in a corner and pretend he's with someone else. Anyway, back to me. You're sure this will be OK?"

"Yes. It's one of our most popular costumes for Halloween. I have half a dozen in stock, and I always rent every one of them. When they come back, the ladies who wore them say they had a wonderful time. That's the last one I have."

"Right," said Philippa. "I'll take it."

She went back into the cubicle and changed into her own clothes, but feeling suddenly mischievous, she kept the wig on. She emerged from the dressing room and took the outfit to the cash desk.

"I'll wear the wig home," she said, "just to get the feel of it." Secretly, she wanted to test the reaction of other people when she passed by. Humour she could take, but if she found herself being propositioned before she had walked back to her car, she would rethink the wig and do something with her own hair.

She looked around the racks of costumes while Katya filled out the rental agreement. The boutique was still well stocked. There were period gowns and soldiers' uniforms, sultans' robes and Cleopatra-like diaphanous draperies, ballerina tutus and tiger suits, but presumably most of the rentals for the evening were already out, for none of the remaining costumes remotely smacked of Halloween. One was the flip side of her own outfit—an angel's gown made of silver thread with huge feathered wings that glittered with sparkling sequins.

"Gorgeous, isn't it?" said Katya, looking up from the rental agreement and following Philippa's glance. "That's one of our most expensive models. I only have two of them. They don't usually go out for Halloween, but the other one is currently in use. There's a fancy-dress ball at Jericho and everyone's going as movie characters. The lady who rented that—she's a widow, a real charmer—is engaged to Harold Morgenstern. He's the H & H Family Restaurant mogul—pots of money there."

"Isn't he married? You always see pictures of him with his wife and family all over the walls of his restaurants."

"He's a widower," said Katya. "He's also a junkie for old movies, and he particularly likes the Eddy-MacDonald musicals. That's probably why he fell for Jane Banks. She looks a bit like Jeanette MacDonald—you know, big blue eyes and masses of long, curly auburn hair. They're going to announce their engagement at the party this evening. As they break the news, the band is going to play 'I Married an Angel'. Romantic, isn't it?"

"Very," agreed Philippa. "The movie theme sounds fun too."

"Yes," said Katya. "Of course, some people are trying to find movies with Halloween themes—Morgenstern's sister and her husband are doing the whole *Dracula* thing, which certainly suits *him* because he's pretty creepy to begin with—but others are snapping up the classic movie costumes. Morgenstern's accountant and his wife are going as Scarlett and Rhett. Mind you, that was *her* choice and it had nothing to do with nostalgia. She chose the green velvet suit that was made from the drapes at Tara because she was getting over the flu and wanted to be covered from head to toe. It can be draughty at the boat club."

"Sensible," said Philippa.

Katya sniffed disdainfully. "Yes, that just about sums up Sue Whitmore . . . and her husband too, come to that. William Whitmore is a born bean counter. A less adventurous Scarlett and Rhett the world will never see. But they pay their bills, so who am I to complain?" Katya prattled on, happy to gossip about her clients. "Morgenstern's brother is a bit of a stick too," she confided, "but I love his wife. Sally Morgenstern is one of my best customers. She's smart too. She's combined Halloween, movies and the current Broadway hit, all in one fell swoop."

"*Wicked!*" crowed Philippa.

"Right on," said Katya. "She's made her husband dress up as the Scarecrow and she's going as The Wicked Witch of the West. There you are," she added, pushing the rental agreement across the counter.

Philippa signed the contract and paid for the costume. Then, still wearing the wig, she left the boutique.

The walk to the parking lot was reassuring. Everyone she passed looked at her, but the smiles were friendly and the jokes good-natured, so she started to feel more comfortable. The pattern continued as she drove home. Halloween was proving to be rather fun, Philippa thought. She heard a high-pitched cry and looked to her left. A station wagon was overtaking her, and the two young girls in the back seat were waving. She waved back, and the car pulled ahead, with the little girls still staring back at the friendly devil in the Chevy Cavalier.

As she turned off the highway onto Canada Way, Philippa saw that the cars ahead were stopped all the way up the hill. She looked at the clock on the dashboard. It was four o'clock, the height of rush hour. Resigned to a slow crawl to New Westminster, she pulled out a Dawn Upshaw CD and popped it into the slot. Soon, the airy lyric tones of the soprano drowned out the noise of traffic and soothed her impatience at the stops and starts as the cars inched forward. After ten minutes, she reached the light at Burris. She just made it through before the light changed to red, but as soon as she cleared the intersection, the traffic ground to a halt. In her rear-view mirror, she saw a man crossing the road with a golden retriever that was leaping about and straining at the leash. Not a well-trained pet, Philippa thought. Even MacPuff, for all his idiosyncrasies, knew to walk properly on his lead.

Suddenly, she sensed eyes on her again. She glanced across to the cars in the oncoming lanes, and then she broke into a smile. A BMW was stopped at the light and Count Dracula was waving at her from the driver's seat. She waved back, and the count gestured to her to roll down her window. He was putting his own window down, and although she felt mildly apprehensive, Philippa lowered her window. After all, he was driving an expensive car and might simply want directions. However, when she leaned out to see what he wanted, she immediately regretted her action, for the count leered and said, "Hey, gorgeous. I already have a date with the devil. Want to make it a threesome? I could really get off on two lady Beelzebubs."

The man was laughing as if he were enjoying a private joke. Philippa froze. Pretending that she had not heard, she gave a frigid smile and looked straight ahead. The light changed and the left-turn signal came on. As the BMW went round the corner, Dracula raised his voice.

"I'll be at the Auto Villa Motel on Kingsway. See you there," he hollered.

Then, to Philippa's relief, his car was gone. A moment later, the traffic in her own lane started to move again, and she drove on, indignantly putting the count and his BMW to the back of her mind. The rest of the drive was uneventful, and by the time she reached her condo and pulled into the underground parking lot, she decided her wig had passed the test. After all, she reflected, there's always going to be one idiot in every crowd. She hopped out of her car, waved to a witch who was unlocking a Volkswagen Jetta at the far end of the stalls, and hurried over to the elevator. Within ten minutes, she was in the shower.

An hour later she was ready for the party. She dispensed with the mask, having put on her stage eyelashes and generous portions of glitter-shadow, liner and mascara. Critically, she surveyed the results, then, as a final touch, added three black sequins for beauty spots. The result was devilish indeed. The legal-eagle blind date might be "hot", Philippa thought gleefully, but she was sizzling. She took once last look before slipping on her coat and heading out the door.

The Halloween dance was being held at the Pan Pacific Hotel, so she took the freeway into Vancouver. She was so used to driving downtown for the opera that her car practically followed the route on autopilot. She was already onto the Georgia Viaduct when she became aware of the sirens behind her. An accident, she thought, pulling over to let the police car pass.

But to her surprise, the squad car stopped behind her. Both the driver and passenger doors opened and two burly Vancouver City Police officers got out, one on either side of the vehicle. Their faces were grim, and there was another expression that Philippa found disconcerting. It almost looked like caution. Slowly they approached her car. She opened the window and leaned out.

"What's wrong, officer? I know I wasn't speeding," she began.

The policeman's expression did not change.

"Get out of the car, miss," he rapped. "Keep your hands in the air."

Wide-eyed, Philippa did as she was told. And then, with a growing sense of bewilderment, as if somehow she had changed from little red devil to Alice in Wonderland and the world had turned upside-down, she heard the officer inform her that she was under arrest.

* * *

Edwina had stopped looking irritated at her daughter's lack of punctuality and was starting to worry.

"Where on earth is Philippa? She should have been here an hour ago."

"Maybe she had second thoughts about our blind date," suggested Günter Sachs. "What did you tell her about me?" he asked Sylvia earnestly.

Beary's eyes rolled up into his laurel wreath, which, having been improvised from the garden hedge, was already wilting and drifting down over his brow.

"My daughter would not fail to show due to cold feet," he said firmly. *Even though,* he reflected, *she probably won't think much of you when she gets here.* Privately he viewed Sylvia's choice of an escort for her sister a poor one. Günter Sachs was certainly handsome, particularly so in the Victorian-era Prussian army uniform that he had chosen as his costume. Probably passed down through his family, Beary thought sourly. Edwina had been instantly won over by Günter's Teutonic courtesy, wavy black hair and what she had rhapsodically described as his "sooty" eyes. However, the man appeared to have absolutely no sense of humour. Beary admitted that this would not be considered a drawback by Sylvia, who tended to be remarkably humourless herself, but would certainly not win him any brownie points with Philippa.

The voluptuous blonde that Richard had brought to the event blinked her round, blue eyes.

"She's probably held up in traffic," she said. "Ricky and I took forever to get here."

Edwina flinched. Beary could read his wife's mind. The word *bimbo* emanated from every pore. However, he noticed that his son did not appear to be offended by the diminutive and, thought Beary, neither would I be. He rather liked the giggly blonde in the Wonder Woman suit.

"As long as she hasn't had an accident," said Beary, who himself was beginning to be quite concerned.

The blue eyes opened even wider.

"Oh, I do hope not!" Wonder Woman looked anxious. "Why don't you call her cell?"

"I did try," said Richard. "She has it turned off. I'm sure she's fine, Trish," he added, patting his date on the shoulder. "She told me that she was having a really hectic week. She didn't even get a chance to find a costume until today."

"That's true," said Edwina. "If she had to get downtown and back, she could have been delayed. But they'll be serving dinner soon. If she doesn't hurry up, she'll miss the meal."

"Yes, well, I'm going to hop over to the bar and get another Scotch," said Beary. "My laurel wreath needs a drink. Anyone else want anything?"

Edwina started to point out that there were two bottles of wine already on the table, but Beary had slipped away. He ambled over to the no-host bar and eased into line behind Spiderman, who turned around and greeted him as if they were old friends. It was Merve Billings from the city council.

"Hello, Beary. No surprise to see you here."

"Yes, but what are you doing here?" grunted Beary. "That isn't a squash court at the centre of the room. It's a dance floor. And since when have you been an opera fan?"

Merve assumed a solemn expression.

"One has to demonstrate support for all areas of the community. Besides," he added. "I like dancing. Marge and I took a course at Arthur Murray last year. Anyway, someone besides yourself has to represent the council. After all, you support the opera because of your daughter's involvement."

"Ah," said Beary. "I get it. The city was sent two freebies, and you nabbed them so you could have a night out at taxpayers' expense and test your new quickstep."

"Well, one could hardly let the tickets go to waste," said Merve piously.

"So where is Spiderwoman?" asked Beary.

"She's over there." Merve pointed to a table on the far side of the room where a woman covered in a voluminous velvet gown perched gingerly at the edge of a chair. "And she isn't dressed as Spiderwoman," he added. "She's Scarlett O'Hara, and given what she paid to rent that costume, it's a good job I did get free tickets."

"Good lord," said Beary. "How do you expect to practise your quickstep with her in that getup? She'll take up the entire dance floor."

"I know," said Merve gloomily. "She really wasn't thinking. I gather the shop had two of those outfits, and when she arrived, there was another woman trying on the same dress, and it looked so stunning that Marge decided to get the duplicate."

"Do women do things like that?" said Beary dubiously. "I thought they went out of their way to make sure they didn't end up wearing the same outfits."

"Oh, Marge checked to make sure the woman wasn't coming here," said Merve. "Evidently there's a big do at the Vancouver Yacht Club tonight. The other Scarlett was going there. I gather she told the saleswoman that she needed something to cover her up because it would be cold near the water."

"Well, that outfit will do it," said Beary. "Marge must be roasting alive."

"So must your good lady," said Merve, nodding towards the Beary table. "Though I must say," he added, "she makes a very good Queen Elizabeth the First. The Prussian officer looks good too, and I like Richard's British bobby—most appropriate." Merve's eye acquired a lascivious glint. "Who's Wonder Woman—the cutie beside him?"

"Her name is Trish. Very sweet girl. She's a cosmetician. She helped Richard pick out a birthday present for Edwina last year."

"Very nice," breathed Merve. "So where is the rest of your brood?"

"Sylvia and Norton are around somewhere. They must have gone table-hopping. They're easy enough to pick out. Just look for Bonnie with a rather weedy-looking Clyde in horn-rimmed specs."

"What about Philippa?"

"She hasn't arrived yet. I'm getting a bit concerned about her."

"Probably caught in traffic," said Merve. "There were games at both stadiums. I had a dreadful time getting downtown."

Merve turned back to the bar as the counter cleared. Beary felt a tap on his shoulder and looked around to see Philippa's friend, Milton. He was dressed in a tuxedo.

"Hello, Mr. Beary," said Milton. "Where's Philippa?"

"Not here yet," said Beary. "How come you're not in costume?"

"I am in costume," said Milton. "I'm Agent 007. Actually there are several James Bonds from the tenor section of the opera chorus. What we didn't spend on costume rentals will cover our bar tabs."

"Now, that was smart," said Beary.

"Not as smart as you," said Milton. "Those bed-sheets look a lot cooler than my tux. Why hasn't Philippa arrived yet?" he added, changing tack. "I passed her on my way in. I wouldn't have recognized her if I hadn't known her car—she's all tarted up like a little red devil—but that licence plate of hers is hard to miss. I could never understand why she had *Can Can* for a vanity plate, but then, of course, she explained that it was her very first show—"

Beary had stopped listening after Milton's third sentence. He cut in impatiently.

"What time did you get here?" he asked.

Milton looked surprised.

"I've been here since the place opened," he said. "I arrived right at six-thirty."

Beary felt a rush of apprehension. He turned away from the bar and was about to return to the table when he saw that Richard was coming across the room towards him. His face was grave.

"What is it?" Beary asked. He felt suddenly short of breath.

"Dad," said Richard. "Brace yourself. Philippa has been arrested."

* * *

Vancouver City Police Detective Constable Robert Miller hated Halloween. The noise from firecrackers and the abundance of masks provided ample cover for the criminally minded at a time when the uniformed branch was kept constantly occupied with complaints from citizens about teenagers using illegally acquired fireworks. So far, the day had brought an armed robbery carried out by a man in a Snoopy mask, a mugging by Superman on the South Slope, and a fire caused by firecrackers that had demolished a hedge in Kitsilano. Then, at five o'clock, when he was due to finish his shift and dutifully pop by his sister's house to admire his niece and nephew in their Halloween costumes, the call came in from the Auto Villa Motel on Kingsway. Dracula had been found dead in unit number five.

The constable who had been first on the scene had immediately called in the Major Crime Section, but he also took it upon himself to corral the trio of twelve-year-olds who had been tossing firecrackers into the courtyard from the vacant lot behind the motel units. For once, juvenile delinquency was to prove useful. The youngsters had been eager to tell what they had seen, and not only to the police, for by the time Miller arrived, along with his partner, DC Phil Ho, he found the motel besieged by reporters. While the motel proprietor had been calling the police, the youths had been calling the radio stations from their cellphones.

The boys' stories had been clear, consistent and precise. During the course of their assault on the motel courtyard, they had seen the dead man arrive. He had driven up in a silver BMW. The car had caught their attention immediately, and they had been even more impressed when a man in a Dracula outfit climbed out of the vehicle. This man had entered the office to register, and the proprietor confirmed the boys' statement that this had occurred around twenty past four. After registering, Dracula went back to his car and drove to the parking spot outside unit number five. The boys decided to wait until he had gone inside before restarting their bombardment, but as they were pulling out another pack of firecrackers, a woman appeared in the courtyard. She did not drive in. She simply walked in off the street, and the boys noticed her right away because she was dressed in a black and red devil outfit, and wore a flaming red wig that had horns sticking out of it and a black mask that hid her face. She went straight to unit number five and knocked on the door. The door opened and she went inside. The youths took great delight in speculating what was happening inside the room, and they decided to spice things up by hurling another volley in front of the unit. They proceeded to set off the firecrackers, but as the sound died away, they heard another muffled bang from inside the room. Almost immediately, the door flew open and the woman in the devil suit ran out, slammed the door shut behind her and took off out of the courtyard.

The boys were wondering what to do, but, at that moment, the proprietor came out from the office and started to lay into them. When they could get a word in edgewise, they told him about the bang that had come from unit number five and how the woman in the devil suit had left immediately afterwards. The proprietor was sceptical, because the boys were known to him as local nuisances, but feeling that he could not take a chance in case they were telling the truth, he fetched his keys and opened the unit. The boys looked into the room over his shoulder. They took ghoulish delight in describing the scene. Dracula lay dead on the bed, still wearing his skullcap and teeth, although the rest of his outfit was piled on a chair in the corner of the room. The motel proprietor had hastily backed out, locked up the unit and called the police. The boys had taken advantage of the hiatus to call the radio stations from their cellphones.

For once, the intrusion of the media had proved beneficial. The details of the shooting had been on the six o'clock news, and shortly thereafter, the police had received an urgent call from a man who had been walking his dog at the intersection of Canada Way and Burris shortly after four o'clock. The man was bubbling over with excitement for he had witnessed the pickup when the victim had made the assignation with the prostitute. He told how he had seen the man talking to the woman in the devil wig when their cars were alongside each other at the intersection, and he had heard the man call out the name of the motel and the unit number as he drove around the corner. Since the woman's car carried a distinctive vanity plate, he was able to give them her licence number—*Can Can*. The call went out right away, and by twenty past six, the car was spotted on the Georgia Viaduct. Within fifteen minutes, the woman had been brought into the station. From there, things had not been quite so easy. Miller was still smarting from the tongue-lashing he had received from the suspect. He had been singularly relieved to hand her over to WPC Anne Watts. Presumably, the fireball in the devil suit would cool off during her stay in the cells.

The door of his office opened and Phil Ho entered.

"We have the victim's identity, subject to confirmation from his family," he said. "His wallet was there, and the car registration confirms that he's Stanley Wells. He's the brother-in-law of Harold Morgenstern who owns the H & H Family Restaurant chain."

"Home and Hearth. Is he indeed? That's a big-money family—and as I recall, Morgenstern is a pillar of the local Christian community and noted for being an outspoken critic of anyone who tries to push for the legalization of prostitution. I heard him once giving a speech at a conference. The way he talked, you'd think Jack the Ripper was doing a public service."

"Then it's going to be very delicate breaking the news to the family, isn't it?" said Ho. "Given the reputation of that particular motel, there's a good chance that this woman is a prostitute."

"Has anyone called his wife yet?"

"I called the home, but I just spoke with the maid. She told me that her employers were at a dance at the Vancouver Yacht Club."

"Did she? Then maybe our victim isn't Wells."

Ho shook his head.

"It has to be him," he said. "The maid said that Mrs. Wells went to the dance with her brother. She said Harold Morgenstern and his fiancée had wanted to go early as they were organizers for the event, and his sister had gone with them to help. They left for the dance at five-thirty. Wells was going to meet them there later. The slimy beggar obviously decided to set up his own event to start off the evening."

"Is Stanley Wells involved in Morgenstern's business?"

"He's a junior partner, but do we have to worry about the family if this is a killing by a prostitute?"

Miller frowned.

"It's pretty unusual for a hooker to kill a client," he said. "The only credible circumstance would be if she walked into a situation and saw she was in danger. Yet the man was in bed. There was no sign of a struggle, and the boys insisted that the shooting happened almost as soon as she entered the room. So unless she instantly recognized Dracula as a john that she knew was violent, it makes no sense that she'd pull a gun on him."

Ho held up a hand.

"Hold on. She made that assignation with him at the intersection. She already knew who he was."

"Not necessarily. He was wearing a mask at that point."

"OK, that's possible." Ho conceded the point. "She might not have recognized him until she walked into the motel room. I'd better get out to the yacht club and break the news to his family. However many ripples it causes, we're going to have to find out more about him. I'll do that while you question our suspect."

"I think you'd better ask the family to come down to the station. I'd like to see if any of them recognize this woman."

"You haven't got anything out of her yet?"

"No." Miller allowed himself a slight smile. "We started rather badly. I made the comment, 'What have we here? Lola from *Damn Yankees*?' and it was as if I'd tossed a grenade into an ammunition dump. She went off with a bang and told me exactly what I could do with my dumb sense of humour. Then she proceeded to give me hell for several minutes, so I basically tuned out. Finally, she clammed up and refused to talk until her lawyer was present, so I'm just waiting until he arrives."

"Has her own lawyer? She must be a high-end hooker."

"Yes, but that's another contradiction. In spite of the harangue she gave me, she's very well spoken, so logically, she'd be an expensive call girl, but in that case, what was she doing in a motel on Kingsway? That's why I want to see if any of the Morgensterns recognize her. We can't just go under the assumption that we're dealing with a prostitute. What if it was simply a case of two people who knew each other hooking up after a chance meeting when they were stuck in traffic? We have to examine that possibility. Anyway, hopefully I'll be able to question her soon. Anne Watts took her to make her phone call so presumably the lawyer will appear any time now."

"Did Anne say who the lawyer is?"

"No. I gather the call was made to the woman's brother, and it was short and sweet—just where she was, what had happened and that she needed a lawyer. Ken Sparks is on the front desk. He'll call me as soon as the man gets here."

As if on cue, the door opened again and an apple-cheeked uniformed constable popped his head around the door. He had an ear-to-ear grin on his face.

"There are some characters to see you out front," he said. He appeared to be suppressing the urge to laugh out loud.

Miller was irritated.

"I don't know what's so bloody funny," he snapped. "Who are they?"

"Well, sir, one of them's a policeman—a British bobby, to be precise. And then there's Julius Caesar, Good Queen Bess, and Bonny and Clyde. Oh, yes," he added, before ducking back out the door, "Clyde is the lawyer, but don't worry—we made him check his machine gun at the front desk. You can go and start your interview now."

* * *

Philippa sat in the interview room and glowered across the table at DC Miller while Norton patiently explained to the detective who she was. She had taken off her wig, and in spite of the elaborate makeup, she looked more like herself. Attractive, thought Miller. Too bad. He looked away from her and concentrated on what the lawyer was saying.

"This is clearly a case of mistaken identity," Norton concluded. "Whoever the woman was in the motel room, it most certainly was not Philippa. She is the sister of Detective Inspector Richard Beary of the RCMP, and the daughter of city councillor, Bertram Beary. She has no idea why she is here, and I demand that you release her immediately."

Miller kept his gaze steady, though inwardly he cursed the complications that were starting to arise in what had seemed a straightforward case.

"She could be the daughter of the prime minister," he said. "That wouldn't guarantee that she was incapable of committing a crime. Your client is a suspect in a murder investigation," he said. "I need to know where she was at four-thirty this afternoon."

"You don't have to answer, Philippa," said Norton.

Philippa looked at her brother-in-law impatiently.

"Oh, for heaven's sake, Norton. I don't have anything to hide. The sooner I answer the wretched man's questions, the sooner I can get out of here." She looked across at Miller. She'd have normally considered him nice-looking, she thought suddenly, but as it was, she had the urge to hurl the cup of coffee that WPC Watts had provided and wipe the smug expression off his face. "I was at home getting ready for the party," she told him.

"Where is home?"

"A condo. Westminster Quay."

"Was anyone there with you?"

"No. I share with a friend, but she's in Vernon visiting her parents."

"So no one can verify where you were?"

"Well, probably not. I'd come from downtown after picking up my Halloween costume. I didn't have a lot of time, and the traffic was bad coming back, so I was in a rush when I arrived home. I ran in, showered, got ready, and left for the party. You know the rest. I was stopped by your goons as I was heading over the viaduct."

"For someone who is related to a police officer, you seem to have a remarkable hostility to members of the force," said Miller.

Philippa folded her arms across her chest.

"Not as a rule, but you seem to be bent on harassing and intimidating instead of serving and protecting, so I've revised my opinion."

Miller ignored the sarcasm and continued his questioning.

"Did you meet anyone on your drive home?"

"No. I've told you. I was in a hurry. I went straight home."

"So you spoke to no one. Not even when you were stopped in traffic?"

"No, I . . ." Philippa stopped. "Well, not anyone I knew."

Norton started to look anxious.

"Philippa," he cautioned her.

"Norton, it's OK," Philippa assured him. "This was a complete stranger." She turned back to Miller. "I wore my wig home from the costume boutique," she said.

"Why did you do that?"

"Oh, really. Don't you have any sense of fun? I just wanted to test it out. Lots of people smiled or waved at me. But when I was stopped in traffic, a man in a Dracula costume wanted me to put down my window. I suppose I thought he was just being friendly, or maybe even needed directions . . . You don't have to look like that," she snapped, seeing Miller's expression. "Anyway, he turned out to be a total sleaze, so I just shut my window, looked straight ahead, and fortunately at that moment, the light changed and he moved on."

Miller leaned forward.

"What exactly did he say to you?"

Norton piped up again.

"Philippa, I advise you to—"

"Oh, shut up, Norton," said Philippa. "I want to know what's going on as much as he does." She leaned in towards DC Miller. "He said something about already having a date with the devil and he asked if I'd like to make it a threesome." She frowned for a moment. "He must have been reasonably well educated because he made some reference to Milton—well, he mentioned Beelzebub, so I immediately thought about *Paradise Lost*, but it could have meant something else. He was laughing as if there was some secret joke."

Miller drew in his breath. It sounded so plausible. Yet he knew from experience that the coolest killers were capable of the most credible lies. He looked steadily at Philippa.

"What was your reply?"

"Nothing. I told you. I looked straight ahead and waited until he'd gone."

"Did he say anything else?"

"He yelled something about a motel as he went round the corner onto Burris, but I was trying to tune him out at that point. I can't recall exactly what he said."

Miller leaned back. His instincts told him that Philippa was telling the truth, but if he went by the book, the evidence told him that she should be charged. He tried another tack.

"Where did you get that costume?" he asked.

"The Masked Ball Boutique. It's downtown."

"Was that the only devil outfit?"

"No. The salesgirl told me they had six in stock. Mine was the last to be rented, so they are all out. You know," she added, leaning in eagerly, "what you should do is send someone down and get a list of all the people who rented the outfit."

Miller felt irritated.

"I don't need you to teach me police procedure," he said. "We'll do that as a matter of course." Before, he could say any more, the door opened. DC Ho came in. He took Miller aside.

"Stanley Well's wife is here," he said quietly. "Her name's Donna. She's pretty angry."

"Is she indeed? So she's not showing sorrow over the loss of her husband."

"No. Her first comment was, 'So he was up to that again. Serves him bloody well right.' And 'that', by the way, referred to the use of prostitutes. She didn't pull any punches. Do you want me to bring her down?"

"Yes. I'll come out." Miller told WPC Watts to remain. He came out into the corridor and waited until Ho returned. Momentarily forgetting it was Halloween, he did a double-take when Donna Wells appeared, for she was dressed as a vampire, with a sleek widow-peaked wig and a long-sleeved black gown, but even the blood-red lips and charcoal-ringed eyes could not disguise the hostility in her expression. Miller wondered who her anger was directed against—the killer, her husband or the police. His guess would be the husband. Her pride must have taken a devastating blow. Miller met her and led her to the one-way window. He pointed at Philippa.

"Do you know that woman?" he asked.

Donna Wells stared long and hard. Then she straightened up.

"So it wasn't a prostitute," she said. "The slime-ball was actually having an affair."

"You recognize her?"

"Yes," she said. Her tone was distinctly vindictive. "I do. That's the singer that starred in *Oklahoma* at TUTS two years ago. My husband and I went to the show. I remember her, because he made such a thing about how charming she was. He made a point of getting an introduction to her at the cast party."

Miller's heart sank. For a moment he had really believed that the girl in the interview room was innocent. It just went to show that a cop who ignored the rulebook was asking for trouble.

* * *

After Miller concluded the interview, he sent for Richard. He laid out the evidence, and then looked him straight in the eye.

"What would you do in this situation?" he asked.

Richard frowned.

"It's damning," he acknowledged. "If I didn't know Philippa, I probably wouldn't believe her."

"There's enough here for me to lay charges," Miller said bluntly.

"Then why aren't you doing that?" asked Richard.

"Because my instincts tell me there's more to this than meets the eye. That's why I want your input. Tell me about your sister. Is there even the remotest chance that she could have got herself into a mess like this?"

Richard shook his head.

"No. I realize you're in a dilemma because you only have my word on this, but Philippa is as straight and honest as they come. For all that she's glamorous and full of pizzazz, she's a very old-fashioned girl with old-fashioned values. She's clever and hard working, and above all, she's decent. That's why she exploded all over you," Richard added solemnly. "She's mortified to be put in this position. She's the last person in the world to be meeting a man in a sleazy motel, let alone putting a bullet in him. And if that's what your instinct is telling you, then your instincts are correct."

"I assume you'll help us sort this out," said Miller. "I'm going to be under pressure to charge her. If I don't, I'm going to have to come up with the solution fast."

"My division will do everything we can," Richard assured him. "We'll pull out all the stops." He stood up and headed for the door. Then he turned back.

"One word of advice," he added. "Philippa is very observant. When she settles down and stops being on the defensive, she could be helpful. Get her to think back to that meeting at the intersection. See if she can remember anything about meeting Wells at the post-show reception. See if there's anything, however small, that she thinks might be significant."

"Why don't you talk to her?" said Miller. "She might be more receptive with you. But in the meantime, I'm going to trace the other people who rented those devil costumes. If there were only six outfits, the pool of suspects will be limited. We'll go from there."

Richard nodded and left the room. Miller thought for a moment. Then he called DC Ho and filled him in.

"So you're going to let her go?" The other detective looked sceptical.

"For the time being," said Miller. "But there's one more test I'm going to try. With the exception of Donna Wells who is waiting to be questioned, the victim's family is still in the foyer. Keep them there.

We'll give Philippa Beary the chance to wash off the fancy makeup. She's wearing a winter coat, so that covers up the devil costume. Then we'll send her out to join her family. I want to see if there's any reaction from the Morgensterns, or from the Beary girl herself. Let's watch the faces and see if anyone shows the slightest recognition of anyone else."

"What if the Morgensterns have heard the Beary clan talking?" said DC Ho. "They may already know that Philippa Beary is our suspect."

"Possibly, but only if the Bearys have been talking at the tops of their voices. I told PC Sparks to keep the two groups on opposite sides of the room."

"OK," said Ho. "It's worth a try. I'll go and get her now."

* * *

Constable Sparks looked around the foyer. He knew the force was dealing with a serious investigation, but he had a great deal of difficulty maintaining a solemn countenance because the police station had acquired a remarkably festive air. Harold Morgenstern was the only person present who did not appear to be in fancy dress, though his red waistcoat, slicked-back hair and old-fashioned dress suit was presumably not his normal garb. The stunner with him, who had been introduced as his fiancée, was dressed as an angel—and a particularly expensive one at that, Sparks thought, assessing the number of sequins adorning her feathery wings and gauzy dress. The victim's wife, who had been taken back for questioning, had looked like a refugee from *The Munsters*, and the rest of Morgenstern's entourage was equally incongruous. One couple appeared to have stepped out of a production of *The Wizard of Oz*, and the other pair was dressed as Scarlett O'Hara and Rhett Butler.

The far side of the room was equally colourful. Good Queen Bess sat, tight-lipped and mercifully silent, though she had given PC Sparks a vituperative earful on her arrival. However, now she had settled mutely on the centre bench, her voluminous skirt taking up most of the space, while a portly and rather dilapidated Julius Caesar with a wilting headdress was squeezed onto the end of the seat. Beside them stood Bonnie Parker, tapping her fingers impatiently on the back of the bench and looking at the clock every couple of minutes. A more petulantly bad-tempered gangster's moll Sparks had never seen, but he supposed her irritation could be attributed to the disappearance of her wimpy-looking Clyde who had remained in the backroom with his client. The British bobby had also disappeared into the back.

WPC Ann Watts came down the hall and leaned over the front desk.

"What's up?" asked Sparks.

"They're letting her go. Oh, and just so you know, The Badger is on his way in."

"Again."

"Yup, drunk as the proverbial skunk. He was weaving along Granville Street telling all the old ladies how much he loved them. He can sleep it off in the cells."

"Sad case," said Sparks. "You know, that old goat used to be a high-school teacher."

A flurry of movement made him look up. Julius Caesar had leapt to his feet, and Bonnie had moved round to help Queen Elizabeth up. Sparks looked towards the corridor. DC Miller and the lawyer dressed as Clyde were coming down the hall, and behind them was Philippa Beary. She looked pale. The elaborate makeup had gone, and her heavy winter coat hid the devil costume. She came through into the foyer and was engulfed by her father in a big hug. Then her mother followed suit, while Bonnie and Clyde closed ranks and appeared to be having a conference. Once her parents released her from their affectionate clasp, Philippa turned and looked speculatively at the group on the other side of the room. Harold Morgenstern and his guests stared back, but their faces seemed only to register interest. There was no indication that they knew the girl who was looking them over so carefully.

Miller watched the scene closely. If the Beary girl had been afraid of being recognized, he thought, she would not have stared at the members of the other family with such intense interest. She appeared puzzled as she looked at Harold Morgenstern's beautiful angel with the auburn hair, tightly coiled and interwoven with silver thread. Then her head tilted curiously as she observed Scarlett O'Hara. But it was Morgenstern's sister who elicited the greatest reaction. As Philippa turned to the witch, she gasped and her eyes flew wide open. Miller felt a wave of anxiety, which quickly changed to bewilderment, for Sally Morgenstern was covered from head to toe in glittering black lamé, and her long hair had been styled into green swirls interlaced with silver streaks. Her make up was so bizarre that the person underneath was completely concealed. No one could have recognized her.

Philippa whirled round to face Miller.

"That's it," she said. "The witch! There was a witch in the underground parking lot. She saw me as I came in. It would have been around four-thirty. She must live in the same complex as I do because her car was parked there. It was a green Volkswagen Jetta. All you have to do is ask around the different apartments until you find her."

With a look of triumph mixed with considerable relief, Philippa turned back to her family.

A uniformed constable came through the front door. He was escorting a derelict-looking old man, who in spite of his rough clothes and unshaven face seemed extremely cheerful. His smile grew wider as his eyes focussed on the medley of characters in the foyer. He weaved towards Edwina and she recoiled as the alcoholic fumes wafted towards her.

Philippa tucked her arm into her mother's. "Come on, Mum," she said. "Let's go home."

"Gladly," said Edwina. "Richard and Sylvia can go back to the party and let the others know we're bowing out."

"The party will be over, Mum," said Sylvia. "It's well past midnight."

"Good heavens, so it is."

"Don't worry." Richard smiled wryly. "Günter practically fell over backwards assuring me that he'd look after Trish and take her home. I don't think we have to worry on that score. Come on, Mum. Follow Dad. This way."

Old Badger's grin had broadened as he listened to the conversation. As Edwina passed by, he leered at her and raised his battered hat.

"I must say, Ma'am," he said cheerfully, "for a Virgin Queen you've been awfully busy."

Like Queen Victoria, Good Queen Bess was not amused, but the look on her face as she swept out of the police station made Constable Sparks' day.

* * *

Miller's investigation progressed quickly over the next few days. Wells had been shot with a 9-mm Glock, probably unregistered, but as yet the gun had not been found. Neither had the devil costume, which had not been returned to Katya's store. However, the Volkswagen-driving witch was traced and she confirmed Philippa's presence in the underground lot at four-thirty, and the renters of the other five devil costumes were tracked down without difficulty. Four of them had alibis and were quickly discounted as suspects, but the identity of the fifth renter turned out to be a surprise, for it was Stan Wells himself. He had told Katya that it was for his wife to wear at a private party. His leer, along with his instruction not to say a word, had implied that it was a party of two.

The interview with Donna Wells revealed a great deal more about the dead man. He had caused his wife a lot of unhappiness over the years. Stan's history of consorting with prostitutes went back to the early days of the marriage when he had made frequent business trips to Nevada. In 1998, when Donna Wells found out that his business was ready to fold, she also discovered that large amounts of money had been spent on visits to the Wild Pony Ranch. She threatened her husband with divorce, and at that point, Harold Morgenstern had intervened in an attempt to save the marriage. He offered Stan a junior partnership and a management position in Kamloops, not because he expected great productivity from his brother-in-law, but simply out of love for his sister. However, a condition came with the partnership. Stan had to mend his ways—and until the police informed Donna Wells of the manner of her husband's death, she had assumed that he had reformed. Her fury at his ultimate betrayal appeared to have eliminated any former feelings she might have had for her spouse.

But having been told that the woman they were looking for must be a prostitute, Miller's investigation ground to a halt again, because no matter how hard they looked, none of his officers could find a link between Stan Wells and any ladies of the night, whether high-end call girls or streetwalkers, either in Kamloops or in Vancouver.

"He obviously knew her," said Phil Ho. "If he provided the costume, then the assignation was not only pre-arranged, but he'd seen the woman beforehand in order to give her the outfit. He had to be a regular client."

"I'm beginning to wonder if this mysterious prostitute really exists," said Miller. "If it weren't for the maid's insistence that Donna Wells was at home during the relevant time, she'd top my list of suspects."

"You mean, if she'd discovered that her husband was up to his old tricks, she might have decided to get rid of him once and for all?"

"Possibly. But remember, she's the one pushing the prostitute angle. Wells told the saleswoman at Masked Ball that the costume was for his wife. Some couples do the oddest things to spice up their sex life."

"But if the outfit was for his wife, he wouldn't have been up to his old tricks, so why kill him?"

"She could have had other reasons. But I don't see how she could have done it. Donna Wells was formerly a hairdresser, and I gather she spent the early afternoon doing hairstyles for her sister and Morgenstern's fiancée. By the time the other women left, it was three-thirty, and the maid said that Donna Wells went to her bedroom to have a rest prior to getting ready. She came out, fully dressed at quarter past five, and was ready to go when Morgenstern and his fiancée arrived to pick her up at five-thirty."

"All right, so we eliminate the wife. What about the other women in his circle? Could he have been having an affair? The costume could have been for someone he knew."

"But if he had a mistress, what was her motive for killing him?"

"Love, money, revenge, blackmail," rattled off Ho. "Must be one of the above. It could be someone from his past too."

"I've thought of that. He spent a lot of time in Nevada, so I've asked the state police to find out what his old acquaintances there know about him—I particularly want to know if he had any regular girlfriends or a favourite filly at the Wild Pony Ranch. We should be hearing back pretty soon if they come up with anything."

There was a knock on the door. It opened and WPC Watts stuck her head into the room.

"Phone call for you," she said. "You might want to take it. It's that girl you arrested for the Wells murder."

Hoping that the call was going to produce information rather than recrimination, Miller picked up the phone. He heard Philippa's clear, crisp voice at the other end.

"DC Miller?"

"Yes." Miller attempted to sound cheerful and businesslike. "Nice to hear from you, Miss Beary. What can I do for you?"

There was a pause at the other end.

"Well, for one thing, you could buy me a new car."

"I'm sorry?"

"Didn't you hear what happened when your underlings had my car towed? It was sideswiped by a drunk driver. It's a complete write-off."

Miller groaned inwardly, but he kept his voice even as he replied.

"That's most regrettable. Let me know if there are any problems with ICBC. We'll make sure that you are properly compensated."

"You certainly will," retorted Philippa. "Anyway, that wasn't why I was calling. Richard was filling me in about the case and something occurred to me. I honestly don't know if it's important—it's pure speculation—but Richard said I should call you."

"Go ahead," said Miller.

"I've been thinking about what Dracula said to me, and I may have figured out what his secret joke was. Remember how I told you he said he could get off on two lady Beelzebubs? Well, it suddenly occurred to me—in *Paradise Lost*, Beelzebub is a fallen angel."

"Go on."

"From the way Wells talked," said Philippa, "it was obvious that he knew the woman he was going to meet, and when I was leaving the police station on the night you arrested me—"

"You saw an angel." Miller sounded sceptical. "That was Morgenstern's fiancée. Are you seriously suggesting that Wells had an assignation with her?"

"I know it sounds crazy, and it probably is, but the killer had to be someone whose hair could be stuffed under a wig. It couldn't have been the witch with the pouffed-up green and silver hair. There's no way she could have crammed that under a wig and kept it looking as fresh as it did. Scarlett O'Hara might have managed it, because her hair was tucked into a snood and she had a hat on—but there was something else that bothered me about the angel."

"I'm listening," said Miller. "What was it?"

"The salesgirl at the costume rental told me that Morgenstern was a big fan of the Jeanette MacDonald/Nelson Eddy movies, and that he and his fiancée were going to dress as the stars of *I Married an Angel*."

Miller started to feel impatient.

"Yes, all right. How is that relevant?"

"Because Katya also told me that the fiancée had gorgeous long curly tresses, and in the movie, that's exactly how Jeanette MacDonald wears her hair. Loose and flowing. But the woman in the angel costume had her hair tightly wound against her head and laced with silver. It didn't really make sense, unless . . ."

"Unless she had to stuff it under a wig."

"Well, yes."

"Why couldn't she just wear one of those stocking caps, and then pull it off and wear her hair loose?" said Miller. "That would have been the most logical thing to do."

"Yes," agreed Philippa, "but women in that money-bracket always have their hair styled for social events, and I gather that Morgenstern's sister insisted on doing everyone's hair for the party. If she'd actually styled the hair into gorgeous puffy ringlets, it would have been instantly obvious that the hairdo had been squashed. No matter how hard you try, you can't restore that sort of hairstyle to the exact same shape once it's been flattened. And from what Richard tells me, Morgenstern's fiancée didn't have a whole lot of time to get back to her apartment, change and fix her hair, because she had to be ready to go by five-thirty. The hairstyle she had would have retained its shape perfectly. I bet if you talk to Donna Wells, you'll find that the fiancée insisted on the coiled hairdo."

"This is pretty slim," pointed out Miller. "I'll certainly ask her, but there's not much to go on. Let's face it, Jane Banks is a forty-year-old widow, about to marry an extremely wealthy and influential man. Why on earth would she jeopardize that by meeting with her fiancé's brother-in-law at a seedy motel?"

"I have no idea," said Philippa. "That's for you to find out."

* * *

As it turned out, Miller only had to wait until the next day to get the answer to his question. WPC Watts came into his office just before noon. She looked excited and she hurried over to Miller's computer.

"Look what the Nevada State Police came up with," she crowed. "Bring up your email. I just sent it over to you."

Miller did as he was told, and then his eyes widened and his face broke into a grin.

"Well, what do you know?" he said. "My fiery little devil's guess was correct."

He stared at the photograph that had come up on the screen. The auburn hair was loose and flowing and the face was made up far more heavily, but the woman in the picture was unmistakably Jane Banks. He scrolled up to the top of the screen to see the message that had come with the picture.

"Janna Bergen," he read. "Wells was one of her regular clients at the Wild Pony Ranch."

The rest of the pieces fell into place quickly. Janna Bergen had been a call girl in Nevada from 1988 to 1999, but she married Nick Banks and got off the game when she was thirty-one. The couple moved to Los Angeles, but Janna soon discovered that her husband was not as well off as he'd led her to believe. In 2001, they both took out large life-insurance policies, and two years later, Banks was killed in a car accident. Janna modified her name to Jane and moved to San Francisco where she bought a townhouse and started mixing with the wealthy set. She met Harold Morgenstern at the Golden Gate Yacht Club when he was on holiday in San Francisco. After he returned to Vancouver, they stayed in touch and the following year, she moved to Vancouver, buying a condo in False Creek. Before long, she and Morgenstern became engaged, but her world started to collapse about her ears when Stan Wells came back to Vancouver. Wells recognized her right away. He didn't want money from her—he had plenty of that—but the thought of having power over his priggish brother-in-law's fiancée appealed immensely, and the price of his silence was for them to resume their old relationship. He took sadistic pleasure in setting up an assignation to take place just before the engagement was to be announced. He was a nasty piece of work, and his victim decided to get rid of him because she knew that Morgenstern would break off the relationship if he ever found out the truth about her background. So she agreed to meet Wells, knowing that no one would be able to recognize her in the devil costume and no one could trace the rental back to her.

DC Miller phoned Richard Beary the following week and recounted the results of the investigation.

"So there it is," he concluded. "Janna Bergen used a disguise to commit murder, but unfortunately for your sister, she had the same costume. I feel pretty badly about the way we dragged Philippa in, but the case against her seemed so strong. I hope she understands that."

"Intellectually, yes," said Richard. "Emotionally, she's still pretty sore."

"She certainly knows how to put people in their places," said Miller. "My ears are still burning from the way she ripped into me."

"She comes by that honestly," chuckled Richard. "Don't ever have a run-in with our mother."

"She said I had a devil-may-care attitude to individual rights. Actually, given the costume she was wearing, I had a hard time keeping a straight face, but I have to admit it stung a bit."

"Well, by now she'll have realized that the devil did care. You did the right thing," Richard told the young policeman. "You kept an open mind. That's the first rule for a detective, and you abided by it. Philippa will get over it."

"Hopefully she'll get some gratification from the fact that she figured out who the killer was."

"True, but you were about to produce the same result yourself. Great combination actually," Richard said thoughtfully. "Her instincts and your systematic police work. I'm impressed."

"Me too," said Miller. "Clever girl, your sister." He smiled. Before he rang off, he added, "Thank her for me, will you?"

MARY POPPINS, WHERE ARE YOU?

We *are breaking in with a special bulletin. Serial killer, Peter Crampton, has escaped from Greystone Jail where he was serving a life sentence for murder. Crampton, along with his girlfriend, Christie Canning, was responsible for the grisly series of murders that shocked the Lower Mainland in the 1980s. Canning, who co-operated with police investigators in return for a guarantee of a reduced charge, was released after serving a twelve-year term. The search for Crampton is being impeded by the weather as heavy rains and windstorms have caused mudslides at several points on the highway—*

Charlene switched off the radio and shivered. She ran her fingers through her tawny blonde hair and wondered if it was going to start all over again. She felt ill as she remembered the trial, and she knew she could never survive such an ordeal a second time. She went to the window. It overlooked the approach to the lodge, and as she rested her hands on the sill, she noticed that her fingers were trembling. She gripped the wood tightly, trying to stop the shaking, and stared out onto the grounds, wondering if Crampton's eyes were staring back at her from the evergreens at the edge of the drive. Although it was only three in the afternoon, the scene outside was dark. The trees were barely visible through the sheets of rain pouring down the windowpanes, and the mountains had completely disappeared, engulfed in a grey haze of mist and cloud. The isolation that had once made the lodge seem a haven had suddenly become a terrible threat.

Margaret Crane came into the room. She was carrying a pile of towels and was slightly out of breath from the effort of coming up the basement stairs. She saw right away that something had happened to distress the owner of Marshlands Lodge.

"Charlene, you're upset. What's happened?"

Charlene turned and looked at her bleakly.

"Peter Crampton has escaped from prison," she said.

Margaret drew in her breath sharply. Then she set down the towels and put an arm around Charlene's shoulders.

"Try not to worry," she urged. "There's no reason why he would come here."

"Greystone Prison is only a few miles from here. What if he finds out that the Morton family is to be here this weekend? He vowed revenge on them too, remember?"

Margaret bit her lip.

"I never liked the idea of the Mortons coming to the lodge," she muttered. "John Graves may be a good gamekeeper, but he's overstepped his position. He had no business inviting that family here."

"Yes, he did. I told him he could try promotional weekends with influential people who could bring us clients. It never occurred to me that the Mortons would be on his list."

Margaret frowned.

"I can't understand why John would set up such an important booking when I was going to be away. He knew I was going to Vancouver for the weekend. Why would he leave you stranded like that? It's not really like him. Couldn't you have used that as an excuse to close for the weekend?"

"Not really, and the Mortons would be far more likely to ask awkward questions if I turned them away without a valid reason." Charlene drew herself up and forced herself to be positive. "It'll be all right," she insisted. "I've arranged for Mrs. Marks to come in. She's quite capable of handling a house party in the lodge. Ronald Morton is the only one who might recognize me, and he isn't arriving until tomorrow afternoon. The rest of his family is coming tonight, but his daughters were much too young to remember the trial, and his current wife wasn't around at the time, so there shouldn't be a problem."

"But what if they find out your maiden name?"

"Why would they? No, I'll be fine. You can leave first thing in the morning as you planned, and I'll stay just long enough to make sure everyone is settled. Then I'll drive into Hope and hole up in a motel until Tuesday."

"I still don't like it," said Margaret. "Do be careful, dear."

She picked up the towels again and left the room. Charlene watched her go. Another wave of nausea overtook her, and she fought to keep her equilibrium. She would go to the kitchen, she decided. She must keep busy to prevent herself from thinking and fretting.

She had gone no more than three steps into the hall when the ringing of the telephone brought her back. She answered the call but there was no one there. She was about to hang up when she became aware of the sound of heavy breathing at the other end. Then, suddenly, a gravelly voice spoke in her ear.

"Mary Poppins, where are you?" it said.

Shaking like a leaf, Charlene could barely get the phone back on its stand.

* * *

"It was a particularly ugly case," said Staff Sergeant Brodie. "Crampton raped and murdered four girls before he was caught."

"I was a teenager at the time," said Richard Beary, "but I remember the sensational headlines. I suppose it was because Christie Canning was a gorgeous, angelic-looking blonde, yet she must have had the soul of a devil to help him procure those girls."

"That was never proved, you know," said Brodie. "That's why she was able to strike a deal with the prosecution. The only abduction definitely linked to her was the last one, and she admitted that, but she'd been so badly beaten up by Crampton that it was obvious she'd been terrified into submission."

"How did she get mixed up with Crampton?"

Brodie had no difficulty in recalling the details. He had worked on the case as a young constable and he still felt revulsion whenever he thought back to the terrible crimes.

"She met him through her boss—Ronald Morton."

Richard recognized the name.

"The real-estate magnate? Wasn't his oldest girl one of the victims?"

Brodie nodded. "Yes, that's right—April. Lovely girl, by all accounts."

"My sister knows Morton's other daughter," said Richard. "Carol Morton is an opera singer. Quite the big-time diva, actually. Philippa says she's pretty intimidating. Late thirties, loaded with confidence and death on anyone who doesn't come up to snuff."

"There were actually three daughters in the Morton family," said Brodie, "though I believe the last one was adopted. April was quite a few years older than the other two, but the combination of a teenager and two young ones was a handful for their mother. That's why Morton advertised for a nanny. The press had a field day when the wording of the advertisement came out in court. The ad read, 'Mary Poppins, where are you?' Given what happened to April, it was very ironic."

Richard flinched.

"God, yes. They sure didn't get the perfect nanny. What a travesty!"

"Yes, well, to answer your question about how they met, Canning was only nineteen when Morton hired her, and Peter Crampton was a real-estate agent who had been at the house on business. He was a smooth, handsome charmer, and Canning was ripe for the picking. You see it turned out she'd been having an affair with Ronald Morton. I suppose she took Morton seriously, but once she realized that he was just toying with her, she began a relationship with Crampton."

"Was she angry with Morton?"

"Possibly. She said not, but who knows. The murder happened when Morton and his wife were in Europe. Canning was left in charge of the children, and on the day of the abduction, she was supervising them in the swimming pool. April had wanted to hang out with the gardener's son—they'd pretty much grown up together—and I guess she was in a snit because Canning had made her stay to help with the younger children. Anyway, at some point in the afternoon, April went inside to put on sunblock and she never came back. Crampton was holding an open house for the property next door, and whether April simply took off defiantly and ran into him, or whether he managed to slip away and subdue her somehow, we've never figured out, but the bottom line is that Christie Canning never left the poolside. She was with the other children the entire time, and when April didn't return, she and the other children searched the house for her. When there was still no sign, Canning phoned all over the neighbourhood and ultimately called the police. Her behaviour couldn't be faulted."

"Didn't Crampton come under suspicion? Surely any male in the vicinity would have been checked on."

"The open house didn't end until six o'clock and April went missing around one, so he had a pretty good alibi. Besides," Brodie added, his face suddenly taking on a dispirited expression, "we had another suspect in our sights. It seemed such a clear-cut case. April's body was found two weeks later in the woods, very close to the small cottage where the Morton's gardener lived. The gardener's son had been adamant that April hadn't come over that day, but the Morton's cleaning lady came forward and told us that there was talk that Edward Marshall—that was the gardener—had been showing an unhealthy interest in April. We went in and carried out a search, and sure enough, the girl's locket was found in Marshall's van. That seemed to clinch the matter. He was arrested." Brodie paused and sighed heavily. "He hanged himself in jail before the case came to trial."

"Crampton set him up?"

Brodie's face was sombre.

"Yes. It was a terrible thing. The bastard must have planted the locket and started the gossip. The whole thing was a pack of lies, but Marshall despaired of ever proving his innocence. We broke the poor man."

"And Crampton went free to kill three more girls before he was caught."

"Yes. That wasn't the only tragedy, either. Once he was apprehended and he and Canning were charged, there were two sensational trials. Crampton and Canning each tried to blame the other, but one of the things that stood in Canning's favour was the fact that Ronald Morton paid to have the best defence lawyer he could get for her. No matter how guilty he might have felt about their affair and the way he'd taken advantage of her, he'd never have done that if he believed she had taken part in the murder of his daughter. But Crampton was furious that Morton helped Canning, and he vowed to get revenge on both Canning and the Morton family. The strain proved too much for Morton's wife. Amanda Morton committed suicide just before the trial began."

"Poor woman."

"She certainly was," agreed Brodie. "Marriage to Morton hadn't been easy at the best of times. The nanny wasn't his only mistress. It transpired that the third daughter—the one that was adopted—was actually the product of a fling he'd had with a model when he was overseas, and he'd brought the child back and insisted that his wife adopt her. After Amanda Morton died, Morton actually married this model. They're a family straight out of the soap operas," said Brodie dourly. "However, nobody can deny that they've seen more than their share of tragedy, and most of it is attributable to Peter Crampton."

"And now he's on the loose again. Have there been any sightings yet?"

"Nothing. He can't have gone far though—unless, of course, he manages to hitch a ride on the highway."

"He might be intending to find Christie Canning. Where is she? Do we know where she's gone to ground?"

"Unfortunately, we don't," said Brodie. "The RCMP did help her get established when she left jail, but she obviously didn't feel safe. Crampton's victims had a lot of relatives who were crying out for revenge and she was terrified of retribution. She went tombstoning on her own, found another identity, and disappeared from view. But you're right. If we could find Canning, we might be able to catch Crampton."

* * *

James Burgess looked anxiously at the tense profile of the woman who was driving him to Marshlands. Carol Morton's hands gripped the wheel of the Mercedes so tightly that her knuckles were white.

"Are you all right, Carol?" he said quietly.

"What do you think?" she snapped. Then her voice softened. "I'm sorry, James," she said. "I didn't mean to snarl at you, but Crampton's escape has brought everything back."

"That's because of that bloody press reporter," said James. "You should have called me to deal with him."

"There wasn't time. He just appeared at the house and announced he was investigating some new information about the case. I had a hell of a time getting rid of him. He kept insisting he might be able to find out the truth about Canning and Crampton—as if we'd want to remember anything about that sadistic pair."

"Find out his name. I'll get an injunction against him."

"Don't bother. I told him exactly where to get off and slammed the door in his face. But I wish Father hadn't insisted on going ahead with this Marshlands visit. We're coming right into the area where Crampton was imprisoned."

"Your father is a stubborn man. He doesn't like other people controlling his actions. Besides, I think he wanted to get your sister away from your current tenor."

Carol's mouth tightened.

"I still can't believe that Jennifer could be stupid enough to fall for Enrico. He has a track record a mile long with women. They don't need the three tenors," she added snidely. "Enrico has enough arms and wind to form a trio all by himself. How can Jennifer seriously believe that he's in love with her?"

"He says he wants to marry her," James pointed out.

"He probably does," Carol said cynically. "We're a very wealthy family."

"Her mother seems to think Enrico is sincere," James interjected gently. "Celia isn't averse to the match."

"Celia is a fool," snapped Carol. "She has the intellectual capacity of a gerbil. I can't think why my father married her."

"Well, she is Jennifer's mother," said James. "And she's a very beautiful woman."

"She is now," grunted Carol, "but it's all Botox and feather stitching. Who knows what she looked like before her car accident? None of us met her until Father brought her back from England. Just like he arrived with Jennifer years before and told my mother to raise her. What a bastard he is."

"Don't talk like that, Carol. I know the circumstances were unhappy, but the fact remains, you love Jennifer and want the best for her."

"Of course I do. Jennifer needs protection. She's fragile." Carol's brow was furrowed with anxiety. "She doesn't sleep well. She has horrible nightmares. No amount of counselling seems to help her."

"Is that surprising? She spent her formative years with a nanny who ended up on trial for aiding and abetting a murderer."

"So did I. It hasn't affected me that way."

James was of the opinion that Carol had been more deeply affected than she admitted, but he let the comment pass.

"You were older and more independent. Jennifer was with Canning constantly for the first three years of her life. Who knows what went on?"

"Actually," Carol said thoughtfully, "I always thought the nightmares were my father's fault."

"Why would you think that?"

"There was an incident in the garden when Jennifer was small. The gardener was burning leaves and my father found a snake on the lawn and threw it on the fire. Jennifer was devastated. She cried for hours afterwards, and that night, she woke up screaming."

"Poor kid."

"My father has a lot to answer for, doesn't he?" said Carol. "We've all been damaged by him in some way, though in my case it worked in my favour because I was determined to show him that I was just as good as he was."

"True." James smiled. "And you love your father too, in spite of everything."

"Do I? I wonder. He was cruel to my mother, and he's unkind to Celia. Not that she cares. She lives in the lap of luxury and she has her daughter back, so she couldn't care less if she sees him from one week to the next. She just drifts along in her designer clothes and does as she's told, but her mind, if she actually has one, is a closed book."

"She's reserved," James acknowledged.

Carol's eyes darkened suddenly.

"What really gets me," she said, "is the way Father treats you. He's been an absolute pig to you over the years. I've never understood why you accepted a job with his company. You'd have done much better to set up in your own practice."

"Perhaps—but the first time I came into his office, there you were, desperately in need of kindness and care. You'd lost your mother, and your father seemed too busy making money to pay you any attention, so I took the job . . . and that's why I stay. You remind me so much of your mother. She was such a wonderful lady . . . so sweet and gentle. She meant the world to me."

"I'm not sweet and gentle," said Carol.

"Underneath," said James firmly. "You have your father's tough edge, which is probably why you've done so well in your career, but you have a lot of your mother in you too."

"You were in love with her, weren't you?" said Carol.

"Yes, but I lost her to your father. I had hoped she was going to wait for me while I went through law school, but I was only in my first term at Harvard when I got the news that they were married."

"Is that why you stayed in the States for so many years?"

"Probably. Who knows?"

Carol sighed. "And by the time you returned to Vancouver, she was dead."

"Yes," said James soberly. "I bitterly regret staying away so long." He hesitated for a moment. Then, cautiously, he continued. "Carol," he asked, "has your father ever said anything to you about your mother's suicide?"

Carol shook her head.

"No. He won't talk about it. I asked him once why my mother took her own life, but he just got a twisted smile on his face and told me that she simply gave up the battle. The way he said it gave me chills. It was almost as if he didn't care. He was like that whenever the subject of April came up too. Maybe that's how he copes, I don't know."

"I hope that's all it is. I don't want to worry you, but you'd better hear this from me rather than someone else. I received an anonymous letter last week. It made a pretty ugly accusation against your father."

"You don't have to spare my feelings," Carol said shortly. "I have no illusions about him. What did the letter say?"

"It told me to ask your father why he drove your mother to suicide."

Carol caught her breath.

"My God. Do you think it's possible?"

"I don't know. He can be very cruel. You know that."

"Don't ask him about it. Let me talk to him. He'll take it from me, but he might turn on you and get really vindictive. Do you want to take that risk?"

"I already have," said James. "I emailed him just before I left. Marshlands has wireless Internet, so I imagine there will be either an indignant rebuttal or a stream of vitriol waiting for me when we get there."

"You shouldn't put up with it," said Carol sadly, "not just because of me. I'm a big girl now. You should have moved on and found someone of your own to love. You should have married and made someone happy. You're such a kind man."

"I never found anyone who matched up to Amanda," James said simply.

* * *

Further along the road, another car was travelling to Marshlands. From the passenger seat, Jennifer Morton looked out at the tree-covered mountains, grey in the late-afternoon light as they soared above the road, disappearing gradually into the lowering sky. To the left, the river glided past, a swollen, tea-coloured stream of smooth water, the very stillness of its surface implying a relentless power, and threatening with the heavy rains to rise over the edge of the bank. Although the car heater was turned up high, there was still a biting chill coming off the windows. Jennifer pulled up her coat collar, huddled low in the seat and tried to focus on the velvet sound of her sister's voice emanating from the car's CD player. How appropriate, she thought, as she mentally translated the lyrics of the aria from *Nabucco*. "Who can know what suffering I have seen?" She wondered if her nightmares would ever cease, or would she be condemned forever to dream of flames surrounding a pair of cruel eyes that never seemed to belong to a particular face . . . and a disembodied laugh that caused her to wake sweating and rigid with fear.

Her mother spoke and pulled her from her reverie.

"Are you warm enough, darling?" Celia pointed over her shoulder towards the back seat. "Why don't you put that blanket over your knees?"

"I'm all right," said Jennifer. "But I wish Father hadn't insisted that we come to Marshlands. This is a dreary, desolate place. I don't like it."

"It'll be all right once we reach the lodge," said Celia. "You can sit by the fire all weekend. I may do some shooting with the men, but I brought lots of books to read and there are several in my bag that you would enjoy."

The road narrowed and began to wind up a steep hill. The river dropped away on the left, but each twist and turn in the road revealed glimpses of the watercourse below. Jennifer could see that the river was running faster and the water was now a mass of turbulent rapids. Suddenly, she became conscious of a dull sound, a constant hum, providing an increasingly intrusive counterpoint to the soprano voice floating from the dashboard. She looked ahead and saw the source of the noise. The road had moved away from the river, but the strip of forest bordering the gorge was narrow, and through the trees she could see a massive cascade of water thundering down the cliff.

"We're nearly there," said Celia. "That waterfall marks the edge of the Marshlands estate. It should only be a few more minutes to the lodge."

As the car reached the top of the hill, the ground levelled out and the road became a twisting ribbon winding through tall stands of pine trees interspersed with spruce and fir. Through the gaps in the trees, Jennifer could see a wide expanse of water ahead. Then the trees on the left disappeared, and for a hundred yards the road ran alongside the lakeshore, with only a strip of gravel separating it from the water. Then it branched away from the lake and cut back through the forest. Just as Jennifer thought that the trees would go on forever, the road widened and the forest opened onto a swath of grassland. The lodge lay straight ahead, a shadowy silhouette against the tall evergreens, but the windows glowed with light.

Celia pulled up in front of the building and reached into the back seat to get the overnight bags. She handed one to Jennifer; then they pulled up the hoods on their jackets, ran to the shelter of the front porch and entered the lodge.

They found themselves in a dark rectangular hall, lit only by a dim yellow ceiling fixture and the small green-shaded lamp which sat on the registration desk. The wall opposite the counter contained a utilitarian steel cupboard which Celia recognized as a gun cabinet. Beyond this, a narrow stairwell led to the lower floor. The far end of the hall opened onto a wood-panelled lounge with a massive stone fireplace. A billowing fire roared in the grate, generating a welcome blast of heat that came all the way across to the front hall.

A woman stood behind the registration desk. She was middle-aged, but well preserved, with blonde hair and a trim figure. She was talking with a tall, dark-haired man and an older lady of motherly appearance. The trio looked up when the newcomers entered. Seeing Jennifer shivering, the older woman murmured something about making her a cup of tea and suggested she go sit by the fire. Then she beckoned to the man to take the cases. He nodded, but said nothing as he picked up the bags. Something about his stare made Jennifer feel intensely uncomfortable.

As she entered the lounge, Jennifer's eyes were drawn to an angular metal sculpture of an eagle that hung from the ceiling on a thick chain. She looked away quickly and, turning her back on the predatory-looking creature, went over to the armchair by the fireplace. As she stared into the flames, she felt a wave of fatigue and her legs became weak. She sat down abruptly and held her hands tightly together in order to keep them still. Uneasily, she looked back towards the hall. The blonde woman was still talking to the man with the cases. Why did she seem familiar? In spite of the heat from the fire, Jennifer found herself shivering. Gratefully she accepted the cup of tea that the grey-haired woman was offering her, but even the hot drink could not eliminate the chill in her bones. The flames flickered in the fireside, and the light cast shadows around the room. Suddenly she felt as if she couldn't breathe, and she knew the nightmare would come again that night.

* * *

By morning, the rain had stopped, but the heavy precipitation had caused several mudslides in the valley. However, the new day brought a stroke of luck for the RCMP.

Staff Sergeant Brodie hung up the phone and looked at Richard triumphantly.

"That was the prison," he said. "One of the inmates has talked. He says Crampton received an anonymous letter that told him where to find Christie Canning, and it's likely that he broke out with the express intention of tracking her down. The letter states that Canning is at Marshlands Hunting Lodge. It's not that far from the prison, but it's very secluded. It's on a lake at the foot of the mountains and there's only one access road which runs alongside the river. We don't know much about the place, but I'm sending someone out there to look into it. We're going to focus the search in that area."

"We should contact the Mortons too," said Richard. "Most likely they will have heard about Crampton's escape, but it would be a courtesy to officially alert them to the fact that he's loose."

"Already been done," said Brodie. "I asked Jean Howe to call them."

The door of Brodie's office opened and the WPC in question popped her head into the room. She looked anxious.

"Sir, I just talked with Ronald Morton's housekeeper. None of the family is at the house." She gulped as if she had caught her breath. "You'll find this as hard to believe as I do," she continued, "but the Mortons are booked into the Marshlands Hunting Lodge for the weekend."

Richard and Brodie stared at her in amazement.

Finally Richard spoke.

"What the hell is going on?" he said.

* * *

James Burgess stared at the message on the screen of his laptop. He had received the answer to his question. Ronald Morton had explained brutally and unequivocally why his wife had killed herself.

Because, you stupid bastard, she was foolish enough to inform me that April wasn't my daughter. She told me shortly before the trial started. She actually thought telling me would ease my pain. But all it did was make me angry—so I punished her. I paid for Christie's lawyer, and I told Amanda that I was going to divorce her and make sure she never saw

Carol again. I expect she felt she had nothing left to live for. By the way, April was your child. I've really enjoyed having you under my thumb all these years, but the entertainment is wearing thin now. After this weekend, you're fired.

James could not take his eyes from the screen, although his vision was blurring and he was no longer reading the words. Then his cellphone rang, bringing him back to the present. It was the police.

"Mr. Burgess, we've been trying to get hold of Ronald Morton but he isn't answering. You're his lawyer, I believe."

"That's correct. Mr. Morton is probably on the road right now. His phone must be turned off."

"You're at the lodge yourself?"

"Yes. Several of us are spending the weekend here."

"Good. Then we'll liaise with you. There have been some landslides on the highway and one is at the junction of the road that leads to Marshlands. That means we can't get anyone there yet, but the road crew is working on the slide and it should be opened up shortly. It's important that Morton be contacted right away, especially if he's still on the road. There's a very good chance that Peter Crampton is somewhere in the vicinity of Marshlands and may be heading for the lodge itself."

"Why would he be coming here?"

"Because there's a very strong likelihood that his former girlfriend lives there."

James felt his head swim. He tried to answer but the words wouldn't come out.

"Sir, are you still there?"

"Yes. I'm sorry. I'm just shocked. Are you referring to Christie Canning? The woman who was implicated in his crimes?"

"Yes, I am. We don't know for certain if the information we received is correct, but it's imperative that you and the Mortons are on your guard. We'll get a unit there as soon as possible."

Stunned, James put down his phone and sat quietly for a moment. He was about to close his laptop, but then he changed his mind and logged onto the Internet. Crampton's escape was at the head of the news page. There was a photograph of two beautiful blonde people, a handsome man and a glamorous young woman—Canning and Crampton as they had been at the time of the trials. Who would believe they had been capable of such evil? James studied the picture closely. In spite of the difference in age, the resemblance to the woman downstairs was unmistakable.

He shut down his laptop and closed the lid. As he stood up, he had only one thought in his mind.

My only child and I never knew her.

* * *

"You know, I keep thinking you look familiar," said Carol. "Have we met before?"

"No," said Charlene. She sat at the desk and pulled out a piece of notepaper.

"That was very definite. How can you be so sure?"

"Your family is well known. I would remember if I had met you."

The front door opened and John Graves entered. He wore a camouflage jacket and was carrying a shotgun. He gave a cursory nod to Carol and walked over to the desk.

"Charlene, I need to talk with you."

"I don't have time. I'll be leaving shortly. I just have to finish these notes for Mrs. Marks." Charlene continued to write, but sensing that John was still standing at her shoulder, she spoke without looking up. "John, I don't think you've met Carol Morton yet. Carol, this is John Graves, our gamekeeper."

John gave Carol a perfunctory glance.

"Oh, *you're* the opera star. I'd assumed it was the gorgeous blonde that arrived last night. She looks so theatrical."

Carol's expression became frosty.

"That would be my stepmother."

"Really? She's very young. She doesn't look much older than you."

"My father likes his women young," Carol said acidly. "While my mother was busy raising myself and my sister, he had teenage mistresses on both sides of the Atlantic—his nanny in Canada and Celia in England. Celia's performances are reserved for real life, and they're hardly operatic, unless of course you add the qualifier, *soap*, in front of it."

"Not a problem," said John. "I don't like opera." Then, seeing Carol's expression, he continued. "But of course, I'd love to hear you sing some time."

Carol's eyes glinted dangerously.

"Perhaps the final act of *Salome*," she said. "You did say your name was John."

She nodded curtly and left the room. As soon as the door closed behind her, John's manner altered and he turned back to Charlene.

"You have to reschedule your trip to town," he said abruptly. "I need you here this weekend."

"John, it's no use arguing. I'm going, and that's final." Charlene finished writing the note and put down her pen. "I'm leaving you in charge."

John scowled angrily.

"But you're the owner. The Mortons will expect you to act as host."

"No, they won't. They're coming to hunt. not have afternoon tea."

"Look, I booked this group for the second weekend in the month because you're always here when it's Margaret's weekend off. How can we entertain high-profile clients with both of you away?"

Charlene stood firm.

"Margaret gave our guests breakfast before she left this morning and she's prepared all the other meals in advance. Sylvia Marks is perfectly competent to manage a house party in the lodge."

John's face darkened in fury.

"I wouldn't have set this up if I'd known you wouldn't be here."

Charlene's eyes flashed. "There's no negotiation on this, John," she snapped. "As soon as I've spoken with Mrs. Marks, I'm leaving."

She turned to go. James Burgess stood in the doorway, blocking her path.

"Is there a problem?" he said.

"No, not at all." Charlene moved towards the door but James remained where he was. He stared at her steadily, as if she had not answered. Charlene faltered. Finally she elaborated. "John is simply concerned because I have to be away this weekend."

"You're leaving before Ronald Morton gets here?"

"Yes, I have to."

James gave a strange smile.

"Yes, I expect you do. Perhaps," he added, "before you leave you could sign us out a couple of rifles. Celia and I thought we might do some target shooting."

Charlene nodded and went to get the key from the desk. "Mrs. Marks will look after your party," she assured him. "Everything will be more than satisfactory."

"I'm sure it will," said James calmly, and waited for her to produce the guns.

* * *

Jennifer left the lodge by the back door and walked down to the lake. A dilapidated-looking building that was either a boathouse or a storage shed jutted out over the water and a trio of ducks swam placidly nearby. Setting off along the trail that followed the shoreline, she breathed deeply, welcoming the cold, damp air, made even fresher by the sodden trees that lined the path. The dream had come back in the night and she felt as if she would suffocate if she remained in the lodge, for a new face had materialized in her restless and tormented sleep. She had dreamt about the ghost of her father's gardener, but the spectre had metamorphosed into the dark-haired gamekeeper who had carried her bags the night before. The dream made no sense. She had been far too young to remember anything about the gardener, other than a vague sense that he had been kind to her and her sisters. She had no recollection of what he had looked like, but she knew that he was dead.

She walked for some time, lost in thought and not noticing how far she had come, but suddenly she rounded a corner and saw that she could go no further. The lake had risen and flooded the trail. There was no way round. She stared down into the silent water. Then, as she peered at the clear, still surface, a leaf slowly drifted by. The stillness of the surface was deceptive, she realized. The lake was in motion. She looked up and gazed towards the distant shore. She could make out a break in the trees, and as she listened and observed the sounds and sights of the terrain, she heard a faint hum in the distance. The leaf was making its slow, inexorable progress towards the waterfall.

She turned and started back in the other direction. She was beginning to feel cold again, and she would have to hurry if she did not want to catch a chill. If Enrico had been there she would have found the weekend easier, but perhaps her father would arrive soon. He wouldn't let anything happen to her. If only she knew why she felt so afraid.

The walk back was longer than she remembered. The trail seemed to go on forever, and she began to wonder if she had taken a wrong turning. She pulled out her cellphone. Maybe Carol would come out to meet her. But before she could dial, she heard voices ahead. She hurried forward. Sure enough, as she turned the next corner, she emerged from the trees and saw the boathouse ahead. The trio of ducks still floated tranquilly near the shore, but there were no people in sight. Whoever had been talking must have gone in the other direction.

The air was very still. Jennifer walked across the grass and approached the lodge. A moment later, a shot rang out on the other side of the building.

With a noisy flapping of wings, the ducks flew up into the air.

* * *

Ronald Morton geared down as he approached the turnoff to Marshlands. There were trucks up ahead, and a road crew, and as he drew nearer he understood why. A section of the mountainside had come down across the road, and although there was just enough clearance to get through, the huge wall of gravel clinging to the rock-face looked sufficiently unstable that it could collapse at any moment. He slowed to a crawl at the corner and waved a thank-you to the man who guided him round the debris. Then he accelerated. The access road to Marshlands wound with the bends in the river, but the day was clear and visibility was good so he revelled in the prospect of a high-speed drive on an isolated country road.

Half an hour later, the Jaguar was climbing the steep hill that led to the top of the gorge. Morton saw the waterfall ahead and realized that he was approaching the boundary of the Marshlands estate. He gave an unpleasant smile as he anticipated his arrival. He was looking forward to the showdown with James Burgess, if, of course, the man had summoned up enough courage to stay and face him.

He had enjoyed the slow process of breaking Burgess down over the years, but he hadn't finished with him yet. The lawyer would never get another position once he was ejected dishonorably from Morton Enterprises, and there were lots of ways that the company accountants could ensure that the dismissal was sufficiently scandalous to cause total ruin. But for now, Morton intended to concentrate on his hunting weekend. He always enjoyed a killing spree.

He noticed that the trees beside the road were starting to sway. A slight breeze was springing up, and he wondered if it would be the precursor to another major storm. The weather forecasts had indicated that rough weather was ahead. Not that it would deter him. He had come to hunt, and he intended to make the most of his stay.

He rounded another corner. The trees disappeared on his left and he found that he was driving along the perimeter of the lake. To his surprise, he saw that someone was standing on the road ahead.

* * *

Constable Terry Blake was intrigued by her assignment. She had been ordered to go to Marshlands and remain with the Morton family until further notice. Although she had only been a child at the time of the Crampton case, she had read about the murder of April Morton. It would be very interesting to meet the people involved. As she headed down the highway, her radio cut in. It was Detective Inspector Richard Beary.

"Terry, how far are you from Marshlands?"

"I should be there in another half hour. I'm about five minutes from the turnoff."

"OK. There's a problem. There's been a shooting at the lodge. I want you to listen carefully. There's been another slide—a relatively small one—but you might be delayed while they clear the road."

"I can still get there faster than anyone else."

"Maybe, but remember, Crampton is in the area and he's highly dangerous. We're sending out a special unit by helicopter, so you'll have backup, but you'll have to be careful. We also have to get a forensic unit out there. The victim is the owner of Marshlands. Her name is Charlene Cook, but we have reason to believe she was actually Christie Canning. Someone fired a rifle shot at her as she was getting into her car."

"Why do we think the victim was Christie Canning, sir?"

Richard explained about the anonymous letter. Then he continued. "It's almost a dead cert that the shooter was Crampton, and that means he's armed. He vowed to get even with Canning after the trial, and he swore revenge on Ronald Morton for helping her. Morton's lawyer is the one who called us. His name is James Burgess. He's assured me that nothing has been touched and he's keeping everyone inside the lodge until we give him the all-clear. Now, there's another complication that you'll have to deal with. The housekeeper is with the traffic officer at the junction by the access road. She's an older lady, and she was actually caught in the second, smaller slide. She isn't hurt, but her car is out of commission. She's very shaken up, and then, on top of her accident, she was with the traffic officer when he received news of the shooting. She's very upset, and it sounds from the way she's babbling that she knew Charlene Cook's real identity. She's been given tea and kept warm, but I want you to take her back to the lodge. A tranquillizer might be a good idea once she gets there. Take care of her as best you can."

The radio cut out. Terry put on her siren and pulled out to pass the line of traffic. As she sped down the centre lane, she felt the car being buffeted by the wind. She suddenly noticed the black clouds hovering over the mountains and saw that the trees on the hillside were starting to dance and sway in the ever increasing breeze. The storm was coming back.

* * *

At the turnoff, the rain had already started. Margaret Crane stood with the traffic officer at the side of the road. She was restless and anxious, preferring to be out in the open rather than in the shelter of the police car, but she was shivering in spite of the blanket around her shoulders.

The policeman remained with her, realizing that she was in a state of shock and needed someone to talk to. He noticed that her teeth were chattering whenever she spoke. He hoped Constable Blake would get there quickly. The road crew had been working steadily and the access road to Marshlands was clear, so the sooner the woman was returned to the warmth of the lodge the better. He peered down the highway again and to his relief, he saw a patrol car approaching.

He moved Margaret onto the verge.

"Look, this will be Constable Blake," he said. "You're going with her. She'll take good care of you."

The squad car sped towards them, and then pulled around the corner and stopped on the road that led to Marshlands. Terry Blake hopped out of the vehicle and, looking carefully in each direction, ran across the highway. She greeted the traffic officer, and then turned to Margaret Crane.

"Mrs. Crane? I'm Constable Blake. I'm taking you back to the lodge. A tow truck has been called for your car. Everything will be taken care of."

She put her arm across the older woman's shoulders and urged her forward.

Relieved to be free of his charge, the traffic officer walked into the middle of the road and waved Terry across. Margaret allowed herself to be led to the patrol car. The rain had started again, and the force of the wind was blowing the drops in under her umbrella. She felt steeped in misery, very cold and desperately tired. Terry Blake solicitously settled her in the back seat. Then she called a thank you to the other policeman and got into the car.

The traffic officer watched as the squad car pulled out onto the access road and disappeared around the first bend. There were no other cars in sight and the road crew was busy, so he wandered to the other side of the highway and looked at the river. The waters were still swollen and moving with an unnerving force towards the junction where the access road met the highway. As the river surged round the bend, the inside of the curve became a series of turbulent rapids. However, on the outer edge, a deep pool had formed and a mass of branches hung over the bank. A log had wedged against the side of the pool, caught in the overhang and partially hidden by the branches that trailed into the water, and it bobbed up and down with the pressure of the moving water. As the constable continued to stare at the log, it seemed to become fluid, and there was something sinister about the shape that kept appearing above the waterline.

Suddenly alert, the policeman walked onto the access road. The slope at the river's edge was less steep at this point, and he scrambled down the bank to get a closer look. The log had submerged again, for the steady stream of water buffeting against the riverbank was being whipped into increased turbulence by the wind and the pounding rain, but after a moment, the object rolled to the surface and the constable saw that his suspicions were correct. A face had appeared amid the branches.

* * *

Carol stood by the window and stared out at the storm. The rain was beating against the glass, and in spite of the noise from the radio in the next room, she could hear the wind whistling and raging as it gusted overhead. It was now past noon and she wondered why her father still had not come. She had tried to contact him, but his cellphone was turned off. He had been looking forward to a weekend of hunting, yet he had seemed in a strange mood before she left. Something was going on, and it probably stemmed from the message that James had sent him. Either that, or he had simply been held up by the storm and the mudslides. She knew her father was not a thoughtful man and that he would not think of calling to let his family know if he had been delayed, but no matter how logically she tried to rationalize his failure to show up, she felt uneasy.

She turned away from the window and came back to the fire. Margaret Crane was huddled in the armchair closest to the grate. The sound of the radio was cut off abruptly, and a moment later, the door opened and James came into the room.

"Where's the police constable?" he asked.

"She's outside talking on her radio."

"The storm is getting worse. It will hold up the search for Crampton."

The door opened again and John Graves appeared. He held the door for Celia to come through. She was carrying a tea tray, which she brought over and set on the end table beside Margaret Crane's armchair. Celia poured the tea. Then she knelt down and gently touched the other woman's arm. The flickering flames from the fireplace turned Celia's golden hair a burnished red and the diamond studs in her ears sparkled in the light. With a sharp intake of breath, Carol noticed that John Grave's eyes did not leave her stepmother's face, but Celia seemed unaware of the gamekeeper's prolonged stare, for her eyes were on the housekeeper.

"Mrs. Crane, I've brought you a tranquillizer," she said. "I think you should take it with your tea. It'll calm you down." Celia placed the pill on the saucer. Then she looked up at Carol and James. "Mrs. Marks has made up sandwiches and there's coffee on the sideboard in the dining room," she told them. "You'd better go and have something to eat."

"What about Jennifer?"

"She's still lying down. I'm going to let her sleep."

The front door opened and Constable Blake entered. Her expression was grim.

"I've just been talking to headquarters," she said. "There's a backup unit and a forensic team on the way, but the weather is causing problems. If they can't get the helicopter out, the unit will have to come via the highway. Everyone is to stay inside. Now, in the meantime, I have some questions." She turned towards John Graves. "Mr. Graves, I want to look at your gun cupboard."

John looked startled.

"Why?"

"It's a precaution. Did anyone have guns out at the time Charlene Cook was shot?"

"Yes. Mrs. Morton and Mr. Burgess were target shooting. Charlene had signed them out a couple of .22 rifles. I had my own shotgun out. I was getting ready to go duck hunting."

"Where are those guns now?"

"Locked away in the gun case."

"The bullet wound looks like a rifle shot," Terry said bluntly. "It could well have been made with a .22." She looked at James and Celia. "Were the two of you together outside?"

Celia flushed and glanced at James. Neither spoke. John Graves answered the question.

"No, they weren't. When I ran out to see what had happened, I saw Charlene sprawled on the driveway. Jennifer was standing a few feet away. She was frozen. The poor girl was in shock, but no one else was in sight. Mrs. Morton appeared almost immediately from the direction of the boathouse, but it was several minutes before Mr. Burgess appeared and he came from the woods on the other side of the drive."

Terry listened dispassionately. Then she walked over to the gun cupboard.

"Open it, please," she told John.

John pulled out his keys and opened the door. He pointed to the row of rifles.

"There they are—two .22 rifles. I fail to see why this is significant," he added. "Crampton is the killer you're looking for. What do our guns have to do with it?"

"Crampton escaped from Greystone less than forty-eight hours prior to the shooting. Someone must have provided him with a gun." Terry pointed to the end of the cabinet. "Is that a separate compartment?" she asked.

"Yes, but that's for Charlene's own guns. She has a shotgun, a rifle and a revolver, and she didn't want anyone else using them. She kept her own key to that section."

"Nobody has a duplicate?"

"I believe she kept one in the safe. I can get it for you."

John went behind the reception desk and opened a cupboard below the counter. Inside was a small safe with a combination lock. He knelt down and turned the dials. The door clicked open, and he reached in and pulled out a small black box. A set of keys lay inside. He took the keys to the gun cabinet and opened the end compartment. As the door swung wide, he gasped. The compartment contained a solitary shotgun. The rifle and the revolver had both disappeared.

* * *

Richard Beary sipped his coffee thoughtfully and contemplated the call he had just received from Constable Blake. Terry had confirmed James Burgess's story. The shot had come from the woods on the far side of the drive, which meant Crampton had somehow managed to arm himself since his escape. The situation was getting uglier by the minute.

The door of his office opened and Jean Howe looked in.

"There's a press reporter to see you, sir," she said. "He's not after a story. He says he has information for you."

Richard felt sceptical, but he asked Jean to let the man in. A moment later, Bob Fenton entered. Richard gestured to him to sit down, but Bob remained standing. He pulled a piece of paper from his pocket and set it on the desk.

"It's an anonymous letter," he said. "Someone thinks Christie Canning didn't deserve to be let out after twelve years."

Richard picked the paper up and perused it.

"I see that," he said, setting the note back down. "According to this, she was helping Crampton from the start. It doesn't give much detail though, does it?"

"Look," said Bob, "this letter says Christie Canning has been living at Marshlands Hunting Lodge. I've been doing some research. I called the place last week, pretending I was interested in a booking, and I managed to get a list of the staff. Then I looked through the old files and did some work on the Internet. Canning is there all right. I thought I should alert you before I head out to Marshlands to get my story."

Richard stood up and his tone became formal.

"Don't even think about it," he said sternly. "You are categorically ordered not to go anywhere near Marshlands."

"Hey, hold on," said Bob. "I didn't have to come here and tell you. I thought I was doing a public service."

"Mr. Fenton," said Richard, "there is every reason to believe that Peter Crampton is in the vicinity of Marshlands. The area will soon be crawling with police, and members of the public will be instructed to keep their distance. And just to make sure you comply," he added, "I'm going to have you wait down the hall as I may have further questions for you."

Richard called Jean Howe back and asked her to escort Fenton to the waiting area. Reluctantly, the reporter followed the constable from the room. As Richard returned to his desk, Staff Sergeant Brodie entered. He looked agitated.

"We've just had a report from the traffic division," he said. "At eleven o'clock this morning, a body was discovered at the bend in the river. It's been identified as Peter Crampton."

Richard was astounded.

"He drowned?"

"No. He was shot in the head. And there's more. His watch was battery-operated but non-digital, so it's waterlogged and the hands are stopped at ten to twelve. He must have been killed and thrown in the water within hours of his escape from prison."

"But that's not possible. That would mean he was already dead before Charlene Cook was shot."

"Exactly. And get this. There were lily pads tangled in his clothing."

"Lily pads? But they don't grow in the river."

"No. But they're abundant in the lake at Marshlands. He must have headed straight for Marshlands as soon as he escaped. He could have reached the estate by late evening. He must have been shot on the grounds and dumped in the lake. The undercurrents will have taken the body across the lake and over the waterfall. And you realize what that means."

Richard looked grim.

"Yes. Someone else at Marshlands is a killer. The Mortons' visit obviously wasn't a coincidence. One of them must have been bent on revenge. Get onto Terry Blake right away and warn her. And alert the unit that's heading out there." Brodie headed for the door, but Richard called him back. "One other thing," he added. "Get that reporter back in here."

* * *

Terry Blake carefully pushed the cabinet door closed without allowing the catch to click into place. Then she turned and looked sternly at the other occupants of the room.

"Is there any chance at all that Crampton could have broken into the lodge?" she asked.

John Graves shook his head.

"I don't see how it's possible. We keep the doors locked. There's no sign of a break-in."

"All right. I don't want anyone to go near that cupboard. The whole cabinet will have to be checked for fingerprints."

Carol looked irritated.

"So what do we do in the interim while we wait for your swat team, or whatever's coming?"

"Sit tight," Terry said shortly. "I have to radio in again. I'm ordering you all to stay inside the lodge. Mr. Graves and Mrs. Crane, you, as staff members, are expected to assist me in making sure everyone stays in and keeps away from the gun cabinet."

"Just because they work at this dump doesn't mean they're any more trustworthy than the rest of us," Carol said snidely. "So if there's nothing else to do, I'm going to have something to eat."

She tossed her head and stalked out of the room. Terry remained outwardly calm, but inside she was apprehensive. Her intriguing assignment was becoming a high-stress situation. There was something more going on than the escape of a convicted murderer. She wished her back-up unit would appear, but the screaming sound of the wind overhead made her realize that she might be on her own for some time. Thoughtfully, she surveyed the other occupants of the room. Celia Morton was breathtakingly beautiful and elegant. Her countenance was serene, and it was hard to believe that she was well into her forties and the mother of a twenty-six-year-old daughter. John Graves stood close to Celia, as if somehow he felt that he had the right to protect her. Was it just the attraction of a beautiful woman, Terry wondered, or was there some connection between them that she did not know about? James Burgess was hard to read, but then he was a lawyer and would be well schooled in the art of giving nothing away. Margaret Crane, on the other hand, was visibly distressed. The woman was clearly in a state of shock and showed no inclination to leave her armchair. Terry noticed that the cabinet was in clear view from the chair by the fire.

"All right," she said briskly. "I suggest you all go and eat. I will need to talk to you, Mr. Graves, once I've reported in. In the meantime, Mrs. Crane, I'd ask that you remain here and make sure that no one touches the gun cabinet. Would you mind doing that?"

Margaret looked surprised, but she acquiesced, and Terry signalled to the others to leave. The room emptied gradually, and Terry, having ascertained that the others were congregated in the dining room, went back outside.

Margaret stayed in her armchair. There was no problem in complying with the police constable's request. Her head was throbbing, and her palpitations had only slightly subsided. She looked at the tranquillizer, but she was apprehensive about taking it. Perhaps more tea would help clear her head. She poured herself a second cup. As she did so, she heard a sound from behind her.

She looked round to see Jennifer coming down the stairs. The young woman's eyes were dazed and she walked like a sleepwalker. She barely acknowledged Margaret's presence, but once she reached the ground floor, she glided across the room towards the hall. She was making for the front door, but as she passed the gun cabinet, she stopped. Her face took on a bemused expression as she saw that the door was slightly ajar. Then she reached out towards the cabinet.

* * *

At the police station, Richard was grilling Bob Fenton.

"Did you pass on the information you unearthed to any member of the Morton family?" Richard demanded.

The reporter looked surprised.

"I did try to get an interview," he admitted, "and I used the tactic that I had information I could share with them. But I never got past the front door. The glamorous harpy who sings opera sent me off with a flea in my ear. That voice may be beautiful on stage but it has one hell of an edge when she's in a paddy."

"So you didn't tell them that Christie Canning was at Marshlands?"

"No. Why?"

"Did you realize that their entire family was going to be at Marshlands this weekend?"

Bob looked astounded.

"No. I had no idea. Good God! Has there been some sort of incident?"

Richard sighed inwardly and weighed the pros and cons of sharing information with a press hound. But the man could be useful, even if he had a tendency to be overzealous in the pursuit of a story. Richard decided to take him into his confidence.

"Both Canning and Crampton have been murdered," he said. "They were both shot on the Marshlands estate. Canning was killed as she was about to get into her car and leave for the weekend. Presumably, she was trying to get away before Ronald Morton arrived and recognized her. Crampton's death is more puzzling. It appears that he was shot within hours of his escape. I need to discover which member of the Morton family knew that Canning was at Marshlands and set this weekend up."

Bob shook his head.

"I can't help you there," he said. "To my knowledge, none of them knew. Why don't you ask the owner of the place? Charlene Cook might be able to give you some idea of who made the initial enquiries."

Richard looked up sharply.

"Charlene Cook can't tell us anything. I just told you. She's dead."

Bob's face paled.

"What do you mean, she's dead?"

Richard started to feel impatient.

"Christie Canning . . . Charlene Cook . . . one and the same person. I told you, she was shot as she was trying to leave the lodge."

"Oh, Christ," said Bob. "We've been talking round in circles. You're looking at this the wrong way round. Charlene Cook wasn't Christie Canning. She was Canning's sister."

* * *

"No, Jennifer. Don't touch that door."

Jennifer looked blankly at Margaret Crane. Seeing the uncomprehending expression on the girl's face, Margaret pulled herself from her armchair. The last thing she felt like doing was helping the police, but at this point there was no alternative. She went over to the gun cabinet.

"The police want to check for fingerprints. Leave the door alone."

Jennifer's head swam. A vision of Charlene's body spread-eagled on the driveway floated in front of her eyes. Then the image dissolved and she found herself staring at the rifles that were just visible through the open door of the cupboard. Her heart started to pound.

"Gun cabinets are supposed to be locked," she insisted.

She reached out to close the door, but Margaret stopped her.

"Jennifer, did you hear what I said? Stay away from that cupboard."

Jennifer froze and stared at the other woman. Then she began to breathe more quickly. Margaret started to feel alarmed.

"What is it?" she demanded. "What's the matter with you?"

Jennifer's fists clenched and she pulled her arms tightly against her chest. "That's what *she* said," she cried. "April was in there! April was in the cupboard on the landing!"

"Jennifer, what are you talking about?"

"When April didn't come back, we went to look for her. We went through the house—but Christie wouldn't let me open the cupboard."

Margaret gave a nervous laugh. "Jennifer, have you gone mad?"

Jennifer's eyes were dark with terror. "Don't laugh!" she pleaded. "*She* laughed . . . don't you see? She was always laughing. She laughed when Father threw the snake on the fire. She—" Jennifer's voice broke off into a sob.

"Stop this," said Margaret sharply. "You're hysterical."

She tried to take Jennifer's arm, but the young woman pulled away violently and thrust her arms out in front of her, holding them rigidly as if trying to create an impenetrable shield.

"Don't touch me!" she hissed. "I know you now. I didn't recognize you before—you look so different—but your eyes are the same."

Margaret took a step backwards but her gaze was riveted on the distraught young woman.

Jennifer put her hands to her head. Her face felt wet, and she knew she was shedding tears for the sister she had lost so young. She could hear the horrible laughter in her ears, although she knew there was no sound coming from the woman opposite. The roaring in her head grew louder and more insistent, and the pounding increased until she thought it would drive her mad. Then, suddenly, she realized that she was not imagining the noises. The incessant beating and throbbing was coming from somewhere outside.

Jennifer looked up. Through her tears she saw that the housekeeper was still watching her, but the motherly façade had slipped away. It had been replaced by an absence of expression that was both terrifying and strangely familiar. Margaret reached into the pocket of her voluminous coat and pulled out a revolver.

Slowly Jennifer backed away.

"Oh, God . . . my beautiful sister. How did you do it? You were with us the whole time."

"It was easy," said Margaret calmly. "Peter waved to me when he had a break, and I sent April inside. Peter slipped away long enough to drug her and shut her in the cupboard. Then he went back to his open house. I provided his alibi."

"Why did you do it? Why did you hurt us?"

Margaret's eyes glittered and her voice hardened.

"Because you had everything, and I had nothing," she spat. "Your father used me and dumped me. He deserved to die. He didn't recognize me either . . . until just before I shot him."

Jennifer sank to her knees. "Father? Oh, God, no!"

Margaret nodded coldly.

"He thought he was pulling over to help a harmless old lady whose jeep was stuck by the lake," she gloated. "I had him like a rat in a trap."

"Why did you have to kill him?" Jennifer sobbed. "You'd served your sentence. You were in the clear. Now you're no better than Crampton."

The air fell suddenly silent. Margaret smiled a chilling smile. Jennifer gradually became aware that the noise she had heard earlier had stopped and an eerie hush surrounded them.

"Oh, you little fool," crooned Margaret. "You still haven't figured it out. Crampton wasn't a killer. He was just a weak fool who used me like your father did. He liked young girls but he was too scared to get rid of them once he'd had his fun . . . so I disposed of them."

"*You* killed April!"

"Yes . . . her and all the others . . . but then the bastard turned on me too . . . he was afraid of the killing . . . he didn't want any more."

"That's why he beat you up . . . he wanted to stop you . . . Oh God, why didn't he kill you?"

"He didn't have the guts . . . even after he broke out of jail. All he could do was make threats."

"So you murdered him too?"

"I had no choice. He called the lodge, you know. Charlene answered, but she didn't know I'd picked up the phone in the library. Once she hung up, I talked to him. I arranged to meet him in the storage shed."

Jennifer felt weak. Margaret continued to drone on as if she were in a world of her own.

"Well, he's dead now. They all are . . . everyone who could identify me . . . Peter . . . Ronald . . . Charlene."

"Who was Charlene?"

"My sister. My stupid, loving sister who always believed everything I told her. Charlene kept her looks, didn't she? But then, she didn't have to hide from the world. I let my hair turn grey . . . my flesh became soft, and I assumed the identity of an elderly cook who had died in a fire in New Brunswick. I thought I was safe, but then everything started again . . . and I knew I had to get away and that Charlene had to be silenced. It was such a perfect plan. But the landslide stopped me from escaping and I found myself coming back under police escort. I still thought I could pull it off, but I never thought you'd be a danger."

Jennifer felt light-headed and the room seemed to be getting brighter. She wondered if she were about to faint, but as she looked up, she saw that the glow was coming from the hall window. The sensor light had gone on outside. Margaret had noticed it too. She waved the gun towards Jennifer.

"Get up."

"Please . . . let me go."

"Shut up and do as I tell you. We're going outside."

Slowly, Jennifer stood up. Margaret backed against the window and waved the gun in the direction of the door. Jennifer started to move down the hall, but before she could reach the door, a shot rang out, deafening inside the enclosed area.

The hall window shattered. Jennifer found she was on her knees though she could not remember falling. She looked up to see a patch of pale grey sky encircled by the few jagged shards that remained in the wooden frame. Beside her, Margaret lay motionless on the hall carpet.

Then the front door burst open and a small troop of officers rushed into the building. The swat team had finally arrived.

* * *

James took Jennifer back to town that night, but Carol and Celia remained at Marshlands while the police carried out their search for Ronald Morton. The rains had stopped, but a cold, deadening mist engulfed the area and progress was slow. Two days later, Ronald Morton's Jaguar was pulled out of the lake. His body was in the driver's seat.

On Wednesday morning, Richard Beary drove out to Marshlands to give his personal condolences to the widow and her daughter. He also wanted to talk with John Graves. When he arrived at the lodge, a patrol car was parked in the driveway, but the engine was running and the constable appeared to be ready to leave. The Mortons were also preparing to go home. Celia stood on the porch of the lodge. She was wearing a heavy winter coat and watching as John Graves loaded bags into Carol's Mercedes. Richard was not surprised to see Bob Fenton also on the premises. The reporter had wasted no time once the area had been opened up to the public. He noted with amusement that Carol Morton appeared to be giving Fenton a tongue-lashing. John Graves, however, seemed oblivious to the altercation at the other end of the porch. He was completely preoccupied with the widow. Hardly surprising, thought Richard. Celia was a very attractive woman.

He had a brief word with the police constable, and then went to pay his respects to Celia. She thanked him graciously and introduced him to John Graves.

The gamekeeper looked slightly uncomfortable. He hesitated, and then, with a rush, he started to talk.

"Look, there's something weighing on my conscience and I'd better come clean. I was going to tell you," he added, turning to Celia, "but then Charlene was killed and it was never the right moment. You see . . . my name isn't really Graves . . ."

His voice petered out. Celia smiled.

251

"I knew that," she said. "You're John Marshall, aren't you? The boy who used to play with April."

John was visibly shocked.

"How could you possibly know that?" he asked.

"I've known Ronald since I was seventeen years old. I wasn't in a position to raise my own child, but surely you realize how closely I must have followed everything that happened to the Morton family. It was my baby's nanny that ended up in the headlines. I read all the news reports, and I saw the pictures of your poor father. You look just like him, John. And your anger is unmistakable every time you speak about what happened to him. How could I not guess? The only thing I couldn't understand was what you were doing here."

"I imagine," said Richard, "that you came here to track down Christie Canning."

John did not attempt to deny it.

"Yes," he said. "She was the one who destroyed my father. I'd always believed that Crampton framed him, but last year my mother died, and when I went through her effects, I came across her diary. Then I learned where the rumour about my father preying on April had started. Christie Canning had been spreading the tale. That evil woman had actually planted doubts in my own mother's mind. And she told other people too, so that the story came back to my mother from other sources. She worked to isolate my father and deliberately set him up as a suspect. She was involved right from the start."

"Why did you stay here if you hated her so much?" Celia asked softly.

John paused. He looked troubled.

"When I met her, I started to have doubts. She seemed so nice . . . so genuine . . . but of course, I had it wrong. I was fixated on Charlene. So I had to be sure before I acted. And then I thought of setting up a confrontation."

Richard looked at him sharply.

"What do you mean, a confrontation?"

John sighed.

"I wrote a series of anonymous letters. I let Crampton know where Canning was living, and I let the media know that there was new evidence to suggest that she was more involved than anyone suspected.

I also wrote to Mr. Burgess because there were things in the diary that I thought he ought to know." He turned back to Celia. "I'm so sorry, Celia. I never meant to put your family in danger."

Richard felt suddenly redundant. He glanced towards Carol Morton. She was still chastising Bob Fenton and had backed him up against the wall of the house. Fenton was making some attempt to defend himself, which surprised Richard. Personally, he would have walked away from such a harangue. He decided it was time to intervene. He stepped over to the other side of the porch and waited for the prima donna to pause for breath.

Carol was in fighting form.

"You don't give a damn about my family," she spat, stabbing her finger in front of the reporter's face. "All Canning and Crampton meant to you was titillating headlines for your newspaper. If you want an exclusive interview, why don't you go to hell, and then you'll be able to interview them in person."

Richard took advantage of the dramatic pause that followed the stream of invective and cut into the conversation.

"Bob may be an aggressive reporter," he said quietly, "but he was the one who provided the information that helped us solve the case. He's the person who found out that Charlene was Canning's sister and that she was sheltering her because she believed her to be innocent."

Carol looked surprised and affronted at being interrupted. She turned her blazing eyes on Richard, but under his steady stare, she faltered and softened her tiger-like pose. Still looking somewhat mutinous, she addressed Bob Fenton again.

"Why didn't you tell us?" she muttered. "You let us walk right into her nasty little hidey-hole."

"When did you give me a chance?" said Bob. "You shut the door in my face—and how was I supposed to know you were going to Marshlands? You're a very private family."

Unable to counter what was undeniably true, Carol changed the subject.

"How did you guess that Margaret Crane was Canning?" she demanded. "Charlene was the one who looked like her."

"I started by going through the old photos of the trial. It didn't take me long to find that Canning had a sister named Charlene, and from there it was easy to discover that Charlene Cook's maiden name was Canning. So obviously, Canning herself had to be one of the other women at the lodge. I didn't expect her to look the same," said Bob. "Logically, if she was afraid of retaliation, she would change her appearance, and if she was going to steal someone's identity, she would opt for a person who looked entirely different. So I researched Sylvia Marks and Margaret Crane. Mrs. Marks had a local history a mile long, but Crane was a mystery. However, the name came up in an article about a hotel fire in New Brunswick, so it seemed likely that the real Margaret Crane was dead and Canning had taken her identity."

"And as soon as he realized that," said Richard, "he came straight to me and passed on what he knew. You owe him an apology, Miss Morton."

Richard nodded politely and walked back to his car. Before getting into the vehicle, he glanced back at the group on the porch. Carol Morton remained by Bob Fenton's side, and the grin on the reporter's face suggested that he was taking full advantage of the prima donna stepping down from her pedestal. But Carol's face revealed a hint of a smile too, and Richard silently wished both the singer and her stepmother well. In spite of their talents and wealth, happiness had been elusive for the Morton women. He hoped life would bring them better things in the future.

Glad to be leaving the bleak estate, he got into his car and started the engine.

As he pulled out onto the drive, he looked into his rear-view mirror. The lodge seemed surreal, its outline hazy and insubstantial in the cloud-like wisps that surrounded it, and he had gone no more than a hundred feet before it faded and evaporated into the mist.

Mary Poppins, where are you? The phrase suddenly flew into his mind. The question was no longer relevant, but if Carol Morton was to be believed, he knew the answer. She was in hell where she belonged.

CHRISTMAS PRESENT,
CHRISTMAS PAST

There were worse things than Christmas shopping with Edwina, Beary thought philosophically, as he waited outside the Guess Store and looked towards Santa's castle where a growing line of small children fidgeted and whined as they inched towards the entrance. At least he could think his own thoughts and grab the occasional cup of coffee, but poor old Saint Nick was stuck on his throne, surrounded by motorized elves and reindeer, with no hope of respite until the next union-dictated break, and doomed like the Ancient Mariner to repeat the same phrases over and over while being drooled on and harassed by wild-eyed tots. Beary watched as a little girl was dragged forward by her mother and coaxed to sit on Santa's lap, whereupon the child emitted an ear-piercing wail and burst into tears. No, thought Beary, I definitely have the better lot.

A prod in his side made him look down. His granddaughter was holding up a shopping bag and pointing gleefully towards its contents.

"Jeans?" said Beary. "Don't you have lots of those?"

"These are Guess jeans," Laura informed him.

"Ah. Very nice." Beary had no notion of the significance, but realized a certain response was called for. "Where's your sister and your grandmother?" he asked.

"Still in the store. Jennifer can't decide which T-shirt to buy. Grandma says she can only have one."

"That debate should be good for another half-hour," said Beary. He gestured towards the glittering ice palace at the centre of the mall. "Why don't you join the line and tell Santa what you want for Christmas?"

Laura looked offended. "I'm eight," she said. "Don't be silly, Grampus."

Beary was tempted to reply that she was also old enough to drop the nickname she had given him when she was two, but since the rest of the family seemed to think the moniker was hilariously appropriate, he accepted the fact that he was stuck with it. Therefore, he simply replied, "So what do you want to do while we wait?"

"Nothing." Laura scowled. "I'm tired."

"You're young," said Beary. "How can you be tired?"

"Because Dad has made us rehearse our show over and over so it's perfect. He's making us work really hard."

"Your parents are working harder," Beary pointed out unsympathetically. "You get to come shopping with us tonight while they're setting up the marionette theatre. At least you only have to work the puppets. I hope you're taking good care of the one I made for you." Beary had made a wooden marionette of his white husky, MacPuff, and he was singularly proud of his contribution to his daughter's entertainment troupe.

Laura's eyes lit up.

"I love MacPuff's puppet," she said. "We've shortened his name to

Max for the show, and he's the star. Dad has written the neatest story. He goes back to Ancient Rome in a time machine and ends up in the Colosseum."

"Who? Your father?"

"No. Max. He gets saved at the very last minute before the gladiators and tigers and soldiers get him."

"I'm glad to hear it," said Beary. "You seem to be taking great liberties with my masterpiece. How did your father manage to write a time machine into the show?"

"There's a naughty boy called Cedric and he invents a time machine because he wants to go back to Rome to meet Nero."

"Another naughty boy. I see. There is a certain logic in that. I hope it all comes right in the end."

"Yes. Everyone gets back to the present in time to sing the title song."

"Which is?"

"'The Christmas Present of Christmas Past'. It's really pretty. Dad wrote the songs for Aunty Philippa and her opera friends."

"That much I knew. Philippa gave me a recording of the music. I imagine it's the semi-operatic nature of the show that enabled your mother to land a prestigious engagement in Shaughnessy. It's quite a coup to be asked to perform for Miriam Fearing's Christmas gala."

"Aunty Philippa is going to be singing live as well as on the puppet soundtrack. It's going to be a really neat party. Why aren't you and Grandma coming?"

"At two thousand dollars a ticket? Not on your life. You can tell me all about it afterwards."

Edwina materialized on Beary's other side.

"It's too bad," she snapped. "With Sylvia's family in Hawaii and Richard flying to New York with that Dolly Parton female, there's only Philippa and Juliette left in town. I don't mind them doing Miriam Fearing's symphony fundraiser—that's a big career boost for them— but going back to perform at her private party on the twenty-fourth is a bit much. We'll be all alone on Christmas Eve. And don't start quoting Omar Khayyám at me," she added, seeing the glint in her husband's eye. "We'll be in a three-story house in a suburb, not in a desert oasis. It's all most annoying." She turned her gimlet eye on Jennifer and

Laura, both of whom were attempting to pass their shopping bags to their grandfather. "Carry your own parcels, girls," she said firmly. "Come along. Two more stops and then we're done." She set off down the mall and the girls obediently fell into line behind her.

"I'm surprised Miriam Fearing can maintain her lifestyle, let alone all the projects she sponsors," said Beary as he followed Edwina towards the escalator. "She must have done some highly successful investing over the years. She can't possibly be doing it from the proceeds of Garden World and that cheap chain of hairdressing joints that her old man established."

"Why not?" said Edwina. "Lots of people get their hair done at Trims, and the garden shops have been around for seventy years. They're a Vancouver institution."

"Exactly," said Beary. "And they were tremendously successful during the forties, fifties and sixties, but times have changed. Stores like Costco are putting them out of business. Three Garden World outlets have been closed in the past decade. In fact, ever since old man Fearing died, there have been signs of cutbacks. And the hairdressing business isn't going to save the day. There was an article in *Financial Post* last week. Trims is facing a hostile takeover from some other quick-cut outfit."

"Shingles?"

"That's the one. Trims must be in even worse trouble than the garden shops. Everything points to the fact that money is tight."

"Not on the society page," declared Edwina. "Miriam Fearing must be over eighty, but she's always popping up in the paper, dripping with diamonds and wearing some gorgeous evening gown that was probably purchased in Paris or New York. Her jewellery alone is estimated to be worth more than a million dollars."

"Maybe that's why money is tight," suggested Beary. He eyed the shopping bags swinging from his wife's arm. "On that subject . . ." he began.

His words fell on deaf ears. Edwina accelerated around two shoppers who were chattering in Chinese and moving at a snail's pace as they pushed strollers and eyed shop windows. Jennifer and Laura trotted after her and hopped onto the descending escalator. By the time Beary reached the moving staircase, there were half-a-dozen shoppers between him and his group, so he settled back, listened to the piped-in carols and contemplated the faces of the shoppers riding in the opposite direction. The expressions glided by, one by one—fatigue, dogged determination, high-stress, bug-eyed greed and boredom. Definitely not a merry lot, thought Beary. It might be the season to be jolly, but the hilarity obviously hadn't made it to Metrotown Mall.

* * *

While Beary was trekking around the mall, his youngest daughter was walking through the maze of cul-de-sacs and crescents that nestled at the heart of Shaughnessy. In spite of the darkness of the evening, the sparkling Christmas lights created an artificial twilight. The air was cold and dotted with sporadic snowflakes that drifted down and disappeared as they reached the pavement. The sparse snowfall, thought Philippa, looked like a low-budget production of *La Bohème*. She strolled by an imposing residence that was surrounded by a low brick wall and a high, but neatly trimmed hemlock hedge. As she progressed along the wall, she came to a set of concrete gateposts with glowing white lamps mounted on top. Curiously, she peeked through the ornate wrought-iron gates. Every shrub was ablaze with golden fairy lights and the driveway was lined with illuminated candy canes. A gleaming Frosty held pride of place at the centre of the lawn.

Near the end of the property, a huge willow tree draped its branches over the hedge, screening the small street that branched off behind it. Philippa ducked through the branches and saw the street sign on the corner. Duchess Crescent. This was where the Fearings lived.

As she turned the corner, she heard a low growl. She stiffened and looked round, but there was no dog in sight. Then she saw a van on the far side of the road. The driver had opened the sliding door at the side of the vehicle. It had been the sound of the door that she had heard.

The Fearing mansion was halfway along the block. Philippa's first thought was disappointment, for unlike so many of the other homes, there were no Christmas lights ornamenting house or garden and even the windows were dark except for two gleaming rectangles on the main floor. The house itself was huge, a turn-of-the-century establishment with four floors culminating in a turret room high overhead. A stone wall surrounded the property, but a small gate gave access to a side path, so rather than continue to the main drive, Philippa stepped through and made her way across the garden. It was too dark to make out more than the size and shape of the building, but as she neared the front door, the light from the porch spilled onto the bushes and revealed tiny bulbs intertwined amid the branches. Presumably, the lights were being saved for the party. She climbed the steps and rang the doorbell. While she waited, she viewed the section of the grounds that abutted the driveway. To the left of the blacktop square in front of the porch stood an old coach-house that had been converted to a three-car garage with a suite on top. A light shone from the window of the suite, and the silhouette of a woman could be seen against the blind. A black van was parked in front of the centre garage door.

Suddenly Philippa heard the same menacing sound she had heard earlier. She looked towards the van, but there was no sign of anyone nearby. Then she jumped out of her skin as a voice spoke from behind her.

"Are you the singer?"

Philippa spun round. She had not heard the door open. A youth, who looked to be about twelve years old, stood in the hall, his hand firmly gripping the collar of an Irish wolfhound that was almost as tall as he was. The growling intensified, and the dog strained forward, its eye fixed on Philippa.

"Shut up, Verdi," said the boy. "Sit!" He bellowed at the dog and yanked on its collar, and the animal's hind end landed solidly on the doormat. "He's OK," the boy added to Philippa. "He'll be fine once you're inside. Just don't try to pat him. Ignore him. That's the best way to get on with him if he doesn't know you. Come on in. Grandy asked me to show you around. She's busy yapping on the phone to the caterers."

Philippa clenched her teeth and inched her way into the hall. She was too preoccupied with keeping a watchful eye on the dog to take in much of her surroundings, but she could not help noticing the twelve-foot ceilings, the Persian carpets, and the stately oak staircase stretching to the next floor. She turned to her guide who had now released the dog. Keeping her eye resolutely on the boy and avoiding the wolfhound's louring stare, she said, "And what's your name?"

"Mason. What's yours?"

Philippa introduced herself. "Is Miriam Fearing your grandmother?" she asked.

"Great-grandmother," said Mason.

Verdi inched forward and sniffed around Philippa's ankles. Philippa remembered the boy's advice and ignored the dog, though it took some effort to keep her voice level.

"Where are your parents?" she asked.

"Up above, along with my Grandma." Mason pointed his finger in the direction of the ceiling.

"Upstairs?"

"No. Dead. Up there in Heaven."

"Oh, I'm so sorry." Philippa was mortified to have asked. However, Mason seemed unperturbed.

"That's OK," he said cheerfully. "They were killed in a car crash when I was four. So was my Grandmother. Gramps and I came to live with Grandy afterwards. Stop it, Verdi," he added, using his knee to push the dog away from Philippa.

Philippa eyed the dog warily. "Is that creature yours too or does he go with the house?"

"He's Grandy's dog. She's opera mad. I'd never call a dog a dumb name like Verdi. Come on, this way."

Mason disappeared through a set of double doors at the side of the hall. Verdi padded after him. Philippa followed and found herself in a vast salon where rows of velvet-upholstered Queen Anne chairs had been arranged, fan-like, facing a concert grand. The side walls were a mass of high, gilt-framed mirrors, and opposite the entrance were three sets of French doors topped by fanlights and framed in vaulted sidelights. Four gleaming chandeliers hung from the ceiling. Philippa felt as if she had stepped back in time to the era of Liszt and Chopin. The room was magnificent.

"This is where you'll be singing," said Mason. "The concert starts at eleven. There's a pianist first who's going to bang out some Beethoven, followed by a little squirt with a violin who's going to show off with a Paganini piece—he's some prodigy Grandy discovered through the Clef Society—and then a quartet is doing a bit from the *Christmas Oratorio*. You get to do your stuff last because you're singing carols that people will actually recognize, even if they are operatic ones. That's all before lunch."

"Lunch! I was told there would be a hundred people. Isn't it just finger food?"

"No way. Grandy likes a sit-down meal. The food is laid out in the dining room, but the furniture is taken out of the living room and replaced with round tables. We put tables in the conservatory too. That's the best spot. I'll save you a place out there if you like. That way I can dodge our family table and I won't have to put up with the twins."

Philippa refrained from enquiring who the twins were and why they had to be avoided. Instead she asked, "What's the program for the afternoon?"

"The dancers are on at one-thirty. They have to perform after lunch because the chairs have to be re-arranged in the salon. Then there's another break for coffee and dessert. Don't miss that because the dessert buffet is going to be awesome."

"When's the puppet show?"

"At three-thirty, right after dessert. After it ends, you get to sing again for the finale. That's at five o'clock when they light up the garden. Grandy always wants 'Oh, Holy Night' for the lighting of the big tree. We open up the doors so everyone can go out on the terrace. You don't have to worry about freezing your vocal cords," Mason added, seeing Philippa's expression. "The terrace is heated."

Philippa felt awed. "This event must cost a fortune," she said. "Is there anything left over for the symphony once the bills are paid?"

"Lots," said Mason. "Grandy picks up the tab for everything."

"Your great-grandmother is extremely generous," observed Philippa. "Especially since the economy is in such tough shape right now."

"Grandy says it's good to spend money during a downturn, though she has cut back a bit. She always used to have an open bar with a ton of sample bottles of alcohol, and the wine was put on the tables so people could help themselves, but this year there's no hard liquor, and the wine is being served by waiters."

Mason grinned.

"You're another of her economies," he said bluntly.

"Oh?"

"Yes. Usually she books big names for the concert, but this year, except for the pianist, you're all locals with good reputations and cheap rates."

Philippa refused to be drawn.

"Are you going to watch the concert?" she asked equably. She was impressed by the boy's knowledge of the program in spite of his off-hand manner.

Mason looked scornful.

"Are you kidding? The only carol I like is 'Jingle Bells'. Besides, I'll get a free hour to play computer games. I'll come down for lunch and the puppet show."

"Where are the marionettes performing?"

"Downstairs. That's your sister's show, right? I've been watching them set up. It looks cool."

"It is," said Philippa. "It has a clever little boy in it just like you."

"Yes, I know . . . Cedric . . . the one who makes the time machine. I saw a bit while they were practising. Max was fighting the wolf and saving the empress's cat and then she made him Friend of Felines. It looked a bit like *Androcles and the Lion*."

"It's supposed to be like *Androcles and the Lion*," said Philippa. "When Max faces the big cats in the Colosseum, they refuse to eat him. You're remarkably well educated for one so young," she added.

"Gramps has a Master's degree in literature," Mason said gloomily. "He wanted to be an English professor, but he was needed to run the business so he spent his life dealing with Garden World instead."

"And drilling you in the finer points of English literature."

Mason grinned. "He's OK, though. He and I play chess a lot. Well, we did until *she* came along."

Philippa was curious. "Who is *she*?"

"Here, I'll show you." Mason shot out of the room, closely followed by Verdi. Philippa went after them.

Mason pointed to a set of double doors on the opposite side of the hall.

"That's the dining room," he said. "You should scoot across as soon as you finish singing because it'll be really crowded." He walked round to the far side of the staircase and indicated a second set of glass doors. "That's the living room. You have to cross it to get to the conservatory.

Come on, through here." He led Philippa through an archway and into a narrow hall. After a few feet, they rounded a corner, and then the passage widened into a long oak-panelled chamber. The walls were lined with oil paintings of couples, the men sporting morning clothes and the women resplendent in white gowns.

"They're wedding pictures!" cried Philippa. "What a lovely idea. Are these all family members?"

Mason nodded. "That's Grandy with Great-Gramps," he said. "He's in his navy uniform 'cause they were married during the war. And the next one is my grandmother with Gramps. Then there's Gaunt and Guncle." He grinned at Philippa's expression. "Great-Aunt Grace and Great-Uncle Rupert," he explained. "She's bossy and bad-tempered and he's a wimp. He was her German prof when she was at UBC."

Philippa stared more closely at the portrait. The thin, bearded man with the bushy grey hair and slightly myopic stare looked familiar.

"Isn't that Professor Harte?" she said.

"Yes." Mason looked surprised. "How do you know? He's been retired for ages."

"He did some private language coaching for the singers in the opera school. I took a couple of sessions with him. He was very charming."

"That's why Gaunt fell for him. Gramps says Gaunt was determined to marry Guncle, but she's bullied him ever since because he doesn't make enough money to pay for the lifestyle that she's used to."

Philippa believed her young host. The set of Grace Harte's mouth looked distinctly waspish and her husband appeared cowed rather than proud. Privately she considered that Gaunt was the perfect nickname for the sour-faced woman in the portrait.

"She's your grandfather's sister?" Philippa asked.

"Yes. Gramps has a younger brother too. Great-Uncle Mark, but he's not on the wall because he never married. He lives in London. He thinks he's really cool. We call him the wicked uncle because every time we see him he's with some bimbo who's half his age. He used to be a racecar driver, and now he works for Mercedes. Grandy spoils him, but they're always getting in fights."

"Why?"

"He wants money and Grandy gets fed up with giving it to him."

Mason swung round and pointed to the opposite wall.

"That's my parents," he said. For a moment he sounded wistful. "My mom was pretty, wasn't she?" he said.

Philippa looked at the couple on the wall. The bride was indeed lovely—fair and elegant in an exquisite bare-shouldered taffeta gown with pearls and camellias ornamenting her hair. Before Philippa could comment, Mason was at the next portrait, which portrayed a plump, amiable-faced blonde in pale cream lace, and a thin, dark-haired man whose beady eyes glared morosely from behind wire-framed glasses.

"That's Gauntlet with Aunt Helga," he told her.

Philippa took an educated guess. "Gauntlet would be Great-Aunt Grace's son?"

"Yes. His name's Eric and he's every bit as mean as Gaunt—he's a stockbroker—but he can't be a very good one because he's always on about needing money. Aunt Helga's OK, though, or she would be if she hadn't produced the twins." Mason looked gloomy again.

"Who are these twins that you're so anxious to avoid?"

"Lisa and Lotte. They're ten and they're totally stupid. All they care about is clothes and DVDs and rock groups. They're coming to stay tomorrow and they won't leave until after New Year's Day. It's going to be awful because all everyone does is fight about money and try to persuade Grandy to sell this house and get rid of the garden shops."

"Does your grandfather think she should sell up?"

Mason nodded. "Yes, but he's trying to hold on for a bit. Grandy is eighty-five and her heart isn't too good, so she probably won't live much longer. Even though Gramps knows she's spending down the family fortune, he doesn't want to force her to change when she doesn't have much time left. Grandy is living in the past," Mason said solemnly. "She keeps talking about Christmas in the old days and she wants to make it the same. But Gauntlet says Grandy's going to bankrupt us all and there won't be anything left to inherit. He says she needs to be shaken up and dragged into the present, but Gramps doesn't want to hurt her, so he just finds other ways to cut back."

"So the big party goes ahead and your entire family gathers round and pretends to enjoy it."

"Pretty much, except this year Uncle Mark is going to miss the party. He isn't arriving until Christmas Day. But everyone else will be here."

"That's too bad. I was looking forward to meeting the dashing racing driver."

"I'm not looking forward to any of it," said Mason.

Philippa glanced back at the portraits.

"So which one of these is *she*?" she asked, remembering the boy's earlier comment.

"We haven't got to her yet," said Mason. "Come round the corner."

Philippa followed him into a second, much narrower hall. A painting, similarly framed and the same size as the wedding portraits, hung in an alcove. However, this picture was a surreal painting of what appeared to be a serpent rising out of a patch of stinging nettles.

"There she is," said Mason. "B.B."

"Well, she's obviously not a gun, so what do the initials stand for?"

"Bad Babs, currently the Countess Terrazi. She was my grandfather's first wife," Mason explained. "She walked out on Gramps after six months, and she's been through three more husbands since then. The last one was the Italian count, and he lasted about as long as Gramps—just long enough to get her a title and half his money. Her name is mud with the whole family."

"I gathered that from the adjective," said Philippa, "but how did she get to be a serpent?"

"That used to be their wedding picture. It had been put away in the attic, but when we were in England last year, B.B. turned up again. She lives in Paris but she travels all over, so it could have been a coincidence, but later Grandy found out that Babs had actually arranged to meet up with Gramps in London, so there was a big blow-up. Grandy was furious. She said B.B. would come back into the family over her dead body, and she dug out the painting and commissioned an artist to paint over it."

"Trying to remind your grandfather of the personality beneath the glamorous surface?"

"Sort of."

"Wouldn't it have been cheaper to have used Photoshop to doctor a snapshot?"

Mason acquired a gleam in his eye.

"That's a great idea. Are you good with computers?"

"Yes, but I'm not offering my services. That was a quip, not a suggestion."

"I wouldn't need help," said Mason scornfully. "I can do anything I want on my computer. And on B.B.'s too, come to that. I know where she keeps her passwords," he said complacently. "She has a black binder in the pocket of her laptop case, and she writes her codes on the plastic cover. All you have to do is slide a white sheet of paper underneath and you can see everything. I break into her admin site whenever I want to."

Philippa looked severe.

"Mason, that's illegal. You'd better cut that out before you get into trouble."

"Someone has to keep tabs on her now that she's sucking up to Gramps again. He seems to have forgotten how awful she was to him before."

Philippa looked back at the serpent on the wall. "So I take it that your great-grandmother's stratagem didn't work."

"No, not at all. Gramps got all huffy about the picture, and now things are even worse. B.B. came out to Canada two months ago. She says she's here on business and she's staying at the Hyatt, but ever since she arrived, she's been hanging around Gramps like a hungry hornet and I haven't had a game of chess with him since she arrived."

"What business is she in?"

"Internet sales—BarbaraGrey.com—high-end lotions and health stuff. She runs a modelling agency too."

"In Paris? That must be exciting."

Mason looked scornful.

"Not designer-gowns-on-runway models," he said. "Just the vacant ones with big boobs that sell underwear and fast cars. I think that's just a side business though. The health products are her big thing. She has all these pictures of herself on the front page of her website . . . evening gown, swimsuit, jogging suit . . . as if anyone believes she got that figure through exercise."

"Health and beauty is a major industry these days," Philippa pointed out. "But it's also a highly competitive field. She has to be a walking demonstration of what she sells."

"Maybe, but one thing's for sure, there's nothing about her business that would justify all those meetings with Gramps."

"Well, if she's based in France, she'll go home sooner or later. You'll get your chess games again."

"That's not the point. I wanted Gramps to marry Eloise, but now he's completely sidetracked."

"Who's Eloise?"

"She's Grandy's private secretary. She used to work at Garden World, but after she retired, she came to work here."

Philippa suddenly remembered the silhouette on the blind above the three-car garage.

"Does she live in the suite over the garage?"

"No. That's the Digbys. They're the only live-in help Grandy has left. She can't really afford them, but she keeps them on because they've been with her for years. Mr. Dee looks after the grounds and drives her around, and Mrs. Dee organizes the household. They're not much younger than Grandy so everything happens in slow motion. That's why it's a good job Eloise is around. She makes sure things run smoothly. But she doesn't live here. The office wing has an outside door into the service courtyard, so she comes and goes quite independently, but she has access to the house if she needs it." He pointed to a door on the left side of the hall. "That's her office there. If you have any questions, just go in. She'll drop whatever she's doing and help you out."

"You really like her, don't you?"

"Yes. She's perfect for Gramps. She's a widow, and she's the right age for him. They'd be really happy together."

"Doesn't that rather depend on how your grandfather feels about her?"

"He likes her a lot," said Mason. "If it hadn't been for B.B. reappearing, they'd be together by now."

"Well," said Philippa, "if Babs is really as bad as you say, I'm sure your grandfather will see the light."

"He might, but I'm not taking any chances," Mason said smugly. "I have plans. I'm going to fix B.B. once and for all." Philippa's interest was piqued, but aggravatingly, Mason changed the subject. "Now, you see those doors at the end of the hall?" Philippa nodded. "The first one on the right leads to the kitchen, and the one beyond it is a washroom. The one right at the end goes out to the service patio, but you want the door on the left side. It goes to the back stairs. The dressing rooms for the performers are going to be on the very top floor, and you can't get there from the main stairs because they stop at the third floor. So when you arrive on Saturday morning, you'll come the way we just did, then go up the service stairs until you reach the top. Then you can nab any room you like—except the tower room. That's mine, but all the others are up for grabs. There's a washroom up there too. Got all that?"

"Yes, very clear. Thank you."

"Now, I guess you want me to take you down to your sister," said Mason. "She said you were coming by bus and getting a ride home with her."

"That's right. I've been downtown all day so it worked out perfectly. I wanted to see the layout ahead of time so I said I'd meet her here. Thank you for showing me around. You've been a most courteous host . . . and very interesting. I was fascinated by all the family stuff you told me."

Mason looked suspiciously at Philippa.

"Are you trying to suck up so I tell you what my plans are?" he asked.

"Yes, actually," said Philippa honestly. "What are you planning to do to this awful female who's dug her claws into your grandfather?"

"You'll find out in good time," said Mason. "Or maybe not. Depends on how quickly my sources come through. Come on. The puppets are down here."

He led Philippa back into the main hallway and round to the other side of the oak staircase. Verdi padded alongside.

"Does this dog always stick this close to guests?" Philippa asked.

"Always. He's herding you . . . making sure you behave."

"Is he, indeed? And who makes sure *he* behaves?"

"Me."

"How will you do that with a hundred guests in the house?"

Mason looked glum.

"I won't have to. Grandy says he has to be shut in the service-yard shed for the party."

Mason led Philippa into a second passage and down a narrow flight of stairs. When they reached the bottom, Philippa found herself in a huge basement room that ran the width of the house. Here too, rows of chairs had been set out, but in this case the lines were straight. At the far end of the room, Philippa saw her sister standing at the base of a ladder. Steven was perched on top. Juliette passed an extension cord up to her husband, then turned and waved to Philippa.

"How's it going?" Philippa asked.

"Good. We're almost done. Two more lights to hook up. Then we just have to position the sets and we're through."

"Where are the girls?"

"Shopping with Mum and Dad. Steven and I can concentrate better on our own. This is a pretty big engagement for us. We want to make sure everything goes smoothly."

"You and me both," said Philippa. "It's going to be quite a party."

Juliette furrowed her pretty brow.

"Yes," she said, "but we're not coming until half an hour before our show. If we're here for the whole event, it'll be too much excitement for the girls. I don't want them to get distracted before we perform."

Mason had moved to the side of the marionette stage where a pile of scenery leaned against the wall.

"What's this piece for?" he asked Philippa. He held up a frame that contained a picture created from pieces of gel.

"That goes in the shadow screen," said Philippa. "There's a light at the back, and from the audience, it will appear to be a stained-glass window."

"What's it supposed to be?"

"The lady at the centre is Saint Flavia. At the start of the show, Cedric's history teacher tells him about the miracle of Saint Flavia. She was a beautiful Christian who was sent to the Colosseum, but the Lord took pity on her and took her up to Heaven to save her the agony of death in the arena."

Mason looked suspicious.

"I've never heard of a Saint Flavia."

"No, you wouldn't have. She's a character that was invented for the show."

"Oh. Why does she have those other creatures with her—the owl and the white wolf and the man in flames? Are they part of the miracle?"

Philippa attempted to bargain.

"I'll give you a complete run down of the story if you let me in on your own Christmas plot," she offered.

Mason looked nonchalant.

"That's OK," he said. "I'll wait to see the show. And if you're lucky, you might get to see mine."

He wandered to the back of the theatre and picked up the Cedric puppet.

Appropriate, thought Philippa. They appeared to be two of a kind—clever, devious, and contrary.

* * *

On the day of the party, Philippa arrived an hour before the concert was due to begin. Her hostess greeted her in the front hall. Miriam Fearing might be eighty-five and in questionable health but nobody would have guessed it. She was slim and vivacious, with silver hair and sparkling blue eyes. She greeted Philippa warmly.

"I believe I've met your brother," she said. "Inspector Beary. Such a charming young man. My son and I were at his table at the policeman's ball last year. He told me all about you."

Her eyes twinkled, and Philippa suddenly realized how she and Juliette had won their coveted engagements.

"We've set up dressing rooms for the performers on the top floor where the servants' quarters used to be," Miriam continued. "I'm sorry to make you climb all those stairs, but I have my family staying for Christmas, so all the other bedrooms are occupied. Can you manage?" she added, eyeing the dress bag over Philippa's arm.

"Yes, of course," Philippa replied, but her hostess was already moving away in the direction of the dining room where, through open doors, Philippa could see an impressive stretch of white linen and gleaming silver. Mrs. Fearing's question had been a directive rather than a statement of concern.

The door of the salon opened and a woman came out. She was quietly elegant in a grey wool dress, and her salt-and-pepper hair was neatly styled. The one-colour effect ought to have been drab, thought Philippa, but instead it was pleasing, like an attractive monochromatic photograph. The woman's expression was serene, and the lines on her face looked as if they had been created from laughter and not sorrow. She came directly to Philippa and smiled.

"I'm Eloise Arden," she said. "Do you know how to get to the top floor?"

"Yes, I was here two days ago. Mason showed me around."

"Good. Now, you know you're invited to join the party once the concert is over. The guests like to socialize with the performers. That's part of the perk they get for the exorbitant ticket price. So you must feel free to help yourself at the buffet—and if you want anything prior to your performance, there's juice and water and hot drinks in the little servants' kitchen at the very end of the hall where the dressing rooms are situated."

"Thank you. I must say it's a privilege to be invited to sing for this event. It's incredibly grand."

Eloise smiled. "Mrs. Fearing remembers Christmas the way it was when her husband was alive, and she's determined to carry on the same traditions. Her memories are extremely precious to her."

The front door opened and the sound of voices filtered through from outside. Eloise paused. She glanced over Philippa's shoulder and her expression altered.

"Excuse me," she said stiffly. Without another word, she moved away and disappeared into the passage on the far side of the stairs.

Philippa turned to see what had caused the secretary's hasty departure. A couple had entered the house. The man was grey-haired and appeared rather worn and tired, but he had a quiet dignity and a kind face that was appealing. The woman looked younger, but as Philippa stared more closely, she discerned that there was little difference in age between the two. The woman was extremely well preserved; the casually styled hair with blonde and silver streaks was tossed artfully around a skillfully made-up face that appeared to have been stretched equally artfully to minimize the lines of age. She wore a spectacular blue mink coat, which hung open to reveal a low-cut pink gown and a figure that had either been toned and exercised to model proportions, or had had the benefit of liposuction and breast implants. Her hands were encased in long evening gloves, and draped around her shoulders was a heavily beaded stole. Her left hand clasped a sequined clutch purse. Every accessory was a perfect match for the pink chiffon gown.

Mason came up behind Philippa and hissed in her ear.

"That's her! Bad Babs. Awful, isn't she?"

"I wish you'd stop startling me like that," said Philippa. "Actually, she's pretty sharp-looking."

"Not when you get close. She has eyes like a pit viper."

Philippa was too busy admiring the woman's clothes to look closely at her face.

"Her mink must have cost a fortune," she said, "and that gown didn't come out of a bargain basement. Look at the beading on it. The count must have given her a hefty payoff. Either that, or her line of health and beauty products is a winner."

Barbara Terrazi slipped the mink off her shoulders and smiled seductively as Bruce Greystone helped her out of the coat. Then she murmured something softly in his ear and excused herself. Completely ignoring Mason and Philippa, she passed them by and disappeared into the passage behind the stairs.

Mason pulled a face. "I don't care what she wins as long as it isn't my grandfather," he said. "And speaking of Gramps," he added, his face suddenly assuming an angelic repose, "here he comes."

Bruce Fearing came over to Mason, ruffled his hair, and smiled at Philippa.

"Who's this charming lady?" he asked his grandson.

"Philippa," said Mason. "She's the singer."

Bruce Fearing shifted the mink coat to his left arm and took Philippa's hand.

"Inspector Beary's sister. Delighted to meet you. I look forward to your performance."

With a polite nod, he moved away and disappeared into the cloakroom.

Mason eyed Philippa suspiciously.

"Inspector?"

"My brother is a detective with the RCMP."

"So why didn't you tell me your brother was a policeman?"

"The subject didn't come up," said Philippa serenely. "But perhaps you should wait until you know people better before you start boasting about your hacking skills."

Mason grinned.

"I'm not worried," he said. "You're not going to rat on me. Come on, I'll show you upstairs. Here," he added, gallantly taking her make-up case, "I'll carry that."

Philippa followed Mason down the maze of halls that led to the back stairs. As they turned the final corner, they saw Barbara Terrazi ahead. Her flowing pink gown glowed softly in the amber light. She stopped at the first door on the left side of the passageway, knocked loudly, and then disappeared inside.

"That's odd," said Mason. "Why would she be going to Eloise's office? What's she up to?"

"Why does she have to be up to anything?"

Philippa found herself talking to the air, for Mason had forged ahead and opened the door of the office. He leaned in briefly, then drew back and closed the door again.

"It's OK," he said, frowning. "Eloise is in there. I can't imagine why they'd be talking though."

"Why don't you ask Eloise later?" suggested Philippa. "The straightforward approach often works best."

"Eloise won't tell me," said Mason. "She has this thing about discretion. Grandy says that's why she's the perfect assistant, but it's really annoying. Come on. Let's head up."

He opened the door to the service stairs and ushered Philippa through. The stairway was steep and narrow, and Philippa had to clutch her dress bag close to her body in order to negotiate the corners. As they approached the top of the first flight, they heard raised voices. Mason indicated a narrow archway at the side of the landing.

"That goes through to the second-floor. Gaunt and Guncle have the end room. You can hear a lot from the stairwell. I listen in all the time."

Mason's great-aunt was on a roll. Her voice was shrill and angry.

"Did you see the bill from the caterers?"

The man who replied kept his voice low. He sounded nervous, as if he were afraid of being overheard, but Philippa could still hear his words clearly.

"Keep calm, Grace. There's nothing we can do about it, and there's no point in causing a scene."

"I don't give a damn who hears me. The sooner the old witch drops dead, the better. This rotting pile of real estate should have been sold off years ago, and that archaic chain of flowerpot mausoleums too. She's going to bankrupt us all before she goes. Bruce is insane the way he gives in to her."

Mason nudged Philippa with his elbow.

"See. I told you."

"She sounds pretty upset."

"She's always upset over something," said Mason. "It's the drugs and the nicotine. Everyone tries to get her to quit smoking and cut down on the pills, but of course, she never does."

"What sort of pills is she on?"

"Blood pressure, stomach stuff and anti-depressants."

Another outburst came from the other side of the wall.

"My goodness," said Philippa. "No wonder she needs stomach pills. That much acid would burn out anyone's digestive system."

"Her son is just as bad," said Mason. "If you walked down the hall, you'd probably hear the same conversation coming from Gauntlet's room at the other end. He's as ticked as she is."

"You're not worried about your own inheritance?" asked Philippa.

"No. I hope Grandy spends every penny. She's already set up a fund to pay for my education, and I'm going to get rich by myself, so I won't need her money. Gramps and I will be fine as long as I can get rid of B.B. Come on. Only two more flights."

"Who's on the third floor?"

"Grandy. Her suite takes up the whole floor." He pointed to another door as they reached the next landing. "You can't get through from here though," he added. "That door's kept locked. There will be a security guard in the suite too, just for today, and another one on the main staircase. No one will be allowed up except family. Grandy has tons of jewellery, and she refuses to keep it at the bank. That's another thing that gets up Gaunt's nose."

Philippa followed the boy up to the top floor. The passageway here was even narrower than on the floors below. The servants' quarters were Spartan and utilitarian. However, they were well equipped with all the necessities, and Philippa saw that long mirrors had been set up in the small rooms that were allotted for change areas.

"There you go," said Mason, plopping the case down in the first empty room. "And if you need me, I'm down there at the end. I'm going to hide out until lunch time."

With a breezy wave over his shoulder, he marched down the hall and disappeared into his room. Philippa sighed. She was becoming quite fond of her strange young acquaintance, but she was willing to bet that whatever was planned for Barbara Terrazi, it would be devastating, effective and slickly enacted. She was beginning to feel sorry for Bad Babs.

* * *

In spite of the underlying tensions, the party was a great success. The morning concert was rapturously received, which was hardly surprising considering the calibre of the concert pianist who was internationally renowned, the violin prodigy who was amazing, and the oratorio quartet, which was comprised of a stellar group from the Vancouver Chamber Choir. Philippa felt awed to be in such company, but to her delight, her renditions of "Oh Bethlehem" and "Mary's Boy Child" appeared equally to enchant the audience of connoisseurs that Miriam Fearing had assembled—and when she noticed Mason peeking through the doors at the end of her performance, she winked at the accompanist, went into a lively rendition of "Jingle Bells" and signalled the audience to join in. Mason's gleeful smile indicated she had made a friend for life.

As the rush for the lunch buffet began, Philippa held back to let the paying guests go first. Mason sidled up to her and grinned.

"Hey, was that just for me?"

Philippa admitted it was.

"Cool. You look really nice too."

Philippa glanced down at her pale ice blue satin. It was her latest concert gown, bought with hard-earned dollars, but tax-deductible and breathtakingly glamorous. However, from Mason she realized that *nice* was about as high a compliment as she could expect.

"Thank you," she said. "So what have you been doing all morning?"

"Nothing," he answered, with an air that belied his words. "Don't you want to eat?" he added. "There won't be anything left if we don't get in there. Come on. Fill up a plate and then come out to the conservatory. I've saved you a spot at my table."

Philippa followed Mason into the dining room. The buffet was even more lavish than she had anticipated. One table was laden with turkey and all the trimmings, a second displayed a gourmet spread of seafood, and the third was a varied and exotic salad bar. However, she found it impossible to pay attention to the food as so many people wanted to talk with her. She helped herself to a few tidbits from the seafood trays and resolved to slip back later when everyone was watching the ballet dancers. Mason waved to her from across the room. He was holding a plate piled with turkey, stuffing and potatoes.

"Through here," he called, pointing at the connecting door to the living room.

Conscious that she still had another number to sing, Philippa was glad to escape the noisy chatter in the dining room. She went through to the living room and saw that the tables were filling rapidly. Mason was nowhere in sight, so she wove her way across the room and went into the conservatory. Here, the tables were still empty, and the long glass atrium was pleasantly airy after the crush in the other areas. Mason hailed her from the far end of the room. He had commandeered a small rattan table that was tucked in the corner behind a row of potted palms.

"I thought you'd like this spot," he said solemnly, pulling out a chair for Philippa and then seating himself opposite her. "You have to sing again so you probably don't want to be talking a lot, especially over all the noise in there." He stabbed his fork in the direction of the living room.

Philippa looked at him in amazement.

"That's remarkably considerate," she said. "I'm impressed. You're a mind-reader as well as a computer whiz."

"Eat up," said Mason. "I'll talk and you can listen." He took a mouthful of turkey, chewed reflectively, swallowed, and then resumed speaking.

"Have you noticed how Eloise is behaving?" he said.

Philippa shook her head. She popped a scallop into her mouth and waited for Mason to continue.

"She's really happy," said Mason. "All smiles. Absolutely glowing. I can't figure out why."

Philippa swallowed her mouthful and said, "Did you ask her why Mrs. Terrazi came to speak with her?"

"Yes. She just said B.B. needed to make a call and had forgotten her cell."

"That's hardly a reason for jubilation," said Philippa.

"I know. I don't get it. She had this silly smile on her face."

Philippa rested her fork on her plate.

"Maybe it's bravado," she suggested. "If someone you love isn't interested in you, the best thing you can do is sparkle and be vivacious. At worst, it stops people from feeling sorry for you, and at best, sometimes it makes the object of your affections pay attention."

"Oh well," said Mason, "B.B. is going to get her come-uppance pretty soon, in more ways than one."

Philippa looked sternly at her young friend.

"Mason, what have you done?"

"Wait and see," said Mason. "Now," he added piously, "you came out here to rest your voice, so I'm not going to talk any more."

Without another word he turned his attention to the serious work of demolishing his mountain of turkey.

* * *

By the time Philippa left the conservatory, the dining area was even more congested. Guests in search of second helpings were heading back to the buffet, while others were table-hopping or moving purposefully in the direction of the front hall where the washrooms were located. White-jacketed waiters darted back and forth refilling wine glasses while caterers wearing shirts that sported Paradise Parties logos cleared the empty dishes.

Before the concert, Philippa had been too preoccupied to pay much attention to the various members of the Fearing family, but now she attempted to match the faces on the gallery wall to the people in the room. She saw Bruce Fearing sitting at a table with two men, one of whom she recognized immediately. It was Professor Harte. The second man was also easy to identify. Grace Harte's stockbroker son looked just like his portrait. He was stouter than in his wedding picture but the slick black hair and the petulant expression were exactly the same. His florid complexion suggested that he was either a heavy drinker or had high blood pressure like his mother. His fingers drummed irritably on the tablecloth as he glanced around the room. Spying a waiter, he waved him over and pointed at the glasses around the table. The waiter poured wine for the men; then filled the glasses at the empty places.

Miriam Fearing was on the other side of the room. She seemed to be in her element. She had changed into a long-sleeved, high-necked magenta gown, which glittered with sequins and rhinestones. Around her neck was a diamond choker that blazed with light as it caught the beams from the chandelier overhead. She moved among her guests with charm and ease. The contrast between Miriam Fearing and her son was almost painful to behold, for he remained seated at the table, his fatigue evident to anyone who looked at him.

Philippa noticed Eloise Arden solicitously moving to Bruce Fearing's side. She was carrying two glasses and a bottle of Perrier. The secretary was still in grey, but now her dress was a simple pleated satin, subdued but elegant. Mason was right. Eloise did look happier. Bruce Fearing patted her hand as she poured him a glass of mineral water and there was a flash of understanding between the two of them. As Philippa watched, she felt a growing certainty that Mason's anxieties about his grandfather and Barbara Terrazi were unfounded. If her instincts were correct, Bruce Fearing and Eloise Arden were two people very much in love.

A high-pitched shriek of laughter drew Philippa's attention to the end of the room where Barbara Terrazi, wine glass in hand, was holding court amid a circle of admiring gentlemen. Bad Babs might be anathema to Mason, thought Philippa, but none of the adult males in the room were impervious to her charm. A doddery elder with a lugubrious expression that made him resemble an abandoned basset hound joined the cluster of men surrounding the countess, and as she turned the full force of her flamboyant personality on him, the drooping jowls quivered and he broke into a broad smile. Flirtatiously, she patted him on the cheek, whispered something that made him chuckle, and then slipped away to continue her circuit around the room.

There were a surprising number of young people present considering the price of entry to the party, but two little girls who were darting back and forth between the buffet and the dining tables were identical in appearance, even down to their sparkling purple mini-dresses, so Philippa surmised these must be the twins. A Rubenesque blonde in floral chiffon was attempting to curb their excesses. The good-natured Helga had also gained a few pounds since her marriage, but her expression was as serene as it appeared in the wedding portrait. Eventually she managed to corral the twins and brought them to sit on either side of her husband, who promptly picked up the wine glasses by the girls' placemats and lined them up beside his own.

A tall, angular woman entered from the lobby. The peevish countenance was unmistakable. It was Grace Harte. She was clutching a cumbersome purse and holding an empty bar glass, and she looked as cross as she had sounded during her tirade upstairs. She was tanned, with a weathered face that was indicative of too many holidays in the sun. Her dress was simple, expensive and smart, but without a trace of glamour. She crossed to her family table and hung her bag over the back of a chair. Then she frowned at the wine glass in front of her placemat and moved it aside. Holding up the empty bar glass in her other hand, she turned to speak sharply to her husband. He started to get up, but Eloise Arden waved him back to his seat and poured Grace some mineral water. Then she took the offending glass of wine for herself.

A voice in her ear made Philippa jump. Mason was at her elbow. Unable to point because his hands were holding another plateful of food, he tipped his head towards his great-aunt.

"Gaunt can't drink when she's on medication. It's too bad, because she's even crabbier when she's alcohol-deprived. Hey, I don't get it," he added. "Look at that."

Miriam Fearing and Barbara Terrazi were approaching the table, apparently in perfect harmony. Bruce Fearing had stood and moved to Eloise Arden's side, and Barbara Terrazi slipped between them. She set down her glass and gave both her ex-husband and the smiling secretary a big hug. Then she picked up her glass again and stepped back. Miriam Fearing spoke briefly with her son, who smiled and nodded, and then she looked around the room, her eyes sweeping the crowd until they lit on Mason at Philippa's side. She beckoned to him, and then picked up her wine glass.

"You're being paged," said Philippa. "Better get over there and find out what's going on. If I'm not mistaken, I think one of your wishes is about to come true."

But Mason was already on his way. He moved to his great-grandmother's side, and Philippa was warmed to see the obvious affection between the elderly lady and the young boy. Miriam Fearing whispered something in Mason's ear. His eyes flew wide, and then his face brightened into a smile that could have illuminated the entire room. His great-grandmother raised her wine glass in a toast and the other family members followed suit. Philippa smiled. Even from across the room it was obvious what was happening. Bruce Fearing and Eloise Arden were being congratulated. An engagement was being announced.

Philippa remained where she was, hoping that Mason would return and fill her in. There was a lot of laughter and movement as the various relatives distributed hugs and good will. Even Grace Harte and her dour-looking son appeared elated. But after a moment, Miriam furrowed her brow and peered into her wine glass. Then she handed the glass to her great-grandson and bent down to speak to him. Mason nodded. Then carefully holding the glass, which was still half-full, he came across the room. When he reached Philippa, he jerked his head towards the door. Assuming the gesture meant that she should follow him, Philippa left the dining room.

"In here," said Mason, rolling his eyes towards the salon.

They went into the salon, which was empty except for an immaculately coiffed woman with an artificial smile who was directing two flunkies as they rearranged chairs. Philippa assumed she was the event planner.

"So let me guess," said Philippa as she followed Mason to the far end of the room. "You had it all wrong about your grandfather and Bad Babs. He's going to marry Eloise Arden just like you hoped."

Mason was bug-eyed.

"Yes. I don't get it. It came right out of the blue."

"So Babs really was here on business?"

"Yes. She's pulled off a coup that's going to help us a lot. That's why Gaunt and Gauntlet were looking so pleased. They wouldn't get excited just because Gramps was going to be happy."

"Then," Philippa pointed out, "you no longer have any reason to do anything to drive Babs away, have you?"

Mason looked uncomfortable.

Philippa looked at him sternly.

"Mason, have you already done something?"

"Nothing much. Don't look like that. I can fix it . . . maybe. You could call it revenge for all the chess games I missed. I still don't like her—or trust her, come to that. Whatever deal she's swung, it's bound to be to her own advantage. Anyway, that's not what I wanted to talk to you about." He held up the wine glass and looked at Philippa anxiously.

"Grandy said she didn't want to finish her wine," he said. "She asked me to get her a glass of water instead."

"Did she say why?"

"Yes. She thought her palate was off because she'd taken an anti-inflammatory for her arthritis, but she's done that before and it hasn't stopped her drinking wine."

"What are you suggesting?" said Philippa.

"What if someone put something in it?"

Philippa looked at him suspiciously.

"Mason, this isn't another of your schemes, is it? Are you quite sure you're not still trying to discredit Barbara Terrazi?"

Mason's expression became indignant.

"Of course not. I'm dead serious. Grandy said her drink tasted funny."

Philippa was reluctant to encourage Mason's lurid fantasies, but on the other hand, the boy looked genuinely worried. She bit her lip, not sure what to advise.

"Your brother's a policeman," Mason persisted. "What would he tell me to do?"

Philippa sighed.

"He'd probably tell you that your great-grandmother's assessment was right," she said finally, "but to make sure, he'd suggest you took her a fresh glass of wine to try. Get her another one and see if it tastes the same."

Mason perked up.

"Now that's smart," he said. "I will. Here. You hold this one."

He thrust the glass into Philippa's hand and left the room. Philippa followed, casually holding the wineglass. Mason wove his way over to a waiter who was serving a noisy group of revellers and whisked a glass of wine from his tray. Then he headed back to the living room and delivered the drink to his great-grandmother. Philippa watched closely as Miriam Fearing took a sip of wine, then smiled and nodded. Mason turned to look towards Philippa. Even from across the room, his expression spoke volumes. He hurried back, his eyes wide as saucers, and ushered Philippa back to the salon.

"Grandy said the drink was fine." He stared at the glass in Philippa's hand. "What should we do?"

Philippa raised the glass to the light and peered closely at the wine. The red cabernet gleamed a deep crimson. It looked perfectly normal, yet she felt a growing sense of unease.

"Is there somewhere we could get a small container?" she said.

"In the kitchen. Will you go? Use the back entrance . . . the one by the back stairs. Then you won't get run over by waiters coming in and out. I want to stay and make sure Grandy's all right."

"That's a good idea," said Philippa. "And if there's even the smallest sign that she's unwell, you must tell your grandfather about the drink."

Mason shot off in the direction of the living room. Philippa went more slowly. A stream of people was emerging from the dining area and moving towards the salon. She looked at her watch. It was twenty past one—nearly time for the ballet performance to start. She made her way along the maze of passages, passing the wedding portraits and the closed door of Eloise Arden's office. When she reached the kitchen door, she knocked, but to her surprise, the woman who opened it refused her entry, coolly directing her to the recycling tubs in the service yard.

Irritated, but not wanting to make a fuss, Philippa continued to the end of the hall and tucked the wineglass into a corner. Then she slipped out through the back door, shivering as the biting air nipped at her bare shoulders. A black van was parked so close to the house that it was partially blocking the door, but once she moved around it, she saw that the service patio was a vast concrete lot, fully enclosed by a brick wall which was connected to the two wings of the L-shaped house. The only entrance from the street appeared to be a set of wrought-iron gates at the far end and a single gate directly opposite from where she was standing. To the left of this gate was a low shed. The area was full of trucks and caterers' vans, and sure enough, a row of recycling tubs lined the wall. Two men were loading the bins into one of the vans. Philippa hurried over and repeated her request, and this time she was met with cheerful courtesy. The drivers fished in the bins and extracted a small jar. They found a matching lid, and insisted on rinsing both at the outdoor tap and drying them thoroughly before presenting them to her. She thanked them and returned the way she had come.

As she passed the shed, she was startled by a low growl. So that was Verdi's prison for the day, she thought, moving past quickly before the dog erupted into barks. As she approached the house, she was startled a second time, for a shadowy figure was standing by the black van. It was Grace Harte. She was huddled in a heavy wool coat and smoking a cigarette. She glared as Philippa approached.

"What are you doing out here?" she demanded.

"Retrieving a jar," Philippa said truthfully, and swept inside before she could be questioned further. To her relief, the wineglass was still in the corner where she had left it. She slipped into the washroom, washed the jar again using soap and hot water, and transferred the wine into it. Then she tucked the glass and the jar inside the bathroom cupboard and started to make her way back. She could hear ballet music drifting through the passageway, and she breathed easier realizing that the party was still in progress. Everything must be all right, she decided. Miriam Fearing was safe and well, enjoying the performance along with her guests.

But as Philippa turned into the portrait gallery, she realized that her sense of security was unfounded, for Mason was hurrying to meet her, his face white and strained. He clutched her arm and pulled her towards the front hall.

"Come on," he said. "They haven't left yet. We have to give Gramps the jar. Where is it?"

"In the bathroom at the end of the hall. I left it in the cupboard, along with the wine glass."

Mason dropped Philippa's arm and scurried past her. He shot down the hall and Philippa hurried after him.

"What's happened?" she asked.

"Grandy started to feel unsteady. She said she didn't feel well and was going to her room. Gramps wanted to call an ambulance, but she wouldn't let him. But then her head started to feel strange, so she agreed to go to the hospital. It's only five minutes away so Mr. Dee is taking her in the limo and Gramps is going with her. Grandy's insisted that nobody is to be told and she wants the party to continue."

"Did you tell your grandfather about the wine?"

"Yes. That's why he's so worried."

Philippa went into the bathroom and retrieved the jar. Mason grabbed it from her.

"Here, give it to me," he said. "You can't move fast enough in that dress." He sprinted off down the hall.

"Tell your grandfather to give the wine to the doctor at the hospital," Philippa called after him. "They'll need to know what she's taken."

Mason waved an acknowledgement. As he disappeared around the corner, Philippa felt her throat constrict. She was suddenly afraid that Mason's precious Grandy was not going to make it to Christmas. And she wondered which member of the Fearing clan had taken steps to speed up his or her inheritance. She hoped whole-heartedly that the lively matriarch had a strong enough constitution to foil the would-be murderer's plans.

* * *

Detective Constable Robert Miller turned into Duchess Crescent just before five o'clock. Miriam Fearing was going to pull through, thanks to the quick wit of her great-grandson and the expertise of the emergency team at Vancouver General, but the doctor who had notified the police made it quite clear that there had been an attempted murder at the Fearing Christmas Gala. Analysis of the wine had revealed a lethal dose of anti-depressants, and it was likely that the matriarch of the Fearing family would not have survived if she had drunk the entire contents of her glass.

Miller sighed. This was the sort of case that was a policeman's worst nightmare—a society function for the wealthiest glitterati of the city, not to mention a couple of MP's and the Premier of the Province. DC Phil Ho glanced across from the passenger seat. He correctly interpreted the sigh.

"This is going to be touchy," he said. "Most likely the culprit is a member of Mrs. Fearing's family, but we can't ignore all the other people who were present. How many are there? Did you find out?"

"Close to a hundred guests," said Miller tersely. "Then there are a dozen-or-so performers, plus three household staff and a raft of employees from the catering company. We could be there all next week."

Phil looked gloomy.

"I hope we don't have to drag the Premier and the local MP down to the station. What a thankless bloody job this is going to be."

"Fortunately, we're only dealing with attempted murder," said Miller. "We can get some initial statements, then take names and addresses and deal with the guests later. What we must do is find out from the waiters who served the wine, and we have to give the family the gears. We need to make it hot enough that whoever tried to get rid of the old girl won't try again. Miriam Fearing has given permission for a search of the house, which may not please her relatives, but it's her property so they can't object. That'll rattle them a bit. And the grandson sounds like a smart kid, so he'll probably be able to fill us in. The doctor also indicated that one of the performers sent the wine down to the hospital, so we'd better talk with her too. Here we are," he added, pulling into the circular drive at the front of the mansion. "This is the place."

"There's a kid on the front steps," said DC Ho. "That's probably the grandson. God, he looks like a little Harry Potter!"

"Let's hope he's as smart," said Miller. "Hey, look at that," he added, pointing to the side of the house.

They climbed out of the car and stood spellbound. The garden was gradually changing from black shadows to glowing greens as fairy lights lit up bushes and trellises, and then flashed along pathways, culminating in a gradual ascent up a huge cedar tree at the far side of the lawn. The party guests were gathered on the terrace, and over the awed murmur of the crowd, a clear soprano voice could be heard floating ethereally on the night air. The combined effect of the music and the light show was magical. Miller thought he had never witnessed anything quite so lovely. Forgetting the purpose of his visit, he stood still, listening and watching, until the garden was transformed and the last glorious note had sounded. A moment of silence followed, and then the watchers on the terrace erupted into applause.

Then the crowd parted and Miller saw the person who was receiving the accolade. Amazed, he looked more closely, hardly believing his eyes.

"Is that who I think it is?" said Phil Ho. "Quite the contrast from the first time we saw her." He chortled. "I'll never forget that devil suit."

"Neither will I," said Miller. "And I know who the performer was that preserved the doctored wine."

* * *

An hour later, Miller was ensconced in Eloise Arden's office with Mason. The secretary had left, after providing lists of guests, staff and caterers, and a detailed outline of household routines that promised to be extremely helpful. Mason's cheerful lack of discretion in describing the relationships between his relatives had also been enlightening. Miller anticipated some interesting interviews ahead. He had already met the middle-aged Barbie who Mason described as Bad Babs for she had been in the study when Eloise Arden had shown him in. Countess Terrazi had been calling the hospital for news, and she had turned solicitously to Mason before she left and assured him that there was no need to worry. Mason received this news in silence, and Miller was curious to know the cause of the boy's reserve. However, when asked, Mason clammed up and simply muttered something about interference with his chess games. Deciding that there was nothing more to be learned from the boy at present, Miller sent him to get Philippa Beary.

When Mason arrived in the salon, Philippa was sitting with her sister. Juliette's eyes twinkled when Mason repeated Miller's request.

"I wonder if he's going to arrest you again," she said mischievously.

Mason's eyes widened.

"Again? What's she talking about?" he asked Philippa.

"Nothing," snapped Philippa.

"DC Miller's very good-looking," Juliette continued. "You didn't tell me what a charmer he was."

"That might be because he wasn't the least charming," said Philippa coolly.

"You know him?" asked Mason.

"I've met him," Philippa said briefly. She stood up and left the room. Mason remained behind. He intended to stay until he'd pried the story from Juliette.

When Philippa arrived at the office, Miller stood up courteously and ushered her in. He made no reference to their first meeting, but politely and formally, pulled out a chair for her. Philippa sat down, carefully arranging the folds of her long gown, and waited for Miller to speak. His first comment took her completely by surprise.

"I heard you singing when I arrived," he said. "You have a lovely voice. You look wonderful too," he added. "That's quite a gown."

Philippa was stunned into silence, but before she could respond, Miller began the interview.

"Mason tells me you might be able to help us with our enquiries," he said.

When she had regained her equilibrium, Philippa replied.

"I can certainly tell you what I observed at the party. Mason alerted me very quickly, so I've had lots of time to think about the placement of the wine glasses."

"Excellent," said Miller. "What exactly did you see?"

Philippa described the scene, giving every detail that she could recall.

"I saw the waiter refill all the glasses at the table," she began. "None of the women were there, but there were three men present: Bruce Fearing, Professor Harte, and his son, Eric. Eric Harte was the one who called the waiter over. He had the waiter fill all ten glasses, even though three people at the table weren't drinking alcohol. In the next few minutes, all the ladies reappeared. His wife, Helga, came back with their children, and as soon as the twins sat down, Eric Harte helped himself to the glasses of wine by their placemats. Then Eloise Arden came over with some mineral water. She gave a glass to Bruce Fearing, but before she could pour one for herself, Grace Harte joined them. She moved aside her own glass of wine—according to Mason, when she's on medication, she can't drink alcohol—"

"Yes, he told me that. Where did she put it?"

"Next to her mother's glass. Miriam wasn't there at that point, but she and her daughter had been seated next to each other at lunch. Anyway, the glass of wine wasn't there very long because Eloise Arden took it and gave Mrs. Harte some mineral water instead. Then Miriam Fearing and Barbara Terrazi came to the table. Terrazi had a glass of wine. She set it on the table while she was there and took it with her when she left."

"Did anyone hover around the glasses?"

"Not for long enough to dissolve pills in the wine, but I suppose the killer would have ground up the pills ahead of time and kept them in a small amount of alcohol."

"Most likely. Are you sure Grace Harte's glass was empty when she came in?"

"It was certainly colourless. It might have had some water in it, but definitely not red wine."

"How full were the wine glasses on the table? Was there enough room to add a couple of ounces?"

"Probably. The waiter who served me only filled my wine glass a little more than half full. Mrs. Harte could have slipped the remains of the bar glass into the wine glass."

"You don't know where she was before coming into the room?"

"I'd assumed she'd gone to the washroom, but given that she was staying here, she'd have been more likely to go to her own suite. Mason said there was a security guard on the first landing. You'd easily be able to find out if she went upstairs."

"I will. There's another possibility too," said Miller. "You said Grace Harte moved the drink to the spot where her mother would have been sitting. Is there any chance that either Terrazi or Arden picked up the wrong drink?"

"It's definitely possible. There was a lot of bustle and movement around the table. Bruce Fearing and Eloise Arden had just announced their engagement."

"I heard about that," said Miller. "Eloise Arden told me that Fearing proposed to her just before the concert started. It was quite a surprise, because she had thought he was taking a personal interest in his ex-wife again."

"That's what Mason thought," said Philippa.

"I think the whole family assumed that," said Miller, "but they were wrong. Terrazi was here on business. She wants to come in as a partner and upgrade the family's chain of hair salons—turn them into high-end spas—and she's ready to put in the necessary cash to shore up the company. I gather there was the possibility of a hostile takeover, and the deal that Mrs. Terrazi has pulled off is going to stop it in its tracks. But it's all been kept hush-hush until everything was finalized. The only two people in on the negotiations were Terrazi and Bruce Fearing himself."

"So when did Eloise Arden find out the truth?" asked Philippa. "Even first thing this morning, she seemed very uptight . . . oh, wait a minute. Terrazi went to see her in her study. She must have told her then."

"Yes, that's right." Miller smiled. "Terrazi was waiting for confirmation from her lawyer that the contract had been signed, so she went to the office to make the call in private. Once the deal was through, she told Eloise Arden the good news. She also told Arden that Bruce Fearing was head over ears in love with her, and I gather she also let Fearing know that his feelings were reciprocated. Quite the little matchmaker."

Philippa looked thoughtful.

"Astonishing," she said. "Mason painted Terrazi as a horrible person—he calls her Bad Babs—yet she's sailed in, saved one of the family businesses, and helped her ex-husband find romance. Very different from the impression I was given of her."

"She seems like a pretty industrious woman," said Miller. "After lunch, she borrowed the office key from Arden so that she could slip in for ten minutes and update her website with the news. But there's no doubt that most of the family members mistrust and dislike her, and they were all suffering misconceptions about her right up until the announcement of the engagement." Miller frowned. "Given what you've told me about the juggling of the wine glasses," he said, "there's a possibility that Terrazi was the target. If someone had poisoned her wine and she was too busy talking to drink it, it could have been her glass that Mrs. Fearing drank from. Or come to that," he added, "Terrazi could have doctored her own glass and made the switch, except she doesn't appear to have a motive."

"No. It would have been different if she'd intended to remarry her ex-husband," said Philippa. "Then she'd have had a powerful motive. Mason was adamant that Miriam Fearing did not want her back in the family. Plus with Mrs. Fearing gone, Bruce Fearing would inherit a big chunk of the family wealth, but now that he's engaged to Eloise, Terrazi has nothing to gain from her ex-mother-in-law's death."

"That's right," said Miller. "She'll soon be heading back to her life in Europe."

The door opened and Phil Ho entered.

"Guess what PC Jones found in Grace Harte's bedroom?" he said.

"What?" Miller's eyes glinted.

"An empty pill container—supposed to hold ninety anti-depressants, but not a thing in it."

"Could be an old bottle," said Philippa.

DC Ho shook his head.

"The date on the prescription was from last week. Furthermore, we questioned the security guard on the stairs and, except for Eloise Arden and Eric Harte, Grace Harte is the only person who went up to the first floor once the party started."

"What time did she go upstairs?"

"Around noon."

"Did he happen to notice if she was carrying a glass with her, either on the way up or down?"

"He said she had her purse. That was all."

"She has a big handbag," said Philippa, "but she couldn't have carried an open glass in her purse. She must have had a container."

"We're searching the garbage bins," said DC Ho. "And the recycling tubs."

Philippa remembered her trip to the service yard.

"A lot of the tubs are out back," she said. "They were being loaded into the caterers' vans. And come to think of it, I saw Grace Harte out there around quarter to one. She was having a cigarette. I noticed her because I was passing the shed, and that big galumphing beast growled at me through the door. I jumped and backed away, and that's when I saw her by the van."

"What big galumphing beast?" asked Miller.

"Verdi. Mason told me he had to lock the dog away during the party."

"That's interesting," said Miller. "The kid told me he'd snuck the dog out of the shed during the concert and taken him up to his room. So unless there's another galumphing beast in the household, whatever you heard wasn't a dog growling."

Philippa's eyes grew wide.

"Oh, good grief," she said. "I should have thought of that. It wasn't a growl. It was the sliding door of the van. It must have been the one parked by the back door. It's right outside this room. If you look in there, you just might find the container you're looking for."

"I'll go right now," said Ho. He stood up and started towards the hall.

"You don't have to go that way," said Miller. He pointed to a door at the far end of the wall. "That's Eloise Arden's private entrance. It goes directly to the courtyard."

Ho left the room and Miller turned back to Philippa.

"Are you quite sure that Grace Harte was the only person in the courtyard?"

"Yes, other than the employees who were loading the vans. I didn't see anyone else. There was nobody in the hall either."

"Then," said Miller, standing up, "it's time to bring Mrs. Harte in for questioning."

* * *

On Sunday, the snow started in earnest. By the beginning of the following week, the Lower Mainland was blanketed with white. Vancouverites, unused to heavy snowfalls, stayed home if they didn't have to go out, thus decimating the usual pre-Christmas visitors to malls or theatres. Many who did venture out were not equipped with proper tires and caused havoc on the roads, so that even those with four-wheel drive had difficulty getting around the abandoned vehicles that blocked the lanes that had been cleared for passage.

Miller sat in his office and looked gloomily at the fat snowflakes drifting past his window. A stack of reports and statements were piled on his desk, and every piece of evidence contained therein pointed to the fact that Grace Harte had attempted to murder her mother. A search of the caterer's van had revealed an empty 125-millilitre vodka bottle and analysis had shown traces of drugs in the residual liquid. According to the men working in the service yard, the only party guests who had come outside were Grace Harte and Philippa Beary. Professor Harte had inadvertently damned his wife further by telling the police that he had seen her take her medication at ten o'clock on the morning of the party and that the bottle had been almost full at the time. Once the police knew that the critical period when the pills went missing was between ten and twelve-thirty, things looked even worse for Grace Harte. The only other people who had been upstairs during that period were Eloise Arden and Eric Harte, and neither had gone anywhere near the Hartes' suite. However, the guard admitted that someone might have slipped through from the back stairs since both the connecting archway and the door of the Hartes' suite were hidden by the curve of the corridor. Around one-thirty he had heard a toilet flush from the far end of the hall, so someone must have been in the suite then—but he insisted that the morning had been quiet. The delivery foreman who had been in the back hall between ten and twelve reinforced the security guard's story. No one could have slipped up the backstairs without being seen.

But in spite of the facts glaring him in the face, Miller was troubled, for Grace Harte's hysterical indignation and vigorous denials rang true. Miriam Fearing had stated baldly that someone must be trying to frame her daughter, and the young detective knew that if he recommended charges, he would be facing opposition from the mother as well as the daughter, not to mention a defence funded with enough dollars to guarantee the very best law firm in town. He had to be sure before he proceeded.

A question suddenly occurred to him. He flipped the pile of evidence statements open and jotted a phone number on the pad in front of him. Then he picked up the phone. He glanced at his watch.

Ten o'clock. Well, Philippa Beary was a theatre type. With any luck he'd catch her at home in the morning.

He was in luck. Philippa was just getting ready to go out. She sounded surprised, but not displeased when she heard who was calling her.

"I'm glad you called," she said. "I'm on my way to see Mason. He wants to talk to me. He sounded very mysterious and he wants to meet at Starbucks so that the other family members don't find out. I think he might know something important."

"You're not driving to Shaughnessy in this blizzard, are you?" Miller sounded concerned.

"Downtown, actually. He's at Science World with his aunt and the twins."

"That's even worse. It's bedlam down here. Half the time the Skytrain freezes and quits, and half the drivers on the road don't have proper tires. Can't whatever he wants to say be handled over the phone?"

An acerbic note crept back into Philippa's voice.

"You know," she said, "I really wish the police and the media would stop telling everyone to stay at home. My friend Milton just called and told me the panto audiences are down fifty percent from last year. This weather is going to kill all the Christmas shows."

"Are you performing in any of them?" Miller asked.

"Not this year, but my sister's marionette show has three public performances starting next Sunday, and her run will be wiped out if this continues."

"Sorry to hear that, but I don't control the weather. Let me know if you're in any shows though," he added. "I'd love to hear you sing again."

"Then you should come to Juliette's show," Philippa pointed out. "My voice is on the soundtrack. I'm going on Boxing Day."

"A puppet show? I don't think so."

"It's a very sophisticated puppet show. It's for grown ups as well as children. You'd enjoy it."

"I'd never live it down," said Miller. "Anyway, the reason I called is to ask you a couple more questions about the Fearing case. I'm still not entirely satisfied that Grace Harte is the culprit. It's possible someone tried to set her up. We know her pills couldn't have been taken by anyone else during the morning, but someone might have been able to slip up to her room via the back stairs after lunch. You were in the corridor around one-thirty. Did you see anyone?"

"No. The area was deserted. But what are you suggesting? That someone already had a batch of pills and they stole Mrs. Harte's later to throw suspicion on her?"

"I know it's far-fetched, but the guard heard a toilet flush in the Harte suite around half past one."

"If the killer flushed Mrs. Harte's pills away and left the empty jar to incriminate her, he must really have a grudge against her. That's pretty calculating and vindictive."

"True," said Miller, "but it can't be the son or the husband, because if Grace Harte was found guilty of murder, she wouldn't be able to inherit and they'd automatically lose out on her share of the family fortune. So if you're determined to go out and meet Harry Potter today, ask him if his great-aunt has any enemies."

"I will. What was the other question? You said you had two."

"Right. We did find a container in the van by the back door. It was an empty 125-millilitre vodka bottle and it had traces of antidepressants and wine in the bottom. As you know, the van was parked in the corner where the office annex joins the main part of the house. The side with the sliding door was facing the wall of the office and the rear doors were just a couple of feet from the house."

"Yes, that's right. I had to hold my skirt up and wriggle round carefully to get by."

"So which side of the van was Mrs. Harte standing on?"

"She was by the back door of the house," said Philippa.

"The side opposite the sliding door?"

"Yes." Philippa felt a surge of excitement. "So why would she go round to the sliding door when she could just toss the bottle in through the back doors?"

"Exactly—and the way you described it, you saw her almost immediately after you heard the rumbling sound."

"Yes, I did. She wouldn't have had time to move round to the other side of the van."

"Yet you didn't see anyone else?"

"No, but I wasn't far enough over to see if anyone was lurking on the other side." Philippa paused. "What about Barbara Terrazi?" she asked suddenly. "I know she doesn't appear to have a motive, but didn't you say she was in the study after lunch? The outer door of the office was on the other side of the van."

"I thought of that," said Miller, "but the timing doesn't work. Eloise Arden indicated that Terrazi asked for the office key at twenty past one and returned it within fifteen minutes. She just wanted to update her website with the announcement about the new spas. Even if she only took five minutes to post the information, there's no way she had time to slip upstairs, empty Grace Harte's pill container, come back to the office, and go out the side door to dump the vodka bottle."

"Why didn't she do the update as soon as she made the call that morning? She was in the study. Why come back later?"

"Arden said Terrazi was in a hurry to join the family as the guests were beginning to arrive, so they arranged that she would pop back later during the ballet performance."

"Are you sure she was on the computer? What if she did the update later on? If you go into her admin site, you could find out exactly when she posted the news. And," Philippa added, "if your computer people need help accessing Terrazi's codes, get your hands on the black binder that goes with her laptop. Her passwords are written on the plastic cover. All you have to do is slide a sheet of white paper underneath and they'll all appear."

There was a momentary silence at the other end.

"I won't ask how you know that," Miller said finally. "Anyway we've already checked. The site was updated at twenty-five past one, exactly as Terrazi told us. But," he added, "if that enterprising delinquent tells you anything else of interest over coffee, do call me back. And drive carefully."

"I'll be fine," said Philippa. "I now own a second-hand Jeep with four-wheel drive. As you might recall, I recently had to replace my Chevy."

Miller ignored the dig. "Sounds a much better vehicle than what you had before," he said. "I guess we did you a favour when we towed your car."

He hung up the phone and smiled. Then he stood up and left his office.

Partway down the hall, he paused. After a moment, he pulled out his cellphone and dialled his sister's number.

When she answered, he said, "Any chance I can borrow the kids on Boxing Day. I thought I'd take them to see a show."

* * *

The drive into Vancouver was slow, but the main roads were clear so Philippa did not have to use her four-wheel drive until she turned into the parking lot. Once out of the Jeep, she called Mason on her cellphone and asked him to order her a non-fat caramel macchiato. Then, glad of her boots, she picked her way across the snow piles and made her way to Starbucks. She found Mason sitting at a corner table, tucked obscurely behind a stand loaded with shiny red packages of Christmas Blend. He was nursing a hot chocolate and guarding her drink. She sat down and put some change on the table. Mason shoved the coins back towards her.

"You're a singer," he said. "I probably get more allowance in a week than you make in a month."

Philippa smiled and thanked him, but there was little response. She looked hard at her young friend. His expression was dejected.

"You look down-in-the-mouth," said Philippa. "Something wrong?"

"Everyone's mad at me."

"So what did you do?"

Mason looked indignant. "How come you assume I did something?" he said.

"Because you probably did. What happened?"

"I just had a bit of fun with B.B.'s website."

Philippa looked at him sternly. Mason shrugged.

"Well," he said, "I had nothing else to do on the morning of the party."

"You could have come to the concert."

Mason's tone was scathing.

"Classical music, forget it. Anyway, how was I to know she'd done something to help the family? I was still mad at her."

"Don't keep me in suspense," said Philippa. "What did you do?"

Mason's eyes shone with a satisfied glint.

"I copied the pictures on her website and made a few adjustments. Then I replaced the originals."

"What sort of adjustments?"

"I just expanded her a bit." Mason started to look more like himself. "It was really neat. I made her look like she'd gained about sixty pounds. You should have seen her when she saw what I'd done. I thought she'd have a heart attack, she was so red in the face."

Philippa managed to keep a straight face and simulate disapproval.

"You can't blame her for being angry," she pointed out. "She's in the beauty industry. You don't know how many people looked at that site before she was able to fix it. Honestly, Mason, it's no wonder you get yourself into trouble. You must have realized—"

Philippa stopped. The significance of Mason's prank suddenly registered.

"Wait a minute," she said slowly. "When did you say you mucked up her website?"

"Saturday morning. The day of the party."

"And when did she explode?"

"Two days later. She hadn't been on her computer for a couple of days because she's been busy Christmas shopping."

"But that's not possible," said Philippa. "She was online the afternoon of the party. She used the computer in Eloise Arden's office."

"Maybe she was just checking her email."

"No. She was updating her website."

Mason shook his head.

"She couldn't have been. You can't update a website without bringing up the actual site as well as the admin site. She'd have seen the pictures. And I know she hadn't because she was being really nice to me when Grandy was ill. It was totally fake, but she'd never have managed it if she'd seen what I'd done. She couldn't have been on the Web."

Philippa sighed.

"But she told Eloise and the police that she'd been posting the news about the spas."

"Then she was lying."

"But they checked. The site was updated at the time she'd indicated."

"Then someone else did it," said Mason. He paused. Then, conscious that he was delivering a bombshell, he announced, "It was probably her boyfriend in London."

Philippa's eyes bulged. She could hardly believe what she was hearing.

"What boyfriend in London?"

"That's what I've been trying to find out. That was my big plan . . . to discover who he was and tell everyone. You see, Tony Johnson—he's my best friend—moved to England two years ago and he came up to town when we were there on our trip, so he met B.B. the day we went to the Tower of London. Anyway, he emailed me after we'd flown home and told me he'd seen her at the country hotel in their village. She was with some guy and they were holding hands and kissing, so I knew she was two-timing Gramps. That's why I've been going into her computer because I was hoping I could get proof. That would have finished her with Gramps . . . but it doesn't matter now because he's marrying Eloise."

Philippa frowned. "I think it does matter," she said.

Mason nodded slowly. "I guess you're right, because if she was lying to the police, there has to be a reason."

"Yes. The police are already having doubts about charging your Aunt Grace, and if they know B.B. is lying, she'll become a suspect again. She was in the perfect position to dump the container that held the drugged wine. It was a small vodka bottle. It had been dumped in a recycling tub in the van by the office door."

"A vodka bottle?"

"Yes. One of those little sample ones."

"That's weird. We *used* to have those at the parties, but this year Grandy cut back and only served wine. It would have made sense last year, because if there were sample bottles at the party, it would have been the perfect container for the poison. The killer could have left it on a table anywhere in the house and it wouldn't have stood out at all.

But Gaunt knew that we weren't having hard liquor, so why would she make a mistake like that?"

"Well, that would make Barbara Terrazi an even more likely candidate. She wasn't staying at the house so, unlike your Aunt Grace, she wouldn't have known about the change."

"But she wouldn't have known about the sample bottles anyway," protested Mason. "She's never been to one of our Christmas parties. She was only married to Gramps for six months, and she ran out on him on his birthday, which happens to be in November."

"Could someone have told her?"

"I suppose so. There are lots of people who come every year." Mason frowned. "You know," he said thoughtfully, "it's not really fair to accuse Gaunt just because her pills went missing, but it's kind of odd, because her pills disappeared once before."

"When?"

"When we were in England. We were all staying with a friend of Grandy's who has a big country house in Kent."

"Who is 'all'?"

"Me, Grandy, Gramps, Gaunt and Guncle, Gauntlet, Helga and the twins . . . and Eloise too."

"Bad Babs wasn't there?"

"No."

"So when did the pills disappear?"

"Uncle Mark drove down for lunch one day, and after we finished eating, he went onto the terrace for a cigarette, so Gaunt went out to join him, and when she came back, Grandy started going on about her smoking. Gaunt got all indignant because Grandy was bugging her and wasn't criticizing Uncle Mark. Grandy said Uncle Mark could get away with smoking because he didn't have all the other toxins going through his system. So then the big battle started over the pills."

"But if your Aunt Grace has high blood pressure and stomach problems, she'd need her medication. That's not unreasonable."

"I know, but it's the anti-depressants that Grandy gets on about. Anyway, later that evening, Gaunt kicked up a big fuss because her anti-depressants were missing and she figured that Grandy had taken them, so then there was another fight."

"Did the entire jar go missing, or just the pills?"

"The whole container was gone."

"Couldn't your aunt have simply mislaid them?"

"That's what Grandy said, but they were never found. Gaunt had to get a new prescription. Do you think it's important?"

"Yes. We have to pass this on to DC Miller," said Philippa.

"You call him," said Mason. "But remember, B.B. wasn't there when the anti-depressants went missing, so how could you link the pills to her?"

"I don't know. I don't know how she would know about the sample bottles either."

"Yeah . . . and why she'd want to kill Grandy. The only way she'd get hold of Grandy's money would be to marry back into the family and she isn't going to marry Gramps . . . Oh, wow." Mason's eyes bulged. "Are you thinking what I'm thinking?" he said.

Philippa nodded.

"How well does Bad Babs know your Uncle Mark?" she asked. "Obviously they met years ago when she was married to your grandfather, but have they been in touch since?"

"They met once when we were in London. They didn't do any of that long-time-no-see stuff, but they weren't all over each other either. They mostly talked business. She provides some of the models who do shoots for Mercedes. Uncle Mark had some twenty-something bimbo on his arm . . . but that could have been a big front."

"Your uncle would definitely know about the sample bottles?"

"He sure would. He used to polish off half a dozen of them every Christmas party. Geez," he said. "Maybe I really do have a wicked uncle."

Mason pulled out his Blackberry.

"I have a picture of him stored on this. I'm going to send it to my friend in England," he said. He waved towards the front door. "You go call Miller. You'll have to shout if you stay in here."

Mason turned to his Blackberry, and Philippa stepped outside where it was easier to hear. She called the police station and was put through right away to DC Miller. He sounded pleased to hear from her.

"Don't tell me Harry Potter really does know something," he said.

"Does he ever," said Philippa. "Believe me, he's a mine of information."

She explained why Mason thought Barbara Terrazi was lying about her actions on the afternoon of the party, but before she could finish her story, the detective interrupted her. His voice had a peculiar edge.

"Am I hearing this right? He hacked into her website and doctored her pictures?"

"Don't be too hard on him," said Philippa. "He's a nice boy really. He was just dreadfully upset about the prospect of Terrazi moving back into their lives."

"I'm not going to be hard on him," said Miller. "I should offer him a job on the force. Look, it sounds like you have a lot to tell me. Could you both come by the station and fill me in?"

Philippa hesitated. The pause spoke volumes. Miller began again.

"I guess not," he said. "That was pretty tactless of me. You probably never want to come near this place again. I tell you what, could you handle another latte? I can join you at Starbucks. You're at the one on Main?"

Philippa paused again. Her information could easily be given over the phone, but she suddenly found that she wanted to see the young detective again. Juliette was right. He was nice-looking, and now that he was also behaving nicely, she found that her icy reserve was beginning to thaw. She agreed, and was gratified to hear the pleasure in Miller's voice. She ended the call and went back inside. After a trip to the washroom to comb her hair and freshen up her lipstick, she returned to the table.

Mason was still playing with the Blackberry.

"Any luck?" she asked.

"Not yet. It's evening over there. He might be out. But he'll get back to me. I've left an email, a phone message and a text message. Did you get hold of Miller?"

"Yes. He's coming to join us. He'll be here any minute. He's only a few blocks away."

Mason looked uncomfortable.

"What did you tell him?"

"Don't worry. He's not going to run you in for hacking, though you might get a lecture. He wants to hear what you told me."

"Why couldn't you have filled him in over the phone?"

Because, thought Philippa smugly, DC Bob Miller would obviously like to see me again. However, to Mason, she simply replied, "Just cooperate, and be glad he's impressed with what a clever kid you are."

"No one in the family will think I'm clever if Bad Babs ends up in jail. The spa deal will probably go under."

Philippa sighed.

"I suppose so, and your Grandy will be distressed if your Uncle Mark turns out to be involved too."

"Not necessarily," said Mason. "He's upset her a lot over the years. She's numb by now. She always used to say he'd end up in jail, so she wouldn't be that surprised if the cops carted him away. Hey, speaking of cops, here's yours."

"He isn't my cop," said Philippa sharply.

Mason's expression remained impassive. "Ask him if he'll buy me another hot chocolate," he said.

"I thought you had lots of money."

"I do, but I want to see if I can get an informant's fee."

Philippa rolled her eyes. She stood up and joined Miller at the counter. The cashier was waiting to take his order.

"What does Harry Potter want?" asked Miller.

"Hot chocolate, and I'll have a—"

"Non-fat caramel macchiato, right?" said Miller.

Philippa blinked.

"You *are* a good detective," she said with a smile.

"Not really," said Miller. "I phoned your brother. By the way, he was pleased to hear you've forgiven me for Halloween."

"Who said I have? Anyway, let's not talk about that. Wait until you hear what Mason has to say."

Miller paid for the drinks and, with a hand on Philippa's elbow, steered her over to the barista's counter. While they waited, Philippa looked out through the plate-glass windows. The snowflakes were larger and fluffier, and the Expo bubble had almost completely disappeared behind the white curtain outside. The high-pitched whine of spinning tires struggling through snow and the whirr of the Skytrain overhead periodically cut through the piped-in music and noisy chatter inside the coffee shop.

Miller spoke suddenly, cutting into her thoughts.

"So where is this Boxing Day show that has your voice coming out of a string puppet?" he asked. "I have a six-year-old niece and an eight-year-old nephew—my sister's children—they'd probably love it."

"It's at the Burnside Arts Centre. Your sister can find the address on the Internet. If she wants, I can reserve tickets for her and she can pick them up at the door. How many would she want?"

"Just three. Actually she isn't coming," Miller added casually. "I thought I'd bring them myself. She's always on at me to improve my uncle skills."

Philippa smiled inwardly but wisely remained silent.

Miller picked up the drinks that the barista had set on the counter. As he turned to take them to the table, there was a whoop from behind the display of Christmas Blend. Mason's head popped into view. He was waving his Blackberry and stabbing his finger towards the message on the tiny screen.

"Jackpot!" he cried. "Tony recognized him right away."

"What's he talking about?" asked Bob Miller.

"Go over and let him tell you," said Philippa, taking her own drink from him. "I think you'll find that young Mason has really earned that hot chocolate."

Philippa held back. Mason deserved his moment of glory. She watched as Miller strolled to the table, plopped down the drinks and ruffled Mason's hair. Mason grinned as the detective sat down, and within minutes, the two were engrossed in an amicable exchange.

As she sipped her drink, Philippa glanced down at the pile of newspapers on the stand by the counter. The headlines were predictions of worse weather and a dire economic downturn. It was promising to be the most dismal Christmas that Vancouver had seen in years, yet she found herself feeling illogically happy.

* * *

Beary hung up the telephone and went to join Edwina in the living room. MacPuff followed close on his heels. The dog flopped onto the carpet, eyes and nose fixed on the base of the tree where his squeaky elephant lay wrapped amid the gleaming parcels.

"That," said Beary, having inserted Philippa's new recording into the CD player, "was our daughter. Would you believe there was an attempted murder at the symphony fundraiser? Miriam Fearing's youngest son tried to pop her off. He teamed up with his mistress, some creature Philippa referred to as B.B.—"

"Bad Babs," said Edwina, without looking up from her book.

"What?"

"Bad Babs. That's what the initials stand for."

"Well, I knew it wasn't Brigitte Bardot," said Beary reproachfully. "You obviously know all about it."

"Philippa called me this morning," said Edwina. "I gather Miriam Fearing is fully recovered and the family is still having their Christmas Eve party tonight. Apparently it's questionable whether or not there's enough proof to lay charges, but it's unlikely there will be another attempt. Miriam Fearing stopped at her lawyer's office on the way home from hospital and changed her will. The homicidal son has been disinherited."

"So is there anything you don't know?" Beary grunted.

"Probably not," said Edwina blithely. "Do I have to pour my own glass of sherry?" she added pointedly.

"Actually," said Beary, going through to the kitchen and putting on the kettle, "since it's Christmas Eve, why don't I make you a Spanish coffee? Aha," he smirked, glancing back into the other room, "that made you look up from your book."

Edwina smiled.

"Spanish coffee would be very nice," she said. "Then I won't have to listen to the 'jug of wine' and 'loaf of bread' quotes. You know," she added more amenably, "it's not so bad spending Christmas Eve by ourselves, is it? The house is decorated, the lights look lovely, the presents are wrapped, and everything is tidy and ready for tomorrow. It's really rather peaceful . . . and very Christmassy with the snow drifting down outside the windows."

"Very daunting, since we've spent most of the day shovelling the driveway and sidewalk," growled Beary, putting coffee into the filter and pulling a bottle of kahlua out of the cupboard. He fetched a couple of wine glasses from the cabinet and ringed the tops with sugar.

"It's certainly proving to be a labour-intensive Christmas," Edwina called through the door, "though Juliette and Steven are having a much worse time. What a year to be touring their marionette show. Poor things must be exhausted."

"Yes, but you can feed them tomorrow and stoke them up for their post-Christmas run. I just hope they get an audience. The weather is going to make it tough for them." Beary poured hot water through the filter, set down the kettle and went to the fridge for the whipped cream.

"Yes, it's too bad. Philippa says the reservations are very low."

"In that case," said Beary, stirring the drinks and squirting cream on top, "we'll join Philippa and form a cheering section on Boxing Day."

Edwina smiled enigmatically.

"We don't have to sit with Philippa," she said. "My, that looks nice," she added, as Beary came back into the living room and placed the drinks on the coffee table.

"What do you mean? We don't have to sit with Philippa?"

"Well, she sounded as if she might have a friend with her."

"Oh?" Beary's antennae twitched. "Judging by the smirk on your face, there's something else I don't know. Could it be a new young man on the horizon?"

"Yes," said Edwina. "He's asked her out for New Year's Eve too."

"Let's hope she manages to stick to one date this year," said Beary with a chuckle. He settled himself on the couch and patted MacPuff on the head. "So who is this new gallant?" he asked. "Being the father, of course, I'm always the last to know."

"Oh, you've met him," said Edwina. "It's that young detective from VPD. Bob Miller."

Beary's jaw dropped.

"The one who arrested her? You're joking."

"No," said Edwina. "He's actually very nice."

"How can you possibly know that?"

"I asked Richard to check up on him. It's easy for him to do that . . . being a policeman. Miller sounds most satisfactory."

"Satisfactory for what?"

Edwina picked up her drink and took a sip.

"For Philippa, of course. I think this one might do. I must say," she purred, "this drink is absolutely delicious."

The music emanating from the CD player changed from lively to lyrical as the title song of Juliette's new show began. MacPuff gave a contented sigh and closed his eyes.

"Well," said Beary, "that is nice to hear." He waved his left hand gently in time to the music. "Christmas past may have been less wintry and more prosperous," he mused, "but it sounds as if Christmas present isn't shaping up too badly."

Edwina smiled and nodded.

She set down her book and raised her glass to Beary. Then, having taken a long draught of her Spanish coffee, she leaned back in her armchair, listened to the sound of her daughter's voice floating across the room, and looked with pleasure at the gleaming lights of the Christmas tree.

ALSO BY ELIZABETH ELWOOD

MYSTERY STORIES

To Catch an Actress and Other Mystery Stories
A Black Tie Affair and Other Mystery Stories

PLAYS

Casting for Murder
Renovations

WATCH FOR THE NEXT BEARY ANTHOLOGY

The Agatha Principle and Other Mystery Stories

An amateur production of *The Mousetrap* tests both the acting and the detecting skills of the Beary family, for when a leading player falls to his death, the unexpected twists and turns of the real-life plot emulate every trick and contrivance of the play itself.

Enjoy this intriguing story and other mysteries in the next Beary anthology.

Website: www.elihuentertainment.com

AUTHOR'S NOTE

The stories in this volume are set in the Greater Vancouver area, on the Sunshine Coast of British Columbia, in the B.C. Interior and in the city of Boston. Therefore many of the settings described may be familiar to residents of those areas. However, the assorted political groups, theatrical associations and characters in the various stories exist only in the imagination of the author and bear no relation to organizations or people in real life. Also, some of the settings, including Barnet Village in "The Beacon" and the city of Burnside where Beary resides on Council, are composites of several different locations and do not really exist.

The plot twist in "The Beacon" stemmed from a near-fatal incident that almost resulted in me and my husband ending up at the bottom of the inlet, and once I had recovered from my shock, I realized that the experience could be utilized in a mystery story. "Reflections on an Old Queen", was inspired by a ferry crossing on the *Queen of Tsawwassen*, which was officially decommissioned at Deas Pacific Marine Inc. in Richmond on September 27, 2008. She has since been sold for use as a logging camp on the coast. The fictitious ship, the *Queen of Tofino*, was based on the stately old vessel that ended her days on the Earl's Cove to Saltery Bay run.

The Black Bandit Inn in "Echo of Evil" does not really exist. However, the creation of the imaginary site resulted from a delightful visit to the Quilchena Hotel, which is a charming tourist destination on the southern shore of Nicola Lake.

"Who Killed Lucia?" owes a great deal to Sir Walter Scott's *The Bride of Lammermoor*, along with the intriguing prologue that precedes the novel. I should also acknowledge our friendly taxi driver, Bobby, in New York, who not only ferried us back to Jersey City after our nights at the opera, but also took great delight in giving me a book on the Sikh religion and customs to assist me in my research for the story.

The final story in the collection, "Christmas Present, Christmas Past", describes a marionette show which is performed by Juliette and her children. The details about the show do come from life, as I did write a show called *The Christmas Present of Christmas Past* for

Elwoodettes Marionettes, and when, during the summer of 2008, the trailer that contained our theatres and much of our equipment was stolen, the devastating loss of so much carefully crafted artwork was very much on my mind when I was writing this book. Therefore, the urge to have the show performed, albeit in print, was irresistible. The description of the show is accurate, and those who want to know the end of the story can go to www.elihuentertainment.com and find more information under Elwoodettes Marionettes Theatre Productions.

I would like to extend my thanks to my husband, Hugh Elwood, for researching material on a variety of topics and for providing guidance and information from his wealth of knowledge of outdoor recreational activities. Last, but definitely not least, a big thank you goes to Lorraine Meltzer for her invaluable assistance in proofing and editing my manuscript.